P9-DCD-896

BROTHERHOOD OF WAR

A sweeping military epic of the United States Army that became a New York Times *bestselling phenomenon.*

THE CORPS

BOOK IV

BATTLEGROUND

W.E.B. GRIFFIN

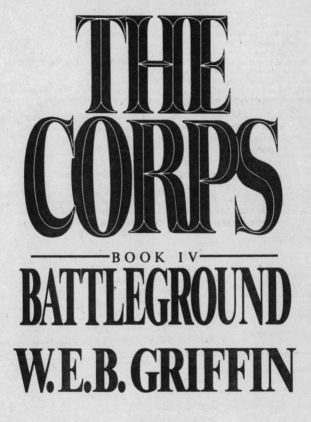

JOVE BOOKS, NEW YORK

THE BERKLEY PUBLISHING GROUP
Published by the Penguin Group
Penguin Group (USA) Inc.
375 Hudson Street, New York, New York 10014, USA
Penguin Group (Canada), 90 Eglinton Avenue East, Suite 700, Toronto, Ontario M4P 2Y3, Canada
(a division of Pearson Penguin Canada Inc.)
Penguin Books Ltd., 80 Strand, London WC2R 0RL, England
Penguin Group Ireland, 25 St. Stephen's Green, Dublin 2, Ireland (a division of Penguin Books Ltd.)
Penguin Group (Australia), 250 Camberwell Road, Camberwell, Victoria 3124, Australia
(a division of Pearson Australia Group Pty. Ltd.)
Penguin Books India Pvt. Ltd., 11 Community Centre, Panchsheel Park, New Delhi—110 017, India
Penguin Group (NZ), 67 Apollo Drive, Rosedale, North Shore 0632, New Zealand
(a division of Pearson New Zealand Ltd.)
Penguin Books (South Africa) (Pty.) Ltd., 24 Sturdee Avenue, Rosebank, Johannesburg 2196,
South Africa

Penguin Books Ltd., Registered Offices: 80 Strand, London WC2R 0RL, England

This is a work of fiction. Names, characters, places, and incidents either are the product of the author's imagination or are used fictitiously, and any resemblance to actual persons, living or dead, business establishments, events, or locales is entirely coincidental. The publisher does not have any control over and does not assume any responsibility for author or third-party websites or their content.

BATTLEGROUND

A Jove Book / published by arrangement with the author

PRINTING HISTORY
G. P. Putnam's Sons hardcover edition / January 1991
Jove mass-market edition / September 1991

ISBN: 978-0-515-10640-4

JOVE®
Jove Books are published by The Berkley Publishing Group,
a division of Penguin Group (USA) Inc.,
375 Hudson Street, New York, New York 10014.
JOVE and the "J" design are trademarks belonging to Penguin Group (USA) Inc.

PRINTED IN THE UNITED STATES OF AMERICA

35   34   33   32   31   30   29   28   27   26

The Corps *is respectfully dedicated to the memories of*
Second Lieutenant Drew James Barrett III, USMC
Company K, 3rd Battalion, 26th Marines
Born Denver, Colorado, 3 January 1945
Died Quang Nam Province, Republic of Vietnam,
27 February 1969
and
Major Alfred Lee Butler III, USMC
Headquarters 22nd Marine Amphibious Unit
Born Washington, D.C., 4 September 1950
Died Beirut, Lebanon, 8 February 1984.

And to the Memory of Donald L. Schomp
A Marine Fighter Pilot who became a legendary U.S.
Army Master
Aviator
RIP 9 April 1989.

"Semper Fi!"

I

William Charles "Bill" Dunn, USMCR, of Point Clear, Alabama, was twenty-one years old, five feet six inches tall, and weighed 142 pounds; he'd been a First Lieutenant, USMCR, twelve days, and a Naval Aviator not quite six months; and in all that time—in all his twenty-one years, even—he'd never had a night as hard as the last one. By the time he threw off the sheet that morning and swung his feet onto the floor, he did it with the sinking conviction that he was a coward. That conviction didn't come as a surprise to him. The thought, if not the conviction, had been there when he crawled into bed, and more times than he wanted to count he'd woken up during the night with it.

Just about every time he did that, he'd had to rush to the head to move his bowels. As far as he was concerned, that made him—literally—"scared shitless." It did not strike him as amusing. Now that his bowels were empty, he had an urge—suppressed only with enormous effort—to throw up.

1

And every couple of minutes he felt a cold and clammy sweat on his back and on the seat of his skivvy shorts.

The reason his body was acting so wild was that today he was going, as the Naval Service so quaintly put it, "In Harm's Way." The Japanese were about to attack the islands where Dunn was stationed, with the objective of capturing them; the United States Navy was determined not to lose them. Both sides had sent formidable naval forces toward the area. And both forces were closing in on one another. Bill Dunn's role in this vast exchange was to fly a single seater fighter off this tiny little airfield to see if he could shoot at least some of the Japanese airplanes down.

All for the sake of a circular atoll surrounding a pair of tiny dots of land (total area, two square miles) lying just east of the International Date Line, 1,300 miles Northwest of Pearl Harbor. The dots themselves were named Eastern Island (1.25 miles long) and Sand Island (1.75 miles); and the whole thing, including the atoll, was called Midway.

Midway had been an American possession since just after the Civil War. But, with the exception of a cable station, it had been essentially abandoned and forgotten until 1936. That year, Pan American Airways instituted scheduled service between Hawaii and the Philippine Islands using Midway as a midpoint stop. Once that facility was in place, the strategic importance of Midway began to grow apparent, until in 1939, the Navy Hepburn Board (named after its senior member), charged with evaluating Navy facilities in the Pacific in case of war, determined that those tiny dots of land were "second only in importance to Pearl Harbor" itself.

In 1940, the Navy started construction of extensive facilities to service both aircraft and submarines on Midway. A Navy dock was completed on 1 September 1940, and on 29 September, about a third of the 3rd USMC Defense Battalion arrived with one battery of two five-inch naval cannons and some machine guns to defend the atoll.

The decision was made to build an airstrip (only facilities for seaplanes were originally planned) and Army Engineers began to dredge the channel between the islands and undertook other construction work.

The Japanese, meanwhile, attacked Midway at 2135 hours 7 December. The destroyers *Sazanami* and *Ushio* under

Captain Koname Konishi shelled the tiny islands for twenty-three minutes, causing minimal damage. The three- and five-inch naval cannon of the 6th Defense Battalion (which had replaced the 3rd) returned the fire and claimed damage to both vessels.

This first Japanese attack was hardly more than a nuisance, but other attacks, including an amphibious assault, were expected. And so by the end of May, Midway had received meaningful reinforcement: The Marine Corps had furnished five anti-aircraft batteries, ranging in size from twenty-mm to three-inch; two companies of the 2nd Marine Raider Battalion; and even a platoon (five) of light tanks.

During the same time, the small airstrip on Eastern Island had become home to an odd mixture of aircraft: In addition to the original fourteen Navy Consolidated PBY Catalinas, there were two Royal Dutch Navy Catalinas, which had attached themselves for service after they were unable to return to their base; the U.S. Army Air Corps had flown in from Oahu four twin-engine Martin B-26 Marauder medium bombers and seventeen four-engine heavy bombers, Boeing B-17 "Flying Fortresses"; while the Navy had sent six torpedo-carrying Grumman TBF Avengers.

Most of the aircraft, however (sixty-four), were Marine: nineteen Douglas SBD-2 Dauntless dive bombers; seventeen (virtually obsolete) Vought SB2U-3 Vindicator dive bombers; twenty-one (obsolete) Brewster Buffaloes; and seven of the new Grumman F4F-3 Wildcat fighters.

In the days before this particular morning, Navy Intelligence, whose information in this instance Bill Dunn trusted, had provided a good deal of information about the enemy, all of it alarming:

Their Midway Strike Force, under Admiral Chuichi Nagumo, was built around four aircraft carriers: The Akagi (at 36,500 tons, Japan's largest carrier); *Kaga* (36,000 tons); and *Hiryu* and *Soryu* (both much smaller at 16,000 tons). The force also included two battleships, three cruisers, destroyers and other screening vessels, and transports for 1,500 men of the Special Naval Landing Force and 1,000 soldiers of the Ichiki Detachment.

There were going to be large numbers of Japanese aircraft: "Probably in excess of one hundred," the skinny, bespectacled, school-teacherish Navy full Lieutenant Intelligence Officer had announced at the most recent briefing, sounding as bored as a guide in the Atlanta Zoo telling visitors about the wonders they could find in the reptilarium.

If the Japanese followed their usual practice, based upon the normal complement of aircraft aboard their carriers, three types of aircraft would be in the striking force, and in roughly equal numbers.

There would be an element of Nakajima B5N1 Torpedo Bombers, single engine, low wing monoplanes, which some Navy Intelligence bureaucrat had decided should be known as Kates. Since torpedoes cannot sink an island, even little, bitty ones like Sand and Eastern Islands, Intelligence had cleverly deduced that the Kates would probably be operating in their bomber and not their torpedo role. That meant the Kates would have large bombs, probably enormous bombs, slung beneath their fuselages, and they would carry three men aboard, instead of the usual two. When it was used to deliver torpedoes, the pilot aimed the single torpedo Kates could handle; when it was used as a bomber, there was a bombardier. The pilot could also fire the two 7.7mm machine guns in his wings. And there was always a gunner, who fired a single 7.7mm machine gun from the back seat.

They could also, according to the Atlanta Zoo guide, expect an element of Vals. The Val was officially the Aichi D3A1 Navy Type 99 Carrier Bomber Model 11. Bill Dunn vaguely remembered hearing someplace that Type 99 (or was it Model 11?) made reference to the year in the Japanese calendar, which was different from the calendar used in the West.

He did remember that the Val had a nonretractable landing gear . . . the wheels had pants. These made Vals look something like the Gee-Bee Racer Jimmy Doolittle used to fly in air races. Jimmy Doolittle was one of Bill Dunn's childhood heroes.

Bill hadn't thought of Jimmy Doolittle in years, until word had come six weeks ago that Doolittle had flown B25s off an aircraft carrier, bombed Tokyo, and wound up a Brigadier General with the Medal of Honor. He didn't understand how the hell Doolittle had managed to get B25s off an aircraft carrier; it was hard enough getting a Wildcat off.

The news of the Tokyo raid brought back to him his adolescent hero worship of Doolittle racing his Gee-Bee around pylons. The Gee-Bee was much like the Wildcat, a little airplane with a big engine, and thus very fast. And correspondingly hard—dangerous—to fly.

By the time Bill Dunn was fifteen, he knew he would never emulate his father and his two brothers who'd been football heroes at the University of Alabama: He weighed 105 pounds and was dubbed "The Runt." Things were in fact looking bad for him in the manhood department in general until the U.S. Navy—specifically, the Naval Air Station, Pensacola—came to his rescue. The Navy showed him a way to do manly things, even if he wasn't going to be well over six feet and two hundred pounds when he reached full growth.

The Navy hoped to build auxiliary and emergency landing strips on land the Dunns owned just across the border from Florida in Alabama. Though the Navy had no funds to lease, much less buy, the necessary land, the Admiral at Pensacola thought there was a good chance that he could appeal to the Dunn family's patriotism.

The Admiral had read his history and suspected—correctly—that Lieutenant Cassius Alfred Dunn, gunnery officer of the Confederate Ship *Alabama,* probably had a familial connection with the Dunns of Mobile and Point Clear, shipping agents and land owners. The *Alabama,* under Admiral Raphael Semmes, was the greatest Naval Raider of all time.

"You must come see us at Pensacola," the Admiral said to C. Alfred Dunn IV, Bill's father. "And bring your boy. I think he'd like it."

When the Dunns came to Pensacola, the Admiral laid on them a little demonstration of the capabilities of the Grumman F3F-1, the last Navy biplane fighter to be produced. Bill Dunn's awe of the F3F-1 was exceeded only by his shocked realization that the pilot who climbed out of the cockpit and walked over to be introduced to the Dunn family was no taller and not much heavier than he was.

I bet they called him "Runt" too, when he was fifteen.

That summer, and the next, Bill spent long hours with his

feet dangling off the family pier, watching the sun set over the smooth waters of Mobile Bay. A lot of the time he was there he was thinking about flying. He would have cheerfully swapped all his worldly possessions, present and future, for a chance to climb in the cockpit of a fast and powerful little airplane and shove the throttle as far forward as it would go.

The dream endured . . . though he changed part of it. By the time he entered the University, he'd decided that if there was anything in the world better than being a Naval Aviator, it was becoming a *Marine* Naval Aviator.

Now that he was a Marine Naval Aviator and rated in the Grumman F4F, which was a little larger than the Gee-Bee, but just about as fast, he understood that flying hot aircraft as fast as they would go, as close to the ground as you could get them, was a pretty dumb thing to do. He realized now why there had been such a hell of a hue and cry to stop the National Air Races because those guys had kept flying into each other, the pylons, or the ground.

The Val, like the Kate, had two forward firing 7.7mm machine guns in the wings and a single 7.7mm in the aft cockpit. It could carry about nine hundred pounds, total, of bombs, a big one under the fuselage and two smaller ones under the wings.

Neither the Val nor the Kate was any match for the *Wildcat,* which was faster, and far more heavily armed (six .50 caliber Browning machine guns) and armored. One on one, that is.

Was one Wildcat equal to two Vals? Or three?

That was an uncomfortable question.

And that wasn't the whole problem.

"We may certainly expect the Vals and Kates to be accompanied by a roughly equal number of Zeroes," the Navy Zoo Guide had said matter-of-factly.

The Zero (technically the Mitsubishi A6M2 Model 21) was an interesting airplane . . . interesting, that is, if you could sit back and compare it dispassionately with the Wildcat. It was a low wing monoplane fighter, with a fourteen-cylinder radial engine that gave it a top speed of about 315 mph at 16,000 feet. The Wildcat had a top speed a couple of miles an hour faster at 18,000.

But if you could not consider it dispassionately—for

example, if you were about to go fight twenty-five to thirty-five of them—the Zero seemed immensely formidable. From everything Bill Dunn had heard, the Zero was a better airplane than the Wildcat. That the Navy pretended otherwise did not change the facts. The Navy also pretended that the Brewster F2A Buffalo was only "marginally inferior" to the Wildcat, and that was bullshit, pure and simple.

It was common knowledge, anyhow, that the Zero was far more maneuverable than the Wildcat, except at sea level, where the more powerful Wildcat engine gave it an edge. And in addition to the two 7.7mm machine guns it had in the wings, it had two 20mm machine cannon. The projectile from a 20mm machine cannon had greater range than a .50 caliber bullet. Thus a Zero pilot could shoot at a Wildcat before the Wildcat pilot could shoot at him; and because it was larger, a 20mm did more damage.

If it was true that no matter how bad a situation is, it could always be worse, Bill thought, *then whenever we sally forth into harm's way, I could be flying a goddamned Buffalo. There are three times as many (twenty-one) Buffaloes on Midway as there are Wildcats.*

The Navy didn't want the Buffaloes, of course, knowing that they are no fucking good. So naturally, they are good enough for the Marines. But at least I will be flying a Wildcat.

Which raises the interesting question, how come?

Did Major Parks put me into a Wildcat because he felt I can fly one better than the other guys? Or because he thought, being the nice guy he is, that I stand a slightly better chance of living through this morning flying a Wildcat than I would flying a Buffalo?

And that raises the question of relative pilot skill, which is a real chiller. Christ only knows how much time Major Parks and Captain Armistead and the other old timers have—several thousand hours anyway—but Mrs. Dunn's Little Boy Billy has 312.5 hours, which ain't very much, especially considering how little of that is in the Wildcat, and that somehow Navy Intelligence has learned enough about the Japs to estimate their average carrier pilot has 800 hours, including some in combat. I have zero hours in combat.

After he rolled out of bed, Dunn dressed quickly by pulling

on what the Marine Corps called a "Suit, Flight, Tropical," and which he somewhat irreverently thought of as his rompers. Next came ankle high boots, which he thought of as his clodhoppers, because the rough side of the leather was on the outside. Some of the guys flew with low-quarter shoes, but he preferred the clodhoppers. He slipped a leather flight jacket over the flight suit, and then put on a shoulder holster with a Colt Model 1911A1 pistol in it.

Some of the guys carried .38 Special caliber revolvers, which were somewhat smaller weapons, arguing that they didn't get in the way as much as the Colt. Bill carried the Colt because that's what they had issued him, and because he thought the chances of his ever having to take it from the holster to shoot anybody with it ranked right up there with his chances of being named Pope.

Last came a canvas helmet with flaps folded up so his ears were free. It always reminded him of the helmet he'd worn to grammar school, goggles in place, imagining that he was Jimmy Doolittle flying the Gee-Bee to racing glory around the pylons.

He looked at the photograph of his parents standing outside St. Luke's on some long ago Sunday morning. It shared a folding leather frame with a photograph of Miss Sue-Anne Pendergast, who had been the 1941 Queen of the Mobile Mardi Gras. Sue-Anne was a nice looking girl . . . for that matter, a nice girl, period. But she was not, as Bill suggested to his peers, his beloved, almost his fiancée.

He had known Sue-Anne all of his life. They'd climbed trees and gone swimming and thrown mudballs at each other since about the time the two of them could talk. Now she was doing her bit for the Boys In Service by writing him faithfully once a week. While she signed her letters, "Love," it wasn't the sort of love Bill had so far in his life been denied.

Another of the reasons it was a dirty rotten fucking shame he was probably going to get killed today was that he was, with one exception, a virgin. Just before he'd dropped out of college to join the Marines, he and half a dozen fraternity brothers had gone down from Tuscaloosa to the Tutweiler Hotel in Birmingham, where they had pooled their money and hired a whore from the bellhop. He was so drunk he didn't remember much about it, except that it was not what he expected it to be, and not very pleasant either.

It seemed to Bill common justice that a man should be able to get decently laid before he got himself killed. But that hadn't happened.

The Officer's Mess was an open-sided tent with benches and tables, the food was served cafeteria style. Breakfast was the standard fare: Spam and powdered eggs served any way you wanted them, which meant that you could either have little squares of fried Spam with powdered eggs on the side, or you could have the Spam cut up and mixed into powdered eggs. Plus toast, with your choice of apple or cherry flavored jelly. And coffee, with your choice of canned cow or no canned cow.

He had taken a mug of black coffee and a piece of cold toast and walked out to the flight line. He was afraid that he would throw up and didn't want to vomit in the cockpit.

The plane chief was there, looking over the armorer's shoulders as he checked the Brownings and the links and placement of the belted .50s. They exchanged salutes. The plane chief, a stocky Italian from Florida whose name was Anthony Florentino, was about as old as Bill was, and took his work and the Marine Corps seriously. He was a corporal.

"Good morning, Sir," he said.

"Good morning. Everything shipshape?"

"Yes, Sir. Just checking the guns, Sir."

Funny, it looked to me like you were playing chess.

"You got the word, Sir, that we're to start engines at 0540?"

"No, I didn't."

Jesus, I have to take another dump!

"The Skipper wants the engines warmed up for when the word comes, Sir."

He looked at his watch. It was 0533. In seven minutes he would have to climb in that cockpit and hope that he didn't have nausea or diarrhea.

He walked around the plane and did the preflight, trying to act as nonchalant as possible. When he finished he had four minutes to wait. He leaned against the Wildcat, just behind the cowl flaps.

"I didn't see you in the mess, I wondered where you were,"

Major Parks said, startling him. He hadn't seen The Skipper coming up.

"Good morning, Sir."

"Everything all right? You feeling OK?"

"Yes, Sir, fine."

"You got the word about warming the engines?"

"Yes, Sir. I was about to get in."

"A PBY radioed at five-twenty-five that it had spotted the Japanese fleet," Parks said. "I expect word anytime now that the Navy radar has picked up aircraft. I want to get off the ground as soon as we get a heading. Hit them as far away from here as possible."

"Yes, Sir."

"You're a good pilot, Bill. That's why I put you in a Wildcat. You don't get excited. That's a good thing for a fighter pilot. Excited pilots forget what they've been taught."

"Yes, Sir."

Translated, that means you have had second thoughts about putting me in a Wildcat, because I am very likely to get excited and forget what I've been taught, and would probably change your mind if there was time and put me in one of the goddamned Buffaloes. That being the case, you have decided to inspire the troops with confident words.

Shit!

Major Parks touched his arm.

"Good luck," he said. "Good hunting."

"Thank you, Sir."

Major Parks was both a professional warrior and a realist. He knew that until the shooting actually started there was no way to predict how Lieutenant Dunn, or any of his pilots, would behave in combat. Even so, he had a belief that he could devise guidelines that would give him some indication—a hint if not a prediction—about which pilots could handle best the stress and terrors of combat. With that goal in mind, he had collected as much data as he could about the behavior of British fighter pilots during the Battle of Britain, the battle Churchill had described both accurately and eloquently: "Never in the history of human conflict have so many owed so much to so few."

Parks wondered what the few were really like.

Not without difficulty, he had learned that by and large they were no older than his young officers, and they'd been trained no better. They had also gone up against pilots with more experience than they had, yet they'd done very well.

He'd found two notable differences between the British pilots and his own, perhaps the most important being that the English were defending their homes, literally fighting above their mothers and their girlfriends, where his kids would be fighting halfway around the world from theirs. They would be protecting their mothers and their girlfriends, too, but abstractly, over a wide and empty ocean.

Secondly, the Brits had flown Spitfires against Messerschmidts. Both were splendid aircraft; it was a matter of opinion which was the better. One could charitably call the Wildcat the equal of the Zero, and perhaps when they had enough experience against the Zero to make a bona fide analysis, it would turn out to be so. But that could not be said about the Buffalo, which was hopelessly outclassed by the Zero, and probably by even the Kate.

With no data worth a damn to really go on, Parks realized he would have to go with his gut feeling. He thought that commanders had probably been forced to go on their gut feeling from the beginning of time, but that offered little reassurance. His gut feeling (which he desperately hoped was not wishful thinking) was that his kids—and perhaps Bill Dunn in particular—would acquit themselves well.

He had given Bill Dunn one of his precious few Wildcats because of that gut feeling. And perhaps, he thought, because sometimes when he saw Dunn on the flight line, a spunky little crew-cutted, clean-cut kid who looked more like a cheerleader than a Marine Officer, he reminded him of those young English kids standing beside their Spitfires in an East Anglian field.

(Two)

Lieutenant Bill Dunn watched The Skipper walk down the flight line to the next aircraft, which happened to be a Buffalo, and pause for a word with its pilot.

I can't remember that guy's name! I'm about to go get killed with him, and I can't even remember his name. I wonder if he knows mine?

He climbed up on the wing root.

Corporal Florentino had already opened the canopy. As Bill lowered himself into the seat, Florentino climbed onto the wing root and watched, prepared to help, as Bill fastened his shoulder and lap belts, and then as Bill set the clock, the altimeter, and the rate of climb indicator to zero. He waited until Bill had checked the stick and rudder pedals for full movement, and then jumped off the wing root.

Bill checked the emergency canopy release and the fuel gauge, then glanced out the canopy.

"Ignition switch off, throttle open, mixture at idle cut off," he called. "Pull it through."

Florentino grasped a propellor blade and pulled on it, then the next blade, and the next, until the engine had been turned through five revolutions. Otherwise, oil that had accumulated by gravity in the lower cylinders would still be there when the engine fired. Since oil does not compress, lower link rods would have been bent or broken.

Bill put the Fuel Selector Valve handle to MAIN TANK and turned the crank opening the engine cowl flaps. He checked the propellor circuit breaker switch and then set it on AUTOMATIC. Outside, Corporal Florentino had charged the starter mechanism with a Type C cartridge, a kind of super-sized blank shotgun shell. When it fired, its energy would turn the engine over until it started.

Bill set the supercharger on LOW, pushed the Carburetor Air handle in so that air would be delivered directly to the engine, and set the throttle for 1000 rpm.

He looked to make sure that no one was near the propellor and that a ground crewman had a fire extinguisher ready to go.

"Clear!" he called.

Florentino made a wind-it-up motion.

Bill turned the battery switch to ON, turned on the Emergency Fuel Pump, and watched as the fuel pressure gauge rose to fifteen pounds. Then he held the primer switch on for three seconds, turned the ignition switch to BOTH, and fired the starter cartridge.

The propellor began to turn, and then there was the sound, rough, of the engine catching. The Wildcat shuddered, and the engine gave off a small cloud of blue smoke. He moved the mixture control to AUTO RICH and flicked the primer switch a couple of times until the engine smoothed out.

He idled the engine at 1000 rpm, and then teased the throttle further open until it indicated 1200 rpm. There was nothing to do now but wait for the oil pressure and inlet temperature needles to "move into the green." This made reference to little green arcs painted on gauges and dials to show where the indicator needle should point, if things were as they were supposed to be. There were also little red arcs that indicated a dangerous temperature, or pressure, or the like.

The oil pressure gauge almost immediately indicated 70 psi (Pounds Per Square Inch) and then the oil inlet temperature gauge needle came to life. It slowly began to move across the dial to the green arc, stopping at an indication of 86° Fahrenheit.

Then he checked the magnetos, which provided the ignition spark to the engine, by switching from their normal BOTH position first to LEFT and then to RIGHT. The tachometer showed a drop of less than 100 rpm, which meant he had no problem there.

The goddamn airplane is not going to suffer some fatal internal malady and keep me on the ground. That would have been nice. Not exactly heroic, but nice.

He let it run another minute and then shut it down. It was warmed up and ready to go. He sat in the cockpit for another minute, listening to the creak of metal as it cooled, and then a Jeep came down the flight line with Captain John Carey at the wheel. He signaled down the flight line. Dunn had expected this. The word had come, and there would be last minute instructions and probably a pep talk.

"We've been over this before," Major Parks conceded. "You all know where you're supposed to be when we get in the air. What we have now is where the enemy is: bearing 310, about 90 miles. Radar reports too many of them to count."

Now he's going to say, "Go out there and give them hell,

*men! Win one for the Gipper! Semper Fi! To the Halls of
Montezuma!"*

Major Parks said, "I'll see you all later at the debriefing."

Bill was a little surprised to find himself trotting, almost
running, back to the Wildcat. As he climbed in, he saw for
the first time that something had been stenciled below the
canopy: 1ST LT W C DUNN USMCR CPL A M
FLORENTINO, USMC.

That wasn't there yesterday. He must have painted it on
there last night. And I didn't see it before because I had other
things on my mind, like getting killed.

"Great-looking sign, Florentino," Bill said when the plane
captain appeared at the side of the cockpit.

"Thank you, Sir."

He fastened his seat and shoulder harness again and went
through the start-up procedure. The engine caught
immediately and quickly smoothed down. He checked the
Manifold Pressure Regulator and the Propellor Operation;
then he de-sludged the supercharger. After that he followed
the Buffalo which had been parked beside him toward the
runway.

When he was lined up with the runway, he went through
the final take-off checklist, which takes longer to describe
than to do: He checked to see that the indicator in the wing
root showed the wings were properly spread and locked. He
locked the tail wheel; made sure the sliding portion of the
canopy was locked open; set the aileron and elevator tabs in
NEUTRAL and the rudder tab a couple of marks to the right.
He checked to see that the fuel selector switch was on the
main tank and that the cowl flaps were open. He made sure
the propellor governor control was pushed all the way in; that
the supercharger was set to LOW, the mixture control set to
AUTO RICH, and the Emergency Fuel Pump to ON. He pushed
the Carburetor Air Control all the way in and finally pushed
the throttle to FULL.

The engine roared, the plane began to strain against the
brakes, and the needle on the Manifold Pressure Gauge rose
to indicate about fifty-two inches. He released the brakes and
the Wildcat started to move down the runway, as if it was
chasing the Buffalo in front of it.

He dropped his eyes momentarily to check the oil and fuel

pressure, the oil and cylinder head temperatures, and the indicated airspeed. The needles were all in the green. He thought he saw the airspeed indicator needle flicker to life, which usually happened about 40 knots, but he wasn't sure. It didn't really matter. He would sense in the seat of his pants when the Wildcat wanted to fly.

The rumble of the landing gear suddenly stopped. The Wildcat, having reached an airspeed of about 70 knots, had decided to fly. Without thinking about it, Bill swapped hands on the control stick, using his left hand on the stick to counter the Wildcat's tendency to veer to the right on take-off and freeing his right hand to crank up the landing gear. It took twenty-seven revolutions of the crank, hard turns, to get it up.

When he had finished and put his right hand back on the stick, he looked around for Major Parks, spotted his Wildcat, and maneuvered to get into his assigned position behind him. He was not at all surprised when he was in position and had adjusted the throttle, the mixture, and the trim, to see that he was climbing at 1,000 feet per minute, indicating 125 knots, and with his cylinder head temperature right at 215° Centigrade. That's what the book said was the most efficient climbing attitude, and Major Parks flew by the book.

As they passed through 12,000 feet, he put the black rubber mask over his face, readjusted his headset to accommodate it, and turned on the oxygen. It felt cool in his mouth and throat, and somehow alien. At 14,000 Parks leveled his flight out.

Several minutes after that, Parks wiggled his wings, seeming to point with his right wing tip. Bill followed the line down, and there they were, two thousand feet below them.

He was surprised at the color scheme. The Kates' fuselages, wings, and rear appendages were painted a lemon yellow. And the red ball of Japan was not readily visible on either fuselage or wings. From the windscreen forward, the Kates were painted black. And so was the bomb hanging under the fuselage.

Jesus Christ, there's a lot of them!

I'll be goddamned, the Zeroes are below them! What the hell is that all about? Didn't they think we'd try to intercept?

Following Parks's lead, he put the Wildcat into a dive,

correcting without thinking about it for the Wildcat's tendency to drop the right wing and turn the nose to the right.

As he approached his first target, Bill could clearly see the aft-facing gunner bringing his machine gun to bear on him.

That bastard is shooting at me!

That triggered two other—alarming—thoughts:

Christ, I didn't test my guns!

I forgot to pull my fucking goggles down!

The Wildcat shook with the recoil of the .50 caliber Browning machine guns in the wings. And two other thoughts came:

Jesus, my tracer stream is way out in front of him!

I'll be goddamned! He blew up! How the hell did that happen?

And then he was through the layer of Kates and approaching the layer of Vals beneath them.

I fucked that up! I didn't get a shot at any of them, and here come the fucking Zeroes!

Our Father, who art in heaven—

I don't think I can turn this sonofabitch enough to lead him—

I'm skidding all over the fucking sky! You're a real hot pilot, Mr. Dunn. In a pig's ass you are!

Oh, shit, there goes one of our guys. His right fucking wing just came off!

For yea, tho' I walk through the valley of the shadow of death—

That's right, you miserable cocksucker, just stay right there another five seconds, four, three—

Gotcha!

Holy shit, there's somebody on my tail! A fucking Zero, what else?

I can't get away from him.

Our Father, who art in heaven, hallowed—

Chop the fucking throttle, stupid! Put it in a skid, let him overshoot you!

Oh, my God, the windshield's gone. I can't see a fucking thing. I'm going to die. Where the fuck are those goggles? Where the hell is that Zero? Why does my leg feel wet? Did I piss my pants?

Not unless you're pissing blood, you didn't.
I thought it was supposed to hurt when you got wounded.
Oh, shit, it hurts! I wonder if it's broken?

(Three)

"How do you feel, Dunn?" the tour guide from the Atlanta Zoo asked, pulling up a folding metal chair to the side of Dunn's bed. "Well enough to talk to me?"

What if I said "no"?

"Yes, Sir."

"The more you can tell me about what happened out there, the better," the tour guide said. "You want to take it from the beginning?"

"We were at fourteen thousand, about thirty miles out, when Major Parks spotted them. He showed us where they were and went into a dive, and I went after him."

"And?"

"And that's all I remember."

"Come on."

"I remember being surprised that the Zeroes were on the bottom of the formation, not the top."

"OK. That was unusual. They apparently intended to use the Zeroes to strafe the field here. I guess they didn't think we had anything to send up against them. When you went in the dive, then what happened?"

"I shot at a Kate."

"You got it. It was confirmed."

"The Kates were on top. Then there was a layer of Vals. I went right through them without firing a shot. And then I was in the Zeroes."

"And?"

"I don't know. I don't remember much."

"You are credited with shooting down one of them. You don't remember that?"

"Who says I shot down a Zero?"

"I don't immediately recall."

"The Skipper?"

"Major Parks didn't make it back, I'm sorry to say."

"Shit."

"I was hoping that perhaps you might have seen him go in."

"I saw somebody go down. His right wing, most of his right wing, came off. I don't know who it was."

"When was that?"

"I don't know. Toward the beginning."

"That was the only time you saw one of ours go down?"

"Yes."

"You're sure?"

"I told you, that was it. How many of ours went down?"

"A good many, I'm sorry to have to tell you."

"How many is a good many?"

"We lost fifteen. Two Wildcats—not counting yours, although yours has been surveyed and is a total loss—and thirteen Buffaloes."

"We only had nineteen Buffaloes with us."

"In addition to yourself, Captain Carey, Captain Carl, and Lieutenant Canfield came back. Of Major Parks's flight, I mean."

"You mean the rest are dead?"

"Do you remember when you were hit?"

"You mean everybody but the four of us is dead?"

"I'm afraid so."

"Oh, my God!"

"Do you remember being hit?"

"No. I remember the windshield going."

"In other words you don't know who shot you down, whether it was a Zero or some other type aircraft?"

"It had to be a Zero. I was in the Zeroes."

"But you don't know for sure?"

"I don't even know how I got back here."

"You came back and made a wheels-up landing."

"I found my way back here by myself?"

"How else?" the Naval Intelligence debriefing officer asked, a tinge of sarcasm in his voice.

"The last thing I remember is when I lost my windshield. And got hit."

"You don't remember heading back here?"

"The last thing I remember is trying to pull my goggles down after the windshield went."

"You were apparently flying with the canopy open—"

Christ, I forgot to close the canopy, too?

"Was I?"

"The shell, most likely a 20mm, apparently entered the cockpit from the side—"

"Just one round?"

"There were others. In the engine nacelle. Another just forward of the seat. But the one—the one which entered the cockpit—apparently exploded going through the windshield, from the inside out?"

"Yeah," Bill said, understanding.

"What they took out of your face and leg, legs, was debris from the windshield and control panel. Perspex and aluminum fragments."

"Then it was a Zero."

"Presumably." The Intelligence officer looked directly at him. "You have no memory of breaking off the engagement and heading back here?"

"No."

"Could you determine, do you have any memory of determining, from your instruments, or from a loss of control, that your aircraft was no longer airworthy?"

"No," Bill said, and then, thinking aloud, "That's an odd question."

"You were seen leaving the area."

"So?"

"The officer who saw you leave could not tell whether you had lost your windshield. You were too far apart."

"Who was that?"

"I don't think we'd better get into that."

"But he thought I was running, right?"

"Were you?"

"I don't know."

"That's not a very good answer, you realize?"

"Sorry about that."

"You don't seem overly disturbed at what could be an accusation of cowardice in the face of the enemy."

"Fuck you, Lieutenant."

"You can't talk to me that way!"

"If I'm to be charged with cowardice in the face of the enemy, what's the difference what I say to you?"

After a long pause, the Naval Intelligence Officer said, "I didn't say anything about you being charged with anything."

"No witnesses, right? Everybody's dead?"

"If you're through with my patient, Lieutenant," another voice said, from behind Dunn, "I'd like to put him aboard the PBY."

"You're being flown to Pearl Harbor," the Intelligence Officer said to Dunn.

"I'd prefer to stay with the squadron," Bill said.

"You won't be flying for a while. Three weeks anyway," the voice behind him said.

"And there's no squadron to stay with," the Naval Intelligence Officer said.

"Moving is going to be painful," the voice behind him, now much closer, said. "I can give you some morphine, if you like."

"How painful?"

"You're pretty well stitched up, particularly on the legs. Any movement will be painful."

"Then you'd better give me the shot," Bill Dunn said.

II

(One)
MENZIES HOTEL
MELBOURNE, AUSTRALIA
1040 HOURS 8 JUNE 1942

When the knock came at his door, Captain Fleming
Pickering, USNR, was relaxing with his jacket off and his
tie pulled down, tilting back in a chair, his feet on the
windowsill of his seventh-floor suite, and balancing a cup of
coffee on his stomach. Even that way he looked tall and
distinguished; and it would have taken a moment of
indecision before you concluded he was a man in his early
forties. At first glance he appeared younger than that.

Rooms—much less suites—in the Menzies Hotel, now the
Headquarters of General Douglas MacArthur, Supreme
Commander, South West Pacific Ocean Areas, were not
ordinarily assigned to lowly Navy Captains. But Captain
Pickering was not an ordinary officer, or for that matter, an
ordinary man.

Six months before, he had been Chairman of the Board,

Pacific & Far East Shipping Corporation. He had been known as Captain Pickering then, too, preferring the title to the more grandiose Commodore which many ship owners adopt, whether or not they have ever gone to sea. Fleming Pickering had received his Master, Any Ocean, Any Tonnage, license from the U.S. Coast Guard when he was twenty-six. He was entitled to be called Captain.

The Corporation he chaired was in many ways as singular as he was. P&FE did not for instance issue an annual stockholders' report detailing the financial condition of its assets (which included fifty-two ships and a good deal of real estate in the United States and abroad). The majority stockholders did not consider such a report necessary. Captain Pickering and his wife owned seventy-five percent of the outstanding shares, and controlled voting rights to the other twenty-five percent, which had been placed in trust for their only child.

Captain Fleming Pickering, USNR, was, in other words, an important and influential man in his own right. But what made him unique, in the military pecking order, were the orders he carried in his pocket:

THE SECRETARY OF THE NAVY
WASHINGTON, D.C.

30 JANUARY 1942

CAPTAIN FLEMING W. PICKERING, USNR, OFFICE OF THE SECRETARY OF THE NAVY, WILL PROCEED BY MILITARY AND/OR CIVILIAN RAIL, ROAD, SEA, AND AIR TRANSPORTATION (PRIORITY AAAAA-1) TO SUCH POINTS AS HE DEEMS NECESSARY IN CARRYING OUT THE MISSION ASSIGNED TO HIM BY THE UNDERSIGNED.

UNITED STATES NAVAL COMMANDS ARE DIRECTED TO PROVIDE HIM WITH SUCH SUPPORT AS HE MAY REQUEST. OTHER UNITED STATES AGENCIES ARE REQUESTED TO CONSIDER CAPTAIN PICKERING THE PERSONAL REPRESENTATIVE OF THE UNDERSIGNED AND TO PROVIDE TO HIM APPROPRIATE SERVICES AND AMENITIES.

CAPTAIN PICKERING HAS UNRESTRICTED TOP SECRET SECURITY CLEARANCE. ANY QUESTIONS REGARDING HIS

MISSION WILL BE DIRECTED TO THE UNDERSIGNED.
   FRANK KNOX
   SECRETARY

Very soon after the attack on Pearl Harbor, Navy Secretary Frank Knox came to realize that the information about Naval operations in the Pacific he was getting—and would get—from regular Navy officers was understandably slanted to reflect well on the U.S. Navy. These reports tended to gloss over any facts or opinions that might suggest that the Navy was less than perfect. What he needed, he concluded, was someone to report to him directly, and someone who not only was not a member of the Navy establishment, but who would know what he was looking at.

Knox met Pickering through their mutual friend, Senator Richmond Fowler (Republican–California). He decided immediately that Pickering was the man he was looking for. It was less Pickering's nautical experience that appealed to him than Pickering's strongly stated conviction that after Pearl Harbor, Knox should have resigned and the admirals at Pearl Harbor should have been shot. It was *in vino* truth: The day Secretary Knox met him, Pickering was treating a sorely bruised male ego with large doses of Old Grouse Scotch whiskey. The P&FE Chairman, a much decorated Marine corporal in France during the First War, had just been told the Marine Corps could not use his services in World War II.

Two weeks later, Knox offered Pickering a commission as his personal representative, with captain's stripes to go with it. To Knox's surprise, Pickering immediately accepted. Shortly thereafter he left for the Pacific.

"Come!" Captain Pickering called; and carefully, so as not to spill the coffee, he looked over his shoulder.

A youthful-looking Navy officer somewhat hesitantly stuck his head in the door.

"Captain Pickering?"

"Yes," Pickering said. "Come on in."

His visitor's sleeves, Pickering saw with surprise, carried the stripes of a full commander. He didn't look old enough to be a commander, Pickering thought. Even more surprising was the manner in which the commander carried his large, apparently full briefcase. It was attached to his wrist by a chain and a handcuff.

"You *are* Captain Pickering?" the young-looking commander asked.

"Guilty," Pickering said. "Who are you?"

"Sir, may I trouble you for some identification?"

"Jesus," Pickering said, and carefully removing himself from the tilted back chair, went to his uniform jacket and took out a wallet. The breast of the jacket carried ribbons for both valor and for wounds received in action in what had now become the First World War. He offered the young commander his Navy Department identification card, and then, because he already had his hands on it, his local identity card.

That one, with red diagonal stripes across the photograph and data blocks, told the Military Police he had been authorized unlimited access to all areas of MacArthur's headquarters. The red stripes seemed to awe people, Fleming had noticed. It should satisfy this young man.

"Thank you, Sir, I just had to be sure."

"I understand," Pickering said. "Now who are you?"

The commander did not reply. Instead, he reached into an interior pocket of his uniform jacket and came out with an envelope. As he did so, Pickering saw the butt of a revolver and the straps of a shoulder holster.

"This is for you, Sir," the commander said.

"What is it?"

"Captain, I suggest that when you've read that, you burn it as soon as you can," the commander said.

Pickering tore the envelope open. Inside was another envelope. He opened that and took out a thin sheath of onion skin carbon copies of a typewritten document. There was no heading, and neither was there what he expected to find, in these circumstances, the words TOP SECRET stamped in red ink on the top and bottom of each page.

"What the hell is this?" Pickering asked. "It doesn't even look like it's classified." When there was no immediate reply, he added, a little coldly, "And for the last time, Commander, who are you?"

"I think you'll understand when you read it, Sir," the commander said. "Sir, I'm a friend of a friend."

Pickering ran out of patience. Both his eyes and his voice

were cold when he replied, "In case you haven't heard, Commander, I'm a friendless sonofabitch around here."

While Pickering had established a good, even warm, relationship with MacArthur, the officers on MacArthur's staff were barely able to conceal their hostility toward a man who was not part of their clique; was not subject to their orders; and who could be accurately described as Frank Knox's spy.

The commander baffled him with a warm smile. "That's not exactly the scuttlebutt I heard, Sir," he said, adding, "Our mutual friend is Captain David Haughton. If you don't mind, Sir, I won't give you my name. Then you can truthfully say you never heard of me."

"OK, sure," Pickering said, far less icily. Captain David Haughton was Administrative Assistant to Secretary of the Navy Frank Knox. If Haughton was involved, there was certain to be a satisfactory explanation for all this.

"I'll say 'Good morning,' Sir," the commander said. "I hope to meet you—for the first time—while I'm in Melbourne."

Now Pickering chuckled.

"We can walk through the looking glass together, right?" he said.

"Sir?" the commander asked, confused.

"Alice in Wonderland? Lewis Carroll?"

" 'Curiouser and curiouser,' Sir." the commander replied, now understanding.

"I would say 'Good-bye,' " Pickering said, "but you're not here, right?"

The commander smiled again and walked out of Pickering's suite. Pickering unfolded the sheets of onion skin and started to read them. The salutation was brief, and it was meaningful only to him. He was obviously FP. EF was Ellen Feller, who had been assigned as his secretary when he had been in Washington. But Ellen Feller was more than that, actually; for she'd been his administrative assistant, with the same relation to him as David Haughton had to Secretary of the Navy Knox. Ellen was now in Pearl Harbor, serving as his conduit to Knox, when she wasn't working as a Japanese language linguist in the ultrasecret Navy cryptographic office. The Commander, Pickering now guessed, was some sort of officer courier between Pearl Harbor and MacArthur; that would explain the pistol and the briefcase.

FOR FP FROM EF

This is a back channel summary prepared for PH by an officer here and sent to you on PH's authority.

A Midway-based PBY spotted the transport element of the Japanese assault force 700 miles West of Midway at 0900 3 June. B-17s were immediately dispatched from Midway. They later reported hits which still later proved to be wishful thinking. At 0145 4 June, another PBY hit a Japanese oiler with a single bomb as the Japanese moved closer.

At 0555 4 June, Navy landbased radar on Midway picked up reflections from a large aerial force about ninety miles away. Four Army Air Corps B-26 Marauders and six Navy TBF Avengers were launched from Midway against the carrier(s) which had presumably launched the Japanese aircraft.

Marine fighters and dive bombers on Midway were airborne within ten minutes of the alert. Major Floyd Parks led seven Buffaloes and five Wildcats directly toward the Japanese aircraft. Captain Kirk Armistead led the remaining Wildcat and a dozen Buffaloes to a position ten miles away, where it was believed another flight of Japanese would be found.

Thirty miles off Midway, Parks found a 108-plane Japanese force, divided into three waves of thirty-six planes each, and attacked. Several minutes later, Armistead joined up. They shot down sixteen horizontal bombers of the first Japanese echelon, and eighteen of the second echelon of dive bombers.

Fifteen of the twenty-five Marine fighter pilots were shot down, including Major Parks. Only three of the pilots with Parks survived the attack. Thirteen Buffaloes and two of the four Wildcats went down. For all practical purposes, Marine Fighter Squadron VMF-221 has been wiped out.

The Japanese force, although weakened, continued onto Midway and dropped its bombs. They destroyed the powerhouse on Eastern Island and the PBY hangars and some fuel tanks on Sand Island. Thirteen Americans were killed and eighteen wounded.

Meanwhile, the Marine dive bombers sent to attack the Japanese aircraft carrier approached their target. Major Lofton R. Henderson led the first, faster, echelon of SBD Dauntless Dive Bombers, and Captain Elmer C. Glidden led the slower Vought SB2U-3 Vindicators.

Apparently because neither he nor any of his pilots were really proficient in the Dauntless, Henderson ordered that greater accuracy would be obtained by glide (as opposed to dive) bombing. At 0800, from 8,500 feet, he began a wide "let down" circle. At 8,000 feet, Japanese fighters from the carriers attacked his force.

Henderson's plane was the first to take fire and begin to burn.

Captain Glidden's echelon, arriving shortly afterward, began to dive bomb at five-second intervals. Of the sixteen planes in both echelons, eight were lost. Damage to the enemy was minimal.

Fifteen B-17s from Midway arrived at 0810, somewhat naively trying to hit now wildly maneuvering warships from 20,000 feet.

We believe that on learning that he had lost about a third of his attacking force, Admiral Nagumo ordered a second attack. This required that he put his aircraft carriers into their most vulnerable condition, as they were refueled and rearmed. He apparently decided the prize, the neutralization and capture of Midway, was worth the risk.

At 0940 the first torpedo bombers from American aircraft carriers arrived above the Japanese carriers, whose decks were crowded with aircraft being rearmed and refueled.

Fifteen Devastator torpedo bombers from Hornet attacked first. They were all shot down. Fourteen Devastators from Enterprise attacked next. Ten of these were shot down. Next came a dozen Devastators from Yorktown. Eight of them were shot down.

It was a slaughter, and little damage was done to the Japanese fleet.

Thirty-seven Dauntless dive bombers from Enterprise under Lieutenant Commander Clarence McCluskey remained available. McCluskey led half in an attack on the carrier Kaga, and ordered Lieutenant Earl Gallagher to attack the carrier Akagi with the remainder. They sank both Japanese carriers.

Next, seventeen Dauntlesses from Yorktown dive bombed the carrier Soryu, causing severe damage, and she was later sunk by the submarine Nautilus. Finally, the fourth, and last, Japanese aircraft carrier, Hiryu, was successfully attacked and sunk.

I regret to inform you that Kate torpedo planes broke through the defenses of Yorktown and sank her, with great loss of life.

The entire Japanese fleet has withdrawn beyond range of our land- and sea-based aircraft. We believe that Admiral Nagumo has transferred his flag to the cruiser Nagara.

KLW

Pickering strongly suspected that the two "we believe" statements, that Nagumo had ordered a second attack on Midway and that he had transferred his flag to the cruiser *Nagara,* meant that "we"—almost certainly a Naval Intelligence officer in Hawaii—had obtained the information from interception and decryption of Japanese radio messages.

Navy cryptographers had broken several important Japanese codes. Keeping that knowledge from the Japanese was of great importance. Reference would not be made to it even in documents which would be hand carried by officer couriers.

He considered briefly, and then forced from his mind, the painful images of the terrible loss of American life, and wondered what he should do with the information he had been given.

It took him just a moment to decide to give it to General MacArthur. Commander Nameless certainly was carrying with him, among other things, the official Navy after-action report. But that was certain to be wordy, and written in the knowledge that in addition to being at war with the Japanese, the Navy felt itself to be at war with the Army.

What he had in his hand was what General MacArthur wanted—and certainly was entitled to have—a concise, unvarnished description of the first major Japanese naval defeat of the war.

He picked up the telephone.

"Yes, Sir?" a male American voice answered. The hotel's Australian switchboard operators had recently been replaced by U.S. Army Signal Corps soldiers.

"Six One Six," he said. That was MacArthur's private number. It wasn't much of a secret, but there were few who dared to call it directly and run the risk of annoying The General.

"Six One Six, Sergeant Thorne speaking, Sir."

"This is Captain Pickering, Sergeant. I'd hoped to speak to The General."

"Sir, the General is in his quarters, and will go from there to the Briefing Room. Shall I switch you, Sir?"

"No, thank you," Pickering said. "I'll try to see him at the briefing."

He quickly pulled up his tie, shrugged into his uniform jacket, tucked the onion skin sheets of paper in the side pocket, and left his suite.

(Two)

The Briefing Room, once one of the Menzies Hotel's smaller "Function" Rooms, was on the mezzanine floor. Pickering momentarily debated going down the stairs, which would almost certainly be quicker, but decided against it. Around Supreme Headquarters, SWPOA, it would not be considered good form for a Navy Captain to race down five flights of stairs three steps at a time, when an oak paneled elevator was available.

His hope was to meet MacArthur as The General strode off the elevator reserved for his use and marched toward the briefing room. With a little luck, he would be able to ask for a couple of minutes.

Luck went against him; MacArthur was nowhere in sight. So he had no choice but to get in line with the others waiting to pass the muster of the MPs guarding the door to the Briefing Room. Once inside, he took a seat at the rear, beside the door. The man in the seat beside him was a Cavalry Colonel who nodded coldly at him.

Pickering wondered what the Cavalry Colonel's function was. The only U.S. Cavalry in the Orient had been the 26th Cavalry in the Philippines. They had been dismounted and their horses butchered and issued as rations fairly early on in the war.

The door beside him was flung quickly open, hitting Pickering on the shoulder. An officer stepped inside; he was wearing a tropical worsted uniform and the golden fourragère and four-starred lapel insignia of an aide-de-camp to a full general.

"Gentlemen," Lieutenant Colonel Sidney L. Huff announced with a shade more than necessary pomp, "The Supreme Commander."

The thirty-odd men in the room quickly rose to their feet and came to attention.

The Supreme Commander, General Douglas MacArthur, strode into the room and marched down the aisle between rows of folding metal chairs. He was wearing an Army Air Corps leather flight jacket with a zipper front, the four silver stars of his rank pinned to its epaulets; a somewhat battered brimmed cap with faded gold ornamentation around the headband that he had designed for himself when he had been Marshal of the Philippine Army; and wash-faded khakis. Another four stars were pinned to each collar of the shirt. He was tieless, and he had a long, thin, black cigar in his hand.

The corncob pipe he was famous for was most often seen when the Supreme Commander was in public. This gathering was the antithesis of public. Every man in the room—from the three sergeants functioning as orderly, stenographer, and handler-of-the-maps, through the assorted majors, wing commanders, and colonels, to the dozen general and flag officers of five different nations—not only held a TOP SECRET security clearance, but appeared on a list, updated daily, of those authorized to be present at what the schedule called "THE SUPREME COMMANDER'S MORNING BRIEFING."

An Australian Military Police Captain had checked each man against the list before permitting him to enter the room.

The front row was furnished with two blue leather armchairs. There was a table at each end of the row and between the chairs. The center table held a silver thermos of water, two glasses, a telephone, and an ash tray. The table at the left held a coffee cup and saucer; a cigarette box; an ash tray; a lighter; and another telephone. The table at the right held a coffee cup and saucer; a larger (big enough for a corncob pipe) ash tray; a small cigar box; a sterling silver lighter; a glass holding four freshly sharpened pencils; and a small notepad in a leather folder on which was stamped "Douglas MacArthur" and four silver stars.

When he reached his chair, General MacArthur looked around the room at his senior officers, all standing to attention. He found the face he was looking for, toward the rear.

"Captain Pickering," he said. "May I see you, Sir?" He smiled at everyone else. "Good morning, gentlemen," he added. "Take your seats, please."

He sat down.

Captain Pickering came down the aisle to MacArthur.

"Have a seat, Fleming," MacArthur said cordially, gesturing at the other blue leather armchair. The second chair was ordinarily reserved for Mrs. MacArthur. Although she had no official function and no security clearance, she went anywhere in HQSWPOA The General felt like taking her. When she was not present, The General awarded the privilege of sitting beside him to whichever of his officers was at the moment highest in his favor.

To the barely concealed disappointment and displeasure of his generals and admirals, that officer had very often been Captain Fleming Pickering. There were a number of reasons for their annoyance, starting with Pickering's relatively low rank. For another, the initials following his name were USNR; he wasn't even a professional Navy Man. And neither was he actually a member of the staff. Technically, he was assigned to the Office of the Secretary of the Navy, half a world away in Washington, D.C.

"Thank you, Sir," Pickering said and sat down.

MacArthur gestured to the orderly, a swarthy-skinned, barrel-chested Filipino Master Sergeant, who immediately approached the table beside MacArthur and filled the cup with steaming coffee.

MacArthur gestured with his finger that the service should be repeated for Captain Fleming. Then he turned to his side and picked up the small cigar box, opened it, and extended it to Pickering, who took one of the cigars, nodded his thanks, and bit off the end.

So far as MacArthur was concerned, it was simple courtesy. He had mentioned idly, in conversation, that among many other obvious regrets he had about leaving the Philippines, he was going to miss his long-filler, hand-rolled El Matador cigars. The next day, a half dozen boxes of El Matador had been delivered to his office, courtesy of Captain Pickering, who had found them through his contacts in Melbourne. When a friend (and he had come to think of Pickering as a friend) gives you boxes of cigars, and you are smoking one, how could a gentleman not offer him one?

So far as ninety percent of the people in the Briefing Room were concerned, it was one more manifestation of the incredible way that man Pickering (often that Goddamned Sonofabitch Pickering) had wormed his way into The General's intimate favor.

The General waited until his Filipino orderly held a flame to Captain Pickering's El Matador, then nodded at the portly U.S. Army officer in tropical worsted blouse and trousers standing almost at attention beside a lectern.

"Willoughby," he said. "Please proceed."

Colonel Charles A. Willoughby stepped behind his lectern. Willoughby had been MacArthur's Intelligence Officer (G-2) in the Philippines, had escaped with him from Corregidor, the island fortress at the mouth of Manila Bay, and was now the SWPOA G-2.

"General MacArthur," he began, "gentlemen. This morning's briefing is intended to bring you up to date on the Battle of Midway."

He nodded at the sergeant standing by the map board, who removed a sheet of oil cloth covering a map of the Pacific Ocean from the Aleutian Island chain off Alaska to Australia. When the sergeant was finished, Willoughby walked to the map.

"The intelligence we have developed," Colonel Willoughby said, "indicates that Admiral Yamamoto, commanding the entire Japanese fleet, is aboard the battleship *Yamoto* somewhere in this general area."

He pointed roughly between Midway and the Aleutian Islands.

You phony sonofabitch, Captain Fleming Pickering thought, in disgust. *"Intelligence we have developed" my ass. You didn't develop a goddamn bit of that. It came from the Navy. After the fact, of course, much later than they should have told us,* but *they came up with it.*

"The Japanese fleet was divided into two strike forces," Willoughby went on. "One intended to strike at the Aleutian Islands, and the other to attack and occupy Midway. As The General predicted when we first developed this information, the Aleutian operation was in the nature of a feint, a diversion, and their real ambition, as The General predicted, was to attack and occupy Midway, rather than, as some senior Navy officers believed, to launch another attack at the Hawaiian islands.

"The Midway Strike Force, under Admiral Nagumo, was made up of two battleships, four aircraft carriers, with a screening force of three cruisers, a half dozen destroyers and other ships, and of course the troop transports and other ancillary vessels."

The Supreme Commander leaned his head toward Captain Pickering and, covering his mouth with his hand, waited until Pickering had leaned toward him, and then said,

"Mrs. MacArthur would be pleased if you would come for a little supper and bridge."

"I would be honored, Sir."

"And could you have that Korean Signal Officer come too? After supper, of course?"

"I'm sure I can, Sir."

The "Korean" Signal Officer was Lieutenant "Pluto" Hon, a New York-born, MIT-educated mathematician, assigned to the staff as a cryptographic officer and Japanese-language linguist. A mere lieutenant was far too low in the military social hierarchy to be asked to dine with The Supreme Commander and his lady, but his bridge playing skill got him into The Supreme Commander's suite for bridge after dinner.

"Good," MacArthur said. "I'll give *you* to Jeanne this time, and he and I will whip you badly."

"Sir, will you take a look at this please?" Pickering asked.

"Something you want, Pickering?" MacArthur asked, suspiciously.

"Something that just came to hand, Sir," Pickering said, and handed the onion skins to him.

MacArthur took the sheets from him. Pickering saw the distress in Colonel Willoughby's eyes that showed he no longer had The Supreme Commander's attention.

MacArthur read the summary carefully, grunting once or twice, and shaking his head.

"You believe this is accurate?" he asked.

"Yes, Sir. I think that's the best information presently available."

"You're an amazing fellow, Fleming," MacArthur said. "I'd love to know where you got this."

MacArthur handed the onion skins back to Pickering and stood up. Pickering saw in that—with relief—that MacArthur did not expect an answer.

Colonel Willoughby interrupted himself in mid-sentence as everybody in the room stood up and came to attention.

"Willoughby, something has come up. Captain Pickering and I have to leave. That was a first-class briefing. Make me a one-page summary, would you please, at your first opportunity?"

"Yes, Sir," Colonel Willoughby said.

"Keep your seats, gentlemen," MacArthur ordered, and

then marched back up the aisle with Pickering and then Lieutenant Colonel Huff trailing after him.

"What was that you gave The General?" Huff asked.

"I'm sorry, Sid," Pickering said. "I can't tell you."

"I'm The General's aide," Huff argued.

"I'm sorry, Sid," Pickering repeated.

He saw the anger in Huff's eyes.

He really hates me, Pickering thought. *Hell, if I was in his shoes, I'd hate me, too. But he really doesn't have the Need to Know what those onion skins say, and I don't want him asking questions, of me or anyone else, about how I got them.*

The elevator was waiting. They rode up in it to MacArthur's office.

"Sid," MacArthur ordered, as he swept through the outer office, "will you get us some coffee, please? And have Sergeant Thorne bring his book? And then see that we are not disturbed?"

"Yes, Sir," Huff said.

Pickering saw that Sergeant Thorne already had his stenographer's notebook and a half dozen sharpened pencils in his hand. He still had time to make it to the inner door and open it for MacArthur.

Once in his office, MacArthur waved Pickering into a leather sofa. He walked to his desk, laid his gold encrusted cap on it, and then sat on the forward edge of the desk, supporting himself with his hands, looking upward, obviously deep in thought.

A staff sergeant appeared with a silver coffee set, put it on the coffee table in front of the sofa, and left.

When the door closed, MacArthur looked at Pickering.

"Pickering," he said solemnly, "my heart is so filled with thoughts of the nobility of the profession of arms that words may fail me."

Pickering, not having any idea how he was expected to respond to an announcement like that, fell back on the safe and sure: "Yes, Sir," he said.

"The first message," MacArthur went on, now looking at Sergeant Thorne, "is to Admiral Nimitz."

"Yes, Sir," Thorne said.

"My dear Admiral," MacArthur began. "Word has just

come to me of your glorious victory and of the incredible courage and devotion of your men which made it possible."

He stopped abruptly. He looked at Pickering. "Pour some of that coffee for us, will you please, Fleming? Thorne, will you have some coffee?"

"Not just now, thank you, Sir," Sergeant Thorne said.

MacArthur pushed himself off the desk and walked to the window.

"Read that back, please," he said.

Sergeant Thorne did so.

"Strike 'admiral,' make it 'Chester,' " MacArthur ordered. "Strike 'made it possible.' "

"Yes, Sir," Sergeant Thorne said.

MacArthur walked to the coffee table, picked up the cup Pickering had just poured, and stood erect.

"Read it, please."

"My dear Chester, Word has just come to me of your glorious victory and of the incredible courage and devotion of your men."

"Move 'has just come to me' to the end of the sentence," MacArthur ordered, "and read that."

"Word of your glorious victory and of the incredible courage and devotion of your men has just come to me."

MacArthur considered that a moment.

"Better, wouldn't you say, Fleming? Not yet quite right, but a decent start."

"I think that's fine, General," Pickering said.

"I would be grateful for any suggestions you might care to offer," MacArthur said. "This sort of thing is really very important."

Gracious and considerate, Pickering thought. *But important?*

And then he realized why it was important.

And not only as a footnote in the History of World War II, he thought, *when someone got around to writing that. That cable is an olive branch being offered to the Navy. Nimitz is supposed to be a salty sonofabitch, but he's human, and getting a cable from MacArthur addressed, 'My dear Chester' and using phrases like 'glorious victory' and 'the incredible courage and devotion of your men' is going to have to get to him.*

Is MacArthur aware of that? Is that the reason for this? Or is it just what he said, that his heart was 'filled with thoughts of the nobility of the profession of arms' and nothing more?

It's probably both, Pickering decided. *And I'm going to give him the benefit of the doubt and think it is mostly emotion. But he is not unaware of the ancient tactic of putting your enemy off guard, either.*

"General, I wouldn't presume to attempt to better that," Pickering said.

MacArthur didn't hear him.

"The Battle of Midway will live in the memory of man—strike 'memory of man,' make it 'hearts of our countrymen, alongside Valley Forge,' " he dictated. "Got that, Thorne?"

"Yes, Sir."

"I am having trouble," MacArthur said, "recalling significant U.S. Naval victories. If only he'd said something, I could compare that to 'Don't give up the ship,' or 'Damn the torpedoes, full speed ahead.' "

For God's sake, Pickering. Don't chuckle. Don't even smile. He's deadly serious.

"If I may say so, Sir, Valley Forge seems appropriate. A small band of valiant men, with inadequate arms, showing great courage against overwhelming odds."

MacArthur considered that for a moment.

"Yes," he said. "I see what you mean. Valley Forge will do. Thorne, add 'forever' after 'live'—'will live forever.' "

"Yes, Sir," Sergeant Thorne said.

"Read the whole thing back," MacArthur ordered.

Master Sergeant Thorne stood almost at attention before General MacArthur's desk as The Supreme Commander read the fifth—and Thorne hoped last—neatly typed version of his Personal for Admiral Nimitz.

MacArthur handed it back to him.

"Give that to Captain Pickering, please."

Pickering read it, although he knew it by heart.

"I think that's fine, Sir," he said. "The language is magnificent."

"From the heart, Pickering. From the heart."

Sergeant Thorne put his hand out for the Message Form.

"I can take it downstairs, Sir," Pickering said. "I have to see Lieutenant Hon anyway."

Downstairs was the Cryptographic Office and Classified Document Vault in the hotel basement.

"Very well," MacArthur said.

"Sir, I have the Personal for General Marshall ready, too," Sergeant Thorne said.

"Well, give that to the Captain, too," MacArthur said. "Two birds with one stone, right?"

Thorne left the office and returned with two envelopes. One was sealed. He took the Personal for Admiral Nimitz Message Form from Pickering and sealed it in the other.

"If that's all you have for me, Sir?" Pickering said.

"I appreciate your assistance, Fleming. See you at six?"

"And I'll tell Lieutenant Hon to stand by from seven, Sir?"

He involuntarily glanced at his watch. It was quarter to two. He had been in MacArthur's office for nearly three hours. That seemed incredible. There had been interruptions, of course, but they hadn't taken much time at all. There had been two calls from Mrs. MacArthur and a dozen officers seeking decisions. MacArthur had wasted little time making them. Most of that time had been spent composing MacArthur's Personal for Admiral Nimitz.

"Seven," MacArthur confirmed.

(Three)

First Lieutenant Hon Song Do, Signal Corps, U.S. Army Reserve (his very unlikely nickname was "Pluto"), and Captain Fleming Pickering, USNR, had an unusual relationship for an Army first lieutenant and a Navy captain. This had its roots in Hon's duties at SWPAO. There was virtually nothing classified SECRET or above in Supreme Headquarters SWPAO with which Lieutenant Hon was not familiar.

Lieutenant Pluto Hon was carried on the books as a cryptographic-classified documents officer. He was one of half a dozen so designated; and he performed those duties carefully and diligently. Only a very few people knew his primary function, however; for Pluto Hon had a MAGIC clearance. He was thus privy to the same information made available in Melbourne solely to MacArthur himself; his Intelligence Officer, Colonel Charles Willoughby; and Captain

Fleming Pickering, Personal Representative of the Secretary of the Navy.

Hon, a mathematician at the Massachusetts Institute of Technology before the war, was directly commissioned into the Army's Signal Corps, where mathematicians were critically needed for cryptographic operations. It had then been learned that not only was he fluent in written and spoken Japanese, he was steeped in the subtleties of Japanese culture.

When word of Hon's knowledge of Japanese culture reached the cryptographic-intelligence community, he was quickly transferred from Fort Monmouth, New Jersey, to Pearl Harbor, where the Navy code-breaking operation was located, and then to MacArthur's headquarters.

In one of the most closely held secrets of the war, Navy cryptographers at Pearl Harbor had succeeded in breaking many—though by no means all—of the Japanese military and diplomatic codes. The operation involved with decrypting the Japanese messages was called MAGIC; it was a major American triumph.

Still, once the intercepted messages were decrypted, most of them did not make complete sense; for the intercepted messages were all deeply impregnated with Japanese culture and traditions. Thus analysts were needed who were not only familiar with the language but who could almost feel and react to the messages the way a Japanese would.

Lieutenant Hon was also one of the very few people who had unquestioned access to the Classified Documents Vault. When a TOP SECRET document was signed out, and later returned, it was his duty to make sure it had been returned in its entirety. It would be impossible to do that without counting pages and looking at the maps.

Additionally, he had other duties involving Captain Fleming Pickering, USNR, personally. Since Pickering had been charged by Secretary of the Navy Frank Knox to provide his assessment of what was going on, and since very often his assessments were not flattering to any number of highly placed people, these assessments had to be kept secret not only from the enemy but from everybody in Supreme Headquarters SWPOA as well.

Hon personally encrypted all communications between

Pickering and Secretary Knox, and was thus privy to information known only to Pickering.

And on top of that, they had become friends. Pickering not only genuinely liked the outsize Korean, he felt a little sorry for him: The nature of Hon's duties shut him off from other junior officers; and off duty, he was in Australia. Australians did not like Asiatics—there were rigid immigration and even tourist regulations against them. It made no difference to them that Pluto Hon was a native-born American and an officer in the United States Army.

Lieutenant "Pluto" Hon stood up when Pickering walked into his tiny office. He was eating a Hershey bar.

"Good afternoon, Sir."

Hon had a thick Massachusetts accent. Pickering, a Harvard man himself, knew the dialect well. Hon was also a large and tall man, which Pickering thought of as another inconsistency. Orientals were supposed to be slight.

"How goes it, Pluto?" Pickering said, "I don't suppose you've got another Hershey bar?"

Hon took a small box of them from a desk drawer and handed it to Pickering.

"Aren't they feeding the brass these days?" Hon asked.

"I was sitting at the foot of the throne," Pickering said, as he unwrapped the Hershey bar. "The emperor was not hungry, so we didn't eat."

Pluto chuckled. "I also have peanuts," he said.

"Thank you, this will hold me. I'm eating at the palace, too. Where you will play bridge starting at about seven."

"I don't mind," Hon said. "He's one hell of a bridge player."

"Tonight it's the Empress and me against you and the throne," Pickering said.

"What have you got for me to brighten my otherwise dull day?"

"Two personals," Pickering said. "Oh, and before I forget it . . ."

He took the onion skins from his pocket and handed them to Hon.

"Burn those for me, will you?"

Hon took them and matter-of-factly started to read them.

"This must be the straight poop," he said. "KLW is a Lieutenant Commander named Ken Waldman. In MAGIC."

"How can you be sure?" Pickering asked, and then, without waiting for a reply, asked, "You know him?"

"Who else would have this much hard data this quick? Yeah, I know him. He was at MIT, too."

He held one sheet of the onion skin over a metal waste basket and touched the flame of his Zippo to it. It caught fire so quickly that Pickering suspected it had been chemically treated to do that.

Hon lit another sheet.

"You get this from that commander who flew in this morning?"

"Yeah. *A* commander."

"Mine had a briefcase chained to his wrist and a gun," Hon said. "He stopped in here and asked where he could find you before he gave me his stuff."

"Must be the same guy."

"What's the personals?"

"One to Nimitz. Powerful words of congratulation," Pickering said, and handed the envelope to Hon.

Hon tore it open and started to read it.

"What's the other one?"

"Personal to Marshall."

"What's it say?"

"I don't know, it's sealed," Pickering said, and handed it to him.

Hon read it, raised his eyebrows, and handed it to Pickering. "Based on my vast professional military experience, I don't think he's going to get away with that."

Pickering was reluctant to take the document, but curiosity overwhelmed his reticence. His curiosity was rationalized by his orders stating that it would be presumed he had the Need to Know anything that interested him. And as Hon turned to his cryptographic machine to encode the Personal to Nimitz, he read the Personal to Marshall.

TOP SECRET

FROM SUPREME HQ SWPOA

TO WAR DEPARTMENT WASH DC

FOLLOWING EYES ONLY GENERAL GEORGE C. MARSHALL CHIEF OF STAFF

PERSONAL FOR GENERAL MARSHALL

MY DEAR GEORGE X I HAVE TODAY DISPATCHED VIA OFFICER COURIER INITIAL PLANS FOR AN OPERATION I WOULD LIKE TO COMMENCE AS SOON AS I CAN OBTAIN AUTHORITY FROM THE JOINT CHIEFS OF STAFF X IT IS MY INTENTION TO STRIKE IN THE NEW BRITAIN DASH NEW IRELAND AREA USING THE US 32ND AND 41ST INFANTRY DIVISIONS AND THE AUSTRALIAN 7TH DIVISION ALL PRESENTLY IN AUSTRALIA X ONCE DRIVEN FROM NEW BRITAIN DASH NEW IRELAND THE JAPANESE WOULD BE FORCED BACK TO TRUK X TO ACCOMPLISH THE INITIAL ASSAULT AND FOR A PERIOD NOT TO EXCEED THIRTY DAYS THEREAFTER MY PLAN WOULD REQUIRE THE USE OF PAREN A PAREN ONE INFANTRY DIVISION TRAINED AND EQUIPPED FOR AMPHIBIOUS OPERATIONS X PAREN B PAREN AIR COVER FROM CARRIER BASED AIRCRAFT X PAREN C PAREN A SUITABLE NAVAL FORCE TO BOMBARD THE HOSTILE SHORE AND GUARD SHIPPING LANES X ONCE THE BEACHHEAD IS ESTABLISHED I CAN QUICKLY BEGIN AERIAL OPERATIONS FROM EXISTING FIELDS AND WILL NOT HAVE FURTHER NEED OF NAVAL ASSISTANCE X I MOST EARNESTLY SOLICIT NOT ONLY YOUR SUPPORT BUT ONCE YOU HAVE READ THE DETAILED PLANS YOUR WISE COUNSEL AS TO THEIR EFFICACY X TIME IS OF THE ESSENCE X WITH MY MOST SINCERE EXPRESSION OF REGARD I REMAIN AS ALWAYS FAITHFULLY DOUGLAS X END PERSONAL TO GENERAL MARSHALL

TOP SECRET

"The Navy's not going to loan him the First Marines and a couple of aircraft carriers," Hon said when he was sure Pickering had had time to read the Personal to Marshall. "Are they?"

His fingers were still flying over the cryptographic machine's typewriter keys as he talked. Hon always baffled Pickering when he did that. How could one part of his brain type while another part engaged in conversation?

"Not willingly," Pickering replied.

"And he doesn't know that?"

"I think he knows it," Pickering said. "I am always astonished when I find something he doesn't know."

And, he thought, *after that cable The Emperor just sent him, when Admiral Nimitz bitterly objects to this plan, he will not be as abrupt as he would otherwise have been.*

"It doesn't even make much sense, does it?"

"Yeah. I think it does. But I agree with you that the Navy will have a fit when they get this. I think they'd rather scuttle an aircraft carrier than loan it to MacArthur."

"What is that shit all about?" Pluto asked. "Can't the brass understand they're on the same side? That the goddamn Japs are whose throats they're supposed to cut?"

"Yours—and mine—Pluto, is not to reason why," Pickering said. "Can I change my mind about those peanuts?"

III

"Bingo!" Technical Sergeant Harry Rutterman, USMC, said softly, nodding his head with satisfaction.

Rutterman, a wiry man in his early thirties, raised his eyes from his desk and looked down the narrow, crowded room to an office at the end. The door was cracked open. That meant Captain Ed Sessions was in there; if he was gone, the door would have been closed and locked with iron bars and padlocks.

Rutterman lifted himself out of his chair and took the uppermost of a stack of yellow teletype sheets from his desk. He was wearing green trousers and a khaki shirt. His field scarf was pulled down, which was unusual for a regular Marine non-com; the manner in which he was armed would also be considered unusual elsewhere in the Corps. The pistol was a standard issue Colt Model 1911A1, but instead of the flapped leather holster and web belt, its standard accou-

44

trements, Rutterman had his pistol in a skeleton holster clipped to the rear of the waistband of his trousers; the pistol was inside his trousers with only the butt in sight.

He went to Captain Sessions's door, rapped it with his knuckles, and announced, "Rutterman, Sir."

"Come," Sessions answered, and Rutterman pushed the door open.

Captain Edward M. Sessions, USMC, was a tall, lithely muscular young officer, not exactly handsome, but attractive to women all the same. Like Rutterman, he had removed his blouse and pulled his tie down; and like Rutterman, he was armed in a manner not common in the Corps. He was wearing a leather shoulder holster, which held a short-barrelled Smith & Wesson .357 Magnum Revolver.

He had expected to spend his career as a Marine officer who followed the usual progression: from infantry platoon leader, to assistant staff officer of some sort at battalion level, and then to executive officer and company commander. He had in fact commanded a platoon, but while serving as an assistant S-2 of Third Battalion, Second Marines, he had attracted the attention of the Marine Intelligence Community by the literary quality of the routine reports and evaluations he was required to write.

These were written in a style that was the antithesis of the fancy prose that the word "literary" usually calls to mind. His words were short and simple; he came right to the point; and there was little chance of mistaking what he meant.

Instead of returning to a line company following his eighteen-month assignment as an assistant S-2, he was relieved from the assignment after only a year. First, he was sent to the University of Southern California at Los Angeles for six months intensive training in Japanese, and then he was assigned to Marine Corps Headquarters in Washington. He was put to work synopsizing Intelligence reports and translating Japanese documents that had come into American hands.

He had done that for six months when a far more experienced officer, a captain, fell ill three days before he was to board the Navy Transport Chaumont. The Captain was being sent to China (where the Fourth Marines were stationed in Shanghai) to have a close look at the Japanese

Army. Having no one else to send, they ordered Lieutenant Sessions to go in his place.

He performed far better than anyone expected. In his basic mission, he handled efficiently and accurately the more or less routine business of seeing how the Japanese Army was organized and equipped. And in a far more important and dramatic way, he knew what to do when the Japanese harassed a Marine convoy by dispatching Chinese "bandits" to rob it on a remote highway.

There was a nasty firefight, during which Sessions proved that he had the one characteristic the Marine Corps seeks in its officers above all others, the ability to function well and calmly under fire.

His promotion to captain came a full year before those who had been promoted to first lieutenant with him; by then it was clear that his career would henceforth be in the Intelligence field. At least twice a day, he dwelled on the thought that he would much rather be a line company commander in one of the regiments. But he was a Marine officer, and good Marine officers do—without complaint and to the best of their ability—what they are ordered to do.

"This is interesting, Harry," Captain Sessions said to Sergeant Rutterman. "The powers that be have determined that former members of the Abraham Lincoln Brigade are to be considered potentially subversive, are not to be granted security clearances, and are to be 'assigned appropriately.' "

"Interesting," Rutterman agreed. "Where'd that come from?"

"This came from G-2," Sessions said, "but it says, 'on the recommendation of the Attorney General.' That means it came from J. Edgar Hoover; I doubt if the Attorney General ever heard of the Abraham Lincoln Brigade."

Rutterman snorted.

"Have we got any, do you think?" Sessions asked.

"You mean us? Or the Corps generally?"

"In the Corps. I don't think we have any, Harry."

"There was 3000, 3500 of them. I'm sure that there's some in the Corps. But I'll bet most of them have already been tagged as Reds. What's that got to do with us?"

"Nothing that I can see; it's a Counterintelligence matter.

Unless you were in Spain fighting fascism and haven't told me. I think we were just on the distribution list."

Rutterman nodded.

"What have you got, Harry?"

"I think I have a Japanese linguist for Major Banning," Rutterman said, handing Sessions the sheet of teletype paper.

Major Edward J. Banning, one of the most knowledgeable-about-the-Japanese officers in the Marine Corps, had been the S-2 of the 4th Marines in Shanghai. He had gone with the Regiment to the Philippines when it had been transferred there just before the war had broken out.

He had been blinded by concussion during a Japanese artillery barrage on Leyte, and evacuated with other blinded men by submarine from Corregidor. His sight had returned as the submarine approached Pearl Harbor. After a month's recuperative leave he had returned to duty, and almost immediately he'd been ordered back to the Pacific as commanding officer of the purposely obfuscatorily titled "Special Detachment 14."

The mission of Special Detachment 14 was to support an organization known as "The Coastwatcher Establishment" of the Royal Australian Navy. When the Japanese had begun their march toward Australia down the islands, the Australians had left behind on the captured islands a motley collection of ex-colonial officials, plantation managers, and the like. They had been equipped with radios and were reporting on Japanese shipping, troop movements, and other matters of critical intelligence importance.

One of Captain Fleming Pickering's first reports from Australia to Secretary of the Navy Knox had informed him both of the existence of the Coastwatcher Organization and of the barely concealed hostility between it and the U.S. Navy. He recommended, strongly, that Knox establish a special unit—not subordinate to "Pearl Harbor brass hats"—to work with the Coastwatchers.

Properly handled, Pickering wrote, the Coastwatcher Establishment would be of enormous value. Knox responded by charging Marine Corps Intelligence with the responsibility of working with the Coastwatchers. The orders to the again purposefully obfuscatorily named Marine Office of Management Analysis had been to set up an outfit, with whatever priorities and funds were required, to do what Captain Fleming Pickering thought should be done. Special Detachment 14 had been the result.

There was a more or less standing requisition from Major Ed Banning for two kinds of specialists: radio technicians and Japanese-language linguists. What Banning wanted, the Marine Office of Management Analysis tried very hard to send him.

"Think?" Captain Sessions asked. "Does he speak Japanese or not? And assuming he wasn't in the Abraham Lincoln Brigade?"

"He's an officer candidate," Rutterman said. "They started sending a bunch of them through Boot Camp at Parris Island."

"So? What's the problem?"

"For one thing, he's five months, maybe a little more, away from being available for assignment. After he finishes Parris Island, he has to go through Officer Basic School at Quantico. And by that time, we'd have to fight for him anyhow; they'd want to send him to a Division. And Banning needs him now."

"So we take him and send him to Banning now," Sessions said. "As an enlisted man." He heard what he had said, and added: "That sounds a little ruthless, doesn't it? But Banning really needs linguists. 'For the good of the Corps,' all right?"

"Those guys who enlisted as officer candidates have a deal, Captain," Rutterman said. "They either get the bar, or they get discharged."

"And then what?" Sessions asked.

"They report him to his draft board, and he goes in the Army."

"What about a direct commission?"

"Two weeks ago, that would have been the answer; but now the word is every second john goes through Basic School at Quantico. No exceptions. We'd only pick up a couple of weeks, *if* we could get a slot for him at Quantico. Of course, if we did that, got him a direct commission, he would belong to us, and we could probably keep him."

"Damn!" Sessions said. "And there are some other questions. Is he for real? Can he get a security clearance?"

"He's got a security clearance. Permanent SECRET. The

FBI ran a complete background investigation on him when he first applied for the officer candidate program. Before they called him for active duty."

"So it would be reasonable to presume that his story that he lived in Japan for—how many years?"

"Ten, in all."

". . . checked out. And if that's the case, maybe he really does read and write Japanese."

"Yes, Sir."

"I think I better go see the Colonel," Sessions said. "And you better come with me."

The Colonel was Lieutenant Colonel F.L. Rickabee, USMC, who was carried on the Table of Organization and Equipment of Headquarters, United States Marine Corps, as a Management Analyst in the office of the Assistant Chief of Staff for Logistics. This had absolutely nothing whatever to do with his actual duties.

Colonel Rickabee, a tall, slight man who was in civilian clothing and didn't, truth to tell, look much like a Marine on a recruiting poster, heard out Captain Sessions and Technical Sergeant Rutterman.

"Ed, there's a courier plane to Parris Island at ten o'clock. Get on it. Go see this young man. First see if he really is fluent in Japanese. If he is, offer him instant sergeant's stripes and five-day delay en route home leave if he waives his current rights as an officer candidate. Tell him we'll arrange a commission for him later. If he gets on his high horse, Rutterman here will personally take him to 'Diego or 'Frisco and load him on the first plane for Australia as a private. Questions?"

"Sir, where are you going to get the authority to promote him to sergeant?" Sessions asked.

"The same place I got the authority to put him on the next plane to Major Banning. Banning desperately needs linguists. This linguist Rutterman found just may keep some Marines alive if I can get him to Banning. If I have to explain that to General Holcomb personally, I will. Questions?"

Captain Sessions was aware that two mornings a week, Lieutenant Colonel Rickabee went to Eighth and "I" Streets, S.E., in Washington. There, with the sliding doors to the Commandant's Dining Room closed, he took breakfast alone with the Commandant of the United States Marine Corps, newly promoted Lieutenant General Thomas Holcomb. If the Commandant was out of town for longer than a couple of days, Rickabee either went wherever he was, or had a private meeting with whoever was running the Marine Corps in Holcomb's absence.

"No, Sir," Sessions said, and then had a second thought. He glanced at his watch. "Sir, it's five past nine. I'm not sure I can make that ten hundred courier."

Colonel Rickabee looked thoughtful for a moment, and then dialed a telephone number from memory.

"Charley, Fred Rickabee. I'm sending an officer, Captain Ed Sessions, to Parris Island on your ten o'clock courier plane. See that it doesn't leave until he gets on it, will you?"

There was a pause, and then Rickabee said, "I don't care who gets thrown off, Sessions goes. And when he comes back, he'll be bringing a private with him. Questions?"

There was another pause.

"I've always been an unreasonable prick, Charley, you know that," Rickabee chuckled. He put the phone in its cradle and looked at Captain Sessions. "Questions?"

"No, Sir."

"Good job, Rutterman," Rickabee said, "finding this guy."

Then he dropped his eyes to the papers, most of them stamped TOP SECRET, on his desk, and shut Captain Sessions and Technical Sergeant Rutterman off from his attention.

(Two)
HEADQUARTERS, 2ND TRAINING BATTALION
UNITED STATES MARINE CORPS RECRUIT DEPOT
PARRIS ISLAND, SOUTH CAROLINA
1555 HOURS 15 JUNE 1942

"Colonel Westman for you, Sir," Major H.B. Humphrey's clerk, a small, stocky, young Corporal in tailored khakis, announced, putting his head in the door.

"Thank you," Humphrey said, reaching for the telephone on the desk of his office. The desk, like the building, was new. The building was so new it smelled of freshly cut pine. The interior walls of the hastily thrown up structure had not been finished; between the exposed studs the tar paper under the outer sheeting was visible.

Photographs of the chain of command—President Roosevelt, Secretary of the Navy Frank Knox, the Commandant of the Marine Corps, and the Commanding General of Parris Island—hung from bare studs. These photos were as much *de rigueur* for a battalion commander's office as the National Colors, the Marine Corps flag, and the battalion colors.

In addition to the desk and its chair, the office was furnished with a small safe, a filing cabinet, and two folding metal chairs.

"Major Humphrey, Sir," he said to the telephone.

He wondered what the hell Colonel Westman wanted. Westman was the Parris Island G-2 Intelligence Officer. There was very little that a training battalion had to do with Intelligence. For that matter, Humphrey had wondered idly more than once what the Parris Island G-2 did at all. The function of a G-2 in the Marines was to provide the Corps with whatever information he could lay his hands on about the enemy. There was no enemy anywhere close to Parris Island.

"One of your boots has attracted the attention of some people who sit pretty close to the divine throne, Humphrey," Colonel Westman announced without any preliminaries. "A man named Moore. John Marston Moore. An officer candidate. You know him?"

Humphrey thought it over a moment.

"No, Sir."

"I have had two telephone calls," Westman said. "The first was official. From Washington. A captain named Sessions was on his way down here to 'deal with' Private Moore. I was told it would behoove me to grease this captain's ways, and if necessary, to run interference for him."

"Sir, I don't think I understand . . ."

"The second call was back channel. From . . . an old friend of mine. An aviator. He said he thought I should know that this Captain Sessions who's coming on the courier plane works for Lieutenant Colonel Rickabee. That name mean anything to you?"

Humphrey thought about that for a moment.

"Sir, there was a Major Rickabee in the class ahead of me at the Command and General Staff College. That was '39. Thin officer. Not very . . . outgoing. I've met him, but I can't say I know him."

"That's him. A very interesting man. I served with him years ago in Santo Domingo. I hear he now has very interesting duties. You take my meaning?"

"No, Sir, I'm afraid I don't."

"He sits at the foot of the divine throne. OK?"

"I take your meaning, Sir."

"I think it would behoove you to give Captain Sessions whatever he asks for, Humphrey. If he asks for anything you don't feel you can give him, call me."

"Aye, aye, Sir. You don't know what he wants with Private Moore?"

"I was not told," Colonel Westman said. "When I asked, I was told that if Captain Sessions wanted me to know, he would tell me."

"Jesus Christ!"

"I had precisely the same reaction, Humphrey," Colonel Westman said. "I would like an after action report, if I don't hear from you in the interim."

"Aye, aye, Sir. When does Captain—Sessions, you said, Sir?—get here?"

"Sessions," Westman confirmed. "The courier plane is due here in thirty minutes."

"Thank you for the advance warning, Sir."

"Good afternoon, Major," Colonel Westman said, and hung up.

Major Humphrey called for his clerk, learned to his scarcely concealed annoyance that the battalion sergeant major had business on Main Post . . . which meant that he was already hoisting his first brew of the afternoon at the Staff NCO Club . . . and was not available.

"Find out what platoon a man named Moore, John Marston Moore, is in," Major Humphrey ordered. "Then send word I want him available; and that I want to see his Drill Instructor here, right now. And then go to personnel and get his record jacket."

"If I leave, Sir, there will be no one to answer the telephone."

"I know how to answer a telephone," Major Humphrey said, more sharply than he intended. "Get moving."

"Aye, aye, Sir."

Staff Sergeant J.K. Costerburg, Private John Marston Moore's Drill Instructor, was not very helpful: Moore had not given him any trouble, but on the other hand he hadn't been an outstanding trainee, either. There had been genuine concern that he was going to have trouble on the rifle range for a while, but he'd finally shaped up. He kept to himself.

"Sir, he's just not . . . *out of the ordinary,*" Staff Sergeant Costerburg said, almost visibly pleased that he'd found the right words.

Private Moore's record jacket, which included a synopsis of the FBI Complete Background Investigation, was more illuminating: Moore was the second of three children born to the Reverend Doctor and Mrs. John Wesley Moore. He had been born in Osaka, Japan, twenty-two years before. There was a notation that under a provision of the Immigration & Naturalization Act of 1912, as amended, Moore was considered to be a native-born American, as his father's service abroad as a missionary representative of the Methodist Episcopal Church was considered to be service abroad in the interest of the United States.

He had lived in the United States, in Washington and Philadelphia, from 1922 until 1929 (Humphrey checked the dates and did the mental arithmetic and came up with from the time he was two until he was eight), and then had returned to Japan with his family, staying there until 1940, during which time he had matriculated at the University of Tokyo. On his return to the United States, he had entered the University of Pennsylvania as a junior and graduated in June of 1941 with a Bachelor of Arts degree in Oriental Languages.

He applied for the Marine Officer Candidate Program in January 1942 and was accepted. He was sworn into the Marine Corps Reserve in February, and ordered to active duty 1 April.

Humphrey was aware that people who spoke Japanese were in great demand, and that a young officer who spoke Japanese would almost certainly be given duties to take advantage of his skill, but that did not explain the attention being paid to him by a lieutenant colonel who "sat at the foot of the divine throne."

He now knew a little something about Private John Marston Moore, but he had no idea what that little something meant. And there was no time to really think it through; for he was still examining the contents of his record jacket when Colonel Westman called again.

"The plane was early," Westman announced by way of greeting. "He's on his way in my staff car with one of my lieutenants."

"Thank you, Sir," Humphrey said. For a reply he got the clatter and click of a telephone being replaced in its cradle.

Captain Sessions appeared ten minutes after that. He was a stranger to Humphrey, but he had a manner that suggested that he had been a Marine before the war.

That didn't annoy Humphrey; but there was something about his attitude that did. He was polite, but superior. It was an attitude that Humphrey had sensed in other officers who worked in Headquarters, U.S. Marine Corps, and who seemed to be very much aware of their own importance.

"Sir, my name is Sessions," Sessions had begun. "I understand that someone telephoned to alert you that I was coming."

"They didn't tell me why," Humphrey said.

"I want to look at the service records of Private John Marston Moore, and then I'd like to talk to him, Sir."

"Have you got some kind of orders, Captain? Or at least some identification?"

"Yes, Sir," Sessions said. He handed Humphrey a small leather folder. It contained a gold badge, and an identity card sealed in plastic with Sessions's photograph and name—but not, Humphrey noticed with curiosity, his rank. And it was not a Marine Corps identity card. It bore the seal of the Navy Department, and the legend CHIEF OF NAVAL INTELLIGENCE. It identified Sessions as Special Agent, not as a Marine Captain.

"That ought to do it," Humphrey said, and then blurted, "I've never seen anything like that before."

"There's not very many of them," Sessions said, matter-of-factly.

"I've got Moore's record jacket here," Humphrey said.

"May I see it, please?" Sessions replied. "And then could you send for him, please, Major?"

"I've got him standing by," Humphrey said. "Is this boy in any kind of trouble, Captain?"

"Not so far as I'm concerned," Sessions replied, and then smiled, "I was about to put that same question to you, Major."

(Three)
UNITED STATES MARINE CORPS RECRUIT DEPOT
PARRIS ISLAND, SOUTH CAROLINA
1615 HOURS 15 JUNE 1942

Private John Marston Moore, United States Marine Corps Reserve, had practiced the maneuver, but he had never before rendered the rifle salute to a real officer: He marched through the door identified by a stenciled sign as that of MAJOR H.B. HUMPHREY, USMC, BATTALION COMMANDER, with his piece at right shoulder arms, determined to do so to the best of his ability.

He stopped eighteen inches from the Major's desk, with his heels together and his feet turned out equally and forming an angle of 45 degrees. He then moved his left hand smartly to the small of the stock, forearm horizontal, palm of the hand down, the first joint of his left forefinger touching the cocking piece of his Springfield Model 1903A4 rifle.

"Sir," he barked, looking at Major Humphrey, a thin, leather-skinned man of about thirty-five who wore his hair so short his scalp was visible, "Private Moore, J.M., reporting to the battalion commander as ordered."

Ordinarily, Private Moore had learned, persons in the Naval Service of the United States do not salute indoors, except when Under Arms. He was obviously, with the Springfield, Under Arms, but he had also learned in his six weeks of service in the Marine Corps that things were most often not as one expected them to be. He had asked the staff sergeant in the outer office what he was supposed to do with the rifle. The reply—"Get your ass in there and report to the Major"—had not been very helpful.

Major Humphrey touched his eyelid with his right hand, fingers together and straight, palm down.

The salute had been returned.

Private Moore cut his left hand smartly back to his right side, fingers extended and together, so that his thumb touched the seam of his utility trousers. He then looked six inches above Major Humphrey, in the prescribed position of attention.

"Order arms," Major Humphrey ordered, and then followed this command immediately with, "stand at ease."

Private Moore moved the Springfield so that it cut diagonally across his body, the center of the rifle just below his chin, held at the point of balance by the left hand. He moved his right hand from the butt on the rifle to a point one-third down from the muzzle, and then moved the rifle beside his right leg, checking the movement with his left hand. When the butt touched the floor, he moved his left hand so that its thumb touched the seam of his utility trousers. Then he leaned the Springfield forward, put twelve inches between the heels of his boots, and set his left hand in the small of his back. He was now At Ease.

"He's all yours, Captain," Major Humphrey said.

"Good afternoon, Moore. How are you today?" the Captain asked.

His tone was conversational, even friendly, which was almost astonishing, but what was genuinely astonishing was that the Captain had asked the question in Japanese.

"Very well, thank you, Sir," Private Moore said.

"Could you reply, please, in Japanese?" the Captain asked. Moore did so.

"Do you read and write Japanese with equal fluency?"

"Yes, Sir."

"Major," the Captain said, switching to English, "I wonder if there's some place I could talk to Private Moore privately?"

"You can use my office, of course," Major Humphrey said.

"Very kind of you, Sir. Thank you, Sir," the Captain said, and then waited for Major Humphrey to get up and leave.

It was not lost on Private Moore that no matter what their ranks, the captain was giving orders, however politely, to the major, and that the major didn't much like it.

Sessions waited until Major Humphrey had left the office, closing the door behind, and then turned to Moore. He opened his mouth, as if to speak, then chuckled.

In English, he said, "I was about to ask you how you find boot camp, but I suppose when you open your eyes in the morning, there it is, right?"

Now he laughed, almost a giggle.

John Marston Moore had no idea how to react. There was no emotion on his face at all. Sessions saw this.

"My name is Sessions," he said. "I'm from Headquarters, USMC."

"Yes, Sir?"

"You're posing something of a problem to the Marine Corps," Sessions began seriously, but then his eyes lit up in amusement. "Usually, with a private, and especially here, that works the other way around, but in this case, you're causing the problem."

"Sir?"

"I'm going to have to take your word that you read and write Japanese," Sessions said. "I suppose I should have brought some document in Japanese for you to read from, but I left Washington in rather a hurry and didn't think about that. And the way I write Japanese . . . that wouldn't be a fair test."

Moore had just decided that Marine Captain or not, this man was an amiable idiot, when Sessions met his eyes. The eyes were both intelligent and coldly penetrating; not the eyes of a fool.

"You do read and write Japanese with fluency, right?" Sessions asked.

"Yes, Sir."

"OK. You ever read any Kafka, Moore?"

"Sir?"

"Franz Kafka? Everyman's problems with a mindless bureaucracy? They kept telling him he was guilty, but they wouldn't tell him of what?"

"Yes, Sir, I know who you mean."

"This is going to be something like that, I'm afraid," Sessions said. "There is a Marine Corps unit somewhere which has a priority requirement for a man with your Japanese language skills. I can't tell you what that unit is, where it is—except somewhere in the Pacific—or what it does, because that's all classified."

"Sir—" Moore began hesitantly, and then plunged ahead. "Sir, I was told that I've been granted a SECRET security clearance."

"Yeah, I know. But then there's TOP SECRET, and above TOP SECRET are some other security classifications. In this case, your SECRET clearance wouldn't get you in the door."

"Yes, Sir."

"I don't suppose," Sessions said, "that based on what little I'm able to tell you, you would be disposed to volunteer for service with this unit, would you?"

I am being asked to do something. This is the first I have been asked, as opposed to being told, to do anything since I got off the Atlantic Coastline train in Yemassee, South Carolina.

An image of that scene popped into his mind, complete to sound and smell; it was the start of his first night of active duty in the Marine Corps.

They had gotten off the chrome-and-plastic, air-cushioned, air-conditioned ACL cars and transferred to ancient, filthy wooden passenger cars resurrected from some railroad junk yard for the spur line trip to Port Royal. From Port Royal, they had been moved to Parris Island, like cattle being carried to the slaughter house, in an open trailer truck.

In Port Royal, he heard for the first time the suggestion that he might as well give his soul to Jesus, because his ass now belonged to the Marine Corps. Those words had subsequently been repeated many times.

From the moment he boarded the spur line train in Yemassee, his every action had been ordered, usually at the top of some uniformed sadist's lungs, his language punctuated with obscenities.

He had once been ordered by a corporal to run around the barracks with a galvanized bucket over his head, his piece at port arms, shouting, "I am an ignorant asshole who can't tell the difference between his piece and his prick." He'd done it, too.

He had only been permitted to stop when he ran full bore into a concrete pillar and nearly knocked himself out. He could not recall, now, the offense.

And now I am being asked *to do something. I am not prepared to make a decision.*

"Sir, I don't know what you're asking me to do."

"Let me throw one more thing into the equation," Captain Sessions said. "It would also mean, for the time being, that you would give up your commission. One can be arranged at a later date, but you would not get one now."

"Sir—"

"The bone I am authorized to throw to you is sergeant's stripes, effective immediately, and a five-day delay en route leave, not counting travel time."

"Sir, I don't mean any disrespect, but could you tell me why I should do something like this? I'm almost through here. When I finish at Quantico, I'll be an officer."

He had clung to that, the belief that when he had endured all that Parris Island, specifically all that his Drill Instructor and his assistants, could throw at him, he would be granted a commission. An officer, even a lowly second lieutenant, was not required to obey the orders of enlisted men.

Captain Sessions didn't reply. He shrugged and opened his mouth as if to speak, but then closed it again.

"Couldn't this assignment wait until I get my commission, Sir?" Moore asked.

"No," Sessions said simply, "it couldn't. You're needed now."

"Captain, what if I tell you 'no'?"

Sessions shrugged his shoulders again, almost helplessly. He did not respond to the question, but after a moment, he said: "I suppose that in your shoes, I would react exactly the way you are. And I would probably snicker, at least privately, if someone like me announced the reason you should do what you're being asked to do is that you're a Marine, and when the Corps asks Marines to do something, they do it."

"I've only been in the goddamned Marine Corps six fucking weeks!" Moore heard himself blurt and was horrified.

The consequences of making a statement like that, especially to an officer, boggled the imagination.

Sessions, to Moore's genuine surprise, did not flare back at him. He looked at him and chuckled.

"Six weeks is long enough, don't you think? Don't you think that six weeks has changed you forever?"

"Oh, Christ," Moore said, and heard himself chuckle. "Yes, Sir, I think I have been permanently changed."

"For what it's worth," Sessions went on, "I've learned that you get back from the Corps whatever you put into it. Sometimes a little more."

He believes that. This man is not a fool, not one of the cretinous savages they make into drill sergeants. He's well educated—Christ, talking about Franz Kafka and Everyman at Parris Island! And he speaks Japanese, and not at all badly. And whatever this is they want me to do, it's important. He really did come down here to see me from Washington.

And what happens if I say 'no'? Since it is important, then obviously they will be annoyed that I have refused. So far as they're concerned, I'm a Marine and Marines do whatever they are asked, or told to do. I will have, so to speak, in their judgment, let the side down. And equally obviously, the consequences of that would be very unpleasant. Am I a Marine? Why do I have the insane urge to go along with this?

Possibly because he is the first man in authority to talk to me as if I were a human being, perhaps even an intellectual equal, since I got on that fucking train from Yemassee to Port Royal.

Fuck it! Why not? What the fuck have I got to lose? The fuckers are right, my fucking ass really does *belong to the fucking Marine Corps!*

Why, John Marston Moore! Listen to *your* language!

"Yes, Sir," Moore said. "Whatever it is you want me to do, Sir, is fine with me."

He had no idea what sort of response his patriotic, "Aye, Aye, Sir! Semper Fi, Sir! We Are All Marines In This Together, Sir!" decision would produce in Captain Sessions, but the one he got was not at all what he expected:

"OK," Sessions said, matter-of-factly, even coldly. "That's it. But don't feel noble. What you just did made you a sergeant and got you five days at home. If you had decided the other way, you would have been on a plane tomorrow as a private."

"Yes, Sir," Moore said, more as a reflex action than a reply.

"This is very serious business, and we can't take any chances with it whatever. Between now and tomorrow, I will come up with some sort of credible story for you to tell your parents when you go home. But from this moment on, you're operating under a whole new set of restrictions. For example, you will not tell anyone that you were pulled out of boot camp and made a sergeant, or that you even met me. If anyone asks you any questions, your response will be, simply, 'I'm sorry, I can't talk about that.' Clear?"

"Yes, Sir."

"Just so that I'm sure you understand me, that includes everybody here, including Major Humphrey. Clear?"

"Yes, Sir."

Sessions got up, walked to the door, and opened it.

"Major Humphrey? May I see you a moment, please, Sir?"

Humphrey came into his office, uneasy, Moore saw, about taking his own chair behind his desk.

"Something I can do for you, Captain?" he asked.

"Yes, Sir. There are several things I'd be grateful if you would do for me. From this point on, you will consider this conversation classified TOP SECRET."

"OK," Humphrey said. Moore had the feeling that Humphrey had only with effort kept himself from saying 'Yes, Sir.' There was now a tone of command, *I Will Be Obeyed,* in Sessions's voice that had not been there before.

"Sergeant Moore will not be returning to his platoon," Sessions said. "I will take his service records jacket with me . . ."

"*Sergeant* Moore?" Major Humphrey interrupted.

Captain Sessions ignored him. "In the next day or two, there will be a TWX from Enlisted Personnel routinely transferring him. You are to discuss the circumstances of Sergeant Moore's departure with no one."

"I understand, Captain," Humphrey said. "Colonel Westman, the G-2, has asked me for an after action report."

"I'll go see Colonel Westman when I leave here. You are not to tell him anything. I'll make sure he understands that I'm responsible for that decision."

"Whatever you say, Captain."

"I don't want the people in his platoon, boots or Drill Instructors, discussing the unusual circumstances of Sergeant Moore's departure," Sessions said. "Do you see any problem there?"

"No, that can be handled, I think. I'll have to tell my sergeant major something. You understand, he will be curious."

"OK. Tell him that there's been an administrative fuck-up—that shouldn't surprise him—and that we're quietly trying to make it right. I would rather you talk to him than me. And also, by the time Sergeant Moore and I get on the courier plane in the morning, I want him to be wearing the insignia of his rank. Which means that someone is going to have to go to his platoon and get his gear and run the shirts and blouses past a seamstress."

"I think the Gunny can handle that without trouble, Captain," Humphrey said.

"Another practical matter. Where is Sergeant Moore going to spend the night?"

"There's a guest house. I don't suppose too many eyebrows would be raised if he was in one of those rooms. He could be waiting for his wife, or mother, whatever."

"Particularly if he went to his room and stayed there until I fetched him in the morning, right?"

Humphrey nodded.

"How is he going to eat?"

"There's a snack bar," Humphrey said.

"Could I stay there, too?"

"It's an enlisted guest house," Humphrey said.

"OK. I'll get a room in the transient BOQ. Moore, you will be taken to the guest house. Your gear will be delivered to you there. You will take supper and breakfast in the guest house. You will not leave your room for any other purpose. I will fetch you at about eight-thirty tomorrow morning. You are to make no telephone calls, or communicate with anyone but myself. I will get you a number where I can be reached. Clear?"

"Aye, aye, Sir."

"Questions?" Sessions asked.

Christ, he thought, *I sound just like Colonel Rickabee.*

There were no questions.

(Four)
ENLISTED GUEST HOUSE
UNITED STATES MARINE CORPS RECRUIT DEPOT
PARRIS ISLAND, SOUTH CAROLINA
0730 HOURS 16 JUNE 1942

Sergeant John Marston Moore was unable to resist the temptation to examine himself carefully in the cheap and somewhat distorting full-length mirror mounted on the door of the closet in his room at the guest house.

He had last examined himself in a small and even more distorting mirror in the head of his barracks twenty-six hours before, after shaving. What had then looked back at him was a hollow-eyed, sunken-cheeked individual in baggy utilities. He had looked very much like every other boot in his platoon, except that he was taller than most of them, and the weight loss and musculature hardening of the physical conditioning had made him look skinnier.

What looked back at him now was a sergeant of the United States Marine Corps, wearing a stiffly starched khaki shirt and a sharply creased green uniform. He moved slightly, so that his left shoulder pointed at the mirror and looked at the reflection of his new chevrons.

Then he met his eyes in the mirror and shook his head. He looked closer. He still had what he thought of as a "boot head"—a head an electric clipper had shorn of all hair, down to the skin, in ninety seconds. His head was by no means recovered from that outrage.

With the boot head I still look like a boot.

He went to the double bed where he had passed the night, picked up his fore-and-aft cap, put that on, and examined himself in the mirror again. That was better. The cap concealed the top of his head from view.

He had woken in the bed at four o'clock, conditioned by six weeks of waking at that hour to the shrill blast of a whistle and the ritual admonition to drop his cock and pick up his socks.

For a moment, he hadn't known where he was, for the room was pitch dark. There had always been some kind of light in the squad bay, if only what came into the long, narrow, and crowded room from the head. And then he had remembered what happened, out of the blue, the previous afternoon.

They would have wondered, the guys in the platoon, what the fuck had happened to Moore, J. He was known as Moore, J. because there were two Moores in his platoon. The other one, from Connecticut, was Moore, A. Moore, J. had never learned what Moore, A.'s "A" had stood for.

"What the fuck happened to Moore, J.?"

"Who the fuck knows. They sent for him. Company, I think."

"What the fuck did he do?"

"Who the fuck knows?"

Eventually, someone's curiosity would overwhelm his good sense and he would ask, waiting until he thought one of the DI's assistants was in an unusually kind mood.

"Sir, permission to speak, Sir?"

"Speak, Asshole."

"Sir, whatever happened to Moore, J., Sir?"

"If the Marine Corps wanted you to know, Asshole, I would have told you. What are you doing, Asshole, writing a book?"

"Yes, Sir. Sorry, Sir. Thank you, Sir."

He had not been able to get back to sleep. After a while, he had gotten out of the double bed and stood at the window in his underwear and looked out at the deserted streets.

Then the sounds of mating had come through the thin walls from the next room. He remembered hearing them the night before, waking him about half past nine.

Someone, he had thought, *was making up for lost time.*

It had been funny for a moment . . . and then somehow erotic, as his mind's eye filled with what was going on next door. And then finally it was terribly sad, although he didn't quite understand why that should be the case. The Marine Corps, he had noticed from signs at the Reception Desk, seemed determined that no Marine should share one of its Parris Island Enlisted Guest House rooms with a lady to whom he was not legally joined in marriage.

He hadn't thought much about sex since he'd been at Parris Island. For one thing, there hadn't been time to think about sex or anything else. For another, he had always been exhausted; he had woken up exhausted. And he thought it was possible . . . he had learned that at Parris Island anything was possible . . . that they did indeed lace the chow with saltpeter as the folklore had it.

There was a knock at the door. He looked at it in astonishment. Since he had been at Parris Island, closed doors, what few of them there were, had been flung open whenever they were noticed.

The door opened. It was the Sergeant Major.

"Good morning," the Sergeant Major said. "You're up."

"Yes, Sir."

The Sergeant Major smiled. He was a bald, barrel-chested man, whose blouse wore the hash marks, one for each four years of service, of two decades in the Marine Corps.

"Sergeant, sergeants do not say 'Sir' to other sergeants," he said. "Only boots do that."

Moore took off his fore-and-aft cap and rubbed his boot head.

"It'll grow back," the Sergeant Major, understanding the gesture, chuckled. "Keep your cap on when you can. Let's catch some breakfast."

Moore had been given a room on the upper floor of the two-story, newly constructed, frame building. As he followed the Sergeant Major down the stairs to the first floor, they ran into Captain Sessions coming up.

"Good morning, Sir," the Sergeant Major said. "I thought I would make sure that Sergeant Moore got his breakfast."

"My mission, too," Sessions said. "The corporal in the BOQ said it would be all right for me to eat in the snack bar."

"Yes, Sir. It's run by the Base Exchange. Neutral territory."

"Good morning, Moore. You packed?"

"Yes, Sir."

"Then let's eat."

"Would I be in the way, Sir?" the Sergeant Major asked.

"Not at all," Sessions said.

"I've got a staff car, too, Sir. I thought I could take you and Sergeant Moore to the airfield. And then you could turn Colonel Westman's car loose."

"Fine," Sessions said.

"I always feel sorry for colonels who have to walk, Sir," the Sergeant Major said, solemnly.

"I'm sure you do, Sergeant Major," Sessions said, and then

laughed. "Take Moore to the snack bar, and I'll go tell the colonel's driver he can go."

The breakfast fare was simple, but the eggs and the hash-brown potatoes were served on plates, and they sat at chairs at four-place tables covered with white oil cloth, and the china coffee mug had a handle; and that combined to make it, Moore thought, the most elegant meal he'd had since he left Philadelphia.

And there was something else. A newspaper. *The Charleston Gazette*. He hadn't seen a newspaper since coming to Parris Island, either.

There was a photograph on the front page of a tall, skinny American officer, a lieutenant general, Moore could now tell. He was seated at a table on what looked like a porch, wearing a tieless, mussed khaki shirt. There were three other American officers sitting with him. On the other side of the table were Japanese officers.

JAPS RELEASE PHOTO OF WAINWRIGHT SURRENDER, the headline over the picture said. Under it, the caption read: "War Department officials confirmed that Lieutenant General Jonathan M. Wainwright, U.S. Commander in the Philippines, sits (center, left) in this photograph, which the Japanese claim depicts General Wainwright's surrender to Japanese General Mashaharu Homma (center, right) May 5. The photo was obtained via neutral Sweden."

"That's a bitch, isn't it?" the Sergeant Major said, tightly.

"I think that must be the toughest thing an officer ever has to do," Sessions said. "God, what a humiliation!"

"It was on the radio last night that General Sharp surrendered Mindanao," the Sergeant Major said. "That's it. The Japs now own the Philippines."

"I know some of the people who are now prisoners," Sessions said, sounding as if he was thinking aloud, "if they're still alive."

"Yes, Sir, I know," the Sergeant Major said.

"How do you know that?" Sessions asked.

Moore sensed that Sessions had been made uneasy by the apparently innocent statement and wondered why.

"I'm an old China Marine, too, Captain. In my last hitch I was the S-3 Operations Sergeant for the 4th."

"Were you?" Sessions asked, and now the suspicion in his voice was evident.

"Yes, Sir. The 4th was a good outfit. Good people. I had sort of a special buddy. Guy named Killer McCoy."

"You're moving into a mine field, Sergeant Major," Sessions said, softly. "Sometimes, playing auld lang syne is not the thing to do."

"Oh, I don't mean to . . . I wasn't trying to pump you for poop, Sir. Really. It was just that Killer and I had the same ideas about who was a good Marine officer and who wasn't."

"Which means?"

The Sergeant Major hesitated momentarily, and then met Sessions's eyes.

"I got three, four staff NCOs who could have taken care of Sergeant Moore for you, Sir. I sort of wanted to do it myself. You know, any friend of The Killer's . . ."

Sessions looked at the Sergeant Major for a long moment before he replied.

"That's very kind of you, Sergeant Major. I'm touched. Thank you."

"No thanks necessary, Sir," the Sergeant Major said. "There's not many of us old China Marines left now. I figure we should try to take care of each other, right?"

"You didn't get this from me, Sergeant Major," Sessions said. "But the Killer made it out. He's with the 2nd Raider Battalion."

"I hadn't heard that. Thank you, Captain."

"What's the word on the courier plane?" Sessions said, obviously changing the subject.

"We better get out to the airport by say nine-fifteen, Sir."

Sergeant John Marston Moore had no idea what the conversation between the Sergeant Major and Captain Sessions was all about, but he understood that Captain Sessions had done something—probably in China, there was all that talk about Old China Marines—that had earned him the respect of the old Marine non-com. And he had the feeling that earning the Sergeant Major's approval didn't come easily.

He wondered about "The Killer." If he was the "special buddy" of the sergeant major and held in high regard by Captain Sessions, "The Killer" was obviously one hell of a

Marine. Hash marks from his wrist to his shoulder, a breast covered with twenty, thirty years worth of campaign ribbons, barrel chested and leather skinned, with a gravel voice to match.

There was something really admirable about these professional warriors, Moore thought. They were latter day Centurions. Or maybe gladiators? Whatever they were, they weren't like ordinary men. For them, war was a way of life.

Captain Sessions looked at his watch.

"Well," he said. "Let's get the show on the road. It never hurts to be early."

"You're all packed, right?" the Sergeant Major asked Moore.

"All packed," Moore replied, stopping himself just in time from replying, "Yes, Sir."

"Go get your stuff then," the Sergeant Major said. "I'm parked right out in front."

"One late thought," Captain Sessions said. "There's always one late thought, too late to do anything about. Have you been paid? Have you got enough money to carry you, Moore? Enough for the train ticket between Washington and Philadelphia?"

"The train ticket between Washington and Philadelphia"? I'm actually leaving Parris Island and going home. Why is that so incredible?

"I haven't been paid, Sir," Moore said. "But I have money."

"You're sure?"

"Yes, Sir."

"Go get your gear, Moore," Captain Sessions said.

IV

As the Sergeant Major drove them to the small airfield that served the Parris Island Recruit Depot, Sergeant John Marston Moore, USMCR, wondered what his father was going to say about his turning down an officer's commission and then going off to God only knows where in the Pacific. His father—to put it mildly—had not been pleased when he joined the Marine Corps in the first place; and he'd probably go into a righteous rage that he was not going to be an officer, at least not for the foreseeable future. To make matters worse, John couldn't even tell his father the reason why he'd made his choice.

All the same, there was no sense worrying about his father. . . . He'd learned not to worry about things he had no control over. And besides, no matter how used his father was to getting his own way, he could not bend the U.S. Marine Corps to his will.

Moore had flown only twice before in his life, both times during the family's last trip home from Japan: They'd left the ocean liner in San Francisco, and then they'd flown on from there via Chicago to New York. The flight from San Francisco to Chicago had been on Transcontinental & Western Airlines, and from Chicago to New York on Eastern. The airplanes had been essentially identical, large, twenty-odd-passenger Douglas DC-3s. Eastern had called theirs "Luxury Liners of the Great Silver Fleet."

John Marston Moore knew he would never forget that trip. He still had a flood of memories from it. He even remembered the name stenciled on the Eastern airplane's nose; it was *The City of Baltimore*. He also recalled watching his father take his mother's hand, bow his head, and mouth a prayer as the TWA airplane started down the runway in San Francisco.

He hadn't forgotten, either, the justification his father put forth for the extra expense of flying: "The Lord is a hard taskmaster," he would intone in his most virtuous voice, "who wants all that I can give Him. 'Missions' needs me in Philadelphia as soon as I can reach there. I've already spent a great deal of time at sea on the voyage from Yokohama, and that has kept me out of touch with 'Missions' for weeks. If I take the train, I'll be traveling another five days, while it will only take thirty-six hours by airplane. Obviously, taking the plane is the clear will of the Lord."

By then, John Marston Moore had long since decided that the Reverend Doctor John Wesley Moore was a pious hypocrite. A number of arguments supported this judgment. His father, for example, had delayed their departure from Japan for nearly three weeks, so they could return to the United States in first class aboard the *Pacific Princess,* the flagship of the Pacific & Far East Shipping Corporation fleet. The alternative would have been to travel on one of the Transpacific freighters which made their comfortable but spartan passenger accommodations available to missionaries and their families at reduced rates.

"Your Uncle Bill would insist," the Reverend Doctor Moore told John Marston Moore and his sisters. "He would know how much I need the rest."

Uncle Bill—William Dawson Marston IV—was president of the family business, Dawson & Marston Paper Merchants.

Dawson & Marston had been in business in Philadelphia since 1781, on Cherry Street, near the Schuylkill River. If John Marston Moore had been a betting man, he would have laid five to one that the first time Uncle Bill heard about the first-class cabins on the *Pacific Princess* was when the bill arrived for payment at Dawson & Marston.

John knew no one in the world who could muster the audacity to ask his father the obvious question: "You could have flown alone at one third the cost, and then the family could have followed by train . . . why didn't you do that?" If someone by chance had dared to ask him such a thing, his father would have replied—with a perfectly straight face, believing every word that poured from his lips—that it was clearly his Christian duty to be with his family and protect them from the well-known hazards of a transcontinental journey.

The Reverend Doctor Moore's concept of his clear Christian duty to his family had also been behind their twelve-room house in Denenchofu; the chauffeured Packard; the semiannual vacations in first-rate hotels in Australia and New Zealand; the monthly crates of canned goods that arrived from Boston; and everything else that made their life saving infidel souls for the Lord in far off Japan far more comfortable than any of their co-religionists in America would have imagined.

It was not as if he was living high on the hog on funds intended to educate and convert Asiatic heathens . . . he did not misappropriate funds; he'd never dream of defrauding "Missions." He was in fact on the whole a very good man. Still, though the salary and living allowance he was paid by "Missions" was not at all generous, the Reverend Doctor Moore didn't complain about his stipend, neither did he make any attempt to live on it. John long ago concluded that most of what "Missions" paid his father went to feed the servants.

Though it was only peripherally connected with most other functions of the Methodist Episcopal Church, "Missions" was more formally known as "The William Barton Harris Methodist Episcopal Special Missions to the Unchurched Foundation." It was founded in 1866 by a grant from Captain James D. Harris of Philadelphia.

Harris Shipping predated the American Revolution and was prosperous before the Civil War. But the war had swelled its coffers beyond anyone's imagination. On Captain Harris's death, the foundation received his entire estate, his wife having died the year before he did; and they'd lost their only son, William Barton Harris, in the Civil War.

The stated purpose of Missions was "to bring the Gospel of Jesus Christ and the Hope of Eternal Life to those who would not normally receive the blessing, such as Merchant Seamen, heathen Asiatics, the natives of the Caribbean Islands, and the former slaves now residing in those same islands."

While it was to be guided by the principles of Methodism, and it was "to be hoped that principal officers will be Methodist Episcopal Clergy and that the Foundation will be supported by the ever increasing generosity of Methodists," it was not to "become part of, or subject to the direction of, any local or national Methodist Episcopal organization." A key phrase of the bequest went on to state, "if at any time it becomes evident that the Foundation cannot continue its Christian mission, as specified herein, its assets will be liquidated and conveyed to the Philadelphia Free Public Library."

The rumor, Uncle Bill had once told John Marston Moore, was that "The Captain" had not seen eye to eye with his Bishop and was not about to give him control of his money. But whatever the truth, "Missions" had evolved into an organization with three major arms: The Seaman's Mission provided services to merchant seamen from Boston to Charleston—primarily cheap, clean YMCA-like accommodations and other related socio-religious services; the Caribbean Mission operated schools and social services in the Caribbean; and the Asiatic Mission performed a similar function in the Orient.

Each arm was headed by a Methodist clergyman, while another served as Superintendent; and two of the seven trustees were also Methodist clerics. The other five trustees were a Presbyterian Minister; an Episcopal priest; and three laymen. From the beginning, one of these had either been a Marston or someone married to a Marston. Uncle Bill had succeeded his father as a Missions Trustee.

Philadelphia Methodist and social circles showed very little surprise when the son-in-law of William D. Marston III, a long time Missions trustee, was married and ordained during the same week that he joined Missions; neither was there much surprise when years later the now Reverend Doctor John Wesley Moore, brother-in-law of Missions trustee William D. Marston IV, was named to head the Asiatic Mission.

But Philadelphia Methodist and social circles would have been surprised, John Marston Moore knew, if it ever became generally known how well the Reverend Doctor John Wesley Moore lived while serving the Lord. His father, of course, was ready with an explanation for it—if that ever became necessary: Though *he* was perfectly willing to live a life of austerity, indeed poverty, while in the Service of the Lord, not only had his beloved wife and adored children *not* been so moved to serve the Lord, but the Lord, in his infinite wisdom, had moved his brother-in-law, that fine Christian gentleman, to extraordinary generosity toward his sister and nieces and nephews.

John Marston Moore wondered now and again just how much of Dawson & Marston Paper Merchants, founded AD 1781, his parents actually owned. And for that matter, he had questions about the amounts involved in the trust funds that had been set up for him and his sisters by grandparents on both sides of the family. But the few times he'd asked, he was told that he need not just now concern himself with that sort of thing. "The Lord has done very well, so far, wouldn't you agree, John, providing for your needs?"

If John Marston Moore didn't know his father as well as he did, he would never have believed it possible for anyone to be such a good man—perhaps even close to a saintly man—and still be a pious hypocrite. But the younger Moore had pages of illustrations in his own personal book of memories demonstrating the truth of that hypothesis.

One evening, for instance, while his father was literally warming in his hand a snifter of Remy Martin cognac at the Union League Club, John Marston Moore had been forbidden to live in a fraternity house at the University of Pennsylvania, because it was common knowledge that the fraternity houses were awash with intoxicants. As the only son of a Man of God of Some Position, he had to be quite careful of appearances.

The airplane parked in front of the wood frame, single-story Operations Building at the airfield was much smaller than the Douglas DC-3s of TWA and Eastern. Captain Sessions identified it for him as a Beech Aircraft D-18. The legend MARINES was painted on the fuselage.

There were more than a dozen would-be passengers already in the wooden operations building hoping to get one of the eight seats on the airplane. Since three of these men were officers senior to Captain Sessions, Moore wondered if that meant they would have to travel to Washington as he had come to Parris Island, by train.

But he quickly found out that the seats on the Beech were assigned not by rank but by priority. It did not surprise him, however, that Captain Sessions had a priority: The first two names called out to board the plane were Sessions and Moore.

As they filed out to the plane, one of the pilots handed each of them a brown bag containing a baloney sandwich and an apple. The pilots were both Marine sergeants; Moore found that very interesting. He thought that only officers were permitted to fly.

If there were sergeants who did things like fly airplanes, perhaps there were other things a sergeant—Sergeant John Marston Moore, for example—could do besides screaming obscenities at boots or conducting close order drill. That made him feel a good deal better about having given up—at least for the time being—his promised officer's commission.

Once they found seats, Moore saw that compared to the plushness of the planes he was used to, the D-18 was rather crudely finished inside. But that didn't bother him. The very idea of flying from South Carolina to Washington on a military airplane was exciting. He tried to muster what savoir faire he could to conceal this from Captain Sessions.

But just after the pilots walked down the narrow aisle to the cockpit and sat down to start the engines, curiosity overwhelmed him, and he turned to Captain Sessions.

"Sir, I thought all pilots were officers."

"Just most of them," Sessions replied. "In the Army," he

went on, "they all are. But both the Navy and the Marine Corps have enlisted pilots; oddly enough, they're called 'Flying Sergeants.' Don't worry, Moore, I personally would rather be flown around by a Flying Sergeant than by some kid fresh out of Pensacola."

After the airplane took off, it flew right over the Recruit Depot. Moore could see the small arms ranges, and even platoons of boots marching around on the parade ground. The thought ran through his mind that it was conceivable that he was looking down at his old platoon.

The flight to the Anacostia Naval Air Station just outside Washington was much too short for Moore's liking. The day was clear, and there was something very nice indeed about being able to look down at the lush spring country. It didn't bother him at all that the sandwiches were dry, the apple mushy, and the coffee in the thermos jug lukewarm.

Technical Sergeant Harry Rutterman was waiting for them when the airplane landed. As they got out of the airplane, he came up to them and saluted Captain Sessions, who smiled as he returned it.

"Nice flight, Sir?"

"Why do I suspect that your meeting me has nothing to do with your all-around admiration for me as an officer and human being?" Sessions replied.

"The Captain, Sir, has for some reason a suspicious nature where I am concerned."

"Come on, Rutterman," Sessions said with a smile. "What's going on?"

"The Colonel wants you right now," Rutterman said. "He even sent his car. I'll take care of Sergeant Moore from here."

"Brief me on that," Sessions said, and then, "Excuse me. Moore, this is Sergeant Harry Rutterman."

Rutterman gave Moore a broad smile, and then—unintentionally, Moore decided—he crushed his hand in an iron handshake.

"Welcome to Never-Never Land, Sergeant," he said.

"OK, Rutterman," Sessions said. "Enough!"

"Yes, Sir," Rutterman said. "As of this morning, Private Moore was transferred to Baker Company, Headquarters Battalion, here. Then, recognizing the enormous contribution to the Corps he is about to make, they promoted him to Sergeant. Then they transferred him to Marine Barracks, Navy Yard, Philadelphia. I checked the travel times. He has forty-eight hours to get here from Parris Island, and twenty-four to get to Philadelphia after he leaves here. When his orders get to Philadelphia, he'll have seven days to get to San Diego. I got him an airplane ticket from New York to Los Angeles, which will put him there in about thirty-six hours. He has to take the train from Los Angeles to 'Diego. So I didn't put him on leave. I mean, why? What's important is that he gets on the plane in 'Diego on the twenty-first, right? This way, he won't get charged any leave time."

"I don't think I want to hear about this," Sessions said.

"It's all according to regulations, Captain," Sergeant Rutterman said, sounding slightly indignant.

"The trouble is, Sergeant, that you read things in regulations that no one else can see," Sessions said. "But he has a seat on the courier from San Diego on the twenty-first, right? That's all locked in?"

"As well as it can be, Sir. You know what happens, sometimes. An unexpected senior officer shows up wanting a seat . . ."

"What's his priority?" Sessions interrupted.

"Six As," Sergeant Rutterman had replied. "The Colonel had to make a couple of phone calls himself, but he got it."

Sergeant John Marston Moore wondered what in the world they were talking about.

"What else can we do?"

"Odd that you should ask, Sir—"

"If you're about to suggest that out of an overwhelming sense of duty, you would be willing to take the Sergeant out there yourself, to make sure he doesn't get bumped out of his seat by 'an unexpected senior officer . . .' "

"That thought . . ."

"No, Goddamn it," Sessions said, but was unable to contain a smile. "We must have somebody already out there who can get him through Outshipment despite your 'unexpected senior officer.' "

"I'll think of someone, Sir," Rutterman said.

"Don't be downcast, Rutterman," Sessions said. "It was a good try. One of your better ones."

"Thank you, Sir," Rutterman said.

Sessions turned to Moore.

"I don't suppose you understood much of that, did you, Moore?"

"No, Sir. I'm afraid . . ."

"Sergeant Rutterman will make it all clear, beyond any possibility of misinterpretation . . . Right, Rutterman?"

"Aye, aye, Sir."

". . . before he puts you on the train," Sessions concluded.

"Yes, Sir," Moore said.

Sessions met his eyes.

"Most of this will make sense when you get where you're going and learn what's required of you," Sessions said. "Until you get there, you're just going to have to take my word that it's very important, and that the security of the operation is really of life-and-death importance . . ."

"Yes, Sir," Moore said.

"Damn," Sessions said. "Security clearance! What about that? A lousy SECRET won't do him any good."

"The Colonel had me get the full FBI report on Moore . . ."

"They gave it to you?" Sessions asked, surprised.

"They owed us one," Rutterman said. "And he reviewed it and granted him a TOP SECRET. What more he may have to have, he'll have to get over there."

Sessions looked thoughtful for a moment, and then put out his hand.

"Good luck, Sergeant Moore. God go with you."

Moore was made somewhat uneasy by the reference to God. It was not, he sensed with surprise, simply a manner of speech, a cliche. Sessions was actually invoking the good graces of the Deity.

"Thank you, Sir," he said.

Rutterman had a light blue 1941 Ford Fordor, with Maryland license plates. But a shortwave radio antenna bolted to the trunk and stenciled signs on the dashboard (MAXIMUM PERMITTED SPEED 35 MPH; TIRE PRESSURE 32 PSI; and USE ONLY 87 OCTANE FUEL) made it rather clear that while the car had come out of a military motor pool, for some reason it was not supposed to look like a military vehicle.

When they got to Union Station, Rutterman parked in a

No Parking area and then took a cardboard sign reading NAVY DEPARTMENT—ON DUTY—OFFICIAL BUSINESS from under the seat and put it on the dashboard.

"If you don't think you'd lose control and wind up in New York or Boston, why don't you buy a Club Car ticket and have a couple of drinks on the way?" Rutterman suggested. "Otherwise, you're liable to have to stand up all the way to Philly."

"You reading my mind?" Moore asked.

"And I do card tricks," Rutterman said with a smile.

Moore bought his ticket and then, bag in hand, headed for the gate.

"You don't have to do any more for me, Sergeant," Moore said. "I can get on the train by myself."

"I want to be able to say I watched the train pull out with you on board," Rutterman replied.

A hand grabbed Moore's arm, startling him.

It was a sailor, wearing white web belt, holster and puttees, and with a Shore Patrol "SP" armband. Moore saw a second SP standing by the gate to Track Six.

"Let me see your orders, Mac," the Navy Shore Patrolman said.

Moore took from the lower pocket of his blouse a quarter-inch thick of mimeograph paper Rutterman had given him on the way to the station and handed it over.

"And your dog tags, Mac," the SP said.

"Slow day?" Sergeant Rutterman asked. "Or do you just like to lean on Marines?"

"What's *your* problem, Mac?" the SP asked, visibly surprised at what he obviously perceived to be a challenge to his authority.

"My problem, Sailor, is that I don't like you calling Marine sergeants 'Mac.' "

"Then why don't you show me your orders, *Sergeant?*" the SP said, as the other SP, slapping his billy club on the palm of his hand, came up to get in on the action.

Rutterman reached in the breast pocket of his blouse and came out with a small leather folder. He held it open for the SP to read.

Moore saw that whatever Rutterman had shown the SP, it produced an immediate change of attitude.

"Sergeant," the SP said, apologetically, almost humbly, "we're just trying to do our job."

"Yeah, sure, you are," Rutterman said, dryly. "Can we go now?"

"Yeah, sure. Go ahead."

Rutterman jerked his head for Moore to pass through the gate.

"Goddamned SPs," he muttered.

"What was that you showed him?" Moore asked.

"You forget you saw that," Rutterman said. "That's not what you're supposed to do with that."

"What was it?" Moore asked.

"What was what, Sergeant?" Rutterman asked. "Didn't Sessions tell you the way to get your ass in a crack around here is to ask questions you shouldn't?"

His voice was stern, but there was a smile in his eyes.

"Right," Moore said.

Rutterman boarded the train with him, saw that he was settled in an armchair in the club car, and then offered him his hand.

"I'll give you a call tomorrow or the next day," he said. "To tell you how the paperwork is moving."

"I'll have to give you my number," Moore said.

"I've got your number," Rutterman smiled, then shook his head. "Don't forget to get off this thing in Philadelphia."

"I'll try," Moore said. "Thank you, Sergeant."

"What for?" Rutterman replied, and then walked out of the club car.

(Two)
HEADQUARTERS, FIRST MARINE DIVISION
WELLINGTON, NEW ZEALAND
0815 HOURS 16 JUNE 1942

On Sunday 14 June, when the first elements of the First Marine Division (Division Headquarters and the 5th Marines) landed at Wellington, New Zealand, from the United States, they found on hand to greet them not only the Advance Detachment, which had flown in earlier, but an officer courier from the United States, who had flown in more recently.

The officer courier went aboard the USS *Millard G. Fillmore* (formerly the *Pacific Princess* of the Pacific & Far East lines) as soon as she was tied to the wharf. He was immediately shown to the cabin of Major General Alexander A. Vandergrift, the Division Commander.

In the courier's chained-to-his wrist briefcase, in addition to the highly classified documents he had carried from the States on a AAAAAA priority, there was a business-size envelope addressed to the First Division's Deputy Commander, Brigadier General Lewis T. Harris, and marked "Personal."

Since it took a few minutes to locate the Division's Classified Documents Officer, who had to sign for the contents of the courier's briefcase, General Harris, who was in General Vandergrift's cabin at the time, got his "personal" letter before the other, more official documents were distributed.

The letter was unofficial—a "back channel communication" written by a longtime crony, a brigadier general who was assigned to Headquarters, USMC. Harris tore it open, read it, and then handed it wordlessly to General Vandergrift.

```
Washington, 11 June

Brig Gen Lewis T. Harris
Hq, First Marine Division
By Hand

Dear Lucky:
  Major Jake Dillon, two officers, and six en-
listed Marines are on their way to New Zealand
to "coordinate Marine public relations." The
Assistant Commandant is very impressed with
Dillon, who used to be a Hollywood press agent.
He feels he will be valuable in dealing with the
more important members of the press, and mak-
ing sure the Navy doesn't sit on Marine accom-
plishments.
  He will be on TDY to Admiral Ghormley's Com-
```

mander, South Pacific, Headquarters, rather
than to the First Division, which takes him
neatly out from under your command while he is
there.

If I have to spell this out: This is the Assistant Commandant's idea, and you will have
to live with it.

Regards,
Tony

The Division Commander read the letter, looked at Harris,
snorted, and commented, "*I* don't have to live with this press
agent, Lucky, *you* do. Keep this character and his people
away from me."

The First Division was already prepared to deal with the
public as well as the enemy. One of the Special Staff sections
of the First Marine Division was "Public Information." It
was staffed with a major, a captain, a lieutenant, three sergeants, three corporals, and two privates first class. It was
natural, therefore, that the question, "just what the hell is
this about?" should arise in General Harris's mind.

"Aye, aye, Sir," he said.

Major Dillon, accompanied by two lieutenants, four sergeants, and two privates first class, arrived by air (priority
AAA) in Wellington on Tuesday, 16 June 1942.

He presented his orders to the G-1, who as Personnel Officer for the Division, was charged with housing and feeding
people on temporary duty. The G-1 informed Major Dillon
where he could draw tentage for the enlisted men, and in
which tents he and his officers could find bunks. He told
Major Dillon to get his people settled and to check back with
him in the morning.

The G-1 then sought audience with the Assistant Division
Commander, who he suspected (correctly) would be curious
to see Major Dillon's orders, which included a very interesting and unusual paragraph: *3. Marine commanders are directed to give Major Dillon access to classified information
through* TOP SECRET.

The G-1, who had earned the reputation of not bothering

the Assistant Division Commander with petty bullshit, was granted an almost immediate audience with General Harris. After he read Major Dillon's orders, Harris inquired, "Where did you say you put this messenger from God? Get him in here right now."

This proved not to be possible. For Major Dillon and his officers were not at the Transient Officer's Quarters. Nor were they engaged in helping the enlisted men erect their tents. Indeed, according to the Quartermaster, nobody asking to draw tentage had been to see him. When the G-1 somewhat nervously reported these circumstances to General Harris, the General replied, "You find that sonofabitch, Dick, and get him over here."

The G-1 and members of his staff conducted a search of the area, but without success.

At 0915 the next morning, however, General Harris's sergeant reported that a Major named Dillon was in the outer office, asking if the General could spare him a minute.

"Ask the major to come in, please, Sergeant," Harris replied.

Major Dillon marched into Harris's office, stopped eighteen inches from his desk, came to rigid attention, and barked, "Major Dillon, Sir. Thank you for seeing me."

General Harris's first thought vis-à-vis Major Jacob Dillon was: *The fit of that uniform is impeccable. He didn't get that off a rack at an officer's sales store. Give the devil his due. At least the sonofabitch looks like a Marine.*

General Harris let Major Dillon stand there for almost a minute—which seemed like much longer—examining him.

"Stand at ease, Major," Harris said, and Dillon snappily changed to a position that was more like Parade Rest than At Ease, with his hands folded in the small of his back.

"Colonel Naye finally found you, did he?" Harris asked softly.

"Sir, I wasn't aware the colonel was looking for me."

"Where the hell have you been, Dillon? Where did you lay your head to rest, for example?"

"At the Connaught, Sir," Dillon said.

"At the where?"

"The Duke of Connaught Hotel, Sir."

"A hotel?" Harris asked, incredulously.

"Yes, Sir."

"Just to satisfy my sometimes uncontrollable curiosity, Major, how did you get from here to town? And back out here?"

"A friend picked us up, Sir. And arranged for the rooms in the Connaught. And has arranged a couple of cars for us."

" *'Rooms'? 'Us'?* You took your officers with you?"

"Yes, Sir. And the men. I thought they needed a good night's sleep. It's a hell of a long airplane ride from Hawaii, Sir."

It had previously occurred to General Harris that if Major Dillon and his two commissioned and six enlisted press agents, and their 1240 pounds of accompanying baggage and equipment had not traveled to Wellington, New Zealand, by priority air it would have been possible to move nine real Marines and 1240 pounds of badly needed equipment by air to Wellington.

With some effort, General Harris restrained himself from offering this observation aloud.

"I wouldn't know," he said. "We came by ship. Who's going to pay for the hotel, just out of curiosity?"

"That's going to require a sort of lengthy answer, Sir."

"My time is your time, Major. Curiosity overwhelms me."

"For the time being, Sir, those of us who are still on salary are splitting the expenses for everybody."

"Still on salary?"

"Most of us are from the movies, Sir," Dillon said.

What the hell does that mean? Tony's letter, come to think of it, said this guy was a Hollywood press agent.

"But one of the photographers and two of the writers came from Pathe—the newsreel photographer—and the wires. AP specifically. Their salaries stopped when they came in the Corps. The rest of us are still getting paid, so we decided to split the tab for Sergeant Pincney and the lieutenants."

"Let me be sure I have this right," Harris said. "Your two officers are having their hotel bills paid by your enlisted men?"

"General, it sounds a lot worse than it is," Dillon said.

"Fortunately, it's none of my business, since you're not in the 1st Marines," Harris said. This had just occurred to him;

it was a little comforting. "But what is my business is your mission here. Can you explain that to me?"

"Well, Sir. When we—the 1st Marines—make their first landing, the men I have with me, broken down into two teams, will go ashore with the first wave. Each team will have a still and a motion picture photographer and a writer. The film they shoot, and the copy the writer writes, will be made available to the press on a pool basis . . . and flown to the States, to see what mileage they can get out of it in Washington."

"You're aware, of course, that we have our own PIO people?"

"Yes, Sir. I tried to make that point to General Frischer. I didn't get very far. And to tell you the truth, Sir, I didn't mind getting shot down. I wanted to come over here."

"You did? Why?"

"I'm a Marine, General," Dillon said.

"I was about to ask about that. I heard you were a Hollywood press agent."

"Yes, Sir. Before that I was a Marine. A China Marine. Then I got in the movie business, and then I came back in the Corps."

"To be a press ag—a public information officer?"

"That was the Deputy Commandant's idea, Sir. I thought, still think, that I could be of more use with stripes on my sleeve."

I like the sound of that. Maybe this character isn't a complete asshole after all.

"Well, Major, I'm sure the Deputy Commandant is right. Now, what can I do for you?"

"Not a thing, Sir. I'm going to try to stay out of your hair as much as possible."

It was an ill-chosen figure of speech. General Harris suffered from advanced male pattern baldness and was somewhat sensitive on the subject. Major Dillon promptly made it worse:

"The only thing on my schedule right now is to see your Division PIO," he said. "To assure him that I'm going to stay out of his hair, too. And then I want to see Jack NMI Stecker. *Major* Stecker."

"I'm acquainted with Major Stecker," Harris said. "What do you want from him?"

General Harris was more than "acquainted" with Major Jack NMI Stecker. Given the chasm between officer and enlisted ranks, they were—as much as possible—lifelong friends. For nearly a quarter of a century, Harris had believed that one of the few mistakes Jack Stecker made in his Marine career was turning down the appointment he was offered to Annapolis in 1918.

At nineteen, Stecker won the Medal of Honor . . . for really incredible valor in France. With the Medal came the Annapolis appointment. But Stecker turned it down to marry his childhood sweetheart, which meant that he would spend his Marine Corps career as an enlisted man.

It was folklore in the Marine Corps that many senior noncoms were just as qualified to command companies and battalions as any officer. Harris believed that one of the few men of whom this was really true was Jack NMI Stecker. And Harris put his belief in action; he went to Marine Corps Commandant Slocomb to make this announcement—a dangerous deviation from the sacred path of chain of command. Even so, his move resulted in the gold leaf now on Jack NMI Stecker's collar points, and his assignment as a battalion commander in the 5th Marines.

"Jack and I were pretty close when he was Sergeant Major of the 4th Marines in Shanghai . . ."

If you and Jack NMI Stecker were really close, that means you really aren't an asshole, Major, after all. I'll call Jack and ask him about this guy.

". . . and I hope to talk him into letting me send some of my people down to his battalion to see if he can make Marines out of them."

Good thinking. If anyone can turn feather merchants into Marines, Jack Stecker can.

"The PFCs, you mean?"

"No, Sir. Everybody *but* the PFCs. They at least went through boot camp at San Diego. I mean the sergeants and the lieutenants. Some of them have only been in the Corps a month."

"And they haven't been—the officers—to Basic School? Or the others to boot camp?"

"No, Sir. General Frischer said that since they wouldn't be commanding troops, it wouldn't matter."

"They were commissioned, or enlisted, directly from civilian life, to do this? And they were sent here without any training whatever?"

"Yes, Sir, that's about the size of it."

I don't think I will bother General Vandergrift with the details of this operation. He has enough to worry about as it is; he doesn't need this proof positive that the rest of the Corps has gone insane. He told me to keep this press agent and his people away from him, and I will.

"Thank you for coming in to see me, Major," General Harris said. "Unless you have something else?"

"Just one thing, General. I know that I must look like a feather merchant to you, but to do my job, I have to know what's going on."

"I will see that you are invited to attend all G-3 staff meetings, Major. And anything else I think would interest you."

"Sir, with respect," Dillon said, even more uneasily, "the general doesn't really know what would interest me or wouldn't."

You arrogant sonofabitch!

"What are you suggesting, Major? That you be given carte blanche to just nose around here wherever you please?"

"I'll try to stay out of people's hair as much as possible, General."

There was a perceptible pause as Harris thought that over. Finally, remembering that Dillon's orders had as much as authorized him to put his goddamned feather merchant's nose into any goddamned place where he goddamned pleased, and that Tony had written that this whole goddamned cockamamie operation was the Deputy Commandant's own personal nutty goddamned idea, he said, calmly and politely, "Very well, Major. I'll have a memo prepared authorizing you to attend any staff conferences that you desire to attend."

(Three)
BUKA, SOLOMON ISLANDS
16 JUNE 1942

Buka is an island approximately thirty miles long and no more than five or six miles wide. The northernmost island in the Solomons chain, it lies just north of the much larger Bougainville; and it is 146 nautical miles southeast of Rabaul, on New Britain.

In June of 1942 the Japanese had at Rabaul a large, well-equipped airbase, servicing fighters, bombers, seaplanes, and other larger aircraft. There was, as well, a Japanese fighter base on Buka, and another on Bougainville.

When the Japanese invaded Buka in the opening days of the war, an Australian, Jacob Reeves, who had lived on the island, volunteered to remain behind as a member of the Coastwatcher Service. He was commissioned into the Royal Australian Navy Volunteer Reserve and given a radio, a generator, and some World War I small arms. Thus equipped, he was expected to report on Japanese ship and air movement, from Rabaul down toward the Australian continent. Prior to his commissioning, Reeves had no military experience; and he knew nothing about the shortwave radio except how to turn it on and off.

Inevitably—in early June—what he called the "sodding wireless" failed. Following the orders he had been given for such an occurrence, he—actually he and the girls—stamped flat the grass in a high meadow, forming enormous letters thirty feet tall, R A.

He'd been told that if he went off the air, the Coastwatcher Service would fly over his hideout as soon as possible to look for indication that he was still alive and needed help. There were ten codes in all (Lieutenant Commander Eric Feldt, Royal Australian Navy, commanding the Coastwatcher Service, did not believe his men could remember more than that): R A stood of course for radio; P E would indicate his supply of petrol for the generator which powered the wireless was exhausted; and so on.

As he waited for the Coastwatcher Service to act on his stamped-in-the-grass message, Reeves wondered what the response would be.

His reports on Japanese activity, he knew, had been of great value both tactically and for planning purposes. Now that they were interrupted, getting his wireless station up and running again would be a matter of some priority.

He was well aware that they did not have many options. The only way he could see to get him up and running again was to send him another radio. There were a number of problems with that; most notably: The only way to get him one would be to drop it by parachute. But if the airplane was seen by the Japanese, they would certainly launch fighters to shoot it down.

And even if the plane made it to the meadow, the odds that the dropped radio would survive the shock of landing were slim. If, indeed, he could find it at all.

All the same, he was not surprised on 6 June to hear the sound of the twin engines of a Royal Australian Air Force Lockheed Hudson transport. Five minutes later, he saw the Hudson make a low level pass over the meadow. As it passed, four objects dropped from the aircraft. A moment later these were suspended beneath white nylon parachute canopies.

He was surprised when he made out human forms beneath two of the parachutes. He had mixed emotions about that. On one hand, it probably meant they were sending him people who knew something about how the sodding wireless and its sodding generator worked. And that, of course, would be helpful.

But on the other hand, it would mean he would have to care for two men who had probably never in their lives been out of Sydney or Melbourne, much less been in a jungle. *How can I feed them?* he asked himself. *More important, how can I conceal them from the sodding Nips?*

And then when he made his way to the first one, what he found was a sodding American Marine—a *boy!*—wearing, in the American way, the upside down stripes of a sergeant. The other one turned out to be an American Marine officer, a lieutenant. That one managed to go into the trees, breaking his arm in the process. These two were the first Americans Sub Lieutenant Reeves had ever met. It didn't take him long to conclude that they were an odd, childish lot.

When he reached the boy sergeant, Reeves told him there were Nips snooping around the area, and that they would, unfortunately, have to count as lost the one who landed in the trees.

"We're Marines," the boy told him. "We don't leave our people behind."

It never came to a test of wills; for one of the girls found Lieutenant Howard. As far as Reeves was concerned, that was fortunate. For he not only subsequently grew rather fond of the boy, Steve Koffler, but at the time Reeves was reasonably sure that Koffler would have insisted on looking for his lieutenant even to the point of turning his submachine gun on Reeves.

Not long after that, they found they had to get rid of a Nip patrol who'd heard the Lockheed and probably seen the parachutes; and Koffler did what had to be done then with skill and courage. But the boy threw up when it was over . . . after he looked down at the corpse of a Japanese he'd wounded, and then, because it was necessary, killed.

Later, when Lieutenant Howard explained the reasons for their coming to Buka, the explanation made enough sense to Reeves that he put aside his earlier fears and objections about them.

According to Howard, Reeves's observation point was considered vital. With the three of them there, the odds that it could be kept operational were made greater.

Meanwhile, some weeks before, a small detachment of U.S. Marines was attached to the Coastwatcher Organization. When word that Reeves's wireless was out reached Commander Feldt, Feldt decided to send two men from the Marine detachment to Buka, together with the latest model American shortwave wireless. Koffler was chosen to go because he was not only a radio operator, he was a highly skilled technician as well (he'd been an Amateur Radio Operator before the War), while Howard had once taught courses in recognition of Japanese aircraft and naval vessels. Because of that, and because Koffler couldn't tell the difference between a battleship and an intercoastal freighter, Howard was asked to join him.

The village looked like a picture out of *National Geographic* magazine: A clear stream, about five feet wide and two feet deep, meandered through the center of a scattering of grass-walled huts. The village was populated with about twenty brown-skinned, flat-nosed people, most of whom had teeth died blue and then filed to a point. Cooking fires were burning here and there; chickens were running loose; and bare-breasted women were beating yamlike roots with rocks against other rocks. Most of the men and some of the women were armed with British Lee-Enfield rifles; and many carried web ammunition bandoliers.

Sergeant Stephen M. Koffler, USMC, of East Orange, New Jersey, and Detachment A of Marine Corps Special Detachment 14, had been eating bacon and pork chops and ham and sausage for most of the eighteen years and six months of his life; but if it were in his power he would never do so again.

He had never given pork much thought before. It had always been there in the refrigerated meat display of Cohen's EZ-Shop Supermarket on the corner of Fourth Avenue and North 18th Street, ready to be wrapped and taken to the cash register. All you had to do was pay Mrs. Cohen, who worked the register, and then take the bacon home and put it in a frying pan.

He had spent most of the morning watching the conversion of a living, breathing, squealing, hairy, ugly pig into edible meat products; and he hadn't liked what he had seen at all.

The pig had been brought into the village shortly after dawn by a visibly proud and triumphant Petty Officer First Class Bartholomew Charles Dunlop, Royal Australian Navy Volunteer Reserve. Petty Officer Dunlop, who was known as "Charley," was a native of the island of Buka. When he brought in the pig, he was wearing his usual uniform. That consisted of a brassard around his upper right arm, onto which was sewn the insignia of his rank, and a loin cloth. The loin cloth was something like a slit canvas skirt; and the brassard was placed just below two copper rings. His teeth were black and filed into points. And there were decorative scars on his forehead, his cheeks, and bare chest.

Petty Officer Dunlop was carrying a 9mm Sten submachine gun, two Lee-Enfield .303 Caliber rifles, and a two-foot long machete. The rifles belonged to the other two members of the detail, who were actually carrying the pig. They were uniformed like Dunlop, except that they had no insignia brassards. Canvas webbing ammunition belts, however, were slung across their chests.

They carried the pig, squealing in protest, on a pole run between his tied-together legs.

"Roast pork tonight!" Petty Officer Dunlop announced triumphantly. "And would you look at the size of the bugger!"

Petty Officer Dunlop had been educated at the Anglican Mission School on Buka, and spoke with the accent of a Yorkshireman.

Steve Koffler had not seen many pigs, except in photographs, but the one Charley seemed so proud of didn't seem as large as the ones Steve was used to. It was about the size of a large dog.

"It's beautiful, Charley," Steve said.

"Where's the officers?"

Steve shrugged and nodded vaguely toward the jungle.

How the hell am I supposed to answer that? Out there in the bush someplace?

"I didn't go with them," Steve said, explaining: "I've got to make the 1115 net call. They weren't sure they'd be back in time."

"Well, we'll have a jolly little surprise for them when they do come home, won't we?"

The women of the village, beaming, quickly appeared and watched as the pig was lowered to the ground and the pole between its legs was removed. A length of rope appeared, and this was tied to the pig's rear feet. The pig was then hauled off the ground under a large limb.

A woman produced a large, china bowl and carefully placed it under the pig's head. It looked to Steve like one of those things people put under their beds before there was inside plumbing.

Then with one swift swipe of his machete, Charley cut the pig's throat. The squealing stopped, and arterial blood began to gush from the pig's throat as the pig jerked in its death spasms.

It was only with a massive effort that Steve managed not to throw up. He had to tell himself again and again that he could not humiliate himself, the Marine Corps, and the white race by tossing his cookies.

The butchering process was performed by the women (hunting was a male responsibility; everything else was women's business). It was worse than even the throat-cutting. Intestines (steaming, despite the heat) spilled from the carcass. The hide was peeled off. The carcass was cut into pieces.

And at one point Steve realized with something close to horror that one particularly obscene-looking hunk of sickly white stuff was what he knew as bacon.

Next fires were built; then large steel pots full of water were either suspended over them or set right onto the coals. In one of them, eventually, they dropped the pig's head. Once the water started boiling, the head turned over and over.

By the time the officers returned, just before 1100, the butchering was just about finished. The bacon and hams (they were too scrawny to be *real* hams, Steve thought, but that's what they were) had been suspended over a smokey fire; and the rest of the meat was either being slowly broiled over coals or boiled and rendered. Nothing, Steve saw, was going to be wasted.

Both Reeves and Howard looked exhausted when they arrived. Without a word, Howard dropped his web belt and his Thompson by the creek; and fully clothed, except for his boondockers, he lowered himself into it, carefully holding his splinted arm out of the water. Reeves ordered tea for himself and slumped onto the ground, resting his back against a tree.

They had nothing to report about their patrol—a case of no news being good news: They'd detected no signs of the Japanese looking for them.

Steve took his wristwatch from his pocket, and then from the condom where he stored it. There were two watches in the village, his and Lieutenant Howard's. Since there was no chance of getting replacements, and since there were two times each day that were critical—1115 and 2045—it was crucial that the watches be protected.

The dial read 1059. If he was lucky, the watch was accurate within five minutes. He went in search of Petty Officer Second Class Ian Bruce. He found him in the grass commo shack, already in place on the generator, his skirt spread wide (it wasn't hard to tell that he was a man), ready to start pumping the bicycle-like pedals of the device that provided power for the Hallicrafters shortwave transceiver.

The watch hands now indicated 1102. Steve made a wind-it-up motion with his hand. Ian started pumping the pedals. In a moment, the needles on the Hallicrafter came to life. It was now 1103.

Fuck it, close enough.

Steve put his fingers on the telegraph key.

FRD1.FRD6.FRD1.FRD6.FRD1.FRD6.

Royal Australian Navy Coastwatcher Radio, this is Detachment A, Special Marine Detachment 14.

Today, for a change, there was an immediate response:

FRD6.FRD1.GA.

Detachment A, this is Coastwatcher Radio, Townesville, Australia, responding to your call. Go ahead.

FRD1.FRD6.NTATT.

Coastwatcher Radio, this is Detachment A. No traffic for you at this time.

FRD6.FRD1.NTATT.FRD1 CLR.

Detachment A, this is Coastwatcher Radio. No traffic for you at this time. Coastwatcher Radio Clear.

"Fuck!" Sergeant Koffler said, and signaled for Ian Bruce to stop pedaling. He had hoped—he always hoped—that there would be some kind of message. And he was always disappointed when there was not.

He got to his feet and walked out of the hut. Lieutenant Reeves was nowhere in sight, and Lieutenant Howard was asleep on the bank of the stream. There was no point in waking him up; there had been no traffic.

He walked to one of the charcoal fires. The pig's ribs were getting done. They *looked* like spareribs now, Steve thought, not like parts of a dead animal.

And they smelled good. His mouth actually salivated.

He wondered how much salt from their short—and dwindling—supply Lieutenant Reeves would permit them to use to season the spareribs.

V

(One)
THE CLUB CAR "CURTIS SANDROCK"
THE PENNSYLVANIA RAILROAD "CONGRESSIONAL
LIMITED"
16 JUNE 1942

Sergeant John Marston Moore, USMCR, had been in his chair less than half an hour when he had occasion to dwell on the question of saltpeter.

It had been commonly accepted by his peers at Parris Island that the Corps liberally dosed the boots' chow with the stuff. The action was deemed necessary by the Corps, the reasoning went, in order to suppress the sexual drives of the boots, who were by definition perfectly healthy young men who would have absolutely no chance during the period of their training to satisfy their sexual hungers.

Save of course by committing what his father called the sin of onanism, and what was known commonly in the Corps as Beating Your Meat, or Pounding Your Pud—a behavior that was high on the long list of acts one must not be caught

94

doing by one's Drill Instructor . . . considerations of finding someplace to do it aside.

John Moore now realized that all he knew about saltpeter was what he had heard at Parris Island. That is to say, he had no certain knowledge whether such a substance really existed; or if it did exist, whether it did indeed suppress sexual desires, once ingested; or whether the Corps really fed it to their boots.

It was possible, of course.

There was the question of homosexuality, for instance. He had heard that because of the absence of women, a lot of the men in prisons turned queer. . . . There was a large number of other things Parris Island and prison had in common, too. The Corps could certainly not afford to have its boots turn to each other for sexual gratification. Several times the pertinent passages from The Articles for the Governance of the Naval Service, known as "Rocks and Shoals," had been read out loud to them. These described the penalties for taking the penis of another male into one's mouth and/or anus. In the eyes of the Corps, this was a crime ranking close to desertion in the face of the enemy and striking a superior officer or non-commissioned officer.

And if one was to judge from the training time allocated to inspiring talks from Navy Chaplains and incredibly graphic motion pictures taken in Venereal Disease wards, the Corps had a deep interest in even the heterosexual activities of its men. After they were freed from Parris Island, the Corps did not want them to rush to the nearest brothel and/or to consort with what it called "Easy Women." Easy women were defined as those who would infect Marines with syphilis, gonorrhea, and other social diseases, thereby rendering them unfit for combat service.

The conclusions Sergeant Moore reached as he accepted a second rye and ginger ale from the club car steward was that (a) it was likely that the Corps had been feeding him saltpeter at Parris Island; (b) that it had worked, because he could not now recall any feelings of sexual deprivation while he was there; and (c) that once one was taken off saltpeter, one's normal sexual drives and hungers returned within a day.

With a vengeance, he thought, as he tried to fold his leg

over the first erection he'd had in weeks. It seemed to have
a mind of its own, determined to make his trousers look like
an eight-man squad tent, canvas tautly stretched from a stout
center pole.

The source of his sexual arousal, he was quite sure, was
not what the Corps would think of as an Easy Woman. In
the training films, Easy Women had without exception
earned the cheering approval of the boots with their tight
sweaters, short skirts, heavily applied lipstick, and lewdly
inviting mascaraed eyes. Most of them had cigarettes hanging
from their mouths, and one hand attached to a bottle of beer.

This woman demonstrated none of these characteristics.
She wore very little makeup. She held her cigarette in what
Sergeant Moore thought was a charming and exquisitely
feminine manner. She wore a blouse buttoned to her neck,
a suit, and a hat with a half-veil. She was old—at least thirty,
John judged, maybe even thirty-five—but he charitably
judged that her hair, neatly done up in sort of a knot at the
back of her head, was prematurely gray.

And the final proof that she was a lady and not an Easy
Woman came during the one time she raised her eyes from
The Saturday Evening Post to look at him. It was clear from
her facial expression that he was of absolutely no interest to
her at all.

But despite all this, he found her exciting and desirable.
This struck him with particular urgency after she stood to
take off her suit jacket: The light then was such that her torso
was silhouetted by the sun; the absolutely magnificent shape
of her breasts had, for ten seconds or so, been his to marvel
at.

And when she sat down and crossed her legs, there was
a flash of thigh and slip, of lace and soft white flesh; and
instantly, in his mind's eye, she was as naked as the lady in
the club soda ad, sitting on a rock by a mountain lake.

At that instant the sexual depressant effects of saltpeter
were flushed from his system as if they were never there, and
Old Faithful popped to a position of attention that met every
standard of the Guide Book for Marines for stiffness and
immobility.

Had the opportunity presented itself, Sergeant John
Marston Moore, USMCR, would cheerfully have gone with

her then . . . even if the price was the loss of all his money, contraction of syphilis, gonorrhea, all other social diseases, and any chances he had after the war to meet Miss Right and have a family of his own.

He tried, very hard, not to let her know he was watching her. This involved adjusting his head so that he could see her reflection in a mirror on the club car wall. Despite his care, she did catch him looking at her once; in a flash, he desperately spun around in his chair.

A little later, he managed to catch another reflection of her in the glass of his window, but that was nowhere near as satisfactory as the mirror reflection.

Between Baltimore and Philadelphia, she spoke to him. Her voice was as deep, soft, throaty, and sensual as he knew it would be.

"Excuse me," she said, waving *The Saturday Evening Post* at him. "I'm through with this. Would you like it?"

"No!" he said abruptly, with all the fervor the Good Marine had shown in the training film when the Easy Woman offered him a cigarette laced with some kind of narcotic. "It'll make you feel real good," she'd told him breathily.

"Sorry," the woman said, taken aback.

You're a fucking asshole, Moore, J. Out of your cotton-picking fucking mind!

"I don't read much," he heard himself say.

The absolutely beautiful woman smiled at him uneasily.

"Excuse me," Sergeant John Marston Moore, USMCR, said. Then he got up and walked to the vestibule of the car, where he banged his forehead on the window, and where he stayed until the train pulled into the 30th Street Station in Philadelphia.

The woman got off the train there. Fortunately, Moore decided, she didn't see him hiding in the vestibule corner. He exhaled audibly with relief. And then, for one last look at the beautiful older woman as she marched down the platform and out of his life forever, he stuck his head out the door.

She was standing right there, as the porter transferred her luggage into the custody of a Red Cap.

He pulled his head back as quickly as he could.

When it began to move again, and the train caught up with

her on the platform, she looked for and found Sergeant John Marston Moore. She smiled and waved.

And smiled again and shook her head when, very shyly, the nice-looking young Marine waved back.

"North Philadelphia," the conductor called, "North Philadelphia, next."

(Two)
U.S. MARINE BARRACKS
U.S. NAVY YARD
PHILADELPHIA, PENNSYLVANIA
18 JUNE 1942

While the staff sergeant who dealt with Sergeant John Marston Moore, USMCR, could not honestly be characterized as charming, in comparison to the sergeants who had dealt with Moore at Parris, he seemed to be.

"You're Moore, huh?" he greeted him. "Get yourself a cup of coffee and I'll be with you in a minute."

He gestured toward a coffee machine and turned his attention to a stack of papers on his crowded desk. The machine was next to a window overlooking the Navy Yard. As he drank the coffee, Moore watched with interest an enormous crane lift a five-inch cannon and its mount from a railroad flatcar onto the bow of a freighter.

He found the operation so absorbing that he was somewhat startled when the staff sergeant came up to him and spoke softly into his ear.

"You could have fooled me, Moore," he said. "Even with that haircut, you don't look like somebody who was a private three days ago."

Moore was surprised to see that the staff sergeant was smiling at him.

"Thank you," Moore said.

"I checked your papers out pretty carefully," the staff sergeant said. "Everything's shipshape. Shots. Overseas qualification. Next of kin. All that crap. Once you get paid, and after The Warning, all you have to do is get on the airplane at Newark airport on Friday morning."

" 'The Warning'?" Moore asked.

"Yeah, The Warning," the staff sergeant said. "Come on."

He gestured with his hand for Moore to follow him. He stopped by the open, frosted glass door to a small office and tapped on the glass with his knuckles.

A captain looked up, then motioned them inside.

"Sergeant Moore, Sir, for The Warning."

"Sure," the captain said, and looked at Moore. "Sergeant, you have been alerted for overseas movement. It is my duty to make sure that you understand that any failure on your part to make that movement, by failing to report when and where your orders specify, is a more serious offense than simple absence without leave, can be construed as intention to desert or desertion, and that the penalties provided are greater. Do you understand where and when you are to report, and what I have just said to you?"

"Yes, Sir," Sergeant Moore replied.

"Where's he going?" the captain asked, curiously.

The staff sergeant handed the captain a sheaf of papers.

"Interesting," the captain said.

"Ain't it?" the staff sergeant agreed. "Look at the six-A priority."

"I'd love to know what you do for the Corps, Sergeant Moore," the captain said. "But I know better than to ask."

That's good, Moore thought wryly, *because I have no idea what I'm supposed to do for the Corps.*

The captain then surprised him further by standing up and offering Moore his hand.

"Good luck, Moore," he said.

Moore sensed that the good wishes were not merely sincere, but a deviation from a normal issuing of The Warning, which he now understood was some sort of standard routine.

"Thank you, Sir."

The staff sergeant handed the captain a stack of paper, and the captain wrote his signature on a sheet of it.

That's a record that I got The Warning, Moore decided.

The staff sergeant nudged Moore, and Moore followed him out of the office. They went to the Navy Finance Office where Moore was given a partial pay of one hundred dollars.

The staff sergeant then commandeered an empty desk and

went through all the papers, dividing them into two stacks. Moore watched as one stack including, among other things, his service record, went into a stiff manila envelope. The sergeant sealed it twice: He first licked the gummed flap and then he put over that a strip of gummed paper.

He surprised Moore by then forging an officer's name on the gummed tape: "Sealed at MBPHILA 18June42 James D. Yesterburg, Capt USMC"

Yesterburg, Moore decided, was the captain who had given him The Warning and then wished him good luck.

"Normally, you don't get to carry your own records," the staff sergeant said, handing him the envelope. "But if you do, they have to be sealed. There's nothing in there you haven't seen, but I wouldn't open it, if I was you. Or unless you can get your hands on another piece of gummed tape."

Moore chuckled.

"These are your orders," the staff sergeant said as he stuffed a quarter-inch-thick stack of mimeograph paper into another, ordinary, manila envelope. "And your tickets, railroad from here to Newark; bus from Newark station to the airport; the airplane tickets, Eastern to Saint Louis, Transcontinental & Western to Los Angeles; and a bus ticket in LA from the airport to the train station; and finally your ticket on the train—they call it "The Lark"—from LA to 'Diego. In 'Diego, there'll be an RTO office—that means Rail Transport Office—and they'll arrange for you to get where you should be. OK?"

"Got it," Moore said.

"There's also Meal Vouchers," the staff sergeant said. "I'll tell you about them. You are supposed to be able to exchange them for a meal in restaurants. The thing is, most restaurants, except bad ones, don't want to be run over with servicemen eating cheap meals that they don't get paid for for a month, so they either don't honor these things, or they give you a cheese sandwich and a cup of coffee and call it dinner. So if I was you, I would save enough from that flying hundred they just gave you to eat whatever and wherever you want. Then in 'Diego, or Pearl Harbor, or when you get where you're going, you turn in the meal tickets and say you couldn't find anyplace that would honor them. They'll pay you. It's a buck thirty-five a day. Still with me?"

"Yeah, thanks for the tip."

"OK. Now finally, and this is important. You've got a six-A priority. The only way you can be legally beat out of your seat on the airplane is by somebody who also has a six-A priority *and* outranks you. Since they pass out very few six-As, that's not going to be a problem. If some colonel happens to do that to you, you get his name and telephone Outshipment in 'Diego, the number's on your orders, and tell them what happened, including the name of the officer who bumped you. In that case, no problem."

"I understand," Moore said.

"But what's *liable* to happen," the staff sergeant went on, "is that *you're* going to bump some captain or some major— or maybe even some colonel or important civilian—who doesn't have a six-A, and he's not going to like that worth a shit, and will try to pull rank on you. If you let that happen, your ass is in a crack. You understand?"

"What am I supposed to say to him?"

"You tell *him* to call Outshipment in 'Diego, and get *their* permission to bump you. Otherwise, 'with respect, Sir, I can't miss my plane.' Got it?"

"Yes, I think so."

"Somebody pretty high up in the Corps wants to get you where you're going in a hurry, Sergeant, otherwise you wouldn't have a six-A. And they are going to get very pissed off if you hand the six-A to somebody who didn't rate it on their own."

"OK," Moore said.

"Well, that's it," the staff sergeant said. "Good luck, Moore."

"Thank you," Moore said, shaking his hand.

"Oh, shit. I just remembered: You're entitled to a couple of bus and subway tokens. We'll have to go back by the office, but what the hell, why pay for a bus if you can get the Corps to pay, right?"

"I've got a car."

"Oh, shit! I knew there would be something!"

"Something wrong?"

"You want the Corps to store it for you, you'll be here all goddamned day."

"It's my father's car."

At breakfast, Moore had been surprised at his father's reaction to his mother's suggestion—"Dear, couldn't John use the Buick to drive down there?" He would never have bothered to ask for it himself, for the negative response would have been certain.

"I suppose," the Reverend Doctor Moore had said, after a moment's hesitation, "that would be the thing to do."

There was not even the ritual speech about driving slowly and carefully, which always preceded his—rare—sessions behind the wheel of his father's car. It was a 1940 Buick Limited, which had a new kind of transmission that eliminated the clutch pedal and little switches on the steering wheel that flashed the stop and parking lights in the direction you intended to turn. His father was ordinarily reluctant to entrust such a precision machine into the hands of his rash and reckless—as he considered it—son.

And yet, to his astonishment, his father hadn't even put up a ritual show of resistance.

As he put his mind to that, it occurred to Moore that this was not the first time his father had behaved oddly since he had come home from Parris Island. For instance, there had hardly been any questions about why he was going overseas now as a sergeant, rather than to Quantico for officer training.

His father was probably concerned that he was going to be killed in the Orient, Moore decided, and was going out of his way to be kind and obliging. But he sensed there was something else, too; he had no idea what.

"Jesus, you had me worried for a minute," the sergeant said, and then offered his hand again, and repeated, "Good luck, Moore."

Moore had not been able to get his father's car onto the base. It was parked just outside.

And he had to show his orders to the Marine Guard at the gate as he left. He remembered at the last moment that his orders now were the ones the staff sergeant had just given him, not the ones Tech Sergeant Rutterman had given him only a couple of days before.

He took them from the smaller manila envelope and handed them to the guard, who scanned them quickly.

"OK, Sergeant," he said. "If you have to go, that's the way."

Moore smiled at him, but didn't know what he meant. As he walked to the car, he read the orders for the first time.

Marine Barracks
U.S. Naval Station
Philadelphia, Penna

16 June 1942

Letter Orders:
To Sergeant John M. Moore, 673456, USMCR

1. You are detached this date from Headquarters Company, Marine Barracks, Phila. Pa., and assigned 14th Special Detachment, USMC, FPO 24543, San Francisco, Cal.

2. You will proceed by government and/or civilian rail, air and sea transportation via USMC Barracks San Diego, Cal., and Pearl Harbor, T.H. Air Transportation is directed where possible, with Priority AAAAAA authorized by TWX Hq USMC dated 15 June 1942, Subject: "Movement of Moore, Sgt John M." to final destination.

3. USMC Barracks San Diego, Cal., and Pearl Harbor, T.H., and all other Naval facilities are directed to report via most expeditious means to Hq USMC ATTN: GHV3:12 the date and time of your arrival and departure while en route. Once travel commences, any delay in movement which will exceed 12 (twelve) hours will be reported to Hq USMC ATTN: GHV3:13 by URGENT radio message.

By Direction:
Jasper J. Malone
Lieut. Colonel, USMC

He realized that he knew nothing more now than he had

been told by Captain Sessions at Parris Island. He didn't know what Special Detachment 14 was; where it was; or what he would be doing there when he got there. The only thing he knew for sure was that the Corps was going to a hell of a lot of trouble to get him there as quickly as possible.

It was disturbing.

Disturbing, shit! It's frightening.

He looked at his watch. It was quarter to four. All of his business at the Marine Barracks had taken far less time than he had expected, and planned for. It would take him ten minutes to drive down Broad Street to the Union League, where he was to meet Uncle Bill for dinner. That meant he would arrive two hours and five minutes early.

And two hours and five minutes was not enough time to find a movie and watch through the whole thing. It was enough time to take the car home and ride back downtown on the train. That would make the car available to his father when he returned from the Missions office.

Alternatively, he could make profitable use of the time . . . the Reverend Moore believed that profitable use of one's time was a virtue and thus the waste of one's time was a non-virtue, and consequently sinful . . . by making a farewell visit to the Franklin Institute or the Philadelphia Museum of Fine Art.

Or he could go to the Trocadero Burlesque Theater, which was within walking distance of the Union League Club. There, while munching caramel-covered popcorn, he could watch an Easy Woman take her clothing off . . . perhaps as many as four Easy Women in the nearly two hours he had. That was about as close as he was going to get to a naked woman in the foreseeable future.

It was also possible—unlikely, but possible—that he might encounter a real Easy Woman in the Tenderloin, as the area was known . . . a woman in a short skirt and tight sweater who would leer at him and entice him to a cheap hotel as her contribution to the war effort.

He parked the Buick behind the First Philadelphia Trust Company and walked down 12th Street to the Trocadero. He encountered no real Easy Women on the street, and the Easy Women on the stage seemed not only a little long in the tooth but bored as well. One of them actually blew a chewing gum bubble as she moved around on the stage.

And the Easy Women did not appear one after the other. Their performances were separated by comedians and intermissions, during which the audience was offered special deals on wristwatches, fountain pen and pencil sets, and illustrated books portraying life in Wicked Paris—offered today only, by special arrangement to Trocadero Theater patrons.

An hour after he went into the Trocadero, he got up and walked out. He walked back to Market Street and then up toward Broad Street. Just as he came to John Wanamaker's Department Store he saw the incredibly beautiful older woman from the train.

She walked purposefully out of Wanamaker's and turned toward Broad Street. She glanced at him but he felt sure she made no connection with the train.

Why should she? My God, she's beautiful!

I'm not following her. She's going in the same direction I am.

He almost caught up with her as she waited for the traffic light on Broad Street, but he slowed his pace so that he was still behind her when the light changed. He was sure she hadn't noticed him.

She turned left, and he followed her, for that was his direction too. He was going to meet Uncle Bill at the Union League Club for dinner.

I wonder what the hell that's all about?

She walked past the Union League, moving in long graceful strides, her smooth flowing musculature exquisitely evident under her straight skirt. Quickly consulting his watch, Sergeant John Marston Moore decided there was no reason he could not walk for a couple of minutes down South Broad before returning to the Union League to meet his Uncle Bill.

She came to the Bellevue-Stratford Hotel. The doorman spun the revolving door for her, and twenty seconds later for Sergeant John Marston Moore.

She crossed the lobby and went into the cocktail lounge. Sergeant John Marston Moore visited the Gentlemen's Room, relieved his bladder, and then washed his hands. He examined his reflection in the mirror over the marble wash basin.

Just what the fuck do you think you're doing?

He went into the cocktail lounge and took a seat at the bar.

"What can we get the Marine Corps?"

"Rye and ginger," he said, sweeping the room in the mirror behind the bar.

She was at a small table away from the lobby, near a door that led directly to the street. A waiter was delivering something in a stemmed glass. She took a cigarette from her purse, lit it with a silver lighter, and exhaled through her nose.

Like Bette Davis. Except that compared to her, Bette Davis looks like one of those cows in the Trocadero.

"Seventy-five cents, Sir."

He laid a five-dollar bill on the bar. When the waiter brought the change, he pushed the quarter away and put the singles in his pocket. When he found the beautiful older woman in the mirror again, she was looking at him, via the mirror.

And she was smiling.

In amusement, he thought, *not in encouragement, or enticement.*

He found his pack of Chesterfields and lit one with his Marine insignia decorated Zippo, pretending to be in deep thought. He was unable to keep his eyes away from the mirror. Sometimes he got a profile of her face. Twice his eyes were drawn to her legs; they were crossed beneath the table, ladylike, but they still offered a forbidden glance under her skirt.

You are not only about to make a flaming ass of yourself, but you are going to embarrass that nice woman.

He drained his rye and ginger ale.

I will leave by the side door, so that she can't help but see me leave and will understand that I am leaving, and not making eyes at her, or anything like that.

He determinedly kept from looking at her as he walked to the side door. As he reached the door, a half dozen people started to come into the bar from the street. He had to stop and wait for them. He glanced at her. She was no more than five feet away.

She was looking up at him. She smiled.

"The Club Car, right?" she asked. "You don't read very much, right?"

"I just came in for a drink," he blurted.

"I thought it was something like that," she said.

Christ, she knows I followed her in here!

"I have to meet someone for dinner," Moore said. "Just killing a little time."

"So do I, unfortunately," she said, more than a little bitterly. "Have to meet someone for dinner, I mean."

She ground her cigarette out in the ash tray and then looked up at him. Their eyes locked for a moment, and John felt a constriction in his stomach.

She broke eye contact, fished in her purse, and came up with another cigarette.

She just put one out. What is she so nervous about?

He held his Zippo out to her. She steadied his hand with the balls of her fingers. It was an absolutely innocent gesture, yet it gave him immediate indication that he was about to have an erection.

She raised her eyes to his again.

"Well, nice to see you again," she said.

There was nothing to do now but leave.

"I'll remember it a long time," he heard himself say.

She laughed softly, deeply.

"Oddly enough," she said. "I think I will, too."

As if with a mind of its own, his hand went out.

She caught it, as a man would, and shook it. But of course she wasn't a man, and the warm softness of her hand made his heart jump.

"Good-bye," she said as she took her hand away. "And good luck."

He didn't trust his voice to speak. He nodded at her, and then went through the door onto the street.

I'm in love.

No, you're not, asshole. All it is is that you're not getting saltpeter in your chow anymore.

For Christ's sake, she's thirty, you never saw her before the train, and you'll never see her again.

You are *an asshole, Sergeant Moore. There is absolutely no doubt of that.*

He walked up to Broad Street and turned north, back to the Union League Club.

What did she mean "unfortunately" she had to have dinner

with someone? Was she suggesting that she would rather have dinner with me?

Back to Conclusion One, Sergeant Asshole, you're an asshole.

"May I help you, Sir?" the porter asked, barring his access to the Union League.

"I'm meeting Mr. Marston," John said. "William Marston."

"Mr. Marston is in the bar, Sir," the porter said, pointing.

William Dawson Marston IV, forty-six, a tall and angular man in a nicely tailored glen plaid suit, was sitting in a leather upholstered captain's chair by a small table, his long legs stretched straight in front of him and crossed near his ankles.

He smiled and waved when he saw his nephew, then made a half gesture to get up.

"Sit you down, Johnny my boy, and have a drink."

"Hello, Uncle Bill."

"Christ, you even look like a Marine," Marston said.

"Thank you."

"What will you have to drink?"

"Rye and ginger."

"Ginger ale will give you a hangover," Marston said. "I'm surprised you haven't learned that yet. Or are you that impossible contradiction, a teetotal Marine?"

"What would you suggest?" John asked.

A waiter had appeared.

"Bring us two of these, will you please, Charley?" Marston said.

"What is it?" John asked.

"Scotch and water. Very good scotch, and thus with very little water. They call it 'Famous Grouse.' "

That will not be Uncle Bill's second drink. More likely his fifth or sixth.

"I have been here some time," Marston said, as if he had read Moore's mind. "Absorbing some liquid courage. That would annoy your father, but if you report on our conversation, you may feel free to tell him that yes indeed, Uncle Bill was at the bottle."

"Why should I report on our conversation?"

"When you learn the topic, you will understand," Marston said.

He looked around impatiently for the waiter, then turned back to John.

"When are you leaving, John?"

"Thursday."

"Where are you going? Did they tell you?"

"Not specifically. Somewhere in the Pacific, obviously. From here to San Diego, and then to Hawaii."

The waiter appeared. Marston picked up his glass immediately and took a swallow.

"Not surprisingly, when I spoke with him, your father was rather vague about your status," he said. "How is it you're not an officer?"

"I can't talk about that," John said.

"You in some sort of trouble?"

"No. I've been led to believe the commission will come along later."

John sipped his scotch. He would have preferred rye and ginger ale.

But he's probably right about the ginger ale giving me a hangover.

"Getting right to the point," Marston said. "There are those, including your father, who would hold that this is absolutely none of my business, but I have chosen to make it my business: Has your father discussed your trust fund, funds, with you?"

"No," John replied, and then asked, "Is there any reason he should have?"

"That sonofabitch," Marston said, bitterly.

"Excuse me?"

"I shouldn't have said that," Marston said. "I beg your pardon. I really hope you can forget I said that."

"What about my trust fund?"

"Funds, plural. Three of them. Together, two comma trust funds."

"Two comma?"

"Think about it."

What the hell does "two comma" mean? Then he understood. *When figures in excess of $999,999.00 are used, for example, $1,500,000.00, there are two commas.*

"What about my trust funds?"

"There are three," William Dawson Marston said. "The

first is payable on your achieving your majority—how long have you been twenty-one, Johnny?"

"I'm twenty-two," John said.

"Then you should have had the first one turned over to you. You say that hasn't happened?"

"No. I don't know what you're talking about."

"The second is payable on your marriage, or your twenty-fifth birthday, whichever comes first. And the third on your thirtieth birthday, or the birth of your first issue, whichever comes first. Your father hasn't mentioned any of this to you? Even in his marvelously opaque way?"

"No."

"Then I'm very glad that I decided to butt in," Marston said.

"I don't understand you," John said.

"I need another drink," Marston said. "You ready?"

John looked at his glass. It was three quarters full.

"No, thank you," he said, and then changed his mind. "Yes, please, I think I will."

Marston held his glass over his head and snapped his fingers loudly until he had the waiter's attention.

Father often says that Uncle Bill is crude on occasion.

John took a deep swallow of his drink.

"I love my sister," Marston said seriously, and then unnecessarily adding the explanation, "your mother. I really do. But she has a room temperature IQ, and when your father and/or the Bible are concerned, she is totally incompetent to make decisions on her own."

I wonder why I have not leapt loyally, and angrily, to Mother's defense?

"If she has ever raised with your father the question I just raised—and I will give her the benefit of the doubt on that subject—your father doubtless explained that you're only a child, and not nearly as well equipped to handle your financial affairs as he is. And she was surely reassured by those words."

"Why are you bringing this up?" John asked.

"You may have noticed over the years that I am not among your father's legion of admirers," Marston said.

"No, Sir, I never thought anything like that."

"To put a point on it, I can't stand the sonofabitch," Marston said, and then quickly added, "Hell, there I go again. Sorry."

"I think I better get out of here," John thought out loud.

"Keep your seat!" Marston said, so loudly that heads turned. "I have started this, and I *will* finish it."

"I don't like the way you're talking about my parents."

"I'm talking about your money. Two comma money."

"I don't understand," Moore said.

"That's the root of the problem," Marston said. "I presume that you have considered the possibility—God forbid, as they say—that you won't come back from the war alive?"

"Yes, of course."

"And I presume that the Marine Corps encouraged you to prepare a will?"

"Yes."

"And I will bet you a doughnut to a bottle of scotch that you left all your worldly possessions to your parents, yes?"

"Something wrong with that?" John asked, a little nastily.

"Nothing at all, so long as you know what you're doing," Marston said. "But at the time you signed your will, you thought that your worldly possessions consisted of your civilian clothing and your ten thousand dollars worth of government life insurance, no?"

"Yes," John agreed.

"You now know that your estate will be somewhat larger than you thought it would amount to. I want to make sure that you understand you can dispose of your estate in any manner you see fit. You can for example leave all or part of it to your sisters. Or to your rowing club. Or the Salvation Army. Even—God forbid—to Missions."

"Jesus Christ!" John said.

"Him, too, I suppose. But you would have to route that through some churchly body, I think."

John looked at his uncle. Their eyes met. They smiled.

"I'm sure I don't have to say this, but I will. I don't want any part of it," Marston went on. "I want you to come home from this goddamned war and spend it yourself. Preferably on fast women and good whiskey. At least for a while. I . . ."

He reached over and snatched up John's Zippo. He ran his fingers over the Marine Corps insignia.

"This is all I want in way of remembrance, Johnny. May

I have it?" Marston's voice broke, and John's eyes teared. "I'll give it back when you come home."

"Of course," he said, and his voice broke.

There was a full minute's silence as they composed themselves. John broke it: "What should I do? About the trust funds?"

"Change your will as soon as you can," Marston said. "If you're curious about the numbers . . . hell, in any case, go to the Trust Department of the First Philadelphia and ask for Carlton Schuyler . . ."

He interrupted himself to take a card and write the name on it.

"Schuyler's a good sort, and he's probably already a little nervous that your father's 'handling' your affairs for you. If I know it's not legal, he damned well does too. Anyway, Schuyler will have the numbers and can answer all your questions."

Moore nodded, and then asked: "When I have all this information, what should I do with it?"

"You're asking my advice?" Marston asked. "You sure you want to do that?"

"Yes."

"OK. Have Schuyler set up another trust for you, using the assets of the trust fund that should have been turned over to you. Let the bank manage your assets while you're away. I've asked about this. It's a common practice for people in the service. Put all of it, save, say, a thousand dollars, in the trust."

"I don't quite understand," Moore confessed. "What would the difference be? I mean, it's already in a trust . . ."

"Your father has access to it the way it is now. This way he couldn't touch it."

It was a long moment before Moore replied, "I see."

His uncle nodded.

"And why everything but a thousand dollars?" Moore asked.

"Good whiskey and wild women, Johnny, are expensive. Have a good time before you go over there."

"Christ!"

"I didn't exactly have Him in mind," Marston said. "I was thinking more of the long-legged blondes you might bump into. Pity you're not going through San Francisco. The long-legged blondes around the bar at the Andrew Foster Hotel are stunning."

Like that woman, that stunning woman, in the bar at the Bellevue-Stratford?

"OK," John said. "I'll do it first thing in the morning."

"Then I accomplished what I set out to do," Marston said.

"Thank you," John said.

"You mean that, Johnny? Or was I putting my nose in where it had no business?"

"I mean it," John said. "But what I don't understand is why? I mean, why did my father do what he did? Why is he always doing something like that?"

"In this case, it's pretty obvious. Neither his mother or your grandfather left him or your mother very much in their wills. They left everything in trust to the grandchildren. I won't say—though I have a damned good idea—why they chose to do that, but they did."

"Tell me what you think."

"They didn't particularly like *him,* obviously, and they knew that leaving the money to your mother would be the same thing as leaving it to him. Ten minutes after she got it, he would have talked her out of it."

"Oh."

"In his mind, he was right about not bothering you with the details of your inheritance. He was *protecting* you. He's been that way as long as I've known him. He really never questions the morality of anything he does. He thinks I like to buy his goddamned first class cabins on the *Pacific Princess,* and pay his tailor bills, for example. But I shouldn't have called him a sonofabitch, even if he is a sonofabitch, and I'm sorry."

John chuckled.

Marston smiled at him.

"Finish your drink, and we'll have dinner. I'm not sure I'll be able to find the dining room as it is."

William Dawson Marston IV found the dining room without trouble, and he got through the cherrystone clams and half his steak; but then, without warning, he lowered his chin to his chest, dropped his wine glass, and went to sleep.

John was alarmed, but quickly learned that the Union

League was prepared for such eventualities. The maître d'hôtel and an enormous chef quickly appeared, hoisted Marston to his feet, and carried him out of the dining room.

"We'll just put Mr. Marston up overnight, until he feels better," the waiter said softly in John's ear.

John was back across Broad Street and almost to the First Philadelphia Trust Company parking lot before he realized that the last thing he wanted to do now was get in the car and go home, where he would probably have to face his father.

If I go back to the bar in the Bellevue-Stratford, maybe she'll be there.

There you go again, Sergeant Asshole! For one thing, she won't be there, and for another, what do you think you would do if she was?

He went back to the bar in the Bellevue-Stratford and she was not there.

Well, asshole, what did you expect?

He took the same seat at the bar he had before.

"Scotch," John said. "Famous Grouse, if you have it. With a little water."

He laid money on the bar, but when the bartender delivered the drink, he said, "It's on the gentleman at the end of the bar."

John, uncomfortable, looked down the bar. A middle-aged, silver-haired stout Irishman waved friendlily at him.

Well, he doesn't look like a pervert.

He waved his thanks.

"I wondered if you would come back in here," the beautiful older woman said, behind him.

"Jesus!"

"How was your dinner?"

"The food wasn't bad," John said.

"But the rest was awful?" she asked. "Mine, too."

"Can I get you a drink?"

"Yes, please," she said. "But I insist on paying."

"I can pay," he said. "I want to."

"I think I have a little more money than a Marine Sergeant," she said.

"Don't be too sure," he said. "You weren't at my dinner."

"It was a money dinner? Have you noticed that talking about money at dinner ruins the taste of the food?"

He laughed.

"Yes," he said. "Is that the voice of experience?"

"Yes," she said. "Unfortunately. Over a Bookbinder's lobster, my soon-to-be ex-husband and I fought politely over the division of property."

"I'm sorry," John said.

"Yes, Miss?" the bartender asked.

"What are you drinking?" she asked John.

"Famous Grouse," he said.

"Fine," she said to the bartender. She turned to John. "Why is it that now that I see you again I don't think you're a lonely marine, far from home and loved ones?"

"I'm from here," he said. "That may have something to do with it. And I just had dinner with my uncle."

She chuckled. "You are also far more articulate than you were on the train," she said. "What was with you on the train?"

"I thought you had caught me staring at you," he said.

"I had," she said. "Why were you?"

"Because you're the most beautiful woman I've ever seen."

"I can't believe that," she said.

"Why did you come back in here?" John asked.

"Ooooh," she said, and then looked at him. "Right to the bone, right? OK. I thought maybe you would be in here."

"I am."

"Did you come in here to pick up a girl?"

"I came in because I didn't want to go home and face my father," John said evenly.

"You did something wrong?"

"He did."

"That's the money you were talking about?"

He nodded.

"And because I had the crazy idea you might be here."

"I am," she said.

"I think maybe I'm dreaming and will wake up any second," John said.

"It's like a dream for me too," she said. "A bad dream. I had the odd notion that when I met my husband, that we could . . . patch things up. But what he wanted was the

Spode . . . his beloved saw the Spode and wanted it . . . You know what I mean by Spode?"

"China."

". . . and the monogrammed silver. I mean, after all, it would have no meaning for me anymore, would it? I'll certainly remarry in time, won't I?"

"I'm sorry," John said.

"And then here I am, in a bar, more than a little drunk, with a Marine. A boy Marine. Bad dream."

"I'm not a boy," John said, hurt.

"Yes, you are," she said, laughing.

"Well, fuck you!"

There you go, asshole. You fucked it up. Why the fucking hell did you say that?

"Sorry," he said, in anguish.

She opened her purse and he thought she was looking for a cigarette and remembered that Uncle Bill had taken his Zippo so he couldn't light it for her.

But her hand came out of the purse with a five-dollar bill. She dropped it on the bar and stood up.

Now she's going to walk out of here, and I will never see her again.

She looked into his face.

"Come on," she said. "Let's get out of here."

She walked to the side door; and in a moment he followed her. She waited for him to open the door for her, and walked out. Then she put her hand on his arm.

"As long as we both understand this is insane . . ." she said.

"Where are we going?"

"Rittenhouse Square," she said. "We—*I*—have an apartment there."

There was a hand on Sergeant John Marston Moore's shoulder and a voice calling gently, "Hey!"

He opened his eyes. He was lying belly down on a bed, his arm and head hanging over the edge. He could see a dark red carpet and a naked foot, obviously a female foot. This observation was immediately confirmed when he saw that the leg attached to the foot disappeared under a pale blue robe.

He remembered where he was, and what had happened, and rolled over onto his back.

She was standing there, holding a cup of coffee out to him. *I don't even know her name!*

"Hi!" she said.

"Hi," he replied, looking into her eyes. "What's that?"

"Coffee," she said.

"Coffee?"

"You said you had your father's car. I don't want you driving drunk."

"You're throwing me out?"

"I'm sending you home."

"Why?"

"Didn't we both get what we were looking for?"

"We gave each other what the other needed would be a nicer way to put it."

"All right," she said. "Yes, we did. I hope I did. I know you did. But now it's time to come back to the real world."

"And for me to go home."

"Right."

"I don't want to go home. I want to stay here with you, forever."

"That's obviously out of the question."

He sat up. She tried to hand him the cup and saucer. He avoided it.

She touched the top of his head.

"You are really very sweet," she said.

He tilted his head back to look up at her. She smiled.

He reached up for the cord of her robe.

"Don't do that."

He ignored her.

The robe fell open when he pulled the cord free.

He put his arms around her and his face against her belly.

He heard her take in her breath, and her hand dropped to the small of his neck.

"Oh God!" she said.

Her navel was next to his mouth and he kissed it.

"I'm going to spill the coffee."

"Put the coffee on the floor and take the robe off."

"And if I do, then will you go?"

"No."

She dropped to her knees and put the cup and saucer on

the floor, shrugged out of the robe, and then turned her face to him and kissed him.

"Oh, Baby, what am I going to do with you?"

"I don't know about that," he said. "But I know what I'm going to do to you."

He put his hands on her shoulders and moved her onto the bed and looked down at her.

"God, you're so beautiful!" he said.

"So are you," she said.

And then he surprised her very much by pushing himself off the bed. She raised her head to look at him. He walked to the other side of the bed and sat down and reached for her telephone.

"Father," he said into it. "Uncle Bill and I have had a long talk and a lot to drink, and I think it would be best if I stayed over with him at the Union League, rather than driving."

There was a pause, and then Sergeant John Marston Moore, USMCR, said: "You're going to have to understand, Father, that I'm no longer a child. I can drink whatever and whenever I wish."

There was another pause.

"There's something else, Father. My orders have been changed. I have to leave tomorrow afternoon. When Mother's awake, please tell her that I'll be out there sometime before noon to pack. I have to see Mr. Schuyler at First Philadelphia, first."

One final pause.

"I think you know why I have to see Mr. Schuyler, Father," John said.

A moment later, he took the receiver from his ear and looked at it.

It was clear to Barbara Ward (Mrs. Howard P.) Hawthorne, Jr., that John's father had hung up on him. There was pain in his eyes when he turned from putting the receiver in its cradle and looked at her.

"Oh, Baby," she said. "Whatever that was, I'm sorry."

"Do you think you could manage to call me 'Darling,' or 'Sweetheart,' or something besides 'Baby'? . . . I'll even settle happily for 'John.' "

She held her arms open.

"Come to me, my darling," she said.

He didn't move.

"I thought you wanted me to leave."

She put her arms down and pulled the sheet up and held it over her breast.

She found his eyes and looked into them and said, "I want what's best for you."

"You're what's best for me."

"You really have to leave tomorrow? Which is really, now, today?"

"No. Thursday."

"Then why . . . ?"

"I want to be with you until I go."

She took her eyes from his and lowered her head and fought the tears. Then she raised her eyes to his again and opened her arms again and said, "Come to me, John, my darling, my sweetheart."

And this time he went to her.

VI

Lieutenant Colonel Clyde G. Dawkins, USMC, Commanding MAG-21, was a tall, thin, sharp-featured man who wore his light brown hair so closely cropped that the tanned and sun-freckled flesh of his scalp was visible.

He was wearing a stiffly starched khaki shirt with a field scarf tied in a tiny knot. A gold collar clasp held the collar points together and the knot in the field scarf erect. He had heard somewhere that the collar clasp was now frowned upon; but that brought the same reaction from him as the suggestion from Pearl Harbor that since *Navy* Naval Aviators were now discouraged from wearing their fur-collared leather flight jackets when not actually engaged in flying activities, it behooved him to similarly discourage *Marine* Naval Aviators from wearing their flight jackets when not actually on the flight line: He said nothing; thought, *Fuck You;* and

120

wore both a collar clasp and his leather flight jacket almost all the time, fully aware that if he did so, the Marine Naval Aviators of MAG-21 would presume it was not only permissible but encouraged.

He was not at all a rebel by nature. He did not relish defying higher authority, even when he knew he could get away with it. But he was a practical man, and the wearing of flight jackets by aviators seemed far more practical and convenient than forcing his officers to waste time taking off and putting on their uniform tunics half a dozen times a day. And the gold collar clasp, in his judgment, struck him as a splendid means to keep an officer's collar points where they belonged, even if some people in The Corps thought of it as "civilian-type jewelry." An officer with one of his collar points in a horizontal attitude looked far more slovenly than one with his collar points fixed in the proper attitude with a barely visible piece of "civilian jewelry."

The officer standing somewhat uncomfortably before Lieutenant Colonel Dawkins's desk had performed well in the Battle of Midway. His name was Captain Thomas J. Wood. He was young and newly promoted; he was wearing a fur-collared flight jacket and a collar clasp; and he was standing with his hands clasped together behind him in the small of his back.

But there was something about him—an impetuosity, an indecisiveness—that Dawkins did not like. Dawkins believed that a good officer made decisions slowly, and then stuck by them.

"It's time to fish or cut bait, Tom," Dawkins said, not unkindly.

"Uh . . . Sir, I decline to press charges."

"So be it," Dawkins said.

"Sir, I saw what I saw, but I can't . . ."

"That will be all, Captain," Dawkins said. There was now a hint of ice in his voice. "You are dismissed."

The captain came to attention.

"Yes, Sir," he said. He did an about-face and started to march out of the room.

"Ask Major Lorenz to come in, please," Dawkins called to him.

"Aye, aye, Sir."

Major Karl J. Lorenz, who was the Executive Officer of MAG-21, walked into the office. Lorenz looked, Dawkins often thought, like a recruiting poster for the Waffen-SS—in other words like an Aryan of impeccable Nordic-Teutonic heritage, blond-haired, blue-eyed, fair-skinned, and lithely muscular.

"You wanted me, Skipper?" he asked.

"Close the door, please," Dawkins said.

Lorenz did so.

"After some thought," Dawkins said, "he declined to press charges."

"Huh," Lorenz said thoughtfully. "Probably a good thing, Sir. It would have been hard to make those charges stick."

"*Not* a good thing, Karl," Dawkins said.

"You think we should have tried him?" Lorenz asked, surprised.

"I think before young Captain Wood started running off at the mouth, he should have made up his mind whether or not he was prepared to carry an accusation of cowardice through."

"Oh," Lorenz replied. "Yes, Sir, I see what you mean."

"He doesn't really know any more than I do—and I wasn't there—if Dunn ran away from that fight or not. Cowardice in the face of the enemy . . . that's the worst accusation that can be made."

"I presume you told Wood that?"

"No. I didn't want to influence his decision, one way or the other."

"Can I ask what you *think?*"

"I already told you, I don't think Wood really knows. Or, if you were asking, do I think Dunn ran?"

"Yes, Sir."

"I think we're going to have to give him the benefit of the doubt. He says he doesn't remember when, or under what conditions, he broke off the engagement. I don't think he does. He lost his windscreen and he was wounded. The question is, when did that happen? Before or after he started back to Midway? He didn't run before the fight. He got a Kate. There's no question about that. And then he got a Zero. Again, confirmed beyond any question. And then the next time he's seen, he's on his way back to Midway. Close enough to be recognized beyond any doubt, but too far away for anyone to be able to state with certainty that he had, or had not, already lost his windshield."

"I realize, Sir, I haven't been asked, but in those circumstances I would be prone to give him the benefit of the doubt."

"Ascribing Wood's charges to post-combat hysteria?"

"Something like that, Sir."

"Unfortunately, although he elected not to pursue them, Wood's charges are going to be remembered by a lot of people for a long time—made worse in the retelling, of course."

"What are you going to do with Dunn, Sir?" Lorenz said, after a moment.

"You and I are about to visit Lieutenant Dunn in the hospital; there I will express my pleasure that he will be discharged tomorrow, present him with his Purple Heart Medal, and inform him that he is now assigned to VMF-229. I think he will understand why it would be awkward for him to return to VMF-211. I hope he doesn't ask me for an explanation."

"Two-twenty-nine, Sir?" Lorenz asked, surprised.

Dawkins nodded. "Two-twenty-nine."

"Sir, we haven't activated VMF-229 yet."

"It is activated," Dawkins said and paused to look at his watch, "as of 1300 hours today. Its personnel consists of one officer, absent in hospital, and one officer, en route, not yet joined. See that the order is typed up."

"Who did you decide to give it to, Sir?"

"A good Marine officer, Major," Dawkins said, "is always willing to carefully consider the recommendations of his superiors."

"Sir?"

Dawkins chuckled, opened a desk drawer, and handed Lorenz a sheet of yellow teletype paper.

ROUTINE
CONFIDENTIAL
HQ USMC WASH DC 1445 14JUNE42
COMMANDING OFFICER
MAG-21 EWA TH
CAPTAIN CHARLES M. GALLOWAY, USMCR, HAVING RE-

PORTED UPON ACTIVE DUTY, HAS BEEN ORDERED TO PRO-
CEED BY AIR TO EWA FOR DUTY AS COMMANDING OFFICER
VMF-229. WHILE THIS ASSIGNMENT HAS THE CONCUR-
RENCE OF THE COMMANDANT AND THE UNDERSIGNED YOU
ARE OF COURSE AT LIBERTY TO ASSIGN THIS OFFICER TO
ANY DUTIES YOU WISH.
D.G. MCINERNEY BRIG GEN USMC

"I will be goddamned," Lorenz said.

"I thought you might find that surprising," Dawkins said.

"The last time I saw Charley, I thought they were going
to crucify him," Lorenz said. "And I mean, literally. What
the hell does that 'concurrence of the Commandant' mean?"

"I think it means that Doc McInerney went right to the
Commandant. They had Charley flying a VIP R4D around
out of Quantico." The R4D was the Navy designation of the
twin-engine Douglas transport aircraft called DC-3 by the
manufacturer and C-47 by the Army Air Corps. "What I
think is that McInerney went to the Commandant and told
him how desperate we are for people with more than two
hundred hours in a cockpit. As furious as the Navy was with
him, nobody but the Commandant would dare to commission
him."

"The last I heard, they wouldn't let him fly—hell, even
taxi—anything. He was still a sergeant, and they had him
working as a mechanic on the flight line at Quantico. But this
sort of restores my faith in the Marine Corps," Lorenz said.

" '*Restores*' your faith, Major?" Dawkins asked wryly.
"That suggests it was lost."

"Well, let's say, the way the brass let the Navy crap all
over Charley, that it *wavered* a little."

"Oh ye of little faith!" Dawkins mocked, gently.

"When's he due in?"

Dawkins shrugged helplessly. "The TWX didn't say," he
said. "And knowing Charley as well as I do, that means one
of two things: He will either rush over here as fast as humanly
possible, or else he will still be trying to find a slow ship the
day the war's over."

Lorenz laughed.

Dawkins stood up.

"Let's go pin the Purple Heart on Lieutenant Dunn," he said.

(Two)
U.S. NAVAL HOSPITAL
PEARL HARBOR, OAHU ISLAND, TERRITORY OF
HAWAII
1505 HOURS 19 JUNE 1942

When Lieutenant Colonel Dawkins pushed open the door to his room, First Lieutenant William C. Dunn was lying on his back on the bed; his bathrobe was open and his legs were spread; and he was not wearing pajama pants. Dunn was obviously not expecting visitors.

What Dawkins could see, among other things, were several bandages in the vicinity of Dunn's crotch. One of these was large, but most were not much more than Band-Aids. He could also see a half-dozen unbandaged wounds, their sutures visible, on his inner upper thighs. The whole area had been shaved and then painted with some kind of orange antiseptic.

He was almost a soprano, Dawkins thought. *Whatever had come through the canopy of Dunn's Wildcat had come within inches of blowing away the family jewels. From the number of fragments, it was probably a 20mm, which exploded on contact.*

Soon after the door opened, Dunn covered his midsection with the flap of his hospital issue bathrobe; and then when he saw the silver leaf on Dawkins's collar, he started to swing his legs to get out of bed.

"Stay where you are, Son," Dawkins said quickly, but too late. Dunn was already on his feet, standing at attention.

"Well, then, stand at ease," Dawkins said. "Does all that hurt very much?"

"Only when I get a hard-on, Sir," Dunn blurted, and quickly added, "Sorry, Sir. I shouldn't have said that."

"If I had been dinged in that area, and it still worked," Dawkins said, "I think I would be delighted."

"Yes, Sir," Dunn said.

"Do you know who I am, Son?"

"Yes, Sir. You gave us a little talk when we reported aboard."

"And this is my exec, Major Lorenz," Dawkins said.

Lorenz gave his hand to Dunn.

"How are you, Lieutenant?"

"Very well, thank you, Sir."

"Why don't you let me pin this thing on you," Dawkins said. "And then you get back in bed."

He took the Purple Heart Medal from a hinged metal box, pinned it to the lapel of Dunn's bathrobe, and then shook his hand.

"Thank you, Sir."

"That's the oldest medal, did you know that?" Dawkins said. "Goes back to the Revolution. Washington issued an order that anyone who had been wounded could wear a purple ribbon—and in those days that meant a real ribbon—on his uniform."

"I didn't know that, Sir," Dunn admitted.

"You have literally shed blood for your country," Dawkins said. "You can wear that with pride."

Dunn didn't reply.

"Why don't you get back in bed?"

"I'm all right, Sir. And they have been encouraging me to move around."

"They tell me you're being discharged tomorrow," Dawkins said.

"I was about to tell you that, Sir, and ask you what's next."

"You've been assigned to VMF-229," Dawkins said.

"Pending court-martial, Sir?"

"No charges have been, or will be, pressed against you, Dunn," Dawkins said.

"But they don't want me back in the squadron, right, Sir?"

"*I* ordered your transfer to VMF-229," Dawkins said. "The commanding officer of VMF-211 had nothing to do with that decision."

"Yes, Sir," Dunn said, on the edge of insolence, making it clear he did not believe that answer.

Dawkins felt anger swell up in him, but suppressed it.

"VMF-229 is a new squadron. It was activated today. Right now, you are half of its total strength. The commanding officer is en route from the States. I assigned you there because I wanted someone with your experience . . ."

"My Midway experience, Sir?" Dunn asked, just over the edge into sarcasm.

"When I want a question, Son," Dawkins said icily, "I will ask for one."

"Yes, Sir."

"You will be the only pilot in the squadron who has even seen a Japanese airplane, much less shot two of them down," Dawkins said. "I want the newcomers to look at you and see you're very much like they are. To take some of the pressure off, if you follow my meaning. Additionally, perhaps you will be able to teach them something, based on your experience."

"Yes, Sir."

"I'm personally acquainted with your new commanding officer, Captain Charley Galloway," Dawkins went on. "I will tell him what I know about you, and the gossip. And I will tell him that I personally feel you did everything you were supposed to do at Midway, and then, suffering wounds, managed to get your shot-up aircraft back to the field."

Dunn for the first time met Dawkins's eyes.

"Now, you may ask any questions you may have," Dawkins said.

"Thank you, Sir," Dunn said after a moment. "No questions, Sir."

"Unsolicited advice is seldom welcome, Dunn, but nevertheless: Do what you can to ignore the gossip. Eventually, it will die down. You now have that clean slate everyone's always talking about, new squadron, new skipper. If I were Captain Galloway, I'd be damned glad to be getting someone like you."

"Colonel, I really don't remember a goddamned thing about how I got back to the field," Dunn said.

I believe him.

"The important thing is that you got back," Dawkins said.

"Sir, where is VMF-229?"

"Right now, it's on a sheet of paper in Major Lorenz's OUT basket," Dawkins said. "When you get out of here, check into the BOQ. When Captain Galloway gets here, or something else happens, we'll send for you. Take some time off. I was about to say, go swimming, but that's probably not such a hot idea, is it?"

"No, Sir," Dunn said.

For the first time, Dawkins noticed, *Dunn is smiling. I think it just sank in that he's not going to be court-martialed, and maybe even that someone doesn't think he's a coward.*

"Check in with the adjutant, or the sergeant major, once a day," Dawkins said.

"Aye, aye, Sir."

Dawkins put out his hand.

"Congratulations, Lieutenant, on your decoration," he said. "And good luck in your new assignment."

"Thank you, Sir."

Major Lorenz offered his hand.

"If you need anything, Dunn, come see me, or give me a call. And congratulations, too, and good luck."

"Thank you, Sir," Dunn repeated.

(Three)
U.S. NAVAL HOSPITAL
PEARL HARBOR, HAWAII, TERRITORY OF HAWAII
1535 HOURS 19 JUNE 1942

Lieutenant Colonel Dawkins and Major Lorenz left the room, closing the door after them. Dunn lowered his head to look at his Purple Heart Medal—he had seen the ribbon before, but not the actual medal—then unpinned it and held it in his hand and looked at it again. It was in the shape of a heart and bore a profile of George Washington.

He picked up the box it had come in and saw that it contained both the ribbon and a metal pin in the shape of the ribbon, obviously intended to be worn in the lapel of a civilian jacket.

"You're a real fucking hero, Bill Dunn," he said wryly, aloud. "You have been awarded the 'Next Time, Stupid, Remember to Duck Medal.' "

He chuckled at his own wit. Then he put the medal in the box, snapped the lid closed, walked to the white bedside table, and put it in the drawer. As he was closing the drawer, the door opened again.

Lieutenant (Junior Grade) Mary Agnes O'Malley, Nurse Corps, USN, entered the room, carrying a stainless steel tray covered with a wash-faded, medical green cloth.

"Hi," she said and smiled at him.

Lieutenant Dunn was strongly attracted to Lieutenant (j.g.) O'Malley, partly because she was a trim, pert-breasted redhead, and partly because he had heard that she fucked like a mink. He'd heard it so often at the bar in the Ewa Officer's Club that it had to be something more than wishful thinking.

"Hi," he replied.

He thought she looked especially desirable today. When she put the cloth covered tray down on his bedside table, she leaned far enough over to afford him a glimpse of her well-filled brassiere, and the soft white flesh straining at it.

Despite her reputation, Lieutenant (j.g.) O'Malley had so far shown zero interest in Dunn. In his view there were two reasons for this. First, since someone as good looking as Lieutenant (j.g.) O'Malley could pick and choose among a large group of bachelor officers, she would naturally prefer a captain or a major to a lowly lieutenant. Second, but perhaps most important, he knew that his reputation had preceded him: She had certainly heard the gossip that he had run away from the fight at Midway. To a young woman like Lieutenant (j.g.) O'Malley—for that matter, to any young woman—a lowly lieutenant with a yellow streak was something to be scorned, not taken to bed.

"What did the brass want?" she asked.

"The war is going badly," he said. "They came for my advice on how to turn it around."

"I'm serious," she said, gesturing for him to get on the bed. "What did they want?"

"They gave me my 'You Forgot to Duck Medal.' "

"What?"

"Colonel Dawkins gave me the Purple Heart," Dunn said. "And my new assignment. Why should I get in bed?"

"Because I'm going to remove your sutures," she said. "Or some of them, anyway. Where's your medal?"

"In the table drawer."

"Can I see it?"

"You've never seen one before?"

"I want to see yours."

You show me yours and I'll show you mine.

He went to the bedside table and took the box out and handed it to her.

She opened it and looked at it and handed it back.

"Very nice. You should be proud of yourself."

"All that means is that I got hit," he said.

"You realize how lucky you were that it wasn't worse, I hope?"

Does she mean that the 20mm didn't hit me in the head? Or that it didn't get me in the balls?

"Yeah, sure I do," he said.

"Get in the bed and open your robe," she said.

"I'm not wearing my pajama bottoms."

She tossed him the faded green medical cloth.

"Cover yourself," she said. "Not that I would see something I haven't seen before."

He got on the bed, arranged the cloth over his crotch, and opened the robe.

She pulled on rubber gloves, an act that he found quite erotic, dipped a gauze patch in alcohol, and then proceeded to mop his inner thighs.

He yelped when, without warning, she pulled the larger bandage free with a jerk.

"Still a little suppuration," she observed, professionally. "But it's healing nicely. You were *really* lucky."

Without question, that remark makes reference to the fact that I didn't get zapped in the balls.

As she scrubbed at the vestiges of the tape that had held the bandage in place, he got another glimpse down the front of her crisp white uniform at the swelling of her bosom. He could smell the perfume she'd put down there, too. With dreadful inevitability he almost instantly achieved a state of erection.

Lieutenant O'Malley seemed not to notice.

"Where are they sending you?" she asked, as she jerked the smaller bandage free.

"VMF-229," he said.

"Where's that? Or is that classified?"

"Colonel Dawkins said that right now it's in the exec's desk drawer," Dunn said. "It was activated today. Right now it's me and a captain named Galloway, who's en route from the States."

"Galloway?" she asked. "Does he have a first name?"

Dunn thought a moment. "Charley, I think he said. Mean anything to you?"

"I don't know," she said. "I used to date a Tech Sergeant Charley Galloway. He was a pilot. I wonder how many Charley Galloways there are in the Marine Corps?"

Socialization between commissioned officers and enlisted personnel was not only a social no-no in the Naval Service but against regulations, and thus a court-martial offense. The announcement startled him.

"You used to date a sergeant?" he blurted.

"My, aren't you the prig? Haven't you ever done anything you shouldn't?" she asked as she dabbed at the gummy residue of the second bandage. "I think we'll just leave the bandage off of that."

"I didn't mean to sound like a prig," he said. "I guess I was just a little surprised to . . . hear you volunteer that."

"Well, I didn't think you would tell anybody," she said. "You mean you never heard of Sergeant Charley Galloway?"

And then, all of a sudden, he realized that he had. He hadn't made the connection before because of the rank.

"I reported aboard VMF-211 after he left," Dunn said. "That Galloway?"

She chuckled.

"That Galloway," she confirmed.

"The scuttlebutt I heard was that he and another sergeant put together a Wildcat from wrecks of what was left on December seventh, wrecks that had been written off the books, and that he flew it off without authority to join the Wake Island relief force at sea."

"The *Saratoga,*" she said. "Task Force XIV," she said. "They started out to reinforce Wake Island, but they were called back."

"I heard that he was really in trouble for doing that," Dunn said. "That they sent him back to the States for a court-martial. What was that all about?"

"He embarrassed the Navy brass," she explained. "First of all BUAIR." (The U.S. Navy Bureau of Aeronautics, which is charged with aviation engineering for the Marine

Corps.) "They examined the airplanes after the Japanese attack and said they were total losses. But Charley and Sergeant Oblensky . . ."

"Who?"

"Big Steve Oblensky. He was VMF-211's Maintenance Sergeant."

"I know him," Dunn said. "As far as I know, he still is."

"So after the brass said all of VMF-211's planes at Ewa were beyond repair, Big Steve and Charley got one flying; and then Charley flew it out to *Sara,* which was then a couple of hundred miles at sea. The whole relief force was supposed to be a secret, especially of course, where *Sara* was. So the brass's faces were red, and since the brass never make a mistake, they decided to stick the old purple shaft in Charley."

"Why did he do it?"

"Hell," Lieutenant (j.g.) O'Malley said, "the rest of VMF-211 was on Wake and had already lost most of their planes. Charley figured they needed whatever airplanes they could get. The only aircraft on *Sara* were Buffaloes. They could have used Charley's Wildcat, if the brass here hadn't called the relief force back."

Dunn grunted.

It had occurred to him that despite the smell of her perfume, her well-filled brassiere, and the other delightful aspects of her gentle gender, Lieutenant (j.g.) O'Malley was talking to him like—more importantly, thinking like—a fellow officer of the Naval Establishment, even down to an easy familiarity with the vernacular. It was somewhat disconcerting.

"We don't know if we're talking about the same man," he said.

"Probably, we're not," Mary Agnes O'Malley replied, matter-of-factly, "considering how pissed off the brass was at Charley. It's probably some other guy with the same name."

He sensed that she was disappointed.

She put the alcohol swab on the tray and picked up a pair of surgical scissors. Next she bent low over his midsection; and he sensed, rather than saw—her head was in the way, and he was unable to withdraw his eyes from her brassiere— that she was cutting the sutures.

The procedure took her a full ninety seconds. Sensing that she was concentrating, he did not attempt to make conversation.

She straightened, finally, and he was suddenly sure from the look in her eyes that she knew he had been looking down her dress.

She laid the scissors down and picked up surgical forceps and a pad of gauze.

"Now we pull the thread out," she said, and bent over him again. "It shouldn't hurt, so don't squirm."

"Okay."

The green surgical cloth was somehow displaced. He grabbed for it in the same moment she did. She got to it first and put it back in place. In doing so, her hand brushed against it.

"Christ, I'm sorry!" Dunn said.

"Don't be silly," she said professionally.

"I thought, I heard . . ." Bill blurted, "that when something like that happens, a nurse knows where to hit it to make it go down."

She chuckled, deep in her throat.

"I wouldn't want to hurt it," she said, matter-of-factly. "I think it's darling."

He felt a nipping sensation, and then a moment later, another one, and then a third. He realized that she was pulling the black sutures from his flesh.

She stood erect and wiped two short lengths of thread from her fingers with a cloth, and then a third from the forceps. She looked down at him.

"We're supposed to be very professional—I think the word is 'dispassionate'—when something like that happens," she said. "But the truth is, sometimes that doesn't happen. Especially when the patient is sort of cute."

Her fingers slid up his leg, found his erection, and traced it gently.

"You're going to be discharged tomorrow, which means that if you ask for one, they'll give you an off-the-ward pass until 2230."

She took her hand away, wiped the forceps with the gauze again, and bent over him. He felt another series of nips in the soft flesh of his groin, and then she stood up again.

"Cat got your tongue?" she asked.

"I don't suppose you could have dinner with me tonight?"

"I think that could be arranged," she said.

"Put your hand on it again."

"We'd both be in trouble if somebody saw us," she said, and then ran her fingers over him again.

"What time?"

"I go off at 1630," she said. "How about 1730 at the bar?"

"Fine."

"My roommate has the duty tonight," she said.

"She does?"

"If we have gentlemen callers, we're supposed to leave the door open," she said. "But I always wonder, when the door is closed, how anybody could tell if we have anybody in there or not."

"I can't see how they could tell," he said.

"Well, maybe you might want to get a bottle of scotch and pick me up at my quarters. We could have a drink, and then go to dinner. Or would you rather eat first?"

"What kind of scotch?"

"I'm not fussy," she said.

"You better stop that, or I'm going to . . ."

She immediately took her hand away.

"We wouldn't want to waste it, would we?" she asked. "Now be a good boy and let me finish this. Before old Shit-for-brains wonders why it's taking me so long and sticks her nose in here."

(Four)
APARTMENT "C"
106 RITTENHOUSE SQUARE
PHILADELPHIA, PENNSYLVANIA
22 JUNE 1942

Barbara Ward (Mrs. Howard P.) Hawthorne, Jr., slid the frosted glass door open and stepped out of her shower. She took a towel from the rack and started to dry her hair. Then she stopped and wiped the condensation from the mirror over the wash basin.

She resumed drying her hair as she examined herself in the mirror.

It's not at all bad looking, she thought, they're not pendulous, and the tummy is still firm, but ye old body is thirty-six years old. Nearly thirty-seven, not thirty-two, as you told John.

When he is thirty-seven—she did the arithmetic—you will be fifty-one. Fifty-one! My God, you're insane, Barbara!

She finished drying herself, put the towel in the hamper, and went into the bedroom. There she took a spray bottle of eau de cologne and sprayed it on herself, and then she took a bottle of perfume, which she dabbed behind her ears and in the valley between her breasts. She pulled on her robe, walked back to the bathroom, and began to brush her hair, looking into the reflection of her eyes in the mirror.

Why did you put perfume on? There will be no one to smell it. Specifically, John has probably nuzzled you between the breasts for the last time. He is at this very moment ten thousand feet in the air over Western Pennsylvania, or Ohio, or someplace, on his way to the war. Even if he survives that, the chances of his coming back to you are very slim.

What he got was what he wanted, a willing playmate in bed for four days. But when he comes back, what he is going to want is a quote nice unquote girl his own age, not some middleaged woman who he picked up—or vice versa—in a bar.

He says he loves you . . .

And he probably really thinks he does, because he would not say something like that unless he meant it. But what he is really doing is mistaking lust, and a little tenderness, for love.

He's not much used to love, that's for sure. From everything he told me, his father is really a despicable human being. He got no love from him. Or anything like tenderness, either, for that matter. Nor from his mother, either, I don't think. I got the idea that, in the Moore house, hugging and kissing were unseemly.

And while I am not all that experienced in the bed department myself, it was perfectly obvious that he can count his previous partners on the fingers of one hand. He had an enthusiasm factor of ten and an experience factor of one. Maybe minus one.

*I am absolutely convinced that no one ever did to him some
of the things . . .*
So why did you do them?
He probably can hardly wait to get back to the boys.
"So how was your leave?"
"Great. I met this older woman. Not bad looking. But talk
about hot pants! Talk about blow jobs! I'm telling you, she
couldn't get enough, wouldn't let me alone. Once she did it
while I was sleeping."
*I did do it to him while he was sleeping, and I loved it.
Which goes to show, therefore, that beneath your respectable
facade, you are an oversexed bitch.*
*Or, more kindly, just your normal, run-of-the-mill, unsatis-
fied housewife, whose husband has been off gamboling with
a sweet young thing for the past five months. Or maybe longer.
Only he and the sweet young thing know for sure.*
After she finished brushing her hair and rubbing moistur-
izer into her face, she took a paper towel and wiped the mirror clean of vestigial condensation, and then went into the
bedroom. She lay on the bedspread and turned on the radio;
then she turned it off and went into the living room and took
the bottle of scotch—from where John had left it—from the
mantelpiece and carried it into the kitchen and poured two
inches of it into a glass.
She took a sip, and then a second, larger sip, and then she
exhaled audibly.
God, I wish he was here!
The door bell went off. It was one of the old-fashioned, me-
chanical kind, that you "rang" by turning a knob.
She looked at the clock on the wall. It was quarter to nine.
Who the hell can that be?
*Did that damned fool somehow not go? Did the airplane
turn back for some reason and land at Newark again? If that
happened, he would just have time to come back here now.*
She went to the door, just reaching it as the bell rang again.
She opened the door to the length of the chain and peered
through the crack and saw the last person in the world she
expected to see, Howard P. Hawthorne, Jr.
"It's me, Barbara," Howard said, quite unnecessarily.
"So I see," she said, instantly hearing the inanity in her
voice.

"May I come in, or . . . have you guests?"

She closed the door, removed the chain, and opened it fully.

"Come in, Howard."

"Thank you," he said.

"I'm having a drink," she said. "Would you like one? What do you want?"

"Scotch would be fine, thank you."

"You're welcome to a scotch, but that's not what I meant to ask."

"Oh. Yes, I see. I wanted to talk to you."

"Well, come in the kitchen while I make your drink. We can talk there."

"Thank you," Howard said, and then asked, "I'm not interrupting anything am I? Interfering with your plans?"

"My plans are to go to bed," she said. "I've had a busy day."

She poured whiskey in a glass and handed it to him. With the familiarity of a husband, he turned to the refrigerator, found ice, and then squatted looking for the little bottles of Canada Dry soda habitually stored on the lower shelf.

His bald spot is getting bigger.

He opened the soda bottle, mixed his drink, and stirred it with his index finger. Then he raised his eyes to hers.

"I know," he said. "I was here earlier."

"Cutesy-poo think of something else of mine she wanted from the house?"

"I was worried about you," he said.

"I'm touched, but there is no cause for concern. I was visiting friends in Jersey."

"I know about him, Barbara," Howard said evenly.

Oh my God!

"I beg your pardon?"

"I said I know about you and the—young soldier."

Not very much. John is a Marine, not a soldier.

"And I said, 'I beg your pardon?' "

"Honey . . ."

"Don't you call me 'Honey,' you sonofabitch!"

"Sorry."

He took a swallow of his drink.

"Barbara, you're well known in Philadelphia," he said.

"You must have known that someone would see you, recognize you . . ."

Great, now I will be known as the Whore of Babylon as well as Poor Barbara, whose husband dumped her for young Cutesy-poo.

"I have no idea what you're talking about. Who saw me? What soldier?"

"The young one," he said. "The one you had dinner with two nights ago in the restaurant in the Warwick."

"God," she heard herself say, "people have such filthy minds!"

"I don't understand that," Howard said.

"I'm guilty, Howard. I did have dinner in the Warwick two nights ago. But he's not a soldier. He's a Marine."

"What's the difference?"

"In this case, the difference is I'm nearly old enough to be his mother."

"You're not that old," he said. "You're thirty-eight."

Thirty-six, Goddamn you!

"I had dinner with Bill Marston's nephew, Johnny Moore. He's a sergeant in the Marines and about to go overseas, since you seem so hungry for the sordid details. And if I had had him when I was eighteen, I would be old enough to be his mother. He's eighteen. Or maybe nineteen."

"How did that come about?"

"I don't even know why I'm discussing this with you," Barbara said. "You have given up any right to question anything I do. I would love to know who carried this obscene gossip to you, though."

"Friends," he said.

"Some friends!"

"The same friends who have been telling me all along that I was making an ass of myself with Louise," Howard said.

She met his eyes.

"Tell me about this . . . young man, Barbara."

"I'll be damned! What if I said, 'tell me about Louise, Howard'?"

"Then I would say it's all over," he said.

"Since when?"

"Since about nine o'clock this morning," Howard said. "I

told her I was going to see you, and she said if I came over here, it was all over between us. And . . . here I am."

"You've been trying to find me all day?"

He nodded.

After a moment, Barbara asked, "What did you think you were going to do here?"

"I realize that I've hurt you, Barbara . . ."

"Huh!" she snorted.

"I didn't want you to hurt yourself."

She exhaled audibly.

"With . . . my young man, you mean?"

He nodded.

"Bill Marston found out that Johnny's father was—I don't know how to put this—fooling around with Johnny's trust fund."

"His father? Who's his father?"

"The Reverend John Wesley Moore," Barbara said. "He's with that Methodist Missions thing. What do they call it? The Harris Methodist Missions to the Unchurched, something like that."

"The missionaries, right? In the Orient someplace?"

"Right."

"What about it?"

"Bill Marston found out that Johnny's father had not turned over a trust fund from his grandparents to the boy. So, since the boy is on his way overseas, he decided he had to tell him. And did."

"The father, the *minister*, was stealing the kid's money?" Howard asked.

He's interested. More important, he believes me.

"I don't know if 'stealing' is the right word, but he didn't turn it over to him when he should have."

"I'll be damned!" Howard said, outraged.

He's really angry. Why am I surprised? Before Cutesy-poo came along, he never did anything dishonorable.

"So the boy was upset, obviously," Barbara said. "He's really very sweet. He's on a home leave before going overseas, and he couldn't even go home."

"That's absolutely despicable!"

"So I felt sorry for him. And had dinner with him. And took him to the movies."

"Where was the boy staying?"

"Bill got him a room in the Union League."

"And that's where you heard about this?"

"Yes. I met Bill on Broad Street. He was with the boy. And he insisted I have a drink with them . . ."

"In his cups again, I suppose?"

"Don't be too hard on Bill, Howard. It was a terribly hard thing for him to have to do."

"I've always liked Bill Marston. He just can't handle the sauce, that's all."

He's not at all suspicious. He wants to believe what I'm telling him. He's a fool. Obviously. Otherwise Cutesy-poo couldn't have got her claws into him the way she did.

"Where's the boy now?"

"On his way to the Pacific. That's what I was really doing in New Jersey today, Howard. Putting him on the plane. Bill couldn't get off . . ."

"That was very kind of you, Barbara."

"He had nobody, Howard. I have never felt more sorry for anyone in my life."

"I should have known it was something like this. I'm sorry, Barbara."

"It's all right."

He smiled at her.

"I'm sorry things . . . didn't work out between you and Louise."

"And I would expect you to say something like that," he said. "It could have been worse. I could have actually married her."

"And it's really all over?"

"It's really all over."

"So what are you going to do?"

He looked at his watch and drained his glass.

"I don't really know. Except that right now, I'm going to leave here and see if I can catch the 9:28 to Swarthmore," he said.

"You'll never make the 9:28," Barbara said.

"There's another train at 10:45."

"You left some things here. Shirts and underwear. Why don't you stay here?"

"Barbara—"

"What?"

"That's very decent of you."

"Don't be silly."

"But where would I sleep? There's only one bed in this place."

"I know you don't think I'm very smart, Howard, but I really can count," Barbara said.

(Five)
THE ANDREW FOSTER HOTEL
SAN FRANCISCO, CALIFORNIA
22 JUNE 1942

The tall, long-legged blonde shifted on the seat of the station wagon so that she was facing the driver. Her fingers gently touched the beard just showing on his upper jaw, and then moved to trace his ear. When he jumped involuntarily, she laughed softly.

"I learned that from my husband," Mrs. Caroline Ward McNamara, of Jenkintown, Pennsylvania, said to Captain Charles M. Galloway, USMCR, whose home of record was c/o Headquarters, USMC, Washington, D.C.

Mrs. McNamara was wearing a pleated plaid skirt, a sweater, a string of pearls, and little makeup, all of which tended to make her look younger than her thirty-three years. Captain Galloway, who was wearing a fur-collared horsehair leather jacket, known to the Supply Department of the U.S. Navy as "Jacket, Fliers, Intermediate Type G1," over a tieless khaki shirt, was twenty-five. He was a tanned, well-built, pleasant-looking young man who wore his light brown hair just long enough to part.

The jacket was not new. It was comfortably worn in; the knit cuff on the left sleeve was starting to fray; and here and there were small dark spots where oil or AVGAS had dripped on it. Sewn to the breast of the jacket was a leather badge bearing the gold-stamped impression of Naval Aviator's Wings and the words CAPT C M GALLOWAY, USMCR. The leather patch was new, almost brand-new. The patch had replaced one that had identical wings but had designated the wearer as T/SGT C M GALLOWAY, USMC.

Captain Galloway had been an officer and a gentleman for just over a month. Before that, since shortly after his twenty-first birthday, in fact, he had been an Enlisted Naval Aviation Pilot (all Marine fliers are Naval Aviators), commonly called a "Flying Sergeant." He had been a Marine since he was seventeen.

"You learned that from your husband?" Charley Galloway asked, turning to Caroline McNamara. "How to play with his ear, or how to bullshit your way into a hotel?" The hotel they had in mind was the Andrew Foster, one of San Francisco's finest, and therefore also probably already stuffed to the brim with people who had thought to make reservations.

Her fingers stopped tracing his ear.

"Well, fuck you," Caroline said, very deliberately.

"Oh, Christ," he said, sounding genuinely contrite. "Sorry."

In Caroline's mind, Charley's language was too loaded with vulgarisms. A dirty mouth was certainly understandable, she knew, considering his background. But for his own good, now that he was an officer, he should clean it up. Since he did not like to hear her use bad language (except in bed, which was something else), she had settled on doing that as the means to shame him into polishing his own manners.

Every time he said something like "bullshit," she came back with "fuck." He really hated that; and so words like bullshit and asshole were coming out far less often now than they did not quite four months before, when they first met.

At that time Caroline had been divorced for not quite five months. It was far from a glorious marriage, of course; but it ended more or less satisfactorily, as far as she was concerned. . . . In other words, she came out of it, as she put it, "with all four feet and the tail," meaning that she got the house in Jenkintown, the cars, and almost all of the bastard's money. Her prosperous stockbroker husband had an understandable reluctance to reveal in court that the person he'd been having an affair with also wore pants and shaved.

During the divorce process, she had scrupulously followed her lawyer's advice to do nothing "indiscreet," correctly interpreting that to mean she should keep her legs crossed.

When she met Charley Galloway, then Technical Sergeant Galloway, she had been chaste for more than eighteen months.

He had flown into Willow Grove Naval Air Station, outside Philadelphia, in a Marine version of the Douglas DC-3 transport, acting as both pilot-in-command and instructor pilot to two young Marine aviator lieutenants, one of whom, Lieutenant Jim Ward, was her nephew.

Jim had called from the airport, and Caroline had driven out to Willow Grove to fetch him and the others home. The moment she saw Charley Galloway, she knew he might be just the man to break her long period of celibacy. After all, she would probably never see him again.

Until she met him, she had come to believe—after all manner of sobering, painful experience—that the real love of her life was a delightful, wholly improbable fantasy. But what happened between them, the very first time, told her that that very delightful and improbable fantasy had landed six hours before at Jenkintown.

It wasn't long after that before she started worshiping him.

Jimmy Ward worshiped him, too, which had been at first rather difficult to understand. Enlisted men are supposed to worship officers, not the other way around. But when she asked him about it, Jimmy explained that Charley probably would have been an officer—he had all the qualifications— if it hadn't been for what he'd done a few days after Pearl Harbor.

He and another sergeant had put together a fighter plane from parts of others destroyed by the Japanese. Charley had then flown it out to the aircraft carrier *Saratoga,* then en route to reinforce Wake Island. Half of Charley's squadron was on Wake Island. Charley was riding, so to speak, to the sound of the guns.

The reinforcement convoy was ordered back to Pearl Harbor. And so an act that was to Jimmy's mind heroic—dedication worthy of portrayal on the silver screen by Alan Ladd and Ronald Reagan—became quite the opposite. An *enlisted man* had made flyable an airplane *commissioned officers,* in their wisdom, had concluded was beyond repair. He had then had the unbridled gall, against regulations and policy, to decide all by himself to take the airplane off to war.

The only reason that they hadn't court-martialed him, Jimmy Ward told her, was that the witnesses were either dead or scattered all over the Pacific and could not be assembled.

So what they had done was take him off flight status and return him to the States for duty as an aircraft mechanic. It was only a critical shortage of pilots that had found him—the very morning of the day Caroline met him—back in a cockpit. The Marines were demonstrating parachute troops to the press and couldn't run the risk of having a less than fully qualified pilot fly the plane.

After their first night together, Caroline couldn't have cared if Charley was a PFC. Or what anyone thought about her taking up with an enlisted man eight years younger than she was.

On the twelfth of June, ten days before Caroline and Charley were driving into San Francisco, she went to Quantico to be with him. But he wasn't there.

And then two days later he showed up as Captain Galloway, USMCR, having been pardoned and commissioned by the Commandant of the Marine Corps himself. There was a price, however. He had five days leave, plus travel time, to report to San Francisco, there to board a plane for Hawaii, and there to assume command of a newly activated Marine fighter squadron.

Caroline decided she didn't give much of a damn what anyone—God included—thought about her traveling across the country with a man to whom she was not joined in holy matrimony. She was going with him.

And given a little more time, she thought, she would have been able to clean up his vocabulary so that even the Protestant Episcopal Bishop of Philadelphia could have found no fault with it.

Unfortunately, there was hardly any time left at all. And then there was the matter of finding a room to make time in.

" 'Conspire' is the word you were looking for," Caroline said. "We are going to 'conspire' our way into the Andrew Foster Hotel."

"You think it would really work?" Charley asked.

"They make mistakes," Caroline said. "Everybody does.

All we have to do is make them think they made one with us, and we get a room."

"Sound like bull—aloney to me," Charley said.

"Better," she chuckled, "better."

"This hotel is important to you, isn't it?" Charley asked. "What did you do, stay there with your husband?"

"No," Caroline lied, easily. "With my parents."

My conscience, she thought, *is clear. I don't want him in there thinking of me being there with Jack. All I want him to remember about the Andrew Foster Hotel is the luxury, and the food, and the two of us together in one of those lovely beds. Or together in one of those marvelous marble-walled showers with all the shower heads. I don't think Charley has ever seen anything like that. I want him to remember us there.*

"And you think that would work?"

"Yes, I do," Caroline said, trying to put more conviction into her voice than she felt.

"OK, Baby," Charley said. "If that's what you want, we'll give it a shot."

"Good," she said.

"We'll have to pull over somewhere and get a tunic and a tie out of my bag," Charley said. "I can't walk in a fancy hotel wearing a flight jacket. I wish I could shave. I feel as cruddy as the car."

The light oak bodywork of the 1941 Mercury station wagon was covered with five days and several thousand miles of road grime. They had driven practically nonstop from Quantico, Virginia. There had been a light rain during the night, and the half-moon sweep of the wipers showed by contrast just how dirty the rest of the vehicle was.

"Well, when we get to our room, Mommy will wash your ears," Caroline said. "Or anything else you think needs it."

"I told you to knock off that 'Mommy' shit," Charley said, coldly. "I don't think it's funny."

Caroline did not respond with a dirty word of her own. She was wrong, and she knew it.

Why did I say that? I know it angers him. There's probably something Freudian in that Mommy shit. Obviously. We both know I'm thirty-three and he's twenty-five. There is probably a hint somewhere in there of perversion, too. Charley can't understand why I stayed married to Jack for so long after I learned that he was homosexual. First she was married to a fairy, he thinks, and now she's shacked up with a Marine eight years younger than she is and doesn't give a damn who knows it. Obviously, there is something strange about that dame. Strange is not all that far from perverse.

Charley pulled off the highway and stopped.

"I won't say that again, Baby," Caroline said.

And now he will take affront at 'Baby'! Why did I say that? What the hell is the matter with me?

"Forget it," Charley said, and smiled at her. "My bag will be the one on the bottom, right?"

"Probably," she smiled. "Would you like me to drive? I know where the Andrew Foster is."

"Go ahead," he said.

He got in the back and she slid behind the wheel.

There were four men behind the marble reception desk of the Andrew Foster Hotel, flagship of the forty-one-hotel Foster chain, atop San Francisco's Nob Hill. Three wore formal morning clothes, wing collars and tailed coats. The fourth man, older than the others, wore a double-breasted gray coat and striped trousers and had a rose-bud pinned to his lapel.

"Madam, I'm terribly sorry," one of the men in formal clothing said to Caroline McNamara. "I just don't seem to be able to find any record of your reservation."

"Well, as long as you can put us up, I suppose no harm is done," Caroline said.

"That, Madam, I'm afraid, is going to pose a problem," the desk clerk said. "The house, I'm afraid, is absolutely full. I'll call around and see if we can't find something for you . . ."

"Excuse me," the older man said to the desk clerk. "There has been a cancellation." He handed the clerk a key. "Why don't you put this officer and his lady in 901?"

"Yes, of course," the desk clerk said and snapped his fingers for a bellman.

"Thank you," Caroline said.

"I'm sorry about the mix-up with your reservation," the older man said. He nodded at her, and then at Charley, and disappeared through a door in the paneled wall behind the counter.

Nine oh one turned out to be a corner suite consisting of a sitting room, a bedroom, and a butler's pantry.

As soon as Caroline tipped the bellman and he was gone, Charley said, "Jesus, what do you suppose this is going to cost us?"

"What you are supposed to say, Darling, is 'I was wrong and you were right, and I'm sorry I doubted you.'"

"Consider it said," Charley said. "And what do you think it's going to cost?"

"Do you really care?" Caroline asked. "And anyway, I've got a bunch of traveler's checks."

"No. What the hell," Charley said. "Why not?"

"Why not, indeed?"

"I'm going to take a shower," Charley said, and headed for the bathroom. In a moment, he was back. "Hey, look at this, they even give you a bathrobe!"

He held a thick, terry cloth robe in his hands, embroidered with the logotype, "ANDREW FOSTER HOTEL San Francisco."

"Between the hotel and me, Darling, you'll have everything your heart desires," Caroline said.

As soon as I hear the shower running, I'm going to get in there with him. Surprise, surprise!

She looked around the room, hoping that there would be something to drink—preferably something romantic or erotic, like cognac. She was disappointed, but not surprised, to find a liquor cabinet full of glasses, but no booze. She considered calling room service, but decided that getting in the shower with him was the highest priority. She could call room service later.

She found the bottle of scotch they'd bought in Nevada and set it on the bar. Then she changed her mind and took it and two glasses to the bedside table. And then, after taking Charley's clothes from where he had tossed them on the bed and throwing them onto the floor, she took off her clothes, added them to the pile, and went into the bathroom.

When she opened the glass door, she found him shaving. He told her he'd learned how to do that in boot camp at Parris Island when he had first joined the Corps. She found it delightfully masculine.

She wrapped her arms around him from the back.

"I'll wash yours if you wash mine," she said.

"Mine's already clean," he said.

"Bastard!"

He turned and put his arms around her.

"Christ," he said. "This is like a dream."

"If it is, I don't want to ever wake up."

"We have fifty-six hours," Charley said, "before I have to report to Mare Island."

"Say, 'Caroline, you were right about driving straight through so that we would have some time in San Francisco.' "

"You were right, Baby," he said.

"Fifty-six hours?" Caroline said. "*However* are we going to pass all that time?"

"Well, for openers, I'm clean enough," he said, and turned the shower off. "How about a quick game of Hide the Salami?"

"And then what?" she said, dropping her hand to his midsection.

"And then another game of Hide the Salami," Charley said. "The second time we'll start keeping score."

"You're on," she said.

There came the sound of chimes.

"What the hell is that?" Charley asked.

"I think it's the doorbell."

"One of the characters in the fancy costumes is out there, and he's about to tell us they've made a mistake and we'll have to get our asses out of here."

"We're going to have to see what it is," Caroline said.

"Yeah," Charley said.

He turned her loose and stepped out of the shower, put one of the terry cloth robes on, and went out of the bathroom.

Caroline got out of the shower, quickly towelled herself, and pulled on a robe. She wiped the steam from the mirror and looked at herself.

I can't go out there looking like this!

But, of course, she had to. Charley was ill-equipped to deal with people who managed a world-class hotel like the Andrew Foster.

She went out of the bathroom.

There were three people in the sitting room. Two bellmen, one of whom was stocking the liquor cabinet with liquor, and the other in the act of taking the cellophane from a large basket of fruit. Caroline also saw a bottle of champagne in a cooler.

"I'm so sorry to disturb you, Madam," the third man announced; he was the older man who had announced the reservation cancellation downstairs. "But when I checked, I found that the bar wasn't stocked, and I thought I'd better remedy that."

"Thank you," Caroline said.

"And I wanted to make sure you understood that because of our mix-up about your reservation, your bill will be for the room you reserved; I mean to say there will be no increase in price."

"Oh, hell," Charley said. "I can't let you do that."

"It's the pleasure of the Andrew Foster," the old man said.

"No," Charley said. "That would be stealing. I mean, we didn't really have a reservation. I don't mind talking you out of a room, but I couldn't cheat you out of any money that way."

I can't believe, Caroline thought, *that he just said that!*

"Your husband, Madam, is obviously an officer and a gentleman," the old man said.

Charley is *really a gentleman,* Caroline thought. *And touchingly, innocently honest. And not of course, my husband.*

"My husband is on his way to the Pacific," Caroline said. "I wanted to spend our last night, our last two nights, in this hotel. I didn't much care what I had to do to arrange that."

"The Andrew Foster is honored, Madam. And so you shall. As guests of the inn."

"We want to pay our way," Charley said.

"I would be very pleased if you would be guests of the inn," the old man said.

"Why would you want to do that?" Caroline asked.

"How could you fix it with the hotel?" Charley asked.

"I noticed your wings, Captain. I gather you're an aviator?"

"Yes, Sir, I am."

"Are you familiar with the F4F Wildcat?"

"Yes, Sir, I am."

"Charley's on his way to take command of an F4F squadron," Caroline blurted.

My God, don't you sound like a proud wife!

"My grandson, my only grandchild, is training to be an F4F pilot," the old man said. "I don't suppose you've ever run into a second lieutenant named Malcolm Pickering, have you? They call him 'Pick.' "

"He's a Marine?" Charley asked.

"Yes. He's at Pensacola right now."

"No, Sir, I don't know him," Charley said. "Sorry."

"Nice boy. His father was a Marine in the first war, so of course, he had to go into the Marines, too."

"Yes, Sir," Charley said. "That's understandable."

"I don't know anything about the sort of training they give young men like that, or about the F4F," the old man said. "I don't want to know anything I shouldn't know, classified information, I think they call it, but I really would like to know whatever you could tell me."

"Yes, Sir. I'll be happy to tell you anything you'd like to know."

"Perhaps at dinner," the old man said. "If you did that, I'd consider it a fair swap for you being guests of the inn so long as you're here."

"You don't have to do that," Charley said. "And, how the hell could you square that with the hotel?"

"I can do pretty much what I want to around here, Captain Galloway," the old man said, with a chuckle. "My name is Andrew Foster."

"I'll be goddamned!" Charley said.

"I live upstairs," Andrew Foster said. "Just tell the elevator man the penthouse. My daughter, Pick's mother, lives here in San Francisco. I'd like her to join us, if that would be all right with you."

"Certainly," Caroline said.

"Eight o'clock?" Andrew Foster asked.

"Fine," Caroline said, softly.

"My daughter, of course, knows as little about what Pick is doing as I do, and my son-in-law hasn't been much help."

"I'm sorry?" Caroline asked.

"My son-in-law, who is old enough to know better, and

had more than enough to keep him busy here, couldn't wait to rush to the colors."

"He went back in the Corps?" Charley asked.

"The Marine Corps wouldn't have him back," Andrew Foster said. "So he went in the Navy. The last we heard, he's in Australia."

VII

(One)
UNION STATION
SAN DIEGO, CALIFORNIA
1625 HOURS 24 JUNE 1942

"The Lark," as the train from Los Angeles to San Diego was called, was probably one hell of a money maker, Sergeant John Marston Moore thought; it probably should have been called "The Pigeon Roost."

There was not an empty seat on it; and the aisles and even the vestibules between the cars were jammed with people standing or, if they could, sitting on their luggage. At least half of the passengers were in uniform; and there was something about most of the civilian women that told Moore they had some kind of a service connection. They were either wives or girlfriends of servicemen.

He had recently become convinced that air travel was not only the wave of the future, but the only way to travel. Having a good-looking, solicitous stewardess serving your meals and asking if you would like another cup of coffee was far superior to this rolling tenement, where if you were lucky you could sometimes buy a soggy paper cup of coffee and a dry sandwich from a man who made his way with great difficulty down the crowded aisle.

When nature called, he waited half an hour for his turn in the small, foul-smelling cubicle at the end of the car; and then when he made his way back to his seat, he found a sailor in it, reluctant to give it up.

The ride wasn't smooth enough, nor his seat comfortable enough, for him to sleep during the trip; but he cushioned his head with his fore-and-aft cap against the window and dozed, floating in memories of the time he and Barbara spent together. Aware that it was ludicrous to dream of his return from the war before he had actually gone overseas, he nevertheless did just that.

By then, certainly, the temporarily delayed commission would have come through. He would be Lieutenant Moore, possibly even Captain Moore. In any case, an officer. That would certainly tend to diminish the unfortunate differences in their ages. One simply could not treat a Marine lieutenant, or a Marine captain, like a boy. He even considered growing a mustache—once the commission came along, of course.

But most of the images he dwelt on concerned the scene that would take place once he and Barbara went behind a closed and locked door somewhere, either in the apartment on Rittenhouse Square, or preferably, in some very nice hotel suite.

The astonishing truth was that physical intimacy—he did not like to think of it simply and crudely as "sex," because all that he and Barbara had done together was much more beautiful than that—between people who were in love with each other was everything—and more—than people said it was.

Such images were pleasant. But the ride was long, and the seat uncomfortable, and he was glad to hear the conductor announce their imminent arrival in San Diego. Somewhat smugly, he did not join in the frenzied activity to reclaim seabags and luggage and get off The Lark. When all these people left the train, the station was going to be as crowded as the train had been. If he just sat and looked out the window and waited, by the time he got to the station, much of the crowd would be dispersed.

Finally, he jerked his seabag from the overhead rack, carried it out of the car with his arms wrapped around it, hoisted it to his shoulder in the vestibule, and went down the stairs to the platform.

A hundred feet down the platform toward the station, he was surprised to see a Marine with corporal's stripes painted on his utility jacket sleeves holding up what looked like the side of a cardboard box. Written on that in grease pencil was, SGT. J. M. MOORE.

He walked up to him.

"My name is Moore."

"I was beginning to think you missed the fucking train," the corporal said. "Come on, the Gunny's outside in the truck."

He tossed the sign under the train and started down the platform. Outside the main door was a Chevrolet pickup truck, painted in Marine green. A short, muscular Gunnery Sergeant, a cigar butt in his mouth, was sitting on the fender.

"You Moore?" he asked as he pushed himself off the fender.

"Right."

"I was beginning to think you either couldn't read or missed the fucking train," the Gunny said. "My name is Zimmerman. The Lieutenant, Lieutenant McCoy, sent me to meet you. Throw your gear in the back and get in."

"Right," Moore said. "Where are we going?"

"Would you believe the San Diego Yacht Club?"

Moore smiled uneasily. Obviously, he was not supposed to ask where he was going, otherwise he would not have been given a sarcastic reply.

"Sorry," he said.

Gunnery Sergeant Zimmerman grunted and got behind the wheel, Moore got in the other side, and the corporal got in beside him, next to the window.

As they drove away from the station, Zimmerman said, "I checked out how those fuckers at Outshipment work, the way they handle people like you with priorities like yours."

"Oh?"

"What they do when you report in is send you over to the transient barracks, and then get you put on some kind of detail. Then, when they're making up the manifest for the flight, they see who else is on it with rank and no priority, or not so high a priority. If there ain't anybody, then they call you back from the transient barracks and you get on the plane. But if there is some commander or some colonel who's going to give them trouble about being bumped by a sergeant, they 'can't find you' on your detail, you miss the flight, the commander or the colonel gets on it, they don't get no trouble, and everybody's happy."

"I see."

"So I told the Lieutenant, and he said 'fuck 'em, stash him until thirty minutes before the plane leaves and then take him right to operations. Then they can't lose him, he'll be there.' "

"I understand," Moore said, although he wasn't absolutely sure he did.

"So I asks the Lieutenant where he wants you stashed, and he says take you over to the boat, he'll call Miss Ernie and tell her you're coming."

"The boat?"

"I told you, we're going to the Yacht Club," Gunny Zimmerman said, impatiently.

"How'd you know when I was arriving?"

"You ask a lot of fucking questions about things that are none of your fucking business, don't you?" the Gunny replied.

"Sorry," Moore said.

The corporal beside him snorted in amusement.

"Miss Ernie"? "The Yacht Club"? Am I being a snob because I suspect that the yacht club he's referring to is not what usually pops into my mind when I hear the words "yacht club"? Odds are that this yacht club is going to turn out to be a Marine bar somewhere, with a picture of a naked lady and the standard Marine Corps emblems hanging above the bar, and whose proprietress, Miss Ernie, will bear a strong resemblance to Miss Sadie Thompson?

And then another question popped into his mind: *Lieutenant McCoy? He did say "Lieutenant McCoy," didn't he? He damn sure did! Killer McCoy? Am I really going to get to meet the legendary Killer McCoy?*

Discretion, however, overwhelmed his curiosity. Having just been told by the Gunny that he asked too many fucking questions about things that were none of his fucking business, he decided that it would be best to just ride along in silence.

Fifteen minutes later, he was more than a little surprised when the Gunny turned the pickup truck off the highway and through two large brick pillars. On each of these was a bronze sign reading, SAN DIEGO YACHT CLUB—PRIVATE—MEMBERS ONLY.

Three minutes after that, they stopped at the end of a pier.

"You carry his seabag onto the boat for him," Gunny Zimmerman ordered the corporal, "and you come with me."

They walked down the pier until they came to the stern of a large yacht, on whose tailboard was lettered in gold leaf, "LAST TIME, San Diego."

The corporal went up a ladder carrying Moore's bag and went aboard. Gunny Zimmerman touched Moore's arm in a signal to stop.

What the hell is going on? This thing is at least fifty feet long. Without question, by any definition, a yacht.

A startlingly beautiful young woman wearing white shorts and a red T-shirt emblazoned with the insignia of the U.S. Marine Corps appeared at the stern rail. She had jet black hair cut in a page boy, and the baggy T-shirt seemed to do more to call attention to a very attractive figure than to conceal it.

"Hi!" she called down.

"The Lieutenant call, Miss Ernie?" Gunny Zimmerman asked.

"Yes, he did. And I told you the next time you called me 'Miss Ernie' I was going to throw you in the harbor," she said. She looked at Moore. "Hi! Come aboard. I've been expecting you."

"Go aboard. I'll be back for you in the morning," Gunny Zimmerman ordered.

"You want a beer, Zimmerman?" the girl asked.

"Got to get back, Miss Ernie," Zimmerman said. "The Lieutenant said he might be a little late."

"There, you did it again!" she said.

"Jesus Christ, Miss Ernie," he said uncomfortably, "you're the Lieutenant's *lady.*"

"Just don't stand close to the edge of the dock, Zimmerman," she said. "You're warned."

Zimmerman hid his face from the young woman. "You watch yourself with that lady, Moore," he said, with more than a hint of menace.

And then he marched back up the pier to the truck.

As Moore walked to the ladder, the corporal came down it.

"Nice!" he said, as he walked past Moore.

The black-haired girl was waiting on the deck with her hand held out.

"I'm Ernie Sage," she said. "As Zimmerman so discreetly put it, I'm Ken McCoy's 'lady.' Welcome aboard."

"How do you do?" Moore said, taking the offered hand. "I'm Sergeant Moore."

"Have you got a first name?"

"John."

"Would you like a beer, John? Or something stronger?"

"I'd love a beer. Thank you."

As he followed her down the deck to the cabin, Moore observed that she was just as good looking from that perspective.

She opened a refrigerator door and took out a bottle of beer.

"Mexican," she said. "Ken says it's much better than the kind they make in 'Diego. Would you like a glass?"

"The bottle's fine, thank you," he said.

"Where are you from?"

"Philadelphia," he said.

"Oh, I'm from Jersey. Bernardsville. I've spent some time in Philly. I used to go with a guy—nothing serious—who was at U.P."

"I went to the University of Pennsylvania," he said.

"And then you joined the Corps?"

He nodded.

"Ken's from Norristown," she said. "But he's only been back once since he joined the Corps."

"Oh," Moore said, aware that he was tongue-tied.

"I told Whatsisname, Zimmerman's driver, the one he won't let drive, to put your bag in a cabin—second door to the right when you go below—so if you'd like, when you finish your beer, you could have a shower."

"I need one," Moore said. "I've been traveling for forty-eight hours."

"And you've been on The Lark," she said with a smile. "Anyone who's been on The Lark needs a long, hot shower."

She smiled at him, and he smiled back. He had no idea who this young woman was, but he liked her.

Sergeant John Marston Moore, USMCR, came back in the cabin just as Second Lieutenant Kenneth R. McCoy, USMCR, entered it from the deck.

Lieutenant McCoy, who was in dress green uniform, looked not unlike other second lieutenants Moore had seen. That is, he was young—*about my age,* Moore thought—and trim, and immaculately shaven and dressed. But there was one significant difference. Above the silver marksmanship medals which all second lieutenants seemed to have—although McCoy seemed to have more of these, all EXPERT —he had five colored ribbons, representing medals. Moore had seen very few second lieutenants with any ribbons at all.

Moore didn't know what all of them represented, but he did recognize two. One was the Pacific Theater of Operations Campaign Medal. McCoy's had a tiny bronze star, signifying that he had participated in a campaign. And on top was the ribbon representing the Purple Heart. This second lieutenant had already been to the war in the Pacific and had been wounded.

Miss Ernestine Page kissed Lieutenant McCoy. It was a *wifely* demonstration of affection, Moore judged, although it had been made clear that whatever her relationship was with Lieutenant McCoy, she was not his legal spouse.

"I'm Ken McCoy, Moore," he said. "I'm a friend of Captain Sessions. Ernie been taking good care of you?" He put out his hand. His grip was firm, and there was something about his eyes that made Moore decide that this was a good man.

"Yes, Sir, she has."

"Let me get a beer, Baby, and get out of this uniform," McCoy said. "Give Moore another one."

"Aye, aye, Sir. Right away, Sir."

McCoy patted her possessively on the buttocks.

"Be nice," he said.

"I'm always nice," Ernie Page said.

"How about eighty percent of the time?" McCoy said, and, carrying a bottle of beer, went below. By the time Moore had finished his second beer, McCoy reappeared, wearing shorts and a T-shirt. He looked even younger than he had before.

He caught Moore's eye.

"Why don't I loan you a pair of shorts and a T-shirt?" he asked.

"I don't want to trouble you, Sir."

"You'll trouble me in your greens," McCoy said. "Come on."

He took two fresh bottles of beer from the refrigerator and led Moore below again. He sat on the double bed in the cabin as Moore changed out of his greens.

"Zimmerman tell you about Outshipment? The way those feather merchants handle difficult passengers like you?"

"Yes, Sir."

"And that we figured out how to—fuck them—get you on your way to Australia?"

"Yes, Sir," Moore replied, and then took a chance. "Is that where I'm going, Sir, to Australia?"

"Sessions didn't tell you? What the hell is the big secret? He told me you were going to Australia when he called and asked me to make sure you got on the plane."

"No, Sir, he didn't tell me."

"OK. Well, keep your mouth shut, about where you're going, and who told you."

"Yes, sir."

"You're going to Australia. You know the outfit?"

"My orders say 'Special Detachment 14.' I don't know what that means, Sir."

"Well, I guess that's the reason for the secrecy. So I won't go into that. But your new CO is one of the good guys. His name is Major Ed Banning. I used to work for him in Shanghai. So did Captain Sessions. For that matter, so did Zimmerman. What he's doing is very important, and the reason you're travelling on a Six-A priority is that he needs someone, yesterday, who speaks Japanese."

Moore nodded.

And then he put everything together.

"Lieutenant, are you the one they call 'Killer McCoy'?"

The friendly smile that had been in McCoy's eyes vanished. Moore did not like what he saw in them now.

"Where did you hear that?" McCoy asked, and his voice was as cold and menacing as his eyes.

Moore knew that it had been the wrong question to ask, and tried to frame a reply that would be placating. When he did not immediately reply, McCoy, now visibly angry, asked, "Did that fucking Zimmerman run off at the fucking mouth again?"

Moore didn't reply instantly.

"I asked you a question," McCoy snapped.

"No, Sir. I heard that at Quantico. There was a Master Gunnery Sergeant there . . ."

"Name?" McCoy snapped.

"I don't remember his name, Sir," Moore said, and then remembered. "He said he was the S-3 Sergeant of the 4th Marines . . ."

"Nickleman," McCoy interrupted. "He always had a bad case of runaway mouth."

". . . and he was talking about the 4th Marines, and Shanghai, with Captain Sessions."

McCoy stared at him for a long moment. Gradually, the cold fury in his eyes died, and blood returned to his lips.

"I'm sorry, Sir, if . . ." Moore began.

McCoy waved his hand to shut him off.

"To answer your question, Sergeant," McCoy said. "There are some people who call me 'Killer,' including people who should know better, like Mike Nickleman and Captain Sessions. I don't like it a goddamn bit. But you didn't know, so don't worry about it."

Moore's mouth ran away with him. "Why do they call you that, Sir?"

The ice came instantly back into McCoy's eyes, and his lips drew tight and bloodless again. He looked at Moore for a long moment, and then shrugged.

"OK. Let me set that straight. I had to kill some people in China. I didn't want to. I had to. It just happened that way. Some Italians, the Italian equivalent of Marines. Three of them. And about a month later, when Sessions and Zimmerman and I were fucking around in the boondocks, trying to find out what the Japs were up to, we had to kill some Chinese. They were supposed to be bandits, but what they were was working for the Kempae Tai—Japanese secret police. There was about twenty of them got killed. The word got back to Shanghai and some wiseass—I still don't know who—in the 4th heard about it. He didn't know what we were really doing up there, just that we got in a fight with Chinese bandits, so what he did was have a sign painted, 'Welcome Back, Killer' and hung it in the club. The name stuck. It makes me sound like a fucking lunatic, like I go around getting my rocks off knifing and shooting people."

"I'm sorry, Sir, that . . ."

McCoy held up his hand to cut him off again, and then, switching to Japanese, which startled Moore, said, "I'd be damned surprised, Moore, if you haven't figured out you're now in the Intelligence business, that we both are. Rule One in the Intelligence business, and I'm surprised Captain Sessions didn't tell you this, is to disappear into the wallpaper. The one thing you can't afford, in other words, is to have people point you out and say, 'there he is, Killer McCoy, who killed all those people.' Understand?"

"Yes, Sir," Moore replied in Japanese. "I understand."

McCoy looked at him appraisingly for a moment before he went on. "Well, we know that you speak Japanese, don't we? And damned well. Where'd you learn that?"

The subject of Killer McCoy, Moore understood, was closed.

The truth of the story is that he is called "Killer" because, very simply, he has killed people. Three Italians, probably by himself, and "about twenty" Chinese with Captain Sessions and Gunny Zimmerman. It would be hard to believe if I hadn't seen his eyes. I would hate to have Killer McCoy angry with me. Or, hell, just be in his way.

"I'm fairly fluent, Sir. I lived in Japan for a while," Moore replied in Japanese.

"There's damned few people in the Corps who speak Japanese," McCoy said, "for that matter, anything but English. On the other hand, about one Jap—or at least, one Japanese officer—in three or four speaks English. You'd be surprised how important that is."

"Yes, Sir."

"Well, what happens now is that in the morning, Zimmerman will go to Outshipment at the Seaplane base. When he finds out they're making up the manifest for the Pearl Harbor flight, he'll send his driver out here to pick you up. So you'll have to be dressed and ready after, say, seven o'clock in the morning. Standing by. You show up with your orders and they'll have to put you on the plane."

"Yes, Sir."

"Any questions?"

"No, Sir."

"Not even about the boat? Or Ernie?" McCoy asked, wryly.

"They're both . . . very nice . . . Sir."

"Yes, they are," McCoy chuckled.

As if on cue, Ernestine Sage appeared at the door.

"Dorothy and Marty just came home," she said. "He brought abalone. Unless you two would rather stay here and tell some more dirty stories in Japanese."

McCoy switched to English. "Ernie thinks that whenever people speak Japanese around here they're talking dirty," he said. "Not true, of course. I'm perfectly willing to say in English that she has a marvelous ass and spectacular boobs."

"You bastard!" she said, but Moore saw that it was said with affection.

Dorothy and Marty turned out to be a First Lieutenant and his wife, who was heavy with child. The lieutenant's tunic had no campaign medals above his marksmanship badges. And although first lieutenants outrank second lieutenants, it was immediately apparent not only that McCoy gave the orders on board the *Last Time,* but that the lieutenant was just about as impressed with Lieutenant McCoy as Sergeant Moore was.

"I didn't mean to disturb you . . ." the lieutenant said.

"No problem," McCoy said. "Ground rules: This is Sergeant Moore. John. You didn't see him here. You don't ask him where he came from, or where he's going. But feel free to talk about the Raiders. He's cleared for at least TOP SECRET. Moore, this is Marty Burnes and his wife, Dorothy."

Lieutenant Burnes crossed the cabin to Moore and gave him his hand.

"How are you, Moore?"

"How do you do, Sir?"

"Hello," Mrs. Burnes said.

"Hello."

"Is he going to have to call you two 'Sir' all night?" Ernie Sage asked.

"Whatever he's comfortable with," McCoy said.

"I think we can dispense with the customs of the service, tonight," Lieutenant Burnes said to Moore.

"Yes, Sir."

"Hell, he's as bad as Zimmerman," Ernie laughed. "You better not start calling me 'Miss Ernie,' John."

"No, Ma'am," Moore said, but he said it as a joke, and they all laughed.

"I filled the car with gas, Ken," Marty Burnes said.

"You didn't have to do that," McCoy replied.

"Well, hell, we used it."

"Otherwise I would probably have had Little Martin, or Little Mary," Dorothy said, patting her swollen belly, "on the bus on the way to the Maternity Clinic."

"What did the doctor say?" Ernie Sage asked.

"Three weeks," Dorothy said.

"Your mother called," Ernie said. "I told her where you were. You better go call her. She's concerned."

Dorothy heaved herself with effort to her feet and went to a telephone at the far end of the cabin.

"Ken and Ernie took us in," Burnes said to John Moore. "We couldn't find a place to stay, and Dorothy wanted to have the baby here. If it wasn't for Ken and Ernie, Dorothy would have had to go back to Kansas City."

"Ernie took you in," McCoy corrected him. "This is her boat."

"Go to hell!" Ernie said, and then looked at Moore. "The boat belongs to a friend of a friend of my mother's. And since we're being such a stickler about the facts, my mother pretends that I am not living in sin with Ken. But, romantic fool that I am, I pretend that this is our first home, Ken's and mine, our barnacle-covered little boat by the side of the bay."

Moore smiled at her.

"Tell him about the Raiders," McCoy said.

Burnes looked at him in surprise.

"He's going to meet a friend of mine where he's going," McCoy explained. "He'll be curious."

"Then why don't *you* tell him about the Raiders?" Ernie challenged.

"Because I am only a second lieutenant. Everybody knows that second lieutenants can't find their ass with both hands. Isn't that so, Sergeant Moore?"

"Yes, Sir. We were taught that at Parris Island," Moore said.

"I'm almost glad you're not staying here longer," Ernie Sage said. "I think you and Ken would be dangerous if you had time to get your act together."

"Give the sergeant a beer, Dear," McCoy said, sweetly, "while Lieutenant Burnes tells him all about the Raiders."

"Aye, aye, Sir," Ernie Sage said. "Right away, Sir."

(Two)
U.S. NAVY BASE
SAN DIEGO, CALIFORNIA
0815 HOURS 25 JUNE 1942

Sergeant John Marston Moore, USMCR, was the fifth person to board the seaplane, a U.S. Navy Martin PBM-1. Boarding was supposed to be in order of priority, in which case Moore would have been first. But among those ordered to proceed via air to Pearl Harbor, Territory of Hawaii, by government air transport were a Vice Admiral of the U.S. Navy and a Brigadier General, USMC, whose priorities guaranteed them a seat.

Rank hath its privileges and the admiral and the general and their aides-de-camp were boarded first. Moore stepped inside the fuselage of what had been designed as a Patrol Bomber. A sailor in undress blues, with the insignia of an Aviation Motor Machinist's Mate First Class sewn to his sleeve, showed him where to stow his bag and where to strap himself in for the take-off. He found himself seated next to the admiral.

"Good morning, Son," the admiral said.

"Good morning, Sir," Moore replied.

"First flight?"

"No, Sir."

"Then you can reassure me," the admiral said. "I am not wholly convinced that something this big is really meant to fly."

I will be damned. He really went out of his way to be nice to me.

The sailor, a red-haired man in his late twenties who was obviously the crew chief, waited until all the passengers had come aboard and then passed out yellow, inflatable life preservers, first giving simple instructions about using them, and then checking the passengers to see that they had each put them on correctly.

Then he climbed a ladder in the front of the fuselage. A moment later, the airplane shuddered as first one and then the second of its engines started. The plane immediately began to move, but with a curious motion that made Moore wonder for a moment if he was going to get seasick.

Next, one at a time, the engines roared and then slowed to idle. Then they both revved together, and the seaplane began to pick up speed. The noise of the engines was deafening, and the noise was compounded by a series of metallic crashes as the hull encountered swells. Then suddenly there was only the sound of the engines, and the crashing of the hull against the water was gone.

Through the window on the far side of the cabin, Moore saw that the float—there was one on each side—which had kept the wing from dipping into the water was retractable. As he watched, it moved upward and outward until it formed the tip of the wing.

He turned in his seat and looked through the window behind him. They were already out over the Pacific. Some ships were visible, and the wakes of small boats; and then, suddenly, there was nothing outside the window but an impenetrable gray haze.

"I am solemnly assured by my Naval Aviator friends," the admiral said, "that the young men who drive these things are extensively trained in navigation."

They looked at each other and smiled.

Moore put his head back against the metal wall of the fuselage.

He had really had a good time the night before, he thought. And not only because Ernie Sage and Lieutenant McCoy had gone really out of their way to make him comfortable. More than that, they had made it sort of a party for him.

And what he'd heard about the Marine Raiders had been fascinating. With obvious pride in what he was doing, Lieutenant Burnes had explained that they were sort of American Commandos whose mission it was to make surprise landings—raids, hence the name—on Japanese-held islands. The idea was not to capture the islands, but to blow up enemy installations and supplies, and then leave. That, Burnes said, would force the Japanese to station troops wherever they had supply depots or airfields so they could protect them from the Raiders, troops that otherwise could have been used to invade New Guinea or even Australia.

As he went on, Burnes had mentioned on more than one occasion the 2nd Raider Battalion Commander, Major Evans Carlson, and Carlson's executive officer, Captain James Roosevelt, who was the son of the President. Every time the names of these two came up, his voice dropped to nearly reverential tones.

It was also pretty clear that Burnes was very impressed with the legendary Killer McCoy, who had taken out three Italian Marines with a knife, and then killed the Chinese bandits, and who had been wounded in the Philippines. So, Moore admitted, was he.

Moore could also see that Lieutenant McCoy wasn't quite so boyishly enthusiastic about the Raiders as Burnes was. McCoy never said so directly, and his face was in no way easy to read; but Moore sensed that as far as McCoy was concerned, the Raiders might as well be a gang of ten-year-old boys playing war games. At the same time, it was more than pretty clear to Moore that Burnes had no idea McCoy was involved with Intelligence. He wondered what McCoy was doing that had an Intelligence connection, but obviously he couldn't ask.

In fact there was no sense wondering what kind of Intelligence work McCoy was doing, or what he himself would be doing once he got to Australia. The only thing he knew about Intelligence was what he had learned watching spy movies, and McCoy was certainly not going to tell him what Intelligence was like in the real world.

But it had really made him feel good to see how Lieutenant McCoy and Ernie and Lieutenant Burnes and his wife had behaved to each other.

It would, he thought before he dozed off, be that way with Barbara when he came back. He would be an officer then, and maybe they could all get together and have a welcome home party.

(Three)
HEADQUARTERS
MARINE AIR GROUP TWENTY-ONE (MAG-21)
EWA, OAHU ISLAND, TERRITORY OF HAWAII
1105 HOURS 27 JUNE 1942

"The Colonel will see you now, Sir," the staff sergeant said.

Captain Charles M. Galloway, USMCR, hoisted himself out of a battered, upholstered armchair whose cushions had long ago lost their resiliency, nodded at the sergeant, walked to the commanding officer's door, and rapped on the jamb with his knuckles.

"Come," Lieutenant Colonel Clyde G. Dawkins ordered.

Galloway marched into the office, came to attention eighteen inches from Dawkins's desk, and announced, "Captain Galloway reporting as ordered, Sir."

"Good morning, Captain, welcome aboard."

"Thank you, Sir."

"You get settled all right, Charley?"

"I told the kid in the truck to take me to the NCO billet," Galloway said.

"Did you really?" Dawkins chuckled. "Well, I guess being an officer—a squadron commander—will take some getting used to. But I'm sure you can handle it, Charley. Stand at ease, for Christ's sake. Sit down, as a matter-of-fact."

He pointed to an armchair, and Charley sat down. Its cushions were as exhausted as the cushions on the chair in the outer office.

"Thank you, Sir. That was after he told me he'd never heard of VMF-229."

Dawkins laughed.

"That's because most of VMF-229 resides in Karl Lorenz's desk drawer," he said. "You remember Lorenz, of course?"

"Yes, Sir. Sure."

"Right now VMF-229 consists of you, another officer, and eleven F4Fs on a wharf at Pearl Harbor, covered with all the protective crap they put on them when they ship them as deck cargo."

Galloway's eyebrows rose.

"What about men?"

"Lorenz levied the other squadrons for personnel for you. They came up—after a lot of breast beating—with a list of sixteen enlisted men. Some of them are alleged to be mechanics, and there is an alleged clerk, an alleged truck driver, *and* an alleged armorer. None of them is more than a buck sergeant. You have authority, of course, to draw whatever equipment and personnel is authorized for a fighter squadron."

"How much of what is authorized is going to be available when I go try to draw it?"

"Not much, Charley," Dawkins said. "Supply is a little better than it was, but not much."

"What about pilots?"

"Right now there's two of you. They dribble in all the time. Sometimes one at a time on a courier plane, sometimes two dozen when a carrier or cruiser from 'Diego or 'Frisco puts into Pearl, sometimes lately, three or four at a time on tin cans and merchantmen. As you get your planes operational, I'll see that you have pilots. They won't have much time, I'm afraid, they'll be right out of Pensacola."

"Ouch," Galloway said. "I've got some pilots, pretty good pilots, coming. General McInerney authorized me to steal five from Quantico and Pensacola."

"Only five?"

"I sent him nine names. I didn't have to ask for volunteers. When the word got out I was getting a squadron, people came looking for me. Everybody wants to get over here, even if it means being in a squadron commanded by a flying sergeant."

"Hold it right there, Captain," Dawkins said sharply. He had just been thinking that Captain Charles M. Galloway looked like everything one expected a Marine captain to look like. He was erect and trim, neatly barbered, in a well-fitting uniform. There was an aura of competence and command about him.

"Sir?"

"That's the last time I ever want to hear you refer to yourself as a 'flying sergeant,'" Dawkins said. "I don't even want you *thinking* of yourself as a 'flying sergeant.' When you pinned those bars on, you stopped being a flying sergeant. Is that clear enough for you, Captain?"

"Aye, aye, Sir."

Dawkins held Galloway's eyes with his own for a long moment.

"Scuttlebutt going around is that someone interesting personally gave you those bars, Charley. Anything to that story?"

"Yes, Sir. They had me flying a VIP R4D out of Quantico. I'd just come back from a round robin, Pensacola, New River, Philadelphia, and back to Quantico. When I parked the airplane, the Operations Officer told me to report to the VIP quarters. I walked in expecting some congressman or movie star needing a ride, and what I got was the Commandant."

"No crap?"

"Him and General McInerney. Five minutes later, I was a captain."

"Just like that?"

"He gave me a little speech, Sir, that I won't forget for a while."

"Oh?"

"He said that, acting on General McInerney's recommendation, and against his own better judgment, he was going to give me captain's bars, and that I goddamn well better forget thinking I was Errol Flynn or Ronald Reagan and start acting like a Marine captain."

"Sounds like sound advice," Dawkins chuckled. "Christ, you really had the Navy mad at you. For a while, there was guilt by association."

"Sir?"

"There was talk—serious talk—about court-martialing Lenny Martin for being conveniently absent when you flew that F4F out of here to rendezvous with Task Force XIV. 'Dereliction of Duty' was the way they put it."

Captain Leonard Martin had been the senior officer of VMF-211 present (and thus in command) when Galloway reported that he and the maintenance sergeant, Technical Sergeant Stefan "Big Steve" Oblensky, had repaired one of the shot-up F4Fs and that he intended to fly it out to the *Saratoga*.

Captain Martin had reminded Tech Sergeant Galloway that BUAIR engineers had officially classified the F4F as totally destroyed and that therefore, it was obviously unsafe to fly. He had also pointed out that even if there had been an officially flyable aircraft available, orders would have to be issued before it could be flown anywhere. And obviously, since the location of *Sara* was a closely guarded secret, Tech Sergeant Galloway had a practically nonexistent chance of finding it.

Quite unnecessarily, he had informed Tech Sergeant Galloway that his intended flight was against regulations and thus forbidden. And then, as he shook Tech Sergeant Galloway's hand, he had mentioned idly, in passing, that he had business at Pearl Harbor and would not be at the airfield at the time Galloway said he wanted to take off.

"Sir, is Captain Martin—still in trouble?"

"Not anymore, Charley. He was shot down at Midway."

"Shit!" Galloway said bitterly, adding, "I hadn't heard that."

"He was flying a goddamned Buffalo. We lost all of them but one."

"He was a good guy," Galloway said, softly.

"Most of them were," Dawkins said.

Galloway looked at him with a question in his eyes, and then put it in a word: " 'Most'?"

"I didn't mean that the way it sounded," Dawkins said. "But I was thinking—speaking ill of the dead—that it is possible to be both a dead hero and a prick. But you've touched on something else that needs to be discussed."

"I'm afraid you've lost me, Sir."

"The other officer presently assigned to VMF-229, Captain, is First Lieutenant, USMCR, William C. Dunn. He was also at Midway with VMF-211. Flying an F4F. He has—confirmed—both a Kate and a Zero."

"Dunn?" Galloway asked, thoughtfully. "I don't think I remember . . ."

"Nice-looking young kid. He came aboard after you were returned to the States in such glory," Dawkins said dryly. "He took what we think was a 20mm round, an explosive shell, in his windscreen. It almost turned him into a soprano. He managed to get the airplane back to Midway, totalling it on landing. It was full of holes, in addition to the 20mm, I mean."

"Sounds like a good man," Charley said.

"Very possibly he is," Dawkins said carefully. "But there is some question, I'm afraid serious question, about whether he took the round that filled his crotch with shrapnel and fragments while he was engaging the enemy, or after he'd already decided to fly back to Midway."

"You're saying he ran?"

"Listen carefully. What I said was 'serious question.' The officer—there was more than one, but the officer who made the most serious accusations—decided, on reflection, not to bring charges against him."

"Who was that?"

"I don't think giving you his name would be appropriate," Dawkins said.

"What has . . . you said 'Dunn'? . . . got to say for himself?"

"Dunn says that he has no memory of flying back to Midway at all."

"What do you think?"

"I believe that Dunn doesn't remember flying back to Midway."

"How come I get this guy?"

"I'm giving him the benefit of the doubt," Dawkins said.

Galloway started to say something and changed his mind. Dawkins saw it.

"Say it, Charley."

"Nothing, Sir."

"Say it, Charley," Dawkins repeated.

"Actually, I was thinking two things, Sir. The first was that when a good Marine gets an order, even one he doesn't think he can handle, he says 'Aye, aye, Sir' and does his best."

"You mean you don't think you can handle a squadron?"

"I can handle a squadron. But there are squadrons and squadrons, and it looks like mine is staffed with sixteen enlisted Marines who are almost certainly the ones their squadron commanders figured they could do without; plus pickled aircraft that I have to unpickle with somebody else's rejects; plus, of course, an officer one jump ahead of a court-martial."

"Is that all one thought? You said you had two?"

"I was thinking, Colonel, that you wouldn't screw me unless you had no choice. But if the brass *is* making you set me up to fuck up so I can be relieved, why don't we just jump to that? Give the squadron to somebody else, and just let me fly. I didn't ask for the bars; all I ever wanted to do is fly fighters. I mean, I'll take a bust back to sergeant . . ."

"That's quite enough, Captain," Dawkins said furiously. "Shut down your mouth. How *dare* you suggest, you sonofabitch, that I would be party to something like that?"

"Sorry, Sir," Galloway said after a long moment, during which he realized that Dawkins was waiting for a response.

"You're going to have to learn, Galloway, to engage your brain before opening your mouth," Dawkins said more calmly. "Just for your information, I was given the option of *not* giving you VMF-229. I'm giving it to you because you're the best man I have available to take the job."

"Yes, Sir."

"I wish I had an operational squadron I could just turn over to you, fully equipped with flyable aircraft, qualified mechanics, and whatever else is called for. I don't. All I have to give you is what I told you, airplanes sitting on a wharf and a handful of half-trained kids to get them up and running. I'll do my damnedest to get you anything else you think you need, but the shelves are pretty goddamned bare."

They looked at each other without speaking for a long moment.

"Can I have Oblensky, Sir?"

"What?"

"Tech Sergeant Oblensky, Sir," Galloway said. "I know he's here. I asked."

Dawkins looked unhappy. He made three starts, stopping each time before a word left his mouth, before asking, "Do you think it is a good idea, Captain, theoretically or practically, for a non-commissioned officer to be assigned to a squadron commanded by an officer with whom he served as a non-com? Who was his best pal when they were sergeants together?"

"From what you've told me about the men you're going to give me, Sir," Galloway said, "I'll either have to have Big Steve, or somebody like him, or get those airplanes flyable myself."

"Captain Galloway, if I hear that you have been seen with a wrench in your hand, you will spend the rest of this war with a wrench in your hand. Clear?"

"Does that mean I get Oblensky, Sir?"

"I finally have something in common with the Commandant, Galloway. Acting against my better judgment, I'm going to give you something I don't think you should have."

"Thank you, Sir."

"That will be all, Captain Galloway. Thank you."

VIII

(One)

HEADQUARTERS
MARINE AIR GROUP TWENTY-ONE (MAG-21)
EWA, OAHU ISLAND, TERRITORY OF HAWAII
1135 HOURS 27 JUNE 1942

PFC Alfred B. Hastings, who was seventeen and had been in the Corps not quite five months, had just about finished drying with a chamois a glistening yellow 1933 Ford convertible coupe, when he noticed that his labor had attracted the attention of an officer.

The Ford was parked in the shade of Hangar Three. When Hastings was finished, his orders were to return the car to the other side of the hangar, to a parking space lettered MAINTENANCE NCO.

For a long moment, PFC Hastings pretended he did not see the officer, who was a captain and an aviator. He did that for two reasons. First, he had slipped out of the sleeves of his coveralls and tied them around his waist, which left him in his sleeveless undershirt and thus out of uniform. Second, despite the dedicated efforts of his drill instructors at the San

Diego Recruit Depot to instill in him a detailed knowledge of the Customs of the Service as they applied to military courtesy, he was not sure what was now required of him.

The basic rule was that officers got saluted by enlisted men. But it wasn't quite that simple. You were not supposed to salute indoors unless you were under arms. That meant actually carrying your rifle, or a symbol of it like a cartridge belt. And you were not supposed to salute when you were on a labor detail. The NCO in charge of the labor detail was supposed to do that, first calling "attention" and then saluting the officer on behalf of the entire labor detail.

I suppose, PFC Hastings finally decided, *that since I am the only one on this labor detail, I am in charge, and supposed to salute. And that sonofabitch obviously isn't going to go away. He's looking at the car like he never saw a '33 Ford before.*

And I don't think anybody ever got in real trouble in the Corps for saluting when they really didn't have to.

He gave the chrome V-8 insignia on the front of the hood a final wipe, stepped back a foot; and then, as if he had first noticed the officer just then, he popped to attention and saluted.

"Good afternoon, Sir!" PFC Hastings barked. At the same moment, he realized that coming to attention had rearranged his hips so that the bottom of his coveralls was sliding down off them.

"Good afternoon," Captain Charley Galloway said, crisply returning the salute and doing his best not to laugh. "Stand at ease and grab your pants."

"Aye, aye, Sir. Thank you, Sir."

PFC Hastings quickly untied the sleeves of his coveralls, shoved his arms through them, and buttoned the garment as regulations required. When he looked up, he saw that the Captain was carefully inspecting the Ford's interior. He took a chance.

"Nice car, isn't it, Sir?"

"Yes, it is," Galloway said, smiling at PFC Hastings. "And Sergeant Oblensky lets you take care of it for him, does he?"

"Yes, Sir," PFC Hastings said, a touch of pride in his voice. "I try to keep it shipshape for him, Sir."

"And you seem to have done so very well," Galloway said.

"Thank you, Sir."

"Do you happen to know where Sergeant Oblensky is?"

"Yes, Sir. He's inside, in the hangar, I mean."

"Would you please find Sergeant Oblensky and tell him I'd like a word with him, please?"

"Aye, aye, Sir," Hastings said, and started to walk away, then stopped. He had forgotten to salute; and he also hadn't done what Sergeant Oblensky had told him to do with the car when he had finished washing it.

"Sir, I'm supposed to put the car back in Sergeant Oblensky's parking space."

"It'll be all right here," Galloway said. "Just go get him, please."

"Aye, aye, Sir," Hastings said, and this time remembered to salute.

Galloway, fighting the urge to smile, returned it; and then when the kid had disappeared, at a fast trot, around the corner of the hangar, he leaned over the mounted-in-the-front-fender spare tire and raised the left half of the hood.

The engine compartment of the nine-year-old Ford was as spotless as the exterior. The first time Charley had seen the Ford's engine it was a disaster; where it wasn't streaked with rust it had been coated with grease. Now it looked as good as it must have looked on the showroom floor. Better. And mechanically it was better too. The engine had not just been completely rebuilt, it had been greatly modified. The heads had been milled to increase compression. The carburetor had been upgraded. There had even been thought about "blowing" the engine, getting an aircraft engine supercharger from salvage, rebuilding it, and adapting it to the flathead Ford V-8. That probably would have happened had the war not come along.

Captain Galloway lowered the hood, fastened it in place, and stood erect. Technical Sergeant Stefan Oblensky appeared at the corner of the hangar.

He was known as "Big Steve" because he *was* big. He stood well over six feet, had a barrel chest, and large bones. He was almost entirely bald, and what little hair remained around his ears and the back of his neck was so closely shorn as to be nearly invisible.

He was forty-six, literally old enough to be Charley's father. Seeing him, Charley realized with surprise that he had forgotten both how old and how big Big Steve was. And how formidable appearing in his stiffly starched, skin-tight khakis, his fore-and-aft cap perched on his shining, massive head.

There was no suggestion on his face that he had ever seen Captain Charles Galloway before in his life. He raised his hand in a crisp salute.

"Good afternoon, Sir. The captain wished to see me?"

Charley returned the salute.

"Good afternoon, Sergeant," he said. "Yes, I did."

"How may I help the captain, Sir?"

"I think we might as well start by putting this back in my name," Galloway said, waving at the Ford. "Does it run as good as it looks?"

"I don't think the captain will have any complaints, Sir."

"Well, then get in, Sergeant, and we'll go see the Provost Marshal."

"Sir, with the captain's permission, I'll have to inform the maintenance officer that I will be out of the hangar."

"That won't be necessary, Sergeant. I've explained to your squadron commander that we have some business to take care of."

"Yes, Sir."

That's bullshit.

What I did, with absolutely no success, was try to placate his squadron commander after he had been told five minutes before that he had just lost his Maintenance NCO to VMF-229, and that the decision was not open for discussion or reversal. When I walked out of his door, the man was still steamingly pissed off—not only at his Wing Commander but, if possible, even more at Captain Charles M. Galloway, CO, VMF-229. I wonder why I didn't tell Big Steve that he now works for me?

Obviously, because I don't want him to think that Santa Claus has come to town, and that he now has a squadron commander in his pocket.

Galloway got behind the wheel of the Ford. Oblensky, after first removing it from a well-filled key ring, handed the ignition key to him.

The engine started immediately. Galloway slipped it in gear and made a U-turn away from the hangar.

"I heard you were back," Oblensky said.

It starts. "You," not "the captain." No "Sir."

"I got in yesterday," Galloway said. "I got a ride on an Army Air Corps B-17."

"Do they give them guns and ammo now?" Oblensky asked.

Again, no "Sir," Galloway thought. *What the hell is he talking about?*

And then he remembered. During the attack on Pearl Harbor, a flight of B-17s had arrived in Hawaii. Since they had left the United States in peacetime—and to decrease the parasitic drag the weapons would cause if in place—their .50 caliber Browning machine guns had been stowed inside, and they had carried no ammunition for them. They had arrived in the middle of a battle absolutely unable to defend themselves.

"These had ammo," Galloway answered, remembering. "The side positions were faired over, and their guns were on the deck. The turrets were operational."

"I heard they were giving you a squadron."

Of course you did. If you could find out from the Navy the course of the Saratoga *at sea, it was no problem at all for you to find out from the sergeant in Colonel Dawkins's office that I was going to get VMF-229.*

"VMF-229," Galloway said.

It was not far from the hangar to the Provost Marshal's office. Oblensky did not attempt further conversation.

There was a lanky buck sergeant on duty. He stood up behind his desk when Galloway walked into the small frame building.

"Good morning, Sir," the sergeant said. "Can I help you?"

"I want to register a car," Galloway said. "You got the papers, Sergeant Oblensky?"

"Yes, Sir," Oblensky said, taking the vehicle registrations, military and civilian, from his wallet and handing them over.

"Sir," the Provost Marshal Sergeant said, "if the captain is buying the car from the sergeant, you'll need a notarized bill of sale."

"I'm not buying it," Galloway said. "I already own it. I gave Sergeant Oblensky a power-of-attorney to use it when I went to the States."

"It's on file," Oblensky said. "Look under 'Oblensky.'"

"Let me check," the sergeant said, and he went to a vertical file cabinet. In a moment, he found what he was looking for. He returned with a manila folder, reading from it as he walked.

"You're Tech Sergeant Galloway, Sir?"

"No. I'm Captain Galloway. But I was a Tech Sergeant when I signed that power-of-attorney."

"Yes, Sir. That's what I meant, Sir. I'll get the forms, Sir."

He went into a small storeroom.

"I think he knows who you are," Oblensky said, softly.

"Who am I?"

"I mean, I think he knows what happened, who you are," Oblensky said.

The sergeant came out of the storeroom with several printed forms and a small metal plate. He sat down at the typewriter and fed the forms into it. He asked for Galloway's serial number and unit.

"There's a new regulation, Sir," the sergeant said. "You'll need your CO's permission to have a car on the base."

"Colonel Dawkins, you mean?"

"No, Sir, your squadron commander will do."

"I command VMF-229," Galloway said.

"Yes, Sir," the sergeant said, visibly surprised.

Big Steve was right. That guy did make the connection. It will be interesting conversation at the Staff NCO Club tonight—for that matter at the Officer's Club, too—and all over the base by tomorrow:

"Remember that story about the Flying Sergeant of VMF-211 who fixed up the F4F the Japs got on December 7? Fixed it up and flew it out to the Saratoga *at sea and really pissed the Navy off? The guy they sent back to the states for court-martial? Well, he's back, and guess what, he's a* captain, *no shit, and* a squadron commander!"

The sergeant came from his typewriter and handed Galloway forms to sign and then the small metal plate.

"You screw this on top of the Hawaiian plate, Sir," he said. "That'll be fifty cents, please."

Galloway handed him two quarters.

"Thank you," he said.

"Excuse me, Sir," the sergeant said. "You used to be a flying sergeant with VMF-211, right?"

"Right."

"I thought I remembered the name," the sergeant said.

Would you like my autograph? How to Succeed in the Corps: Really fuck up!

He became aware that Oblensky was tugging at the small metal plate, and released it to him. When they went outside, Oblensky opened the rumble seat, took a screwdriver from a small tool roll, and replaced the tag (for enlisted men) above the license plate with the new officer's tag Galloway had just been given.

"Thank you, Steve," Galloway said. "And also for keeping the car so shipshape."

"Don't be silly," Oblensky said. "I was using it, wasn't I? I owe you."

I'm not very good at this psychological bullshit, "How the wise commissioned officer should deal with the enlisted swine." Fuck it!

"Steve, I had you transferred to VMF-229," Galloway said. "Is that going to cause any problems?"

"You're starting with problems," Oblensky said. "What you have is fourteen pickled F4Fs on a wharf at Pearl, Christ only knows what shape they're in; a dozen—maybe fifteen, sixteen—kids who are not sure what a wrench is used for; and a young pilot scuttlebutt says runs from fights."

"I mean with you and me," Galloway said.

Oblensky's eyes narrowed. Galloway knew him well enough to know that meant he was angry. Very angry.

"I don't think I deserved that, *Captain* Galloway," he said, coldly, after a moment. "I would have thought you know me well enough to know that I have been in the Corps long enough to know where the line is between those of us who wear stripes and those of you who wear bars."

"Christ, Steve!"

"If the captain can remember not to call the sergeant by his Christian name where other people can hear him, the sergeant will remember not to remember that he knew the captain when he was a wiseass little fucker who made tech sergeant before he was old enough to be a pimple on a buck sergeant's ass."

"I'll keep that in mind, Sergeant Oblensky."

"The captain would be wise to do just that," Oblensky said.

They met each other's eyes for a moment, and then, Oblensky first, they smiled at each other.

"Thank you, Steve," Galloway said.

"When does my transfer come through?"

"I don't know about the paperwork, but you're in VMF-229 as of now."

"In that case, why don't we ride over and see what shape our airplanes are in? Unless there's something I don't know about, that would seem to be our first order of business."

They got in the Ford. En route to the wharfs at the Pearl Harbor Naval Station, Oblensky asked, "Remember when we painted this thing? And that Lieutenant Commander wanted to know where we got the paint, and you showed him the can from Sears, Roebuck?"

Galloway chuckled. The paint can from Sears had been labeled, HIGH GLOSS YELLOW ENAMEL. $5.95. After they'd bought it, Oblensky had dumped the contents into a five gallon can of Navy yellow paint intended to paint lines on hangar and flight line floors. He had then refilled it—"borrowed" it from Navy stocks—with a very high quality aviation paint that was reported to be worth sixty dollars a gallon on the civilian market.

The Ford's new paint job had been spectacular, as the Lieutenant Commander had noticed. He had run right down to Sears to get a gallon of their $5.95 "High Gloss Yellow Enamel" to paint his own car. His Studebaker, somehow, hadn't come out looking nearly as nice as Galloway's Ford, and he had been disappointed and mystified.

His own reaction at the time, Charley remembered, was that was the sort of stupid behavior you expected from a fucking officer. He was aware now that he had switched sides, that he was now a fucking officer, and considered fair game by old time non-coms like Big Steve.

"I got some more bad news for you," Oblensky said. "Your Lieutenant Dunn's been fucking your girlfriend."

"You mean Ensign O'Malley?"

"Yeah. You mean you forgot her?"

"She was never my girlfriend, Steve."

"Well," Oblensky chuckled. "You were pretty fucking chummy, as I remember."

In the early morning of December 7, 1941, Technical

Sergeant Galloway had been in bed with Ensign O'Malley in a cabin in the hills Technical Sergeant Oblensky had borrowed for the weekend from an old and now retired Marine Corps buddy. When Oblensky had burst into the room to tell Galloway that the Japanese were attacking the Naval base at Pearl Harbor, Ensign O'Malley had been performing on Technical Sergeant Galloway's body a sexual act that he had not even heard of previously, not even in the French movies he had sometimes seen on stag night in the Staff NCO Club.

"What about Flo?" Galloway asked, to change the subject. "You still see her?"

Flo was Lieutenant Florence Kocharski, Navy Nurse Corps, a lady a few years younger and not much smaller than Oblensky. They had met when Oblensky had gone to the Naval Hospital for his annual physical. It had taken them about twenty minutes to decide that it was time to break a rule both had followed for more than twenty years: Officers do not become involved with enlisted personnel.

"I knew you'd get around to asking that, sooner or later," Oblensky replied.

It was not the reply Galloway expected.

"Is there some reason I shouldn't have asked? You were pretty fucking chummy, too, as I remember."

"Off the record, Captain?"

"Off the record."

"We got married," Oblensky said. "The day after you flew out to the *Saratoga.*"

"Married?" Galloway asked, in disbelief.

"We were going to get married when one of us retired anyway," Oblensky said. "We both got our twenty-years in, and then some. So when this goddamned war came along, and they weren't going to let us retire, we figured, fuck 'em. We got married. Flo knew a priest who can keep his mouth shut, and we didn't put ranks or whatever on the marriage license."

"You mean you got married without permission?"

"They don't let officers marry enlisted men, or vice versa, you know that."

"Well, you know I like Flo," Galloway said, honestly. "So the first thing I've got to say is 'congratulations.' "

"Why don't you just stop there, then?"

"Christ, what are you going to do if they find out?"

"Hope they don't, for openers," Oblensky said. "I don't think they'd court-martial us."

"Goddamn, Steve, I don't know."

"After Flo and Hot Pants O'Malley dropped us back at the base on seven December," Oblensky said carefully, "Flo went down to Battleship Row. She was on board *West Virginia* taking care of some sailors when there was a secondary explosion . . . one of the five-inch magazines blew up. She caught some fragments and got burned a little, but she was still able to work, so she stuck around for a while. Some Commander saw her and put her in for a medal and the Purple Heart. We figured the Navy and/or the Corps would look pretty fucking silly court-martialing a wounded hero for marrying a Marine. Or vice versa, a Marine for marrying a wounded hero."

"They're going to be pissed," Galloway said.

"Well, they were pissed at you, too, and now look at you," Oblensky said.

"I didn't think to ask," Galloway said. "Were you in trouble because of what I did?"

"They were pretty excited for a while right afterward," Oblensky said. "But you were the one who flew the airplane, not me. I don't expect to get promoted any time soon, though."

"What are you going to do about the paperwork?" Galloway asked. "Who's the dependent, for example? You, or Flo?"

"We've been a little wary about getting into that," Oblensky said. "The only thing we did was change our life insurance. She gets mine, and I get hers, if anything happens. I changed my home of record to her brother's, in Chicago. And we didn't say we was married. You can leave your insurance to a friend."

"Let me look into this, Steve."

"Don't rock the fucking boat, Charley," Oblensky said.

"I won't, trust me."

"I guess I have to, don't I?" Oblensky said. "You don't seem very pissed off that Hot Pants is fucking Lieutenant Dunn."

Just in time, Galloway stopped himself from saying, "I met somebody special in the States."

I can't tell him about Caroline. If I told him that I actually met a woman from a background like that, that she drove across the country with me, that we stayed at the Andrew Foster Hotel as the guests of Andrew Foster, he would think it was one hundred-percent bullshit, probably concocted because he had just told me Hot Pants O'Malley is now screwing this guy Dunn. If he believed there really was a woman named Caroline who drove out to the West Coast with me, he would be sure she was some tramp I met in a bar. He would not believe the suite in the Andrew Foster at all. Not that he thinks I'm an imaginative liar, but because all of that belongs to a world that he can't even imagine.

Instead, Galloway said, "*You* seem pissed off about it."

"Pussy's in short supply in Hawaii, as you damned well know. A girl like that, she can do great things for morale. But it seems to me that if she wants to pass it around, she could find somebody who's not afraid to fight to pass it out to."

Oh, shit! I can't let him get away with that!

After a moment, Oblensky sensed the tension.

"I say something wrong?" he asked.

"Yeah, Steve, you did," Galloway said. "Did you really think I would just sit here, as your commanding officer, and let you accuse one of your officers—one of my officers—of cowardice?"

"Everybody knows he ran away from Midway," Oblensky said.

"No, goddamnit, everybody doesn't know that. Colonel Dawkins doesn't know, I don't know, and you goddamned sure don't know. You keep your mouth shut about Lieutenant Dunn. Not only in front of me, but everywhere."

Oblensky looked at him in surprise, but said nothing.

"There is an expected reply from a non-com when an officer gives him an order," Galloway said, coldly.

Oblensky wet his lips. There was a just perceptible pause before he said, "Aye, aye, Sir."

That was pretty chickenshit of you, Charley Galloway, pulling rank on him that way, Galloway thought. And then he thought: *Fuck him. He was wrong. And that's why they*

give officers rank, to use it. And then he had a final, more than
a little satisfying, even a little smug, thought: *I didn't handle
that badly at all. Maybe I just can hack it as an officer, a
squadron commander.*

(Two)
OFFICER'S CLUB
PEARL HARBOR NAVAL BASE
OAHU, TERRITORY OF HAWAII
1630 HOURS 27 JUNE 1942

Uniform Regulations of the United States Naval Base, Pearl
Harbor, specified the white uniform for wear after 1700 hours
in social situations, e.g., while dining in the Main Officer's
Club. But because there were exigencies of the service which
brought officers to Pearl Harbor without their whites—such
as for example the fact that there was a war on—there was
a caveat: The words "whenever possible" had been added.

It was a loophole through which most Marine and many
Naval aviators leapt en masse. White uniforms were
expensive to begin with, they soiled easily and often
permanently, and as a general rule of thumb they could be
worn only once before requiring a trip to the laundry/dry
cleaners.

When Captain Charles M. Galloway came into the Main
Officer's Club, he saw at the bar another Marine officer
dressed as he was. They were both wearing a tropical worsted
uniform, shirt, trousers, and the khaki necktie that the Corps
called a "field scarf"—for reasons Galloway never
understood. "TWs" were not only more comfortable than
whites, they did not require very extra careful movement of
cup or fork to the mouth, and could often be worn three times
before a visit to the dry cleaners.

That has to be Lieutenant William C. Dunn, Galloway
thought. *He's a first john aviator, "a good looking kid," as
Colonel Dawkins called him, and he is rubbing knees with
Mary Agnes O'Malley.*

As he walked to the bar, Charley noticed that Dunn was
wearing his wings, but no ribbons. He was entitled to wear

the Purple Heart after the Japs almost turned him into a soprano.

As soon as Lieutenant (j.g.) Mary Agnes O'Malley, Nurse Corps, USN, recognized Charley, she discreetly withdrew the knee she'd draped over Lieutenant Dunn's and smiled at Galloway. There was, Charley thought, more than a little hint of naughty invitation in her eyes.

"Well, look at what the tide threw up on the beach!" she cried, and got off the bar stool.

Just looking at her, you'd never guess what she likes to do— have done to her—in the sack. I wonder if she's doing that to Dunn? Or got him to do it to her?

"Hello, Mary Agnes," Galloway said. She stood on her tiptoes and gave him her cheek to kiss, managing in the maneuver to rub her breasts against his abdomen.

"Charley, this is Lieutenant Bill Dunn," Mary Agnes said, touching Dunn's shoulder with her hand. "Bill, this is Captain Charley Galloway."

"Hello, Dunn," Charley said, offering his hand.

"Good evening, Sir."

Christ, you can cut that Rebel accent with a knife! He sounds like he thinks there's no "e" in "evening" and that "Sir" is spelled "Suh."

"I sort of hoped you would be here," Galloway said. "So I would have my chance to hold my very first officer's call."

It was an attempt at humor, and it failed.

"Yes, Sir," Dunn said, adding, with absolutely no suggestion of invitation in his voice, "Would you join us for a drink, Sir?"

"Oh, of course, he will," Mary Agnes said. "Charley and I are old friends, aren't we, Charley?"

"Absolutely," Charley said. He caught the bartender's eye. "Another round here, please. I'll have whatever the lieutenant's drinking."

"I'll just get in the middle," Mary Agnes said. "Move over a stool, Bill."

Dunn shifted to the adjacent stool; Mary Agnes sat on the one he vacated; and Galloway slid onto the one where she had been sitting. It was still warm from her body, which served to trigger a remarkably clear image of what that bottom looked—and felt—like when not covered with the crisp white of a Navy Nurse's dress uniform.

Galloway looked past Mary Agnes at Dunn.

"I left a message for you at the BOQ," he said. "Did you get it?"

"Yes, Sir. Hangar Three at 0730. I'll be there, Sir."

"I talked Colonel Dawkins out of Technical Sergeant Oblensky," Galloway said. "You know him, I guess? Big Steve?"

"Yes, Sir."

"I told him to find us someplace for a squadron office . . ." Galloway said.

"Yes, Sir," Dunn said, when Galloway paused momentarily to take a breath.

". . . and I'd be surprised if he didn't have us one by 0730 tomorrow," Galloway finished.

"Yes, Sir."

He doesn't like me. I wonder why? I don't think Hot Pants is likely to have told him much about us, if anything. Maybe because he heard I used to be a flying sergeant? And he's not thrilled by having an ex-sergeant for a CO?

"When I was a flying sergeant in VMF-211," Galloway said, "I got to know Oblensky pretty well. He's what they call 'The Old Breed'; he's been in the Corps since Christ was a corporal. Damned good man."

"So I've heard, Sir," Dunn said.

The bartender delivered the drinks.

"Here's to old friends," Mary Agnes said, raising her glass. "The best kind."

"How about here's to VMF-229?" Galloway said. "And particularly to its pilots, both of whom are here with you?"

"All right," Mary Agnes said agreeably; and then realizing what Charley meant, she added, "Is that right? All the pilots there are is you two?"

"That's right," Galloway said and then added to Dunn, "But there was a radio this afternoon . . ." He stopped, took a sheet of yellow paper from his hip pocket, handed it to Dunn, and continued, ". . . with these names on it. They'll be in the next couple of days."

Dunn took the sheet of teletype paper, read it, and handed it back.

"Know any of those people?" Galloway asked.

"I knew a Dave Schneider, went through Advanced with him at Pensacola, but they sent him on to multiengine. Not an F4F pilot."

"It's probably the same guy," Galloway said. "He was learning to fly R4Ds when I met him."

Galloway had met Lieutenant David Schneider on a very important day in his life. Not only was it the first time he had been permitted to fly since he had landed the Wildcat on *Sara*'s deck, but it was the day he met Mrs. Caroline Ward McNamara.

Headquarters, USMC had laid an important mission on Quantico. They were to furnish an R4D to drop parachutists at the Marine Corps Parachute School at Lakehurst, New Jersey. It was important because Major Jake Dillon, a legendary Hollywood press agent who had come back into the Corps when the war started—he had once been a staff sergeant with the 4th Marines in Shanghai—had arranged for *Time-Life* to do a major story on what were being called "ParaMarines."

Colonel Robert T. "Bobby" Hershberger, of the 1st Marine Air Wing, decided that he could not entrust flying the plane to the only two pilots he had who were checked out in the R4D. Lieutenants David Schneider and James L. Ward simply didn't have the necessary experience. On the flight line, however, wrench in hand, removed in disgrace from flight status, was a Tech Sergeant named Charley Galloway who not only had several hundred hours in R4Ds but had graduated from the U.S. Army Air Corps School for dropping people and equipment by parachute from R4Ds.

After a somewhat heated telephone conversation with Brigadier General D. G. McInerney, during which both officers said things they immediately regretted, it was decided that the situation required Galloway's restoration to flight duty for the Lakehurst mission. It was either that or run the risk of allowing a new R4D with MARINES lettered on the fuselage and a load of parachutists aboard to crash in flames before *Time*'s, *Life*'s, and *The March of Time*'s still and motion picture cameras.

Lieutenants Schneider and Ward were called into Colonel Hershberger's office and told that they would fly the mission with Technical Sergeant Galloway, who would be Pilot-in-Command.

Lieutenant Schneider, who was an Annapolis graduate and a career officer, was very unhappy to find himself under the orders of a Flying Sergeant. And he did nothing to conceal his unhappiness. On the other hand, Lieutenant Ward, who was a reservist, was not knocked out of joint because he had to learn from someone who knew more than he did, whatever his rank. And far more importantly, Ward had a just-divorced aunt named Caroline Ward McNamara, to whom he introduced Technical Sergeant Galloway in Philadelphia.

"Schneider's an absolute asshole," Dunn said. "Annapolis. The reason he hates this war is because they have to let civilians into the Corps to fight it. Civilian savages pissing on the Corps's sacred potted palms, so to speak . . ."

Then Dunn saw the look on Galloway's face and stopped.

"My mouth ran away with me, Sir, I'm sorry."

The test of a truly intelligent man, Galloway remembered hearing somewhere, *is the degree to which he agrees with you.*

"The thing about Lieutenant Schneider, Lieutenant Dunn," Galloway said sternly, "is that he not only is a skilled, knowledgeable pilot, but, in my judgment, he is one of those rare people who are natural fliers. With those characteristics in mind, I asked Lieutenant Schneider to join VMF-229, even though he *is* personally an *absolute* asshole. Fortunately for you—and for me too—you outrank him."

Dunn's eyes widened, and then for the first time he smiled.

"Yes, Sir, that thought has occurred to me."

We're going to get along, Galloway thought, *this Rebel kid is all right.*

Mary Agnes swung around on the stool so that she faced Galloway and her knee pressed against his leg.

"Why don't we carry our drinks into the dining room and find a table?" she asked. "They've got a band in there, and I'd like to dance."

"On the table?" Galloway asked.

Her knees pressed harder against his leg, and her hand came down to rest on it.

"No," she said, giving his leg a little squeeze. "With you, silly."

(Three)
THE ELMS
DANDENONG, VICTORIA, AUSTRALIA
1730 HOURS 28 JUNE 1942

When the telephone rang, Captain Fleming Pickering,
USNR, was in the library of The Elms, sitting in a high-
backed red leather armchair, jacketless, his shoes off, his tie
pulled down, and his feet on a footstool. He was just about
ready to take his first sip of his first drink of the day.

He eyed the instrument with distaste; it was sitting out of
reach on a narrow table across the room. It had been a busy
day, and it was his considered judgment that anything
anyone on the phone wanted could wait until tomorrow
morning.

The telephone kept ringing. There was a staff of four at
The Elms: a housekeeper, a maid, a cook, and a combination
yardman, chauffeur, and husband to the housekeeper. They
were all personal employees of Captain Pickering. The house
was leased from a Melbourne banker Captain Pickering knew
from before the war.

The Vice-chairman of the Board of the Pacific & Far
Eastern Shipping Corporation (that is to say, Mrs. Fleming
Foster Pickering) had arranged for the salary and expense
allowance of Chairman of the Board Fleming Pickering to
continue while he was on "military leave" from his duties.
After having been assigned quarters (a small, two-room hotel
suite to be shared with a portly Army Colonel who snored)
Captain Pickering had decided that since he damned well
could afford something more comfortable, there was no
reason not to leave the colonel to snore alone.

Besides, he rationalized, he needed a place where he could
discreetly meet people in connection with his duties. The
brass hats of MacArthur's Palace Guard could give lessons
in plain and fancy gossiping to any women's group he was
familiar with. The gossip was at the least annoying, but it
could also spread information that deserved to be sat upon,
and at worst it could cost people their lives.

"Christ," Pickering asked rhetorically, vis-à-vis his
domestic staff, "where the hell are they all?"

He hauled himself out of the chair and walked across the

two-story library in his stocking feet and picked up the telephone.

"Captain Pickering."

"Major Banning, please."

It was an American voice.

"I'm sorry, Major Banning isn't here at the moment. I expect him within the hour. Can I take a message?"

"Am I correct, Captain, that you're an American officer?"

"Yes, I am."

"This is Commander Lentz, Captain, of Melbourne NATS."

It took Pickering a moment to decode the acronym: Naval Air Transport Service. Next it occurred to him—after a moment spent digesting the superior tone of the commander's voice—that the NATS officer had jumped to the wrong conclusion: *Lentz thinks I'm a Marine captain, and thus inferior in rank, rather than what I really am, an exalted four striper.*

"How may I help you, Commander?"

"We've got an enlisted man down here, Captain, one of your sergeants . . ."

Bingo, I was right. He thinks I'm a Marine. Actually, I wish to God I was.

". . . he just came in from Hawaii on the courier plane. He's headed for some outfit called Special Detachment 14. Ordinarily, I would have sent him over to the transient detachment, but he's traveling on a Six-A priority, so I tried to find this Special Detachment 14 . . ."

"He's there now, Commander? Is that what you're saying?"

"You people really ought to make an effort to keep us up to date on your phone numbers," Commander Lentz said. "I spent an hour on the telephone before I managed to get through to some sergeant, who said Major Banning could be reached at this number."

"Tell the sergeant I'll be there in about thirty minutes to pick him up," Pickering said.

"You're going to come get him yourself?"

"Certainly," Pickering said. "I think it behooves those of us who are Naval officers to concern ourselves with the welfare of the enlisted men of our sister service, don't you, Commander?"

Commander Lentz was not stupid.

"Yes, Sir," he said. "Of course I do, Sir. Sir, it won't be necessary for the Captain to come himself. I'll arrange transportation if the Captain will give me an address."

"I'll be there in thirty minutes, Commander. I know where you are," Pickering said and hung up. His annoyance at having to drive into town was easily overwhelmed by his pleasure at having pricked the Commander's balloon of self-importance.

He was sitting on the footstool in front of the red leather chair tying his shoes when Mrs. Hortense Cavendish, the housekeeper, came in. She was a plump, gray-haired, motherly woman in her late fifties.

"I'd hoped to be back before you got here," she said.

"No problem."

"I bought a couple of nice, fresh barons of lamb," she said. "I know you like to feed Major Banning well when he comes. And Charley and I were in the country buying them, which is why we weren't here."

"I've got to go into town," Pickering said. "There was another young Marine for Major Banning on the courier plane. I'm going to fetch him."

"Couldn't Charley fetch him?"

"I'll get him," Pickering said. "What this boy needs after flying from the States is a hot meal, not a wild ride through Melbourne on the wrong side of the road with a crazy Australian at the wheel."

She laughed.

"There's plenty of food," she said. "I'll just slice the barons before I serve them."

"I'm not going to bring him here," Pickering said, as he stood up. "The one thing that kid does not need is dinner with a Navy brass hat. I'll get him a hotel and let Banning take care of him in the morning."

He drained his glass of scotch and walked out of the library.

First Lieutenant Hon Song Do, Signal Corps, U.S. Army Reserve, arrived at The Elms ten minutes after Pickering left, and Major Edward J. Banning, USMC, arrived five minutes after that. Both men were there at Captain Fleming Pickering's invitation.

Major Banning had called Captain Pickering on the telephone that morning to tell him he had "something interesting" and was about to fly to Melbourne to show it to him. Pickering asked him then to go directly to The Elms, not only because he liked Banning and wanted to have him to dinner, but also because he liked to keep Banning away from MacArthur's headquarters as much as possible. If the gossips didn't see him, they didn't ask questions. Pickering had also asked Pluto for dinner, not only because he—and Banning—enjoyed Hon's company, but also because he believed that Hon should know about anything "interesting" Banning had found.

After Mrs. Cavendish told them that Captain Fleming would be a little late, she set out a half gallon bottle of scotch, a soda siphon, and a silver champagne cooler full of ice for them in the library.

Major Banning had been driven to The Elms from the airfield in a Ford station wagon bearing the insignia of the Royal Australian Navy. He had just flown in from Townesville, Queensland, where he commanded Special Detachment 14, USMC. The very existence of Special Detachment 14 was classified CONFIDENTIAL. Its presence in Australia was classified SECRET. Its mission, "to support the Coastwatcher Establishment, Royal Australian Navy and to perform such other intelligence gathering activities as may be directed by Headquarters, USMC," was classified TOP SECRET.

Lieutenant Commander Eric A. Feldt, Royal Australian Navy, who commanded the Coastwatcher Establishment, had surprised a large number of Australians and Americans by taking an immediate liking to Major Banning. He had previously run off every other American officer sent to work with the Coastwatchers. In the process he often used language so colorful that some thought it inappropriate for a senior naval officer.

But Captain Pickering heard from Rear Admiral Keith Soames-Haley, RAN, a pre-war friend of long standing, that Feldt had described Major Banning as "the first sodding

American officer I've met who could find his sodding ass with both hands."

Admiral Soames-Haley and Captain Pickering both agreed that the rapport between Feldt and Banning was probably based on the mysterious chemistry that sometimes developed between seemingly dissimilar men—each surprisingly recognizing in the other a deep-down, kindred soul, the two of them bobbing along alone and unappreciated in a sea of fools.

Soames-Haley and Pickering also agreed that the friendship between the two men almost certainly had much to do with the long years that Banning had spent in the Orient before the war. Banning understood the Japanese as well as Feldt did—which is to say as well as any Westerner could. Both officers spoke fluent Japanese. And finally, Feldt probably felt a connection with Banning because of Banning's personal stake in the war: Banning had been forced to leave his Russian-born wife behind in Shanghai when war came.

Whatever the reasons, both Saomes-Haley and Pickering were truly delighted that the problems of Australian-US Cooperation vis-à-vis the Coastwatchers was solved. Soames-Haley was all too aware of how valuable that cooperation would be to both allies. For his part, he was not just eager, he was hungry to get his hands on some of the logistical largess available from Americans with the right connections. The Coastwatcher Organization needed desperately the latest communications equipment, as well as access to aircraft and submarines. And for his part, Pickering was fully aware of the value of the intelligence that would now flow from the Coastwatchers. Now that Banning was close to Feldt, and not regarded by him as one more arrogant, sodding American over here to tell us how to run the sodding war, the intelligence Feldt could provide would arrive far more quickly than through standard channels.

Major Banning had been met at the airport by a RAN Lieutenant, and transported to The Elms in a RAN Ford station wagon, because Commander Feldt had spread the word that Banning was "not too sodding stupid for an American." This was, for Feldt, praise of the highest order. Commander Feldt was highly regarded by his peers in the RAN, and any friend of his . . .

Lieutenant Pluto Hon had driven to The Elms in a 1941 Studebaker President, which had the letters USMC on its hood and the Marine Corps insignia stencilled on its doors.

One of the sixteen enlisted men assigned to Special Detachment 14 was Staff Sergeant Allan Richardson, who was a scrounger of some reputation. Richardson had learned that shortly after the war broke out, a transport under charter to the U.S. Navy and loaded with equipment intended for the Chinese had been diverted to Melbourne. The cargo, which included a large number of Studebaker trucks and twenty President sedans, had been off-loaded and turned over to the only U.S. Navy group then in the area, a small Hydrographic Detachment. Richardson reasoned—correctly—that since Special Detachment 14 needed vehicles and had none, and since it was, furthermore, under the control of Captain Pickering, all it would take to get the needed vehicles would be a call from Captain Pickering to the Commanding Officer of the Hydrographic Detachment, a Lieutenant (j.g.). As a general rule of thumb, Lieutenants (j.g.) tend to comply with requests of Naval Captains.

Captain Pickering made the call. Special Detachment 14 got all the trucks and sedans it needed, plus one additional President. Two days after he made the telephone call on behalf of Staff Sergeant Richardson, Richardson gave Pickering the extra President, now bearing USMC insignia.

Pickering's rank entitled him to a staff car. Nevertheless, in order to avoid worrying about a driver, he had borrowed a Jaguar drophead coupe from a pre-war business associate for his personal transportation. Consequently, he promptly turned the Studebaker over to Lieutenant Pluto Hon. Pickering was immensely fond of Lieutenant Hon; he also felt himself to be in Hon's debt, for many courtesies rendered.

It did not surprise Pickering at all that Commander Lentz was waiting at NATS Melbourne, a small frame building plus a warehouse on Port Philip Bay. What surprised Commander Lentz was Captain Pickering's automobile; he was expecting either a Navy or an Army staff car, with a driver; and so a frown crossed his face when the Jaguar drophead coupe with Victorian license plates pulled into his OFFICIAL VISITORS parking space.

But Commander Lentz noticed the gold braid and the four gold stripes on Pickering's sleeves when he stepped out of the car, and he was suddenly all smiles.

"Captain Pickering? Commander Lentz, Sir."

"How are you, Commander?" Pickering replied, returning Lentz's salute with a far more crisp salute than was his custom.

Sergeant John Marston Moore, USMCR, stood at attention beside his seabag.

"Welcome to Australia, Sergeant," Pickering said.

"Yes, Sir. Thank you, Sir."

"Put your gear in the back," Pickering said, and then turned to Commander Lentz. "Do I have to sign for him or anything?"

"No, Sir. Nothing like that. I hate for you to have to have driven all the way down here, Sir. I would have been happy to arrange . . ."

"No problem," Pickering interrupted him. "Thank you for your diligence in finding somebody to take care of the sergeant, Commander."

"My pleasure, Captain."

Pickering got behind the wheel, and after John Moore got in beside him, he drove off.

"My name is Pickering, Sergeant."

"Yes, Sir."

"That's a long flight. I suppose you're tired, Sergeant? Sergeant what, by the way?"

"Moore, Sir."

"Are you tired?"

"I'm all right, Sir," Moore said, although that wasn't the truth. He had had trouble staying awake waiting for Captain Pickering.

"You don't have to be afraid of me, Sergeant," Pickering said. "I'm one of the *good* Naval officers."

"Sir?"

"Major Banning, your new CO, identifies good Naval officers as those who have previously been Marines. I was a Marine Corporal in what is now known as World War I."

Moore looked at him directly, for the first time, and saw that Pickering was smiling. He smiled back.

"And I have a boy about your age in the Corps," Pickering said. "What are you, twenty-one, twenty-two?"

"Twenty-two, Sir."

"How long have you been in the Corps?"

"About four months, Sir."

"You made buck sergeant in a hurry," Pickering said. But it was more of a question than a statement.

"When they took me out of boot camp to send me here, they made me a sergeant, Sir. I was originally supposed to go to Quantico and get a commission."

"Oh, really? You went to college, then?"

"Yes, Sir. Pennsylvania."

"Well, I'm sorry about the commission. But the Corps needed your skill here and now. What is that?"

"Sir?"

"Why did they take you out of boot camp and rush you over here?"

"Captain, I was told not to talk about anything connected with my transfer here."

"I understand, but, for all practical purposes, I'm Major Banning's commanding officer."

"Captain, with respect, I don't know that."

Pickering chuckled. "No, you don't. Good for you, Sergeant."

"Are we going to Special Detachment 14 now, Sir?"

"They're in Townesville, in Queensland, sort of on the upper right-hand corner of the Australian continent. What we're going to do is get you a hotel room. Have you got any money?"

"Yes, Sir."

"You're sure? Don't be embarrassed."

"I've got money, thank you, Sir."

"OK. So we'll get you a hotel. You can have a bath, and get something to eat, and in the morning, we'll get you together with Major Banning."

"Yes, Sir."

"I suppose I'd better have a set of your orders, and your service records, if you have them."

"Yes, Sir, they're in my bag."

IX

(One)
THE ELMS
DANDENONG, VICTORIA, AUSTRALIA
1845 HOURS 28 JUNE 1942

Major Ed Banning and Lieutenant Pluto Hon were on the wide veranda of The Elms when Pickering drove up. It was a pleasant place to watch darkness fall.

They both stood up as soon as the Jaguar drophead stopped. Banning set his drink on the wide top of the railing, and Hon stooped and set his on the floor.

"Good evening, Sir," they said, almost in unison.

Charley Cavendish, in a striped butler's apron, came from inside the house.

"I'd have been happy to go to town for you, Sir," Charley said.

"I know. Thank you, Charley. It was no trouble. I hope you have been taking care of these gentlemen? Lemonade, tea, that sort of thing?"

"Of course, Sir."

"Major Banning," Pickering said dryly, "the Marine

Corps, in its infinite wisdom, has seen fit to increase your troop strength with a Sergeant John M. Moore. I just put him in a hotel. Here's his paperwork."

"How did you wind up with Sergeant Whatsisname, Captain?" Major Banning asked, as he took the service record envelope from Pickering.

"Moore is his name," Pickering said. "I wound up with him, Major, because you have failed in your obligation to keep Melbourne NATS up to date on your telephone numbers. I know this because a Lieutenant Commander named Lentz called up here and chewed me out about it."

"What?" Banning asked incredulously.

"At the time, he thought I was a Marine and one of your subordinate officers," Pickering said.

"And you didn't tell him?"

"Not at first," Pickering said, "but I think I ruined his supper when I dropped 'we Naval officers' into the conversation later on."

"Captain, I could have gone down there and picked him up," Pluto Hon said. "You should have called me."

"Then I wouldn't have had a chance to rub all my gold braid in the Commander's face," Pickering said. "Besides, it was no trouble."

"Well, I'm sorry that this guy bothered you, Captain," Banning said.

"He didn't really bother me. And I was interested to learn how much trouble he had finding Special Detachment 14. That's the way it's supposed to be."

Banning had meanwhile torn open the envelope and was scanning through Moore's service record with a practiced eye.

"Well, he's not a radio technician," he said, and then a moment later, "nor even an operator. And they didn't send him to parachute school. According to this, he just got out of boot camp. How come he's a sergeant?"

"He said they took him out of the officer candidate program to send him here. And made him a sergeant instead," Pickering said.

He held the service record envelope upside down and shook it. A business size envelope fell out. On it was written,

"Major Ed Banning, USMC Special Detachment 14, Personal."

"And what have we here?" Banning said and tore it open.

```
Washington, 16 June 1942
Major Ed Banning

Dear Ed:


  You have no idea how much trouble it was to
find the young man probably now standing in
front of you. He knows nothing about radios,
I'm afraid, or about parachuting, or for that
matter, about the Marine Corps, since I
plucked him out of Parris Island before he fin-
ished boot camp.
  But he speaks fluent Japanese, and I thought
you could find some use for him. The FBI had
quite a dossier on him (and his family) who were
Methodist missionaries in Japan before the
war, and he comes to you with a permanent TOP
SECRET clearance.
  If you can't use him, I'm sure the First Divi-
sion, which should be in New Zealand by now,
could. But you have the priority, so here he is.
I'm working on radio people, parachute quali-
fied, for you, but they're in nearly as short
supply.
  I wish I was there, instead of here. I don't
suppose you could arrange something for me,
could you?
  Best Regards. Semper Fi!
  Edward Sessions, Captain, USMC
```

Banning handed the letter to Pickering, who read it and handed it to Pluto Hon.

"I guess we'd better send him to the 1st Division," Banning said. "Before I came here, I thought that I would need a Japanese linguist, linguists, which is why Ed Sessions went to all this trouble to get this guy for me. But it hasn't turned out that way. A couple of Feldt's people and I can handle what translations we get into. It would be nice to have another linguist, particularly an American, but the First Marine Division really needs him more than I do. What I really need is radio operators, technicians."

"If you don't want him, Major, can I have him?" Pluto Hon asked.

"What do you want him for?" Pickering asked.

"Analysis," Hon said.

"You're talking about MAGIC?" Pickering asked.

Hon nodded. "Analysis needs someone who understands the Japanese mind, their culture."

"Christ, we can't get him cleared for that," Pickering replied.

"He doesn't have to know what it is, where it came from," Hon argued. "All he has to do is compare the intercepts with the translations we get from Pearl, and tell me if that's the translation he would have made."

"I'll have to think about that," Pickering said. "For one thing, we don't know if he speaks Japanese well enough to be of any use to you."

"Let me talk to him a couple of minutes, and I'd know," Hon said.

Pickering looked at Hon a moment, and realized that Hon really wanted Sergeant Moore.

"Well, that's easy enough to arrange. I put him in the Prince of Wales Hotel. We'll call him up and let you talk to him. But first things first. I need a drink. Unless what you've got that's 'interesting,' Ed, won't wait?"

"It'll wait long enough for a drink, Sir. I left it in the library."

"Well, let's go into the library and have a look," Pickering said. "It'll give us an excuse to get close to the liquor, anyway."

They picked up their empty glasses and followed him into the house.

"I'm going to take my coat off," Pickering said, as he did so. "Why don't you two relax, too?"

Then he went to the liquor and made drinks.

When he turned from the table, he saw that Pluto Hon was standing by the telephone.

"I found the number, Sir. Would you like me to dial it for you?"

Pickering nodded, and signaled for Hon to dial the telephone. Then he walked to him and took it from him.

"Sergeant Moore, please. I think he's in 408," he said, and then a moment later: "This is Captain Pickering, Sergeant. They taking care of you all right?" And then: "There's someone here who wants to talk to you." He handed the phone to Hon.

In Japanese, Pluto Hon said, "Welcome to Australia, Sergeant. I suppose that you're pretty beat after that long flight. How long did it take you to get from the States?"

Banning walked quickly to the telephone and put his head close to Pluto's so that he could hear Moore.

"Yes, Sir, I'm pretty . . ."

"In Japanese," Hon interrupted him, in Japanese. "If you will, please, Sergeant."

"Yes, Sir," Moore said, in Japanese. "I'm pretty tired, it was a long flight. And in Hawaii, I got off one plane and thirty minutes later got on another one."

"Where did you live in Japan?" Pluto Hon asked.

"In Denenchofu, Sir. Tokyo."

"And how long were you in Japan?"

"On and off, all my life, Sir."

"You went to school there? I mean Japanese schools?"

"Yes, Sir."

"The University?"

"Yes, Sir. And elementary and middle schools, too. Sir, who am I talking to?"

"My name is Hon, Sergeant. Your commanding officer is here and wants to talk to you."

He handed the phone to Banning, who didn't expect it.

"Sergeant, I'm sorry there was no one at NATS to meet you," Banning began, in English, and then switched to Japanese. "I'll be down to fetch you in the morning. Get yourself some dinner and a good night's sleep."

"Yes, Sir."

"Welcome to Australia, Sergeant," Banning said. "Good night." He hung the phone up, and turned to Pluto. "I didn't want to talk to him."

"I wanted you to be able to tell the Captain how well that kid speaks Japanese," Hon said, unabashed.

"Does he? Speak it well, I mean?" Pickering asked.

"He didn't learn that pronunciation in Japanese 202 at Princeton," Hon said. "He's been in Japan on and off all his life. He went to school there. Japanese schools, I mean. Including the University. I'd really like to have him, Captain."

"He went to Pennsylvania, too, he told me," Pickering said, "so he probably didn't graduate from University in Tokyo. So what? But I'm more than a little uneasy about giving him access to the MAGIC intercepts, even if he doesn't know what they are."

"I could have a fatherly little chat with him, Captain," Banning said. "And tell him that if it ever comes to my attention that he has discussed in any way what Hon gives him to do, or what he's learned, or thinks he's learned, with anyone but Pluto, you, or myself, I will see that he spends the next twenty years in solitary confinement at the Portsmouth Naval Prison."

"On the way to the hotel, he wouldn't even discuss Special Detachment 14 with me," Pickering said. "I don't think he would have a loose mouth. OK, Pluto. You can have him. But you have that talk with him, Ed, anyway. And don't say Portsmouth. Tell him we'll have him shot."

Banning looked quickly at Pickering and saw that he was serious.

"Aye, aye, Sir," Banning said.

Then Pickering changed the subject. "Let's see what you have, Ed, that's so interesting."

"Aye, aye, Sir," Banning repeated.

He pulled a leather briefcase from under the couch and took a large manila envelope from it.

"Would you like me to keep my eyes to myself, Captain?" Pluto Hon asked.

"Oh, no, Pluto," Pickering said. "You only thought I asked you here just for dinner."

Banning chuckled, and spread a dozen ten-inch-square aerial photos out on a library table.

Three of the photos showed a dense cloud of smoke from a grass fire rising from a field, and then, in photographs apparently taken a day or two later, the same field. There were tracks from a truck or some other vehicle crisscrossing the now blackened grassy area.

"What am I looking at?" Pickering asked.

"That's a field on an island called Guadalcanal," Banning said. "It's one of the larger islands in the Solomons chain. . . . Here, I have a map, too."

He took a map from his briefcase, spread it on the table, and pointed out the position of Guadalcanal in relation to New Britain and New Ireland islands, and to the islands nearer to it, New Georgia, Santa Isabel, Malaita, Tulagi, and San Cristobal.

"That field is near Lunga Point, on the north shore of Guadalcanal," Banning said, "between the Matanikau and Tenaru Rivers."

"I heard the Air Corps had taken some aerials of that area," Pickering said. "Is that what these are?"

"No, Sir. These came from the Australians. Feldt passed them to me."

"And does Feldt also think the Japanese are about to build a fighter strip there?"

"Feldt thinks—he's familiar with Guadalcanal—that *when* the Japanese build a field there, it will be able to handle any aircraft in the Jap inventory."

"Jesus," Pickering said softly. "If they get a fighter field going there, they can cover that whole area. And we don't have anything to stop them, and won't until we get that field on Espíritu Santo built . . . and God only knows how long that will take. Can I have these?"

"Yes, Sir, of course. We have Coastwatchers on Guadalcanal, but not in that area. We've radioed them to see what they can find out. But it will take them a couple of days to move over there."

" 'We'?" Pickering quoted.

"I should have said, 'Commander Feldt,' " Banning said.

"Hell, no. 'We' is fine. 'Them' and 'us' is just what I didn't want to hear. I was asking, are any of the Coastwatchers American?"

"No, Sir. The only Marines we have actually in place are Lieutenant Howard and Sergeant Koffler, and they're on Buka, to the Northwest."

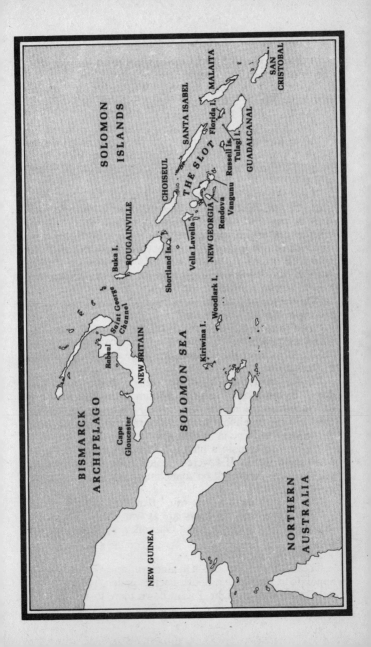

"I thought you told me you were going to try to . . . what's the word? 'insert'? . . . some more of our people."

"So far, no luck," Banning said. "Which translated means that Feldt has shot down every proposal I've made."

"It's his show," Pickering said.

"Yes, Sir. I have been operating under that premise."

"If the Japanese manage to get this airfield up and running, we're in trouble," Pickering repeated, and then asked Banning, "Did Feldt have anything to say about how long that will take?"

"I asked him the same question. 'I'm not a sodding engineer,' he said. 'But they can probably start to land fighters there in maybe six weeks. It depends on what they are using, whether real engineers, with bulldozers and other heavy construction equipment, or whether they will just try to level the field with ordinary soldiers and picks and shovels. If they move in engineers and their equipment, they can build a real airfield in two months or so.' "

"Off the top of your head, Ed, how long will it take to get these pictures to Washington?"

"You're going to send those to Washington, Sir?" Banning asked, surprised.

"I really meant the pictures our Army Air Corps took," Pickering said.

"If they sent them by officer courier, maybe four, five days," Banning said. "Are they that important? To get them to Washington, I mean, rather than a message saying we think the Japs are about to build an airfield on Guadalcanal? A message could be in Washington in a matter of hours."

"A picture, to coin a phrase," Pickering said, "is worth a thousand words. If I were Admiral King and wanted to sell President Roosevelt on something, I'd think I'd want to have the pictures."

"Sir, I don't quite follow you," Banning admitted.

"The Army and the Navy are at war again," Pickering said, bitterly. "Does the name Ghormley mean anything to you?"

"Admiral Ghormley?"

"Yeah," Pickering said. "On nineteen June, Ghormley was appointed Commander, South Pacific, under Admiral Nimitz. Ghormley's all right. I went down there to see him. He was in London on December seventh, and isn't infected with that sense of humiliation that the other admirals from King on down seem to feel."

"Sir?" Banning said, asking for an explanation.

"The others seem to feel that their primary mission in this war is to make amends for Pearl Harbor," Pickering said, bitterly, "ahead of all other considerations, including the best way to fight a war."

"Which is?" Banning asked softly.

"Early this month, when was it Pluto? MacArthur radioed Marshall for permission to attack New Britain–New Guinea. Which would, if successful, remove the threat posed by the Japanese airbase, *bases,* at Rabaul on New Britain."

"Eight June, Captain," Pluto furnished the date. "It was an EYES ONLY for Marshall, and he sent an officer courier with some pretty detailed plans to Washington the same day."

"MacArthur wanted to use two U.S. Infantry divisions," Pickering went on, "the 32nd and the 41st, plus the Australian 7th. Problem One was that they're not trained for amphibious landings. But the First Marine Division, by definition, is. And it was already on its way over here. So MacArthur wanted the 1st Marines to make the landing, and then be replaced by the others. Problem Two was that the beach was way out of range for Army Air Corps fighters. Once the force was ashore, of course, and took the Japanese bases, land-based fighters could be flown in and operate from them. So the solution to Problem Two was to have the Navy furnish fighter support from aircraft carriers until the Army took the Japanese airbases."

"And the Navy didn't like that idea?" Banning asked.

"The Pearl Harbor admirals didn't like it worth a damn," Pickering replied. "Admiral Ghormley, on the other hand, thought MacArthur's plan made more sense than anything else he'd heard . . ."

"Excuse me, Sir," Banning interrupted. "What had he heard? What does the Navy want to do?"

"I'm telling you all this more to get it straight in my mind than for any other reason," Pickering said, a little sharply. "Let me do it my way, please, Banning."

"Sorry, Sir," Banning said, genuinely contrite.

"Ghormley, as I was saying, not only thought Mac-Arthur's plan made more sense than the Navy's, but fired off radios saying so. More important than Ghormley, so did General Marshall. And you know that Marshall and Mac-Arthur agree on damned little. The day MacArthur's courier officer—he was really more than a courier; he was one of the assistant G-3s, a really bright lieutenant colonel, who knew what was in his briefcase. Anyway, the day he got to see the Chief of Staff in Washington, Marshall presented Mac-Arthur's plan to Admiral King. Since New Britain was in MacArthur's territory, logically the operation should be under his command. But he threw in a bone for King: King would appoint an Admiral to actually run the operation, under MacArthur."

"And?" Banning asked.

"On June twenty-fifth, King gave the Navy's plan to Marshall. Instead of MacArthur—or an Admiral under Mac-Arthur's orders—attacking New Britain, King wanted a force under Admiral Nimitz—in other words, not under MacArthur—to make an attack in the Solomons and the Santa Cruz islands, as a first step toward taking New Britain. King wanted MacArthur to stage a diversionary attack against Timor, near the Australian Coast."

"And, of course, the Army doesn't like the Navy's idea?" Banning asked rhetorically.

"No," Pickering replied. "And with good reason. They think that the thing to do is hit New Britain first—specifically, the big Jap base at Rabaul. Our land-based bombers could support the attack, and probably take the airbases out long enough so they wouldn't pose much of a problem for us while we're getting ashore. Then, once we had captured the airbases and got them up and running, Army fighter planes could relieve the Navy's carrier-based fighters. And then once we had Rabaul, we could keep the Japs from supplying or reinforcing their other bases within bomber range. They'd be rendered impotent.

"There's no argument over the importance of Rabaul, just when and how to take it. The Navy wants to start with Tulagi and move to Rabaul gradually. The Army agrees that it would be easier to take Tulagi first than it would be to take Rabaul, but argues that as we move northward to Rabaul afterward, all our operations would be under attack from Rabaul-based bombers. And, further, as soon as the Japanese see what our obvious plans are, they would have time to reinforce Rabaul with both ground and air forces."

"So what's going to happen?" Banning asked.

"Theoretically, the matter is still under consideration by the Joint Chiefs of Staff," Pickering said drily.

" 'Theoretically'?" Banning asked.

"King apparently thinks he will prevail when the decision is made by the President. He's ordered Nimitz to prepare to attack in the Solomons, with or without MacArthur's support. Nimitz relayed that order to Ghormley. So the First Marines are either about to start making up the Operations Orders for the invasion of Guadalcanal, or they already have them now."

"How do you know that?"

"Don't ask, Major," Pluto Hon said softly. "You really don't want to know."

"What do you think's going to happen, Captain?" Banning asked.

"Franklin Roosevelt hates MacArthur, and he loves King and the U.S. Navy. He is probably going to rationalize his decision to go with King by deciding that Marshall's agreement with MacArthur on this is based on Marshall hating the Navy even more than he hates MacArthur. Logic will have little to do with it."

"Jesus!" Banning said softly.

"And of course," Pickering added, "Admiral King is certainly going to walk into the Oval Office and dramatically throw the aerial photographs the Air Corps took of this field on Guadalcanal onto the presidential desk. It will be an effective cap to his argument."

"Isn't it?" Banning asked.

"If we had Rabaul, the Japs could not supply an airfield on Guadalcanal," Pickering said. "And it seems to me that if a B-17 could take pictures of the field on Guadalcanal, B-17s could bomb it, too."

Banning looked as if he was going to say something, but had then decided against it. He held his glass up.

"May I have another of these, Sir?"

"Sure, Ed," Pickering said. "You don't have to ask. Help

yourself." Then he added: "But in any event, the more information we have about the field on Guadalcanal, and the sooner we get it, the better."

Banning, halfway across the room to the liquor, stopped and turned.

"At this moment, as I am about to help myself to another belt of your splendid booze, and about to sit down to a baron of lamb—Mrs. Cavendish told me about the lamb—at least four Coastwatchers are slopping through some of the nastiest mountain jungle in the world to get us that information, Captain."

Pickering grunted. And then he said, "Christ, I'd like to sit all four of them—plus Lieutenant Howard and Sergeant Koffler—down to dinner with King, MacArthur, and the other prima donnas."

Banning chuckled. "Chunk of fire-blackened wild pig, cold rice, and washed down with a nice canteen cup of Eau de chlorine, '42."

Pickering laughed. "Yeah," he said.

(Two)
HEADQUARTERS, 1ST MARINE DIVISION
WELLINGTON, NEW ZEALAND
0815 HOURS 29 JUNE 1942

"Gentlemen," Major General A. A. Vandergrift's aide-de-camp announced, "the commanding general."

The thirty-odd officers in the room, almost all of them field grade, the half dozen senior non-commissioned officers, and the one PFC (there to operate a slide projector), came to attention.

Major General Vandergrift strode into the room.

"Take your seats, gentlemen," he said conversationally, as he stepped behind a rather crude lectern. A bedsheet had been thumbtacked to the wall behind him.

"This won't take long," Vandergrift began when the noise of folding chairs scraping on the floor had died down. "We have a lot to do, and precious little time to do it in, and we can't afford the luxury of wasting any time at all. I have just returned . . ."

He stopped and looked directly at Major Jake Dillon, who was seated in the last row of folding chairs.

"Major, I certainly don't mean to embarrass you, but what are you doing in here?"

"Sir," Brigadier General "Lucky Lew" Harris said, as he got to his feet, "I asked Major Dillon to attend."

Vandergrift's eyebrows rose in surprise.

"Then I suppose we can presume Major Dillon is cleared for TOP SECRET," Vandergrift said, "which is how this meeting is classified, and that he has a Need to Know."

"Yes, Sir," General Harris said.

He suspected, correctly, that the only reason General Vandergrift had not asked Major Dillon, more or less politely, to get his ass out of the room was that Vandergrift paid more than lip service to the military adage that an officer should not be reprimanded or, especially, humiliated, in front of his juniors. Vandergrift was not going to ask his Deputy, before the General and Special Staff officers of the Division, "just what the *hell* did you do that for?"

He probably won't even ask me later, privately. He knows that I know he's displeased. He ordered me to keep Dillon away from him. I wonder if I should tell him about Dillon's orders, which require us to let him stick his goddamned nose in wherever he pleases?

"As I was saying," Vandergrift resumed, "I have just returned from meeting with Admiral Ghormley, COMSOPAC, at his headquarters in Auckland. Admiral McCain, who is COMAIRSOPAC, was also there." (Commander, Air, South Pacific.)

The room was now absolutely quiet.

"Admiral Ghormley has ordered me to prepare the division, less the 7th Marines, which, as most of you know, is on Samoa, for combat in the Solomon Islands on 1 August. For those of you who don't already know, the 1st Marines and our artillery—the 11th Marines—are presently at sea and due to arrive here by the tenth of July. We will be augmented by the 2nd Marines, which will ship out of 'Diego on one July; by the 1st Raider Battalion, now en route; and by 3rd Defense Battalion, which is in Hawaii. When they will ship out of Hawaii isn't known; shipping is in critically short supply. We will probably also have the 1st Parachute Battalion. Because there are no transport aircraft for them, they will function as regular infantry."

There were muted sounds of surprise, audible exhaling and shaking heads. The people in the room were professionals. They knew the division's state of preparedness and its logistical problems. All that added up to the almost unarguable fact that the Division was simply not ready to enter combat in less than two months.

"Son," General Vandergrift addressed the junior Marine present, "would you put map one up on the screen, please?"

The overhead lights went out, and a white beam of light erupted from the slide projector against the bedsheet on the wall, and then a black-and-white map appeared.

"This, obviously, is Guadalcanal," General Vandergrift said, standing in front of the map and pointing to the island that always reminded Lucky Lew Harris of a tape worm. He had been infested with tape worms several times during his Marine service in Latin America. They had left an indelible, unpleasant memory with him.

"While our intelligence, putting it kindly, ranges from lousy to nonexistent," General Vandergrift went on, "we have reason to believe the Japanese are building an airfield here, on the Northern side of the island, near Lunga point."

He paused, and then said, "The comment vis-à-vis our intelligence was not intended as a criticism of Colonel Goettge. I meant to say that there is very little intelligence available to anybody over here, including Admiral Ghormley and General MacArthur."

"Not that MacArthur would give it to the Marines if he had it," someone muttered.

Vandergrift's face tightened.

"I will not ask who made that remark," he said, icily furious. "But I will observe that anyone who makes a similar remark in the future does so at his own, considerable peril."

It had recently become rumored throughout the Marine Corps—and Lucky Lew Harris had taken the trouble to check it out and verify it—that MacArthur had not recommended the 4th Marines, who had fought on Bataan and Corregidor, for the Presidential Unit Citation. The citations had been passed out to almost every other unit in the area. Mac-

Arthur was reported to have explained his action, or lack of it, by saying, "The Marines have enough decorations as it is."

The crack, Harris thought, *is understandable. And probably true.*

When Harris met General Vandergrift at the airport after his return from meeting Admiral Ghormley, Vandergrift told him that MacArthur was opposed to the Solomon Islands operation for two reasons, tactical and personal; he didn't think it was the way to fight the war, and he wasn't to be in command of it.

Under those circumstances, MacArthur would be reluctant to give the Marines the time of day. And the General knows that. But he certainly had to say what he said. If that had been me, I would have called Motor Mouth to attention and really eaten his ass out.

"Now, across this body of water, about twenty-three miles from the airfield we believe they are building near Lunga point," Vandergrift went on, pointing again, "we find these tiny islands off Florida Island, Tulagi and Gavutu. We *know* the Japanese have built a seaplane base on Tulagi, and they have some other installations in the area. The seaplanes could raise hell with our landing craft, so we have to take Tulagi and Gavutu first, by which I mean several hours before we land on Guadalcanal itself, in the Lunga point area.

"A few more points about my general thinking. I think we should divide the division into two regimental combat teams—there would be about 4500 men in each—for the main landing on Guadalcanal. We will use the Raiders and the Paratroops, probably reinforced by one of the battalions of the 5th Marines, for the Tulagi-Gavutu landings, and the RCTs for the landing on Guadalcanal itself.

"What I'm going to do now is turn this over to General Harris and the G-3, and for the next hour—and no more than that—I want you to discuss the major problems as you see them. And then I want you to get to work. As I said before, we have a lot to do, and damned little time to do it in."

He turned from the lectern. Someone called, "Atten-hut!" and everyone came to attention. Vandergrift marched out of the room. General Harris walked to the lectern.

"Take your seats," he ordered. "Try turning the lights on to see if we can still see the map."

(Three)
THE PRINCE OF WALES HOTEL
MELBOURNE, VICTORIA, AUSTRALIA
0930 HOURS 29 JUNE 1942

Major Edward Banning had called Sergeant John Marston Moore, USMCR, at half past six, and somewhat brusquely ordered him to have a quick breakfast, settle his hotel bill, and be waiting for him in the lobby with his gear when he came to pick him up.

"Aye, aye, Sir."

Banning had hung up without a further word.

By 0715 Sergeant Moore had complied with his orders, by dressing hurriedly, gulping down a breakfast identified on the menu as "scrambled eggs with bangers," and paying for his hotel room with a twenty-dollar bill. The cashier looked with great suspicion at that, but he reluctantly accepted it.

When Major Banning did not show up by 0800, Moore checked with the desk to make sure there had been no calls or messages for him. He did so again at 0830, again at 0900, and was about to check again when he saw the Marine officer walking quickly across the sidewalk to the revolving glass door of the hotel. There was little doubt in his mind that it was his new commanding officer, so he stood up, almost in the formal position of Attention.

Each man examined the other carefully. Moore would have been flattered to know that Banning was pleased with what he saw, a tall, good-looking, physically fit kid with intelligent eyes, who really didn't look as if he was fresh from boot camp at Parris Island.

And Moore saw a tall, stocky, tanned man who met his expectation of what a Marine field grade officer should look like. But as a recent graduate of Parris Island, where the only major he had ever seen was on the reviewing stand at a parade, this was not a comforting appreciation. He was more than a little in awe, something approaching fear, of Major Banning.

"Sergeant Moore?" Banning asked.

"Yes, Sir."

Banning offered his hand. There was a momentary test of grip-strength, which Banning, surprising neither of them, won. Banning was further pleased that when he looked intently into Moore's eyes, the kid didn't blink.

"You've had breakfast? Got your bill paid?"

"Yes, Sir."

"Grab your gear, then. I'm parked illegally."

He marched out of the hotel lobby. Moore grabbed his gear and scurried after him.

Banning led him to a Studebaker parked in a No HALTING zone. Marine insignia were on the hood and doors. Banning held open the back door and gestured for Moore to put his gear in the back seat. When he had done so, Banning slammed the door, pointed to the front seat, and said, "Get in."

"Yes, Sir."

Banning got behind the wheel, punched the ignition button, and then looked at Moore.

"Sorry to be late, Sergeant. Captain Pickering had an appointment with General MacArthur at 8:30 and his car wouldn't start. So I had to drive him over there before I came for you."

"Yes, Sir."

Banning had expected to see more of a reaction to the words "General MacArthur" than he got.

Either he's stupid, which I doubt. Or he didn't hear me, which is unlikely. Or he is simply unable to comprehend what I said. It's like being told that someone you know has just had lunch with Saint Peter, if not God himself.

Moore did indeed hear what Banning said. He had also noticed that Banning was wearing the Purple Heart ribbon, making him the second man he'd met (Lieutenant "Killer" McCoy was the first) who had actually seen combat in this war. He supposed that Banning had been wounded in the Philippines, which, aside from Wake Island, was the only place the Marines had seen ground combat so far. But if that was so, he wondered, how had Banning escaped when the Philippines fell?

It was at once possible and incredible to consider that the man driving him around in a Studebaker had actually escaped from Corregidor.

He had not made a response because he could think of none to make.

Banning drove to a hill outside Melbourne overlooking Port Philip Bay and pulled the Studebaker off the road.

"There goes your plane," Major Banning said, pointing. Moore followed the finger and saw a Navy Martin PBM-3R Mariner moving across the blue waters of the bay.

I've ridden on a plane like that, he thought, and then, *Major Banning said, "your plane," so that must be the very plane, headed back for Hawaii.*

The Mariner rose into the air, and then with a tremendous splash fell back into the water. It repeated this twice more before it rose finally into the air. Then it banked, and passed right over them.

Banning offered Moore a cigarette, and then held his Ronson out to light it for him.

"I don't think anyone has to tell you that you're now on the perimeter of the intelligence business, Moore, do they? I mean, you're a bright young man, you *did* think there was *something* a little odd about the way they took you out of Parris Island and sent you here? *Flew* you here, ahead of some pretty senior officers?"

"Yes, Sir."

"And would it be a reasonable statement that you don't know diddly-shit about the Intelligence business? Or for that matter, about the Marine Corps?"

"Yes, Sir."

"You have seen the spy movies, of course, where the sneaky little Jap with the buck teeth and the thick glasses has the plans for the latest aircraft carrier in his briefcase? And is foiled at the last moment by Commander Don Winslow of the U.S. Coast Guard?"

Moore chuckled. "Yes, Sir."

"Commander Winslow of the Coast Guard" was a popular children's radio program.

"Well, for openers, you couldn't get the plans for an aircraft carrier in a boxcar, much less a briefcase. And then, in the real world, I have come to know a number of Japanese Intelligence types who are as large as I am, have perfect teeth and eye sight, and are probably a lot smarter than I am. And I know from personal experience that our Intelligence, and Counterintelligence, fucks up by the numbers far more often than it works at all."

Moore looked at him, expecting Banning to be smiling. He was not.

"For example," Banning said, "all that effort by all those people to get you over here as soon as humanly possible was a waste of time, money, and airspace. I can't use you." He waited for a moment until that announcement had time to sink in, and then added, "Comment?"

Oh, shit! What happens to me now?

"I don't know what to say, Sir."

"But finding you and sending you here the way they did was sound, a good idea, and well carried out."

"Sir?" Moore asked, wholly confused.

"What I'm doing, what Special Detachment 14 is doing, in other words, is very important. Importance is normally judged by how many American lives can be saved, or how many of the enemy can be killed, by what you're doing. Are you still with me?"

"You're saying, Sir, in effect, 'damn the expense'?"

"Just about. When something important is at stake, you can't worry about what it costs, or anything else. So here you are, and I can't use you."

"Sir, what happens to me now?"

"I wondered when you were going to get around to asking that," Banning said. "One of two things: We send you down to the First Division, the initial elements of which just arrived in New Zealand. Your Japanese language skills can be put to good use there."

"Yes, Sir."

"Or, we keep you here," Banning said.

"Sir, I thought you said you don't need me."

"You might be of value working for Captain Pickering, or more precisely, for an officer who works for Captain Pickering."

"May I ask doing what, Sir?"

"It has to do with intelligence, and it has to do with your knowledge of Japanese, and the Japanese culture."

"Sir, I don't understand."

"I said before, if you remember, that importance is usually judged by how many American lives can be saved, or how many of the enemy can be killed. Do you remember that?"

"Yes, Sir."

"What you would be involved in could literally affect the outcome of the war," Banning said evenly.

"I still don't understand, Sir."

"No, you don't. And I will not entertain any questions about what that is."

"Sir, I don't really . . ."

"That's the whole idea, Moore. You're not supposed to know what's going on. You would be expected to do what you were told, and not only not ask questions, but not try to guess. It's that important."

"Wow!"

"No romance. Nobody in a trench coat, but—and I tell you this because it would be self-evident—real world intelligence at the highest level. There would be a high degree of risk to you."

"May I ask how, Sir?"

"If I, or anyone else, ever learned that you had run off at the mouth about any aspect of this operation, you'll be shot. There would be no court-martial, nothing like that. The burden of proof of innocence would be on you. You would be shot out of hand, and your family would get a telegram from the Secretary of the Navy expressing his deep regret that you had been lost at sea. Something like that."

Moore, his eyes wide, looked at Banning for confirmation that he had correctly heard what Banning had just said.

"Yes," Banning said, reading Moore's mind. "I'm serious. Deadly serious, pun intended."

"Sir, when they took me out of Parris Island, they—Captain Sessions—led me to believe that I could ultimately get a commission."

"Maybe you could in the 1st Division," Banning said. "But no way in the billet I'm talking about."

Moore exhaled audibly.

"You want some time to think this over?" Banning said.

If I was this kid, I would think, "Fuck you, Major. Send me to the 1st Marine Division and give me that gold bar I was promised."

"No, Sir," Moore said. "If you think I could do what you want me to do, I'll try. I think I can keep my mouth shut."

"So does Captain Pickering," Banning said. "Don't disappoint him. He told me that you remind him of his son, who's a Marine officer. He wouldn't like to have you shot. But he would, and I'd probably have to do it."

"I understand, Sir."

"The mission of Special Detachment 14 is classified TOP SECRET," Banning said. "What we do is support the Australian Navy's Coastwatcher Operation. What they do is have people on Japanese occupied islands. What *they* do is furnish intelligence information, generally about Japanese air and sea activity, but also about Japanese troop installations, and that sort of thing."

"Am I going to be working with the Coastwatchers, Sir?"

"No. I don't need you. I need radio operators and radio technicians. Who are parachutists. You're none of those things. But having you assigned to Special Detachment 14 will be what is known as a good cover assignment. People who think you're already assigned to a highly classified activity won't be prone to ask questions, or even wonder, about what you're really doing."

"I think I understand, Sir."

"We're in Townesville, Queensland, up North. You will stay here, ostensibly to function as our rear area. Meet courier planes, receive and transship equipment, that sort of thing."

"Yes, Sir."

"There is a headquarters company at Supreme Headquarters, but if we put you in there, questions will obviously be asked as to what exactly you would be doing. So, for the time being, you will live at The Elms."

"Yes, Sir."

"You're not going to ask what 'The Elms' is?"

Moore looked at Banning and smiled, "Sir, you just told me not to ask questions."

Banning chuckled.

"OK, Sergeant, one point for you. 'The Elms' is an estate Captain Pickering has leased, not far from here. He has more money than God, and he was not prepared to share the Spartan quarters provided for Navy captains with an Army colonel who snores. It's equipped with a housekeeper and some other servants, and it's enormous. You'll have no problems making yourself invisible there."

"My God!" Moore said.

"And living there will get you out of the clutches of the headquarters company commander, who would, I'm sure, love to have a Marine sergeant for his guard details. MacArthur is about to move his headquarters to Brisbane—that move is classified SECRET, by the way—so other arrangements will have to made for you when that happens."

"Yes, Sir."

"The officer you will be working for is Lieutenant Hon. He's in the Army Signal Corps and is a cryptographic-classified documents officer at Supreme Headquarters, South West Pacific. He also has other duties he performs for Captain Pickering. You spoke with him on the telephone last night."

"He speaks perfect Japanese," Moore thought aloud.

Banning chuckled again. "He said the same thing about you, which is why you're not on your way to the First Marine Division."

Banning turned the ignition key and started the engine, and then turned and looked at Moore.

"One question, Moore."

"Yes, Sir?"

"Do you believe me when I say we'll have you shot if you breach security? Or do you think this is some sort of bullshit line I'm handing you?"

Moore met Banning's eyes.

"I believe you, Sir."

"Good," Banning said.

He put the gearshift in reverse and turned the Studebaker around.

(Four)
HEADQUARTERS, 1ST MARINE DIVISION
WELLINGTON, NEW ZEALAND
1605 HOURS 29 JUNE 1942

"General," Harris's sergeant said, putting his head in Harris's office door, "Major Dillon is here and wants to know if you can see him for a minute."

I want to see that sonofabitch about as much as I want to break both my legs.

"Ask him to come in, please, Sergeant," Harris said.

Major Dillon, to Harris's surprise, was wearing utilities. Both the utilities and his boots were muddy.

It actually looks like the sonofabitch has been out in the boondocks.

"Hello, Dillon," Harris asked. "What can I do for you?"

"Good morning, Sir," Dillon said, assuming the position of Parade Rest.

"Pull up a chair," Harris said. "But don't get too comfortable. I've got people coming to see me right about now."

Jake Dillon was no fool. He had not been a fool when he was a staff sergeant in Shanghai, and he'd learned a good deal more about people during his time in Hollywood. He was fully aware that General Harris didn't like him personally and regarded his official function as that of a parasite on the body of the First Marine Division specifically and the Corps generally.

"May I get right to the point, Sir?" Dillon asked.

"You'd better," Harris said, tempering it with a faint smile.

"Sir, I've got a pretty good friend in MacArthur's headquarters."

"Why doesn't that surprise me, Major Dillon?" Harris said and immediately regretted it. He saw in Dillon's eyes the hurt the sarcasm had caused.

"Sir, I think he could be helpful with regard to intelligence," Dillon went on.

"He's an intelligence officer?" Harris asked, wondering if Dillon really didn't know that intelligence officers pass out information outside their own headquarters only when specifically ordered to do so, and then did so reluctantly.

"No, Sir. He's . . . Frank Knox sent him over to keep an eye on MacArthur for him."

"You *are* referring to *Secretary of the Navy* Frank Knox and *General* MacArthur?" Harris asked. Dillon nodded, completely oblivious to the oblique reprimand. "And how do you know this?"

"It was all over Washington, General," Dillon said confidently.

This sonofabitch probably was privy to all the high level gos-

sip in Washington. *I wouldn't really be surprised if he calls the Secretary of the Navy by his first name.*

"Who are we talking about, Dillon?"

"Fleming Pickering, General. He's a Navy Captain. He owns Pacific & Far East Shipping."

"And how do you know Captain Pickering?" Harris asked.

"I used to shoot skeet with him in California," Dillon said. "He's a big skeet shooter. I met him through Bob Stack."

I am about to lose my temper. How dare this sonofabitch waste my time like this?

"The actor, you mean?" Harris asked, evenly.

"Yes, Sir. We had a team for a couple of years, me, Stack, Clark Gable, Howard Hawks—the director—and Pickering."

"Major," Harris said, his voice low and icy, "are you actually suggesting to me that because a Navy captain shot skeet with you and some other Hollywood types before the war, he would make intelligence available to you that we could not get through official channels?"

"No, Sir. Not because of the skeet. He was a Marine. He was a corporal in War One. He and Doc McInerney and Jack Stecker were buddies at Belleau Wood. He's got the Silver Star and the Croix de Guerre. He was wounded a couple of times, too."

"By 'Doc McInerney,' Major, I gather you are referring to *General* McInerney?"

"Yes, Sir," Dillon said. "And Captain Pickering's boy is in the Corps. The last I heard he was a second lieutenant learning to fly Wildcats at Pensacola."

I'll be goddamned. This guy Pickering might be damned useful.

"Sergeant!" Harris raised his voice. His sergeant quickly appeared at his door. "Send for Major Stecker, 2nd Battalion, 5th. Get him in here right away. And then pass the word to Colonel Goettge that I may want to see him within the next half hour."

"Aye, aye, Sir."

X

(One)
THE ELMS
DANDENONG, VICTORIA, AUSTRALIA
1430 HOURS 1 JULY 1942

When Mrs. Cavendish put her head in the library and told him that there was a telephone call for him, Sergeant John Marston Moore, USMCR, was sitting at a typewriter set up on a heavy library table. He was writing to his beloved, and he was having difficulty. It was a love letter, of course, and he was highly motivated to write it, but neither his passionate intentions, nor the typewriter, nor the privacy of being alone in the house (except for the servants) seemed to help.

There didn't seem to be a hell of a lot one could say on the subject, beyond the obvious, especially for someone who had absolutely no flair for the well-turned romantic phrase. He couldn't even call to mind much of the established literature on the subject, from which he would have eagerly and shamelessly plagiarized.

He got as far as "How do I love thee, let me count the ways—" and then his mind went blank. A phrase—"Thus

have I had thee" from a poem he thought was called
"Cynara" by Ernest Dowson—kept coming into his mind.
But he wasn't sure that was the title, that Ernest Dowson had
actually written it; and not only couldn't he remember what
came after "Thus have I had thee," but those words seemed
to paint an erotic picture, in the biblical sense . . . as in "Thus
have I had thee, standing up against the refrigerator in the
apartment on Rittenhouse Square." And the last thing in the
world he wanted to do was let Barbara think that all he was
interested in was the physical side of their relationship.

That was fine, marvelous, splendid, of course, but his love
for her was more than that. He loved her because . . .

He knew the one thing he could not write to her about was
what he was doing now in Australia. Even if he could, he
still didn't have all that squared away in his mind. So much
had happened to him so quickly, so much that was so
extraordinary, and so much he could only guess at, that his
confusion was certainly understandable.

Major Banning had driven him from the hill overlooking
Port Philip Bay to The Elms. And Lieutenant Hon had been
waiting for them there, sitting on the wide veranda of the
mansion drinking a beer.

It was the most cordial greeting Moore had ever received
from an officer.

"I'm very glad to meet you, Sergeant," he said in Japanese,
extending his hand before Moore could even begin to salute.
"I owe you a big one."

He looked over Moore's shoulder at Major Banning and
explained his last remark: "The Captain called early this
morning and said, 'Pluto, I've been thinking. Wouldn't it be
more convenient if you moved into The Elms with the
Sergeant? Would you mind?' "

Banning laughed.

"I told him that no sacrifice for the war effort, like moving
into The Elms, was too much to ask of me."

"That was very noble of you, Pluto," Banning said, in
Japanese.

"And I owe it all to you, Sergeant. So welcome, welcome!"

"Thank you, Sir."

Soon after that, a motherly gray-haired woman came onto

the veranda, and was introduced as Mrs. Cavendish, the housekeeper.

"Let me show you where you'll be staying, Sergeant, and then we'll serve lunch," she said.

Moore expected that he would be given a servant's room, probably on the third floor of the mansion. But he was taken instead to a large and airy room on the second floor complete with an enormous tiled bath.

"Get yourself settled," she said. "If you have any soiled clothing, or something that needs pressing, just leave it on the bed."

A luncheon of roast pork, green beans, applesauce, coffee, and apple pie was served in the dining room. The tableware was silver, the plates were fine china, the napkins and tablecloth linen, and the glassware that elegantly cradled Moore's beer was Czechoslovakian crystal.

After lunch, they drove into Melbourne to the Menzies Hotel. Lieutenant Hon told Moore to drive: "That's the best way to learn the route. If somebody else is driving, your mind goes to sleep."

At the Menzies, Hon told him to park in an area marked, RESERVED FOR GENERAL STAFF OFFICIAL VEHICLES.

"Our boss, Moore, ranks right under the Emperor in the pecking order around here. And this is his car."

"Yes, Sir."

At the elevator bank, where Banning left them, Moore saw that one elevator bore a sign, RESERVED FOR GENERAL MACARTHUR. He hoped that he would get a chance to see him.

That would be something to write and tell Barbara about. Oh, shit! I can't do that, either.

They rode the elevator to the basement, and then walked past an OFF LIMITS sign down a low, brick-lined corridor to a steel door guarded by two soldiers armed with Thompson submachine guns.

"This the new man, Lieutenant?" one of the soldiers asked.

"Sergeant Moore, Sergeant Skelly," Lieutenant Hon replied.

"Welcome to the dungeon, Moore," Sergeant Skelly said. "The way this works is that you have to show your dog tags to the guard on duty and then sign the register. He'll check your signature against the one on file, and let you in. If you take anything TOP SECRET out of here, it has to be logged out, and you have to be armed, and you have to carry it in a handcuff briefcase."

"A what?"

Hon leaned behind Sergeant Skelly's desk and picked up a leather briefcase from a stack of them. Attached to the handle was a foot-long length of stainless steel cable welded to half of a pair of handcuffs.

"There's a couple of .45s in our safe," Hon explained.

"You also have to log out CONFIDENTIAL and SECRET," Sergeant Skelly went on, "but you don't need the pistol or the briefcase."

"OK," Moore said.

Hon bent over the register and signed his name, then showed Moore where he was to sign. Sergeant Skelly pushed a 3 × 5 inch card across the small desk to Moore.

"Sign it," he said. "This is the one we keep on file."

Moore signed it.

Sergeant Skelly then went to the steel door and unlocked it with a large key.

"Come by the NCO Club, Moore, and I'll buy you a beer."

"Thank you," Moore said.

When the door had closed behind them, Lieutenant Hon said, "I don't think that would be a very good idea, Moore."

"Yes, Sir."

"I won't tell you to be a teetotal, although that might be a good idea. And I know it would be a good idea if you let Skelly think you are."

"Yes, Sir."

Hon led him to another steel-doored room, the key to which he had on a cord around his neck. Inside was a small room furnished with a small table and two filing cabinets with combination locks.

"Captain Pickering has the only other key to this room and is the only other person to know the combinations," Hon said. "You won't take anything out of here that I don't give you. Understood?"

"Yes, Sir."

"Turn your back, please, while I open this," Hon said, matter-of-factly.

Moore complied.

"OK, you can turn around," Hon said after a moment. "Sit down."

Moore sat down at the small table.

Hon handed him two sheets of paper, both stamped top and bottom, TOP SECRET. They were in Japanese calligraphs.

"We're going to run a little experiment," Hon said. "First, you are going to translate these. Then I am going to give you somebody else's translations. I want to see if they're different, and if they are, whether you think your translation is more accurate than the other guy's. Clear?"

"Yes, Sir. I think so."

"How long do you think it will take you?"

Moore glanced at the calligraphs.

"Ten, fifteen minutes, Sir."

"Can you type?"

"Yes, Sir."

"Well, I'll go see about scrounging a typewriter. For the time being, do these in pencil."

"Yes, Sir."

Hon took a lined pad and a Planter's peanuts can full of pencils from the top of one of the filing cabinets and put them on the table. Then, without a word, he walked out of the room. The door closed and Moore heard the key turning in the lock. He was locked in.

He picked up a pencil and started to read the calligraphs. He became aware of a strange feeling of foreboding and decided it was because he didn't like being locked behind a steel door with no way that he could see to get out.

He read both documents quickly, to get a sense of them, and then again more carefully.

They were obviously Japanese Army radio messages. The first was from the 14th Army in the Philippines to Imperial Japanese Army Headquarters in Tokyo. It was signed HOMMA. The second message was a reply to the first. It was signed, IN THE NAME OF HIS IMPERIAL MAJESTY.

He began to write his translation. It was hardly, he thought, a matter of world-shaking importance. It dealt with captured American weapons, ammunition, and food supplies. Not surprisingly, there was a comment to the effect that most weapons of all descriptions had been destroyed before the

American surrender. Another stated that there was a large stock of captured ammunition, mostly for large caliber artillery, but that it was in bad shape, and that the possibility had to be considered that it had been . . . he had to search for the right, decorous, words in English, for what popped into his mind was "fucked up"—*tampered with? rendered useless? sabotaged?*—by the Americans.

There was another comment that captured American food supplies were scarce, in bad shape, and inadequate for the feeding of prisoners.

The reply from Imperial Japanese Army Headquarters was brief, and far more formal. It directed General Homma to . . . again he had to search for the right words—to *inspect and rehabilitate? evaluate and repair? inspect and salvage?*—the captured artillery ammunition as well as he could using—*facilities? assets? capabilities?*—available to him. It reminded General Homma that shipping, of course, had to be allocated on the priorities of war. And finally, somewhat insultingly, Moore thought, it reminded Homma of the—*duty? obligations? price to be paid? sacrifices expected?*—of soldiers under the Code of Bushido.

Finally, he was finished. He looked at what he had written and heard his mother's voice in his ear, "Johnny, I can't understand how you can do that calligraphy so beautifully, but hen scratch when you write something in English."

He hoped that Lieutenant Hon would have no trouble reading his handwriting and was considering copying what he had written more neatly, when he heard the key in the lock of the steel door. It creaked open—*dungeon-like,* Moore thought—and Hon came back into the room. Moore started to get up.

"Keep your seat, nobody can see us in here," Hon said, and then asked. "Finished?"

Moore handed him the sheets of lined paper.

Hon read them carefully, then opened one of the filing cabinets again and handed Moore two more sheets of paper with TOP SECRET stamped on them.

They were someone else's translations of the two messages. Moore read them, wondering how different they would be from the translation he had made. There were minor differences of interpretation, but nothing significant. Moore felt a sense of satisfaction; he had obviously done as well as whoever had made the other translation.

"OK. Now tell me what the messages mean," Hon said.

"Sir?"

"Tell me what they mean," Hon repeated.

Moore told him and could tell by the look on Lieutenant Hon's face that he was disappointed.

"Look beneath the surface, beneath the obvious," Hon said.

"Sir, I don't quite understand."

"Forget you're a sergeant, forget that you're an American. Think like a Japanese. Think like General Homma."

How the hell am I supposed to do that?

When there was no response after a moment, Hon said, "OK. Try this. What, if anything, did you notice that was unusual, in any way, in either message?"

Jesus Christ, what is this, Twenty Questions?

He went over the messages in his mind, then picked up the original messages in Japanese and read them again.

"Sir, I thought it was unusual . . . I mean, Homma is a general. Why the reminder about the Code of Bushido?"

"Good!" Hon said, and made a "keep going" gesture with his hands.

Off the top of his head, Moore said, "If I was General Homma, I'd be a little pissed—*insulted* that they had given me the lecture."

"Good! Good!" Hon said. "Why?"

"Because it was discourteous. Not maybe the way we would look at it, but to a Japanese . . ."

"OK. Accepting it as a given that the IJAGS . . ."

Hon pronounced this "Eye-Jag-Ess," saw confusion cloud Moore's eyes, and translated:

"—the Imperial Japanese Army General Staff—did insult General Homma by discourteously reminding him about Bushido. He is a General officer who has to be presumed to know all about Bushido." Hon now switched to Japanese: "Why would they do this? In what context? Reply in Japanese."

Beats the shit out of me, Moore thought and dropped his eyes again to the calligraphs.

"The context is in . . ." he said.

"In Japanese," Hon interrupted him.

". . . reference to a shortage of shipping," Moore finished, in Japanese.

"Is it?"

"Homma's message to—What did you say, 'Eye-Jag-Ess'?—said that the food he captured from us was inadequate to feed the prisoners," Moore said. He had in his sudden excitement switched back to English. Hon did not correct him.

"And?"

"IJAGS's reply was that there was a shortage of shipping, and then reminded Homma of the Code of Bushido."

"Right. And how, if you know, does the Code of Bushido regard warriors who surrender?"

"It's shameful," Moore said. "Disgraceful. A failure of duty. More than that, there's a religious connotation. Since the Emperor is God, it's a great sin."

"Meaning what, in this context?"

Moore thought that over, and horrified, blurted, "Jesus, meaning, 'fuck the prisoners, they're beneath contempt, let them starve'?"

"That's how I read it," Hon said. "You did notice that there was just a hint of sensitivity to Western concepts of how prisoners should be treated—the Geneva Convention, so to speak—the reference to the shortage of shipping, which IJAGS uses to rationalize not shipping food?"

"My God!"

"Why are you surprised?" Hon asked. "You grew up there."

Moore's mind was now racing.

"I still can't accept this," he said. "Jesus Christ, can't we complain to the International Red Cross or somebody? Maybe they'd arrange to let us send food."

"We cannot complain to anybody," Hon said.

"Why not?"

"We cannot complain to anybody," Hon repeated. "And stop that line of inquiry."

"We have their goddamn messages," Moore plunged on. "Why the hell not?"

Hon held up both hands, palms out, to shut Moore up.

"In about ten seconds, that will occur to you. And in ten seconds, Major Banning's warning to you will move from the realm of the hypothetical to cold, cruel reality."

Moore looked at him, confusion all over his face. And then, in five seconds, not ten, he understood.

"We've broken their code, haven't we? That was a coded message, and we intercepted it and decoded it, right?"

"Since I didn't hear the question, Sergeant Moore—If I had, I would have to inform Major Banning—I obviously can't answer it."

"Jesus!" Moore exhaled.

"Apropos of nothing whatever, the correct phraseology is 'encrypted' and 'decrypted,' " Hon said. "The root word is 'crypt,' variously defined as 'burial'; 'catacomb'; 'sepulcher'; 'tomb'; and 'vault.' "

"And they don't know we can do that, do they?" Moore asked, more rhetorically than anything else.

"I hope you're about to get your mouth under control, Sergeant Moore," Hon said, "because I feel my memory is returning."

Moore exhaled audibly.

"Jesus Christ!" he said.

"Yeah," Hon said. "OK, Sergeant, we will now proceed to Lesson Two in Pluto Hon's Berlitz in the Basement School of Languages. Just one more thing, apropos again of nothing whatever. There is a security classification called TOP SECRET-MAGIC. There are four people in this headquarters with access to TOP SECRET-MAGIC material: General MacArthur, his G-2, Colonel Charles A. Willoughby, Captain Fleming Pickering, and me. You will not, repeat, not have access to TOP SECRET-MAGIC. I mention it only because if anyone other than the people I just mentioned ever even mentions MAGIC to you, you will instantly tell me or Captain Pickering. Clear?"

What I just read is MAGIC. *There's no question about that.*

"Yes, Sir."

Hon met his eyes for a moment, and then nodded.

"Lesson Two deals with administrative procedures," Hon said. "If you look under the table, you will find a wastebasket. In the wastebasket is a paper bag. The bag is stamped TOP SECRET-BURN in large letters. It is intended for TOP SECRET material that is to be burned. TOP SECRET material includes this lined pad you have been writing on. Not just the pages you wrote on, but the whole pad, because your pencil made impressions on pages underneath the top one. Clear?"

"Yes, Sir."

"I'm about to give you a key to the dungeon and the combination to one of the file drawers. You will memorize the combination. When you come to work here—which will be at any hour something comes in—if I'm not here, you will find that material in your drawer. You will make your translation—one copy only—and when you leave, you will put that in your drawer with the original material and make sure it is locked. Then you will take your notes, if you made any, or if you have written on a pad, anything at all, put them in the burn bag, and, accompanied by one of the guards, take it to an incinerator and burn it. You'll find a supply of burn bags in your drawer. Clear?"

"Yes, Sir."

"You will not, repeat not, burn anything that I give you."

"Yes, Sir."

"You will not take anything from this room, except burn bag material in a burn bag, unless specifically directed to do so by either Captain Pickering or myself."

"Yes, Sir."

"The people around here have been told that you are a cryptographic clerk-typist. If anyone, *anyone,* ever asks you what you're really doing in here, you will tell me instantly. If I'm not available, find Captain Pickering and tell him."

"Yes, Sir."

"To my considerable surprise, when I went to scrounge a typewriter, I managed to get two. I carried one down here. When you are doing MAGIC . . . Shit!" Hon stopped abruptly, and then continued, "When you use the typewriter to do translations for me, you will use a ribbon reserved for that purpose and kept in your file drawer. When that wears out, you will dispose of it via the burn bag. But you will not leave the ribbon in the typewriter when you leave the room . . . even to take a leak. Clear?"

"Yes, Sir."

Lieutenant Hon handed him a large key.

"Wear this on your dog tag chain," he said. "And for Christ's sake, don't lose it."

"No, Sir."

"OK. Go get the typewriter outside, and the box of ribbons, and bring them in here. Then we'll show you the incinerator, and the procedure to burn things. And finally, we'll get the other typewriter, before the supply officer changes his mind, and lock it in the car."

The phone was ringing.

Moore left his—mostly failed—love letter and walked across the library to the telephone.

"Sergeant Moore, Sir."

"Major Banning, Sergeant. I understand you have the car out there?"

"Yes, Sir."

"Is there any reason you could not drive to the airport and pick up some people, and then run past the Menzies and pick me up?"

"No, Sir."

"There'll be two Marine officers waiting for you. A Colonel Goettge and a Major Dillon. Can you leave right now?"

"As soon as I hang up, Sir."

"I'll be waiting in front," Banning said and hung up.

Moore went back to the typewriter, pulled his letter to his beloved from it, read it with very little satisfaction, and started to tear it up. Then he changed his mind.

He laid the letter on the table, took a pen, and wrote, "Duty calls. I have to run. I love you more than life itself."

He addressed an envelope, wrote "free" where a stamp would normally be placed, stuffed the letter in it, and put it in his pocket. There was an Army Post Office Box at the airfield. He would mail the letter to Barbara first and then go pick up the officers.

As he drove the Studebaker to the airport, he thought that "I love you more than life itself" was a pretty well-turned phrase and was sort of pleased that Major Banning's call had rescued him from more time at the typewriter.

(Two)
**SUPREME HEADQUARTERS, SOUTHWEST PACIFIC
HOTEL MENZIES
MELBOURNE, VICTORIA, AUSTRALIA
1600 HOURS 1 JULY 1942**

When Lieutenant Pluto Hon heard the key turning in the
steel door, he quickly covered what he was working on with
its TOP SECRET cover sheet and stood up. There were only
three people with a key to the room, and he had told Sergeant
John Marston Moore to stay at The Elms until he sent for
him. Ergo, whoever was unlocking the door had to be
Captain Fleming Pickering, USNR.

"How are you, Pluto?" Pickering greeted him with a smile.
"What can I do for you?"

"Sir, I just asked your clerk to let me know when you had
a free minute. You didn't have to come down here."

"So she said," Pickering said. "What's up?"

"Well, first, did Major Banning get to you?"

"About tonight?"

"Yes, Sir."

"Yes, he did. And you're invited, too, of course. Is that
what you wanted to ask?"

"No, Sir," Hon said, and then with obvious reluctance he
plunged ahead: "Sir, I'm sorry I let my mouth run away from
me and asked you for Sergeant Moore."

"Oh? How come?"

"Sir, and it's obviously my fault, it's already gotten out of
hand."

"How?" Pickering asked evenly. Hon felt the normal
warmth leave Pickering's eyes.

"Sir, he's already guessed that what I gave him to analyze
was an intercept."

"Guessed?"

"I suppose 'deduced' would be a better word."

"How was his analysis?" Pickering asked.

Hon hesitated.

"Well?" Pickering asked, impatiently.

"Sir, what popped into my mind sounds flippant. And I
realize this is not the place to sound flippant."

"What popped into your mind?"

" 'The true test of a man's intelligence is how much he agrees with you,' " Pluto quoted. "I gave him the MAGIC intercept from Homma to IJAGS, and the reply about prisoner rations in the Philippines."

"Refresh my mind?"

"The one Pearl Harbor thought was a reprimand to Homma, and wondered what about."

"And the one you thought meant, 'prisoners have no right to eat'?"

"Yes, Sir."

"And he agreed with you?"

"Yes, Sir. I had to prompt him a little. But just a little. I didn't give him any . . ."

"I'm sure you didn't," Pickering said. "And he went from that to figure out where it came from?"

"Yes, Sir. I probably handled that badly. I'm very sorry, Sir. I decided I had better tell you."

"Yeah, sure," Pickering said. He reached inside his uniform jacket and came out with a cigar case. He took a long time removing a narrow, black cigar; he then carefully trimmed it with a pocket knife and lit it with a wooden match.

Finally, he exhaled through pursed lips, examined the coal at the end, and said, "We both—me especially—should have seen that coming. Now that I really think about it, it was inevitable. OK. So where does that leave us? Worst possible scenario: What's the greatest damage?"

Pickering paused, not long enough for Pluto to respond, and then answered his own question. "We have added one more man to the loop. I mean the cryptographers at Pearl and here. They know about the existence of MAGIC. So now Moore does too. The only difference between him and them is that he is now analyzing instead of decrypting. They don't have to know that. We won't tell Pearl Harbor . . . we won't volunteer the information, in other words. If we did they would shit a brick. If they find out, I'll take the heat. I'll tell them I ordered you to bring him in on this. I'll say I did so because it occurred to me that if you were unavailable, broke your leg or something, I would need an analyst. That's true, come to think about it."

"Yes, Sir," Pluto said uneasily.

"In for a penny, Pluto, in for a pound," Pickering said. "I'll tell Banning what *I've* done, and tell him to bring Moore in on anything he thinks Moore should know. As far as Moore is concerned, just let things go as they are. As far as you're concerned," he paused and smiled, "since we now have proof positive that he's highly intelligent, just put him to work. To coin a phrase, two minds are better than one."

"Yes, Sir," Hon said.

(*Three*)
THE ELMS
DANDENONG, VICTORIA, AUSTRALIA
1805 HOURS 1 JULY 1942

Sergeant John Marston Moore helped Mr. Cavendish carry Colonel Goettge's and Major Dillon's luggage to their rooms, and then went to his. Obviously, a sergeant was out of place with visiting brass hats, even under the strange circumstances he was now in.

When I get hungry, he decided, *I'll go down the back stairs and see what there is to eat in the refrigerator.*

He had just taken his shoes off and settled himself on the bed when there was a knock at the door.

They probably want me to drive somebody somewhere— maybe go get Captain Pickering or Lieutenant Hon—or maybe serve drinks.

It was Major Banning.

"Yes, Sir?"

"Come with me," Banning said. "I want to show you something. Save your questions until I tell you."

"Aye, aye, Sir. Give me a moment to get my shoes on."

He followed Banning down the back stairs to the kitchen, and then to a small room off the kitchen he had not known existed.

It was not much larger than a closet, and it held a small table with a lamp on it and a simple cushioned chair. Banning put his finger over his lips, ordering silence, and then pointed to foot-square ducts in the walls. Moore realized first that the other end of one of the ducts opened into the library, and then he remembered seeing it when he had been browsing

among the books. It had been hardly visible among the books.
He remembered that there was another duct in the dining
room.

Banning touched his ear and pointed toward the duct
opening on the library. Moore realized that he could hear,
faintly, but clearly, Major Dillon talking to Colonel Goettge
about Captain Pickering's estate in San Francisco. Obviously,
anything said in the library and dining room could be heard
in the small room.

Banning signaled that they should leave the room, and
when they had done so, he closed the door after them. He
went to a coffee pot, helped himself, and then leaned against
a work table under a large rack of pots and pans.

"I think that's where the butler sat," Banning said. "So
he could hear when the lord of the manor needed more ice
or when it was time to serve dessert."

"Interesting," Moore said.

"When you sit in there and listen, you're probably going
to hear all sorts of interesting things."

The notion of eavesdropping on people, especially on
Captain Pickering, made Moore uncomfortable.

"Sir?"

"I want you—as a matter-of-fact, Captain Pickering wants
you—to sit in there and listen."

"Aye, aye, Sir."

"Put your trench coat away," Banning said, laughing.
"This is not high level espionage. You made quite an
impression on Pluto—Lieutenant Hon. He told Captain
Pickering he thought you have a good analytical mind and
that with your knowledge of how the Japanese think and
behave, you were probably going to be damned useful.
Obviously, the more you know, the more useful you will be.
There will be things discussed in there tonight that you
should know, and which would not be discussed if you were
in there, even serving drinks, which was my original idea.
Understand? Or would you rather pass canapes?"

"No, Sir," Moore said with a chuckle.

"There are certain things you should keep in mind,"
Banning said. "Priorities, primarily. And something you
should always have in the back of your mind when you're
involved with intelligence: Who knows what, and who isn't

supposed to know what. You work for Captain Pickering.
Or you work for P1—Lieutenant Hon, which is saying the
same thing. Captain Pickering's interests are therefore your
highest priority. Captain Pickering is here as the Secretary
of the Navy's personal representative. That means he is
authorized access to any information the Navy has. He has
also become quite close to General MacArthur, who has
given him access to everything in Supreme Headquarters. If
you think that through, you'll understand that there's
damned little he does not know.

"I don't know—it's none of my business—what
information he's been getting from the Secretary of the Navy,
or how much of that, if any, he is authorized to pass on to
General MacArthur. Or—frankly—since he has apparently
decided MacArthur is right and Admiral King is wrong, how
much he has passed on to MacArthur without being
specifically authorized to do so.

"Colonel Willoughby, who is MacArthur's intelligence
officer, will be here in a little while. He is not authorized to
know what Pickering may or may not have told MacArthur,
but what MacArthur has decided to tell him anyway will be
interesting.

"And finally, Colonel Goettge: He is obviously not privy
to what either Pickering knows or what MacArthur knows.
He has no Need to Know, for one thing, and for another,
in a sense, at least as far as MacArthur and Willoughby are
concerned, he's the enemy. The First Marine Division is
under COMSOPAC . . ."

"Excuse me?"

"COMSOPAC. Commander, Southern Pacific—Admiral
Ghormley. And Admiral Ghormley is under Admiral
Nimitz. Admiral Nimitz is the senior Naval officer in the
Pacific and is thus MacArthur's opposite number. There are
two wars out here: between us and the Japanese, and between
the Army and the Navy to see who fights the war, and where
it is fought, and how."

Banning could see in Moore's face that the kid was both
a little stunned by what he'd just been told and was
suppressing only with an effort the urge to ask questions.

"And there is one more thing," Banning said, somewhat
reluctantly. He was a good officer, and good officers do not

criticize second lieutenants, much less lieutenant colonels, before enlisted men. But this was the inevitable exception that proved the rule. It had to be done.

"There are intelligence officers and intelligence officers," Banning went on. "Colonel Goettge is very good at what he does—Division Intelligence Officer. What that means is that he advises the Division Commander of his assessment of enemy capabilities and intentions, based on what information he has been given, and what he's been able to develop himself, say from prisoner interrogation, that sort of thing.

"But he has not been trained in, and has no experience with, the kind of—I guess the word is 'strategic'— intelligence that we're dealing with here . . ."

He stopped when he saw confusion clouding Moore's eyes. He realized that he'd been beating around the bush; this was not the place to be doing that.

"To put a point on it, Moore," he said. "In my opinion, Colonel Goettge is not as good an intelligence officer as he thinks he is . . . nor as knowledgeable, nor for that matter as bright. Keep that in mind."

"Yes, Sir," Moore said. Astonishment was all over his face. He never imagined he'd hear an officer say such a thing about another officer.

"Question?" Banning asked. "Questions?"

"Several hundred," Moore said.

"But one in particular?"

"Why am I being told all this?" Moore asked, and then remembered to append, "Sir?"

" 'In for a penny, in for a pound,' " Banning quoted Pickering. "You're now part of the team, Sergeant. In Captain Pickering's judgment, since you have been made aware of the price of a loose mouth, it makes more sense to bring you in on anything and everything that will help you do your job—which you now know is analysis of intercepted enemy messages—than it would be to make a decision every time something came up whether or not you should be told about it."

"I see," Moore said thoughtfully.

"Just one more thing: You are never, under any circumstances, to tell anyone that you have been given access to MAGIC."

"Aye, aye, Sir."

(Four)

Even after all that Major Banning had explained to him in the kitchen earlier, Moore sat for a long time in the butler's cubicle listening to the conversation in the library before he even began to understand what was going on. But finally, it began slowly to make sense:

In about a month the 1st Marine Division would invade several islands in the Solomons. Colonel Goettge, who was the Intelligence Officer of the 1st Marines, had very little intelligence information, maps or anything else, that the Division would need in order to launch the invasion. So he was understandably desperate for whatever information he could get. He'd come to Melbourne after Major Dillon told him that he and Captain Pickering were old friends, and that Pickering could be prevailed upon to use his influence at MacArthur's SHSWPA (Supreme Headquarters, South West Pacific Area).

That wasn't all Moore learned that evening. There were fireworks too.

"Hell, it's all over Washington, Flem, that you and Dugout Doug are asshole buddies," Major Dillon said at one point.

And Captain Pickering jumped all over Major Dillon almost before the words were out of Dillon's mouth.

If Captain Pickering's furious defense of MacArthur's brains and personal courage and his outrage that Major Dillon would dare call him "Dugout Doug" was not so intense, actually frightening, the ass-chewing he gave Dillon would have been funny. Moore was almost pleased to learn that the dignified Naval officer who was now his boss had a completely unsuspected flair for obscenely colorful phraseology. It would have been the envy of any Parris Island Drill Sergeant. Among other things—and there were *many* other things—he told Major Dillon that he wouldn't make a pimple on a real Marine's ass.

But the ass-chewing he gave to Major Dillon was frightening . . . so frightening that at one point Colonel Goettge even tried to apologize and leave.

Probably, Moore decided, because he didn't want to risk exacerbating the already hostile relations between SHSWPA and the Navy, which of course included the Marines.

"No, Colonel, you stay," Captain Pickering told him. "I certainly don't hold you responsible for Diarrhea Mouth here. Let's have another drink to calm down, and then try to figure out how to help the 1st Division."

Five more people came in the library before they all went in for dinner: Colonel Willoughby, who spoke—Moore noted—with a faint German accent and who was introduced as the SHSWPA G-2; then two women, a U.S. Navy Nurse and some kind of Australian Navy enlisted woman; and finally two Australian Navy Officers.

One of them was introduced as "Commander Feldt."

"Commander Feldt, Colonel," Pickering explained to Goettge, "commands the Royal Australian Navy Coastwatcher Establishment."

Moore tried to get a look at Commander Feldt through the duct, but was unable to see him. He decided that the other Australian officer worked for Feldt, or with him anyhow.

The women baffled him for a long time; but from what was said, he eventually understood that they were the girlfriends of two Marines who were off on some island with the Coastwatchers. And that answer raised another fascinating question: What were these women doing at a dinner where all sorts of classified information was being discussed?

The answer to that, when he finally thought of it, was quite simple. Captain Pickering decided who could be told what. In this case, obviously, he had decided that these two women—who were in uniform themselves and whose men were off on a secret mission—could be trusted to keep their mouths shut about that mission, and for that matter, about anything else.

Proof of that came a little later, just before they went into dinner and the women went to "powder their noses."

"Nice girls," Colonel Willoughby said approvingly.

"*Women,* Colonel," Commander Feldt corrected him, somewhat nastily. "Daphne has already lost one man, her husband, to this sodding war."

"He was a Coastwatcher?"

"No," Feldt answered. "He was a sergeant in the sodding

Royal Signals. Our sodding politicians sent most of our men to sodding Africa, which is where he caught it."

He paused, apparently having seen something on Willoughby's face. "Did that remark offend you, Colonel?"

By now Moore was convinced that Feldt was more than a little drunk.

"No, of course not," Willoughby replied, somewhat unconvincingly.

"I was thinking of a conversation I had yesterday with Banning," Feldt went on, "as I watched her walk out of here just now."

"Oh?" Willoughby asked uneasily.

"He asked me what I thought the chances were of getting them back alive—Banning's men on Buka, Lieutenant Howard and Sergeant Koffler, who has been comforting the widow Farnsworth in her grief. I told him the truth: From slim to sodding none."

"Is it that low?" Willoughby asked.

"Commander Feldt underestimates the Marine Corps," Major Banning said, trying to temper Feldt's bitterness.

"Sod you, Banning," Feldt said cheerfully. "What I was thinking, Colonel, was that it is a bit much to ask of a pretty young *woman* like Yeoman Farnsworth to lose two men to this sodding war."

"I think they'll come back," Pickering said. "They are both very resourceful young men."

"I think we had better change the subject," Banning said. "They're liable to walk in here any moment."

"They wouldn't hear a sodding thing they haven't sodding well thought of at least once a sodding day themselves," Feldt said. "What the hell are they doing here anyway? Whose brilliant sodding idea was that?"

"Mine, actually," Pickering said.

Feldt snorted. "Until just now, Pickering, when you said that, I was beginning to believe I had finally met one American who really had enough brains to pour piss out of a sodding boot."

"Banning suggested that the company of a pretty woman just possibly might put you in a mellow frame of mind," Pickering said.

"Shit!" Feldt said. "Why? Banning, you bastard, what do you want from me?"

The women came back in the room. There was an awkward silence, and then Feldt said, "Major Banning was about to tell me what he wants from me."

"A dozen Coastwatchers to be attached to the 1st Marine Division," Banning said.

"That's a marvelous idea," Colonel Goettge said enthusiastically. Moore sensed that it was the first time he had heard of the idea.

"What for?" Feldt asked.

"Captain Pickering and I think they could be very helpful to Colonel Goettge," Banning said. "Dealing with the natives, among other things. Colonel Goettge doesn't speak Pidgin too well."

"I'll bet he sodding well doesn't," Feldt snorted. "From what I've seen, he's living proof of the old saw that 'intelligence officer is a contradiction of terms.'"

"That's quite enough, Feldt," Pickering snapped. "You're in my home, and you owe the colonel an apology."

There was a long, silent moment.

"No offense, Goettge," Feldt said finally. "A little down-under humor."

"No offense taken, Commander," Goettge said.

Neither of them sounded at all sincere.

"Interesting thought, Major," the other Australian officer said, in an obvious attempt to spread oil on the troubled waters.

"Don't encourage Banning, for Christ's sake," Feldt said. "There's no telling what the bastard'll ask for next." He fell silent for a moment, and then said, "OK. I don't know about a dozen. But I can come up with six or eight people."

"Why don't we go in to dinner?" Captain Pickering suggested.

"Are you trying to separate me from the booze, by any chance, Captain?"

"Absolutely not," Pickering replied. "You give us eight Coastwatchers to attach to the 1st Marine Division, and I'll give you all the sodding booze you can sodding well handle."

There was a moment's silence, and then Feldt laughed.

"You're a devious bastard, Pickering," he said. "I like you."

When Major Jake Dillon, more than a little hungover, went down to breakfast, he was surprised to find Fleming Pickering's driver, or orderly, or whatever the hell he was, sitting at the dining room table finishing up what looked like steak and eggs.

Until he had been accused (with justification) of helping himself to the booze, Corporal Jake Dillon of the 4th Marines had once served as an orderly to a captain named Jerold in Shanghai. Corporal Dillon had not eaten steak and eggs at the captain's table. What he ate was leftovers, and he had done that standing up in the kitchen.

Sergeant John Marston Moore started to get to his feet when he saw Dillon.

"Good morning, Sir."

"Keep your seat, Sergeant," Dillon said. "Finish your breakfast."

"I'm just about finished," the kid said. And then he seemed to be stretching his leg under the table. After a moment, Jake understood there was a button on the floor, to summon the help. Proof came a moment later when the door to the kitchen opened and Mrs. Cavendish came out.

"Good morning, Sir," she said. "I hope you slept well."

"Like a drum," Dillon said.

"And what may I get you for breakfast?"

"What the sergeant was eating looks fine, thank you."

"Tea or coffee?"

"Coffee, please."

"Don't drink that," Mrs. Cavendish said to Moore, as he raised his cup toward his lips. "I'll bring you a fresh cup, hot."

She took the cup and saucer from him and went into the kitchen.

"Pretty soft berth, huh?" Dillon said to Moore.

"Sir?"

"I was an orderly once, a long time ago. My officer made me eat in the kitchen." He saw in Moore's face that he had interpreted the remark as a reprimand, and added: "Hey, I don't give a damn where you eat. I told you, I used to be an enlisted man. Hell, I was a sergeant a lot longer than I've been an officer. I was just saying that it looks as if you fell into a pretty soft berth."

"Yes, Sir."

"How long have you been working for Pickering?"

"Not long, Sir."

"Well, don't fuck up, Kid, and get yourself sent down to the 1st Division. They're living in tents, and they are not eating steak and eggs for breakfast."

"Yes, Sir."

Dillon heard the sound of footsteps, turned his head, and saw that Colonel Goettge and Major Banning were coming into the dining room. Moore saw them, too, and started to get up again.

"Good morning," Dillon said. "I told Captain Pickering's orderly to sit down and have a cup of coffee. I hope that's all right, Colonel."

Moore looked at Banning and saw a small smile around his lips and eyes.

"Sure," Colonel Goettge said. "Why not? Good morning, Sergeant. Take your seat."

"Yes, Sir."

Colonel Goettge, Moore thought, *has good reason to be in a good mood. He came here expecting damned little, and he was going to get far more than he could have hoped for.*

Before the evening was over, in addition to the Australians of the Coastwatcher Establishment who were going to be attached to the 1st Marine Division, Colonel Goettge had been offered:

—Intelligence briefings on the Solomon Islands by both the SHSWPA Intelligence Section and the Royal Australian Navy;

—the latest aerial photographs available, Australian and American;

—the latest maps, and in quantities sufficient to equip the

Division. The number of maps required had really surprised Moore;

—permission to send a liaison officer to SHSWPA to ensure that any new intelligence developed would quickly get to the division.

Captain Pickering had been even more obliging about that. When Colonel Goettge admitted that he didn't have an officer of high enough rank to send to Melbourne, Pickering had volunteered to send a radio message to the Secretary of the Navy asking that an officer of suitable rank and experience be flown immediately from the United States.

Captain Pickering walked into the dining room.

"Good morning, gentlemen," he said, as everyone stood up. He walked to the head of the table and sat down. He looked at Moore.

"You look a little beat this morning, Sergeant," he said. "The scuttlebutt is that you were out until the wee hours carousing. Anything to that?"

"No, Sir."

"But you would characterize how you spent last night as interesting?"

"Fascinating, Sir."

Major Dillon snorted. Colonel Goettge smiled tolerantly.

"Well, I hope you can see well enough to drive these gentlemen around town today. They have several errands to run. They'll tell you what they are."

"Aye, aye, Sir."

"But check in every hour or so with Lieutenant Hon, Moore," Pickering said. "I think he may have something he wants you to do."

"Aye, aye, Sir."

"We keep Sergeant Moore pretty busy around here," Pickering said, a smile around his eyes, "with one thing or another."

"Well, whatever you have him doing," Major Dillon said, "it's still a soft berth compared to living in a tent in the mud at Wellington. I just told him, 'don't fuck up, Kid, you've got it made.'"

"You really think so, Jake?" Pickering asked, innocently.

XI

Yeoman Daphne Farnsworth, Royal Australian Navy Women's Volunteer Reserve, walked up to Sergeant John Marston Moore, USMCR. Sergeant Moore was then leaning on the front fender of the Studebaker Commander outside a frame building on a wharf on Port Philip Bay.

Moore recognized her immediately. Last night she was sitting in the dining room directly across from the duct in the butler's cubicle. She had lost her husband in action in Africa, he remembered, and was now a Marine's girl-friend . . . or, in Commander Feldt's words, he was "comforting her in her grief." He also remembered all too clearly what else Commander Feldt said with such bitter cynicism about the Marine, a Sergeant named Koffler now on some Japanese island: His chances of returning alive ranged from "slim to sodding zero."

"Comforting her in her grief" could have meant something sordid. But looking at her the night before, Moore decided she was a nice girl, and that whatever was going on between her and Sergeant Koffler was not cheap.

Looking at her now—just as he realized she had never seen him—the same thing occurred to him again. She was a nice girl, with warm, intelligent eyes. *And damned good-looking.*

"I should be very surprised," she greeted him with a smile, "if you are not Sergeant Moore."

She has a very nice voice.

"Guilty."

"Come with me, Lieutenant Donnelly wants to see you."

"Yes, Ma'am," he said.

She looked at him strangely, and then smiled.

Moore followed her into the building. Lieutenant Donnelly, a tall, sharp-featured, skinny officer with a very pale complexion, and black, unruly hair, had an office on the second floor. Moore recognized Donnelly as the other Australian Navy officer who had been at dinner.

I remember you from last night, but how the hell do you know who I am? And what's this all about, anyway?

"I'm Sergeant Moore, Sir."

"That'll be all, Love," Donnelly said to Yeoman Farnsworth. "Close the door, please."

When the door had closed behind her, Lieutenant Donnelly said, without smiling, "Put your eyes back in their sockets, Sergeant. She already has a Yank Marine sergeant."

Moore looked at him in shock.

"Listen carefully," Lieutenant Donnelly said. "The airfield at Lunga Point is being built by the 11th and 23rd Pioneers, IJN. Estimated strength 450. They are equipped with bulldozers, rock crushers, trucks, and other engineer equipment."

Moore was completely baffled. It showed on his face as he looked at Lieutenant Donnelly.

"What did I just say?" Lieutenant Donnelly asked.

"Something about Pioneers," Moore said lamely, embarrassed.

"Christ!" Donnelly snorted in disgust. He handed Moore a sheet of paper. On it, Moore read what Donnelly had just said. "Try committing that to memory."

Moore read the sheet of paper again. And then again, and again, very uncomfortable under Donnelly's impatient glare. Finally, he said, "I think I have it, Sir."

"Try it," Donnelly said.

Moore repeated what he had memorized.

"Once more, to set it in your head," Donnelly ordered.

Moore repeated it again.

"OK. Repeat that to Major Banning," Donnelly ordered. "Tell him that Commander Feldt said, 'it's as good as gold.' "

" 'It's as good as gold,' " Moore dutifully parroted. "Sir, I don't know when I'm going to see Major Banning."

"You are going to see him right away," Donnelly said. "You get in your car and you go over to the Hotel Menzies, and you repeat to him what you just memorized. And then you forget it, OK? Understand?"

He's talking to me like I'm a backward child. Probably because I am acting like one.

"Sir, I'm driving some American officers around."

"Well, Sergeant, they're just going to have to bloody well wait for you. I'll have Daphne—Daphne being the Yeoman you were ogling—to look out for them and tell them what's happened."

"Aye, aye, Sir," Moore said.

When he got to the Hotel Menzies, Moore realized that he had no idea where to find Major Banning.

Lieutenant Hon will know, he decided. He rode the elevator to the basement and made his way to the steel-doored room.

"I thought you were playing chauffeur?" Hon greeted him.

"I was outside the Australian Navy building when Lieutenant Donnelly sent for me. He gave me a message for Major Banning. Made me memorize it. And then told me to deliver it. I don't know where he is, Sir."

"What's the message?" Hon asked. He saw the look of concern on Moore's face. "Hey, I'm cleared for everything."

"The airfield at Lunga Point is being built by the 11th and 23rd Pioneers, IJN," Moore recited. "Estimated strength 450. They are equipped with bulldozers, rock crushers, trucks, and other engineer equipment."

"Christ!" Hon said, "that's bad news."

"Commander Feldt said 'that's as good as gold,' " Moore added.

Hon looked at Moore thoughtfully. "You don't have the faintest idea what that means, do you?"

"No, Sir."

Hon went to an open file drawer, took from it and unfolded a map of Guadalcanal, and pointed to Lunga Point.

"That's Lunga Point," he said. "We already heard—had aerial photos—that the Japanese had burned the grass off a flat area, a plain, here. Feldt sent Coastwatchers he had on Guadalcanal across the island from here," he pointed, "through the jungle to see what was going on. And now we *know*—Feldt said his information was 'as good as gold'—that the Japanese are making a real effort to build a major airfield there. Pioneers are what we call Engineers. They've got 450 Engineers in there with rock crushers and bulldozers."

"I realize I must sound stupid, but is that really so important?"

"If they can base aircraft there—even fighters, but especially bombers—we're in real trouble. Always keep that airfield in the back of your mind when you're reading the MAGICS. Let me know if anything—*anything*—arouses your curiosity."

"Yes, Sir. Sir, what do I do about getting this to Major Banning?"

"He and Captain Pickering are on their way down here," Hon replied, and then handed Moore a sheet of onion skin. "I just got my hands on this."

OPERATIONAL IMMEDIATE

TOP SECRET
WASH DC 0015G 2JUL42
FROM: THE JOINT CHIEFS OF STAFF
TO: EYES ONLY
ADMIRAL NIMITZ COMPOA PEARLHARBOR
INFORMATION: EYES ONLY
GENERAL MACARTHUR SHSWPA MELBOURNE
VICEADMIRAL GHORMLEY COMSOPAC AUCKLAND
1. NO FURTHER DISCUSSION OF OPERATION PESTILENCE OR ALTERNATIVES THERETO IS DESIRED.
2. DIRECTION OF THE PRESIDENT, EXECUTE OPERATION

PESTILENCE AT THE EARLIEST OPPORTUNITY BUT NO
LATER THAN 10 AUGUST 1942.
FOR THE CHAIRMAN, THE JOINT CHIEFS OF STAFF:
HANNEMAN, MAJGEN, USA, SECRETARY, JCS

"What's 'Operation Pestilence'?" Moore asked, as he
handed the onion skin back.

"The invasion of the Solomon Islands," Hon replied. "Or
three of them, anyway. Tulagi, Gavutu, and Guadalcanal.
Where the Japs are building this airfield. MacArthur and
Ghormley think it's a lousy idea."

The steel door creaked open.

"You should have bolted that," Hon said.

Captain Fleming Pickering and Major Ed Banning came
into the tiny room.

"What was that, Pluto?" Pickering asked.

"Nothing, Sir," Hon said. "This just came in, sir. I thought
you would want to see it right away."

Pickering took the onion skin. His eyebrows rose as he read
it. He handed it to Banning.

"Does General MacArthur have that yet?"

"He and Mrs. MacArthur are having lunch with the Prime
Minister. One of the crypto officers is on his way over there
with it."

Pickering grunted. "What brings you here, Moore?"

"He has a message for me," Banning answered for him.
"Let's have it, Sergeant."

"The airfield at Lunga Point is being built by the 11th and
23rd Pioneers, IJN. Estimated strength 450. They are
equipped with bulldozers, rock crushers, trucks, and other
engineer equipment," Moore recited, and added, "Commander Feldt says 'that's as good as gold.' "

Pickering snorted. "Repeat that, please," he said.

Moore did so.

"What can they accomplish in a month, five weeks?" Pickering asked.

"They can probably have it ready for fighters," Banning
replied. "I don't know about bombers."

"They already have float mounted Zeroes on Tulagi,"
Pickering said thoughtfully. Then he looked at Moore.
"You'd better get back to driving Colonel Goettge around,"

he said. "I don't have to tell you, do I, that Colonel Goettge is not to know about this? Or what you just relayed from Commander Feldt?"

"No, Sir," Moore said. He started to walk out of the room.

"Moore!" Banning called, and Moore turned. Banning held out a thin stack of envelopes to him. "Mail call. It came in on this morning's courier."

"Thank you, Sir."

In the elevator en route to the lobby, Moore thumbed through the half dozen envelopes. There were two letters from his mother; one each from his two sisters; one from Uncle Bill; and one with the return address, Apartment "C", 106 Rittenhouse Square, Philadelphia, Pennsylvania.

His heart jumped. He resisted the temptation to tear Barbara's letter open right there.

I'll save it until I'm alone.

He raised it to his nose and thought he could smell, ever so faintly, Barbara's perfume and then he put the letters in the inside pocket of his uniform jacket.

He walked out of the Menzies Hotel, got in the Studebaker, and drove back to where he was supposed to be waiting for Colonel Goettge and Major Dillon.

They were outside, waiting for him, and Colonel Goettge was visibly annoyed that he had been kept waiting.

"Sergeant," Goettge said, somewhat snappishly, "I thought that you were aware I have a luncheon appointment with Colonel Willoughby."

"Sorry, Sir," Moore said. "I had to do something for Major Banning."

"So we have been informed," Goettge said, as he got in the car. Moore closed the door after him and drove back to the Menzies Hotel.

"Don't disappear again without letting me know," Colonel Goettge said, as Moore held the rear door open for him.

"No, Sir," Moore said.

Moore watched the two of them disappear into the lobby and then took the stack of envelopes from his pocket. He was hungry and knew that he should try to eat, but that could wait.

He carefully opened the letter from Barbara, sniffing it

again for a smell of her perfume, and then unfolded it. It was brief and to the point:

Philadelphia, June 23, 1942

Dear John,
    There is no easy way to break this to you, so here goes: My husband and I have reconciled.
    I'm sure, when you think about it, that you will realize this is the best thing for all concerned. And I'm sure you will understand why I have to ask you not to write to me.
    You will be in my prayers, and I will never forget you.

Barbara.

He felt a chill. He read the letter again, then very deliberately took his Zippo from his pocket and set the letter on fire, holding it by one corner until it became too hot, and then dropping it on the floorboard, wondering, but not caring, if it was going to set the carpet on fire.

Then he banged his head on the steering wheel until the tears came.

(Two)
AOTEA QUAY
WELLINGTON, NEW ZEALAND
5 JULY 1942

It was cold, windy, and raining hard on the Quay, and Major Jake Dillon's allegedly rainproof raincoat was soaked through.

What he faced, he thought more than a little bitterly, was one hell of a challenge for a flack. Even a flack like him . . . The *Hollywood Reporter* had once run a story about the gang that showed up every Saturday at Darryl Zanuck's polo field. The cut line under a picture of Jake Dillon and Clark Gable on their ponies read, "The King of the Movies and the King of the Flacks Playing the Sport of Kings."

For once, Jake Dillon thought at the time, the *Reporter* had stuck pretty close to the facts. He hoped there was still

some truth in the line about him . . . The King of Flacks
would need every bit of his royal Hollywood experience if
he was going to make a success of what he had in mind to
do:

He was going to put together a little movie about the Marine invasion of Bukavu, Tulagi, and Guadalcanal. He'd
made the decision solely on his own authority; nothing about
it was put on paper; and he didn't tell anyone about it except
his cameramen.

His film would come in addition to the footage the combat
cameramen shot when the invasion was actually in progress.
As soon as possible, that would be sent undeveloped to Washington, where somebody else would soup it, screen it, and do
whatever they decided to do with it, passing it out to the
newsreel companies and whatever.

What Jake Dillon had in mind was to have his people shoot
newsreel feature stuff—as opposed to hard news. The empha-
sis would be on the ordinary enlisted Marine. They'd follow
the 1st Division as the Division prepared to go to the Solomons, and then of course, they'd be with them when they got
there.

He had a number of scenes in mind. Training shots, primarily. Life in tent city here in New Zealand. Life in the transports en route to the rehearsal in the Fiji Islands, and then
as they sailed for the Solomons, and then after they landed.
Human interest stuff.

In point of actual fact, it would be the first movie that he
had ever produced. But he had been around the industry for
a long time and knew what had to be done and how to do
it. The idea was not intimidating; God only knew how many
successful movies had been produced by ignoramuses who
couldn't find their own asses with both hands without the assistance of a script, a continuity girl, and two or three assistant directors to put chalk marks on it for them.

He learned early on in Hollywood that a good crew makes
all the difference when you are shooting a movie. If you have
a crew who know what they are doing, all you have to do
is tell them what you want, and they do it. And even if it
was a damned small one, he had a good crew here with him.

They understood what he wanted to do; and, just as important, they thought it was a pretty good idea.

That meant, for example, that he could tell them that he wanted to show equipment being off-loaded from transports, and they would go shoot it for him. He didn't have to stand around with a script and a megaphone in his hand, yelling at somebody to get a tight shot of the sweating guy driving the truck. His people made movies for a living; they knew what was needed, and how to get it.

As Dillon walked down the Quay, he thought, *If I was making a movie called "The Greatest Fuck-Up Of All Time," I could finish principal photography this morning right here on this goddamned dock.*

Jake Dillon had seen some monumental screw-ups in his time, but this took the goddamned cake: The ships carrying the supplies of the 1st Marine Division had not been "combat-loaded" when they sailed from the United States. That meant they all had to be reloaded here, since they could not approach the hostile Solomon Island beaches the way they were originally loaded.

The term "combat-loaded" refers to a deceptively simple concept: Logisticians and staff officers spend long hours determining what equipment will be needed during the course of an invasion, and in what order.

As a general rule of thumb, the ships carrying the invasion force would have in their holds supplies for thirty days' operations. Adequate stocks of ammunition, obviously, had to be put on the beach before the chaplain's portable organ, or the Division's mimeograph machines. But the barges and small boats ferrying supplies from the ships to the beach would be a narrow pipeline. Thus it would not be prudent to fill that pipeline with ammunition and nothing else. For other supplies were no less vital: The men had to eat, for example; so there had to be rations in the pipeline. And all the complex machinery on the beach needed its sustenance too—what the services call POL (Petrol, Oil, and Lubricants). And so on.

When the obvious priorities had been determined, then the loading order was fine tuned. This wasn't simply a case of saying off-load so much ammunition, then so many rations, then so many barrels of POL, and repeating the process until all the important supplies are ashore, after which you could off-load the nonessentials, like typewriters.

For example, while a radio operator receiving messages intended for the Division Commander could take them down by hand, he would be far more efficient in terms of speed and legibility using a typewriter. So, while a typewriter might not seem to be as necessary in the early stages of an invasion as, say, a case of hand grenades, at least one typewriter would head for the beach early on, probably with the first ammunition and rations supplied.

When all the priorities had been established and fine tuned, the ships of the invasion force were ready to be "combat-loaded." This followed the logic of "Last On, First Off": Once The Division was on the Solomon Islands beaches, the supplies needed first would be loaded on last.

Doing this was proving far more difficult than it sounded—the combat-loading planning for an amphibious invasion has been described as a chess game that cannot be won.

One major problem the 1st Marine planners faced—though it was by no means their *only* major problem—was that since the ships were not originally combat-loaded back in the States, the supplies had to be removed from the holds of the ships and sorted out before they could be reloaded.

This problem was compounded by the Wellington Longshoreman's Union, which had very strong views about how ships should be unloaded and loaded; and by whom; and on what days during what daylight hours. They had come to an understanding with management regarding the role of longshoremen in the scheme of things only after long hours on the picket line and extensive negotiations over many years. They had no intention of giving up these hard earned prerequisites for anything as insignificant as a war with the Japanese Empire.

The Americans solved the labor problem by using a cut-the-Gordian-knot approach: American Marines were unloading the ships around the clock, seven days a week. At the same time, they let it be known that armed Marines were posted at various spots around the Quay, with orders to shoot at anyone or anything interfering with unloading and loading of the ships.

Jake hoped the threat would suffice. While it wouldn't have bothered him at all if half the longshoremen in Wellington got shot between the eyes, the flack in him was concerned with how "MARINES MASSACRE THIRTY NEW ZEA-

LAND LONGSHOREMEN IN LABOR DISPUTE" head-lines would play in the papers in the States.

Technically, it was not his problem, since he was not the PIO for the 1st Marine Division. But he was over here to "co-ordinate public information activities," and he suspected that if there was lousy publicity, he would get the blame.

While the supplies were being off-loaded for sorting, an-other major problem had come up: There was no way to shel-ter the off-loaded supplies from the dismal New Zealand July winter weather (the seasons were reversed down under). It was raining almost constantly.

For openers, the supplies for the First Marine Division—not only rations but just about everything else, too—were ci-vilian stuff. The quart-size cans of tomatoes, for example, had been bought from the Ajax Canned Tomato Company, or somesuch. These cans had been labelled and packed with the idea in mind that they would wind up on the shelves of the "Super-Dooper Super-Market" in Olathe, Kansas. They had paper labels with pictures of pretty tomatoes attached to the metal with a couple of drops of cheap glue. There were six cans to a corrugated paper carton. The carton was held to-gether with glue; and a can label was glued to the ends.

As soon as the cases were off-loaded from the cargo holds of the ships onto Aotea Quay and stacked neatly so they could be sorted, the rain started falling on them. Soon the cheap glue which held the corrugated paper cartons together dissolved. That caused the cartons to come apart. Not long after that, instead of neatly stacked cartons of tomato cans, there were piles of tomato cans mingled with a sludge of wa-terlogged corrugated paper that had once been cartons.

And then the rain saturated the paper labels and dissolved the cheap glue that held them on the cans . . .

The people in charge of the operation had put a good deal of thought and effort into finding a solution to the problem. But the best they had come up with so far was to cover some of the stacks of cartons with tarpaulins; and when the supply of tarpaulins ran out, with canvas tentage; and when the tent-age ran out, with individual shelter-halves. (Each Marine was issued a small piece of tentage. When buttoned to an identical piece, it formed a small, two-man tent. Hence, "individual shelter-half.")

As he walked down the Quay, Jake Dillon saw this wasn't going to work: There were gaps around the bases of the tarpaulin-covered stacks. The wind blew the rain through the gaps, and then the natural capillary action of the paper in the corrugated paper cartons soaked it up like a blotter. Moisture reached the glue, and the glue dissolved. The cartons collapsed, and then the stacks of cartons.

Major Jake Dillon found Major Jack NMI Stecker standing behind the serving line in a mess fly tent—essentially a wall-less tent erected over field stoves. A line of Marines was passing through the fly tent, their mess kits in their hands. As soon as they left the fly tent, rain fell on their pork chops and mashed potatoes and green beans.

It was the first time in Dillon's memory that he had ever seen Jack Stecker looking like something the cat had dragged in. He looked as bedraggled as any of his men. In China with the 4th Marines, Master Gunnery Sergeant Jack Stecker used to come off a thirty-mile hike through the mud of the Chinese countryside looking as if he was prepared to stand a formal honor guard.

He walked up and stood beside him.

"Lovely weather we're having, isn't it?" Dillon said.

"There's coffee, if you want some," Stecker replied, and then walked a few feet away; he returned with a canteen cup and gave it to Dillon.

Dillon walked to the coffee pot at the end of the serving line and waited until the KP ladling out coffee sensed someone standing behind him, looked, and then offered his ladle.

The coffee was near boiling; Dillon could feel the heat even in the handle of the cup. If he tried to take a sip, he would give his lip a painful burn. This was not the first time he had stood in a rain-soaked uniform drinking burning-hot coffee from a canteen cup.

But the last time, he thought, *was a long goddamned time ago.*

"What brings a feather merchant like you out with the real Marines?" Stecker asked.

"I'm making a movie, what else?"

Stecker looked at him.

"Really? Of this?"

"What I need, Jack, is film that will inspire the red-blooded

youth of America to rush to the recruiting station," Dillon
said. "You think this might do it?"

Stecker laughed.

"Seriously, what are your people doing?"

Dillon told him about the movie he had in mind.

"I suppose it's necessary," Stecker said.

"I'd rather be one of your staff sergeants, Jack," Dillon
said. "I was a pretty good staff sergeant. But that's not the
way things turned out."

"You were probably the worst staff sergeant in the 4th Marines," Stecker said, smiling, "to set the record straight. I let
you keep your stripes only so I could take your pay away at
poker."

"Well, fuck you!"

They smiled at each other, then Stecker said bitterly: "I'd
like to make the bastards who sent us this mess, packed this
way, see your movie."

"They will. What my guys are shooting—or a copy of it,
a rough cut—will leave here for Washington on tomorrow's
courier plane."

"No kidding?"

"Personal from Vandergrift to the Commandant," Dillon
said.

"Somehow I don't think that was the General's own idea."

"No. But Lucky Lew Harris thought it was fine when I
suggested it."

Stecker chuckled. "I guess that explains it."

"Explains what?"

"I saw General Harris for a moment this morning,"
Stecker said. "I asked him how things went when you took
Goettge to Australia. He said, 'very well. I'm beginning to
think that maybe your pal Dillon might be useful after all.
He's really not as dumb as he looks.'"

"Christ, I better go buy a bigger hat," Dillon said. "How
much did he tell you about what's going on?"

"You mean about the airfield the Japs are building?"

Dillon nodded.

"That we better go try to stop them, whether we're ready
or not."

"And we're not ready, right?"

Stecker waved his hand up and down the Quay.

"What do you think?"

"Well, there'll at least be the rehearsal in the Fiji Islands."

"And because we're not even prepared for a rehearsal, that will be fucked up. And we'll go nevertheless."

"What's going to happen, Jack?"

"You know what the Coast Guard motto is?"

" *'Semper Paratus'?*" Dillon asked, confused.

"No. Not that one, anyhow. What the Coast Guard says when a ship is in trouble. They have to go out. Nothing's said about having to come back."

"You think it's that bad?"

"Even after Wake Island and what happened to the 4th Marines in the Philippines, half the people in the Division think the Japs are all five foot two, wear thick glasses, and will turn tail and run once they see a real Marine. Not only the kids. A lot of the officers, who should know better, think this is going to be Nicaragua all over again."

"Jesus, you really mean that?"

"Yeah, but for Christ's sake, don't tell anybody I said so."

"Of course not," Dillon said.

"Are you going to go?"

"Sure, of course."

"You're not going to inspire . . . what did you say, 'red-blooded American youth'? . . . to rush to the recruiting station with movies of dead Marines floating around in the surf."

Dillon didn't reply for a moment. Then he said, "Straight answer, Jack: I'm not going to show them movies of dead Marines. I'm going to find me a couple, maybe three, four, good-looking Marines who get themselves lightly wounded, like in the movies, a shoulder wound . . ."

"A shoulder wound is one of the worst kinds, nearly as bad as the belly, you know that."

"I know that, you know that, civilians don't know that," Dillon replied. ". . . and maybe have a medal to go with it" he went on, taking the thought forward. "Then I'm going to bring them to the States and send them on a tour with movie stars. People will be inspired to buy War Bonds. Red-blooded American youth will rush to Marine recruiting stations."

Stecker turned to look at Dillon, who saw the contempt in his eyes.

"Most heroes I've known are as ugly as sin and would lose no time grabbing one of your movie stars on the ass," Stecker said. "What are you going to do about that?"

"Present company included, I suppose," Dillon said. It was a reference to Stecker's World War I Medal of Honor. "I'd love to have you on a War Bond tour. Do you suppose you could arrange to get yourself shot in the shoulder, Jack? *After* you do something heroic?"

"Fuck you, Jake."

"Like I said, Jack, I'd much rather be going to Guadalcanal as one of your staff sergeants. It didn't turn out that way, so I try to do what the Corps wants me to do as well as I can."

Stecker met his eyes.

"Yeah," he said. "I know."

He handed Dillon his empty canteen cup.

"I am now going out in the rain again," he said. "Somebody once told me that a good Marine officer doesn't try to stay dry when his men are getting wet."

"Nobody has to tell you what a good Marine officer should or should not do," Dillon said.

"What the hell is that?"

"It was intended as a compliment."

"Don't let it go to your head, Major, but I almost wish you were one of my staff sergeants," Stecker said, and then he touched Dillon's arm and walked out from under the fly tent and into the rain.

(Three)
HEADQUARTERS, VMF-229
MARINE CORPS AIR STATION
EWA, TERRITORY OF HAWAII
7 JULY 1942

If Captain Charles M. Galloway, commanding officer of VMF-229, had been called upon to describe his present physical condition, he would have said that his ass was dragging. He was bone tired and dirty. He had been flying most of the morning. He was wearing a sweat- and oil-stained cotton flying suit. His khaki flight helmet and goggles were jammed into the left knee pocket of the flying suit, and his fore-and-aft cap stuck out of the right knee pocket. He carried his leather flying jacket over his shoulder; his index finger was hooked in the leather loop inside the collar.

He needed a long shower and some clean clothes, he knew, and he would dearly like to have a beer. But beer was out of the question: He would probably put another two hours in the air this afternoon, and you don't drink—not even a lousy beer—and fly.

The door to the Quonset hut which housed both the squadron office and the supply room of VMF-229 was padlocked when Charley Galloway walked up to it. He glanced at his watch and saw that it was just after 1200.

PFC Alfred B. Hastings, Galloway decided angrily, had elected to have his luncheon, and fuck the phone, let it ring. He immediately regretted his anger. Hastings, who had transferred into VMF-229 with Tech Sergeant Big Steve Oblensky, had been promoted from being Oblensky's runner to Squadron Clerk. His only qualification for the job was that he could type, but he had proved to be a quick learner of the fine points of Marine Corps bureaucracy and had been doing a good job. Galloway knew how late at night the kid worked, and obviously he had to eat sometime.

Galloway dipped his hand into the open flap of his flight suit and came out with his dog tag chain. It held his dog tags and four keys—one to his BOQ room; one to the Ford; one to the padlock on the squadron office door; and one to the padlock on the safe in the squadron office. He opened the lock and went inside.

The handset of the telephone was out of the cradle. Not by accident. PFC Hastings had been told by Technical Sergeant Oblensky that it was better to have the brass *annoyed* that you were on the phone when they called than *pissed* because there was no answer when it rang—clear proof that the rule that Squadron Offices would be manned around the clock was being violated.

Captain Galloway walked to the squadron safe, knelt by it, unlocked the padlock, opened the door, and reached inside and took a bottle of Coke from an ice-filled galvanized iron bucket, which at the moment was all the safe held. He knocked the cap off by resting the lip on the edge of the safe and hitting it with the heel of his hand.

He walked to his desk, sat down in the battered, but surprisingly comfortable, office chair Oblensky had scrounged somewhere and then had reupholstered, leaned back in it, swung his feet on the desk, and took a pull at the neck of the Coke. After a moment, he burped with satisfaction.

On his desk, neatly laid out, was a half-inch-thick stack of papers. From experience, he knew that just about every sheet there would require his signature—on the original and the standard four onion skins. Whatever it was, it would have to wait.

His hands were dirty, oily; it would offend the high priests of the bureaucracy if an official document with oily fingerprints on it appeared in their IN baskets for movement to the OUT basket and forwarding to higher headquarters.

He looked at the handset of the telephone and after a moment leaned forward and hung it up. By the time he had rested his back against his chair and raised the Coke bottle to his lips, it rang.

He leaned forward and picked it up.

"VMF-229, Captain Galloway, Sir."

"You guys must live on the phone," his caller said. "I been calling for an hour."

"Well, it'll keep your index finger in shape," Galloway said. "Who's this?"

"Lieutenant Rhodes, at NATS Pearl. I got a couple of warm bodies for you."

"I don't suppose there's any way you could get them a ride over here?"

"No. Not today, anyway. That's why I called."

"What kind of warm bodies?"

"Two intrepid birdmen, fresh from the States. They went into Hickam Field, and the Air Corps sent them here."

"Instead of here. That figures."

"You going to come get them? Or should I put them in the transient BOQ?"

"I'll send somebody for them. Thanks very much."

"Anytime."

Galloway put the phone back in its cradle and talked out loud to himself: "I will not send somebody for them, because

I don't have anybody to drive a vehicle to send for them . . . even if I had a vehicle, which I don't." He thought that over, and added, "Shit!"

He drained the Coke and dropped the bottle with a loud clang into the object he now knew—as a commanding officer charged with responsibility for government property—was not a wastebasket but a "Receptacle, Trash, Office, w/o Liner Federal Stock Number Six Billion Thirteen." Then he swung his feet back onto the floor, burped again, and stood up. He looked at the telephone, took the handset out of the cradle, and laid it on the desk.

He went to PFC Hastings's desk and left him a note. "1205 I went to pick up some replacements at NATS. CMG."

Then he went out of the Quonset hut, closed the padlock, and walked to his Ford. Regulations required that officers leaving installations be in the properly appointed uniform of the day. An exception was made only for officers who were actually engaged in preparing for flight duty, or who were returning from such duty; these men were permitted to wear uniforms appropriate for such duty. Captain Charles M. Galloway decided that he met the criteria for exception. He had been flying, and he was preparing to fly again.

He took his fore-and-aft cap from the knee pocket of his flight suit, put it on, and then slipped his arms into the leather flight jacket and zipped that up. Then he got behind the wheel of the Ford and drove off.

The Marine MP on duty outside the Navy Air Transport Service terminal eyed Galloway suspiciously as he pulled up in the yellow Ford.

"I've got two warm bodies inside," Galloway said when the MP walked up to the car. "Can I leave this here a minute?"

"No, Sir," the MP said. "That would be against regulations. But on the other hand, if I checked around inside, which would take me about two minutes, I wouldn't see it, would I?"

"Thanks," Charley said, and got out of the car.

He smiled when he saw the two warm bodies, the intrepid birdmen fresh from the States, sitting on wooden benches inside the terminal. He knew both of them.

And when they saw him, they both stood up. First Lieutenant James G. Ward, USMCR, smiled and waved. First Lieutenant David F. Schneider, USMC, just about came to attention.

If he outranked Jim Ward, Galloway thought, *he would bark "attention" and announce that he was "Lieutenant Schneider reporting for duty as ordered with a party of one."*

"Welcome to sunny Hawaii," Galloway said, extending his hand. "How was the flight?"

"Long," Jim Ward said.

"Very nice, thank you, Sir," Lieutenant Schneider said.

Oh, that's the way he's decided to play this. He probably sat with his thumb up his ass for a long time, trying to figure the best way to behave when reporting to a squadron commanded by an ex-sergeant.

"I've got a car outside. You can flip a coin to see who gets to sit in the rumble seat. Need any help with your gear?"

"I can manage, thanks," Ward said.

"No, Sir. Thank you, Sir," Schneider said.

He led them outside.

"Great car!" Jim Ward said. "I always wanted one of these. Yours?"

"Yeah. I bought it when I was with VMF-211, tore it apart, and rebuilt it."

Captain Galloway suspected that Lieutenant Schneider was not nearly as enthusiastic about a nine-year-old yellow Ford roadster as Lieutenant Ward was. And he saw that Schneider was almost visibly relieved when Ward settled himself in the rumble seat with their luggage. Riding in the rumble seat of a nine-year-old yellow Ford roadster was not the sort of thing that Lieutenant Schneider felt was appropriate for a Marine officer, especially one who had entered the service from Annapolis.

Galloway got behind the wheel.

"Following the sacred military custom of 'do as I say, not what I do,' " he said, "be advised that wearing flight suits off the flight line is a no-no. A couple of the guys have got themselves written up by the MPs and Shore Patrol."

"What happens then?" Ward asked.

"I reply by endorsement that the offenders have been hung, then drawn and quartered. It's a pain in the ass. We have only one kid for a clerk, and he's not all that good with a typewriter. So don't get caught."

"Got you," Jim Ward said. He leaned forward from the rumble seat and thrust an envelope, a thick one, firmly sealed with scotch tape, at Galloway.

"What's this?"

"A little note from Aunt Caroline," Jim Ward said.

"You hang onto it," Galloway said. "I'm greasy and so is the flight suit. I was about to take a shower when they called and said you were here."

"We could have waited," Schneider said.

"I figured to hell with it," Galloway said. "I'm going to fly again this afternoon anyway."

"We have planes?" Ward asked eagerly.

"Wildcats," Galloway said. "*New* Wildcats. And if you talk nicely to Sergeant Oblensky, he will have your name painted on it, and you can send a picture home to Mommy."

"Who is Sergeant Oblensky?" Ward asked.

"The maintenance sergeant. Best one in the Air Group. At the moment, he's also the first sergeant, the mess sergeant, the supply sergeant, and the motor sergeant."

"How is that, Sir?" Schneider asked.

"Because we don't have anybody else to be the first sergeant, the mess sergeant, the supply sergeant, or the motor sergeant. I'm working on it, so far with a monumental lack of success."

"I see," Schneider said.

"Where we're going now is to Ewa, where I will show you MAG-113 Headquarters,"—Marine Air Group 113; a MAG is the next superior headquarters to a squadron, the aviation equivalent, so to speak, of an infantry battalion—"then the BOQ, and then our squadron office. Then we'll go to the flight line, where I'll get out. You will then drive back to MAG-113. The Skipper—Lieutenant Colonel Clyde D. Dawkins—always wants a personal look at the new meat. When he's finished with you, go to the BOQ and get yourself set up there. And then go to the squadron office, where PFC Hastings will do all the necessary paperwork on you. I'll meet you there, and we can go to the club for our one daily beer and supper. OK?"

"Sounds fine to me," Ward said.

"The penalty for dinging your skipper's little yellow car is death by slow castration," Galloway said. "A word to the wise, so to speak." They chuckled.

"I suppose your flight physicals are up to date?"

"Yes, Sir," they chorused.

"OK. Make sure Hastings gets a copy. And your orders, too, of course. Then in the morning, we'll go flying. Local area checkout if nothing else. There are two IPs. Me and a Lieutenant name of Bill Dunn. He got a Betty and a Zero at Midway. Good pilot. Pay attention to what he says. I do."

"He's almost halfway to being an ace," Ward thought aloud.

"Before you fly away on dreams of glory," Galloway said, "he also took a 20mm round in his window at Midway that damned near made him a soprano, and he totalled the airplane when he set it down. Most of the pilots of VMF-211 who took off for Midway didn't come back. Bear that in mind, too."

There was a moment's silence and then Schneider said, "Sir, we're hardly presentable. To report to the Group Commander, I mean."

"Lieutenant," Galloway said, "we are blessed with a Group Commander who is wise enough to know how mussed people get flying here from the States. He wants a look at your balls, not the crease in your trousers."

Jim Ward laughed.

"Yes, Sir," Schneider said.

If first impressions are important, Galloway thought as he drove the Ford convertible down the taxi road behind the flight line, *Big Steve just blew it so far as Schneider is concerned.*

Technical Sergeant Oblensky was sitting on the ground in the shade of a Wildcat, his back against the left wheel, with a bottle of Coke resting on his belly. He was wearing service shoes and what had originally been khaki trousers, now somewhat raggedly cut off just above the knees. And nothing else. The belly on which the Coke bottle sat sagged over the trouser waistline. His massive chest was streaked with grease and what probably was hydraulic oil, and he needed a shave. His head and neck were sweat streaked.

As Galloway stopped the car and he and the others got out, Oblensky pushed himself to his feet and sauntered over. He glanced at the two young officers with Galloway and dismissed them as unimportant; then he looked at Galloway.

"Those fucking guns need a good armorer," he announced. "Peterson came back this morning with three of his guns jammed after three, four rounds."

There were four .50 caliber air-cooled Browning machine guns on F4F-4 aircraft.

"What's the problem? More important, what do we do about it?"

"If I knew what the problem was, I'd fix it," Oblensky said. "What I did was call a pal—used to be a China Marine, now he's a Gunny with the 2nd Raider Battalion, guy named Zimmerman. He said if I could get them over there, he'd have a look at them."

"OK," Galloway said.

"But I'd have to give him a little present."

"What's he want?"

"An auxiliary generator," Oblensky said. "They're living in tents. He's got a refrigerator someplace, but he needs juice to run it."

"Jesus, Steve, we only have two."

"I think I know where I can get another one."

"Where?"

"You don't want to know, Captain."

"And if you get caught?"

"Then I guess you'd still have some fucked up Brownings, Captain."

"Then be careful," Galloway said.

Big Steve nodded.

Galloway glanced at Ward and Schneider. He saw fascination in Ward's eyes and disbelief in Schneider's, as both came to comprehend what had just been discussed.

"Gentlemen," Galloway said, "I'd like you to meet Technical Sergeant Oblensky, the squadron maintenance sergeant. Sergeant, this is Lieutenant Ward and Lieutenant Schneider; they've just reported aboard."

Big Steve extended his hammy, greasy hand to Ward and Schneider in turn. Ward shook the hand with visible pleasure; Schneider managed a smile only with an almost visible effort.

"Welcome aboard, Sirs," Big Steve said. "The Skipper's told me about you. We didn't expect you so soon."

"I told them you'd paint their names on their airplanes, so we could take a picture," Galloway said.

"Consider it done. Tomorrow, for sure," Big Steve said. He smiled, turned, and pointed at the Wildcat behind him. "This one's ready for a test hop, and if they can replace one more jug in that fucked-up engine in Six-Oh-Three, that'll be ready this afternoon, too." (A "jug" is the engine's cylinder and piston assembly.)

"Is that what you want me to do, Steve, test-fly this one?"

"Lieutenant Dunn took Lieutenant Peterson out again. He said if you got hung up, he'd test-fly this one when he got back."

"What I'd like, Steve, is for six-oh-three to be ready for a test hop when I bring this one back," Galloway said.

"You want to trust Neely to replace the jug himself? I mean, I got to see about that other auxiliary generator."

"We have to push him out of the nest sometime, Steve."

"OK. I'll tell him to have it ready when you get back," Oblensky said. "Things are probably going to be a little tight. You want to change your plans for tonight, Captain?"

Shit! I forgot all about that!

Mrs. Stefan Oblensky, aka Lieutenant Commander Florence Kocharski, United States Navy Nurse Corps, had requested the pleasure of the company of Captain Charles M. Galloway, USMCR, at dinner at the family residence where she and Technical Sergeant Oblensky cohabited with the blessings of God but in contravention of the Rules & Customs of the United States Naval Service.

Charley looked at Big Steve's face.

I can't turn him down again. They've asked me four times, and I've had to turn him down three.

"Hell, no," he said. "I'll be there."

XII

HEADQUARTERS, MAG-21
EWA USMC AIR STATION
OAHU, TERRITORY OF HAWAII
1445 HOURS 7 JULY 1942

Lieutenant David F. Schneider reached out and touched Lieutenant Jim Ward's arm as Ward tried to operate the door latch of Galloway's 1933 Ford convertible. Ward turned and looked at him.

"Don't you really think it would be a good idea if we took a shave and got into a fresh uniform before we go in here?"

"You heard what the man said. The man said the colonel is smart enough to know you lose the crease in your trousers when you spend twelve hours in an airplane. And the man, if I have to point this out, is now our commanding officer."

"But he hasn't changed much," Schneider said, "has he?"

"Meaning what?"

"You did understand that he gave that bare-chested gorilla of a sergeant of his permission to steal an auxiliary power unit generator someplace, from somebody who certainly needs it?"

Ward didn't reply.

"So that he can swap it to some other sergeant in the 2nd Raiders," Schneider went on, "for doing something to the machine guns that he's not competent, or too stupid, to do himself? The last I heard they call that 'misappropriation of government property.'"

"I don't know what you're talking about," Jim Ward said.

"You were standing right there!" Schneider said indignantly, and then understood. "Oh," he said in disgust. "I see."

"I don't think you really do, Dave," Ward said. "Let me tell you something about yourself, Dave. Most of the time you're a pretty good guy; but hiding inside you—I guess all the time—is a real prick struggling to get out. I don't like you much when that happens."

Schneider looked at Ward for a time, and then he said slowly, "Your attitude wouldn't have anything to do with the relationship between Galloway and your Aunt Caroline, would it?"

"Probably that has something to do with it," Ward said. "But what I think it is, what I hope it is, is loyalty to my commanding officer."

Schneider snorted.

"You weren't sent here," Ward said. "You volunteered, so you could get out of flying R4Ds and into fighters. Galloway fixed it. If it wasn't for him, you'd still be at Quantico. You knew what Charley—Captain Galloway—was like when he let you volunteer. All you had to say was no."

"I can't believe that you are actually condoning what you saw him do with your own eyes."

Ward turned away and managed to get the door open. Then he walked quickly around the front of the car and intercepted Schneider as he was getting out.

"I never thought I would enjoy something like this," he said, "but I was wrong. You will recall, Lieutenant, that I am senior to you. By the authority therefore vested in me by the goddamned Naval Service, Lieutenant, I order you (a) to get back in the car; (b) to shut your fucking mouth; (c)

and to sit there and don't move until I send for you. And
be advised, Lieutenant, that if it comes down to it, I will
swear on a stack of Bibles that when Sergeant Oblensky spoke
with us, he was dressed like a fucking recruiting poster and
said not one fucking word about a goddamned generator.
You got that, Lieutenant?"

"Jim," Schneider said. "Obviously, I . . ."

"Your orders, Lieutenant, are to sit there with your
fucking mouth shut," Ward said, spun on his heel, and
walked to the door.

(Two)
THRESHOLD, RUNWAY 17
EWA MARINE CORPS AIR STATION
OAHU, TERRITORY OF HAWAII
1450 HOURS 7 JULY 1942

Captain Charles M. Galloway, USMCR, had a dark secret,
a true secret, shared with no one else. He wasn't sure if it
was a character flaw, or whether it was something that
happened to other people, too. But he knew that he didn't
want it known, and that he could never ask anyone else if
they were similarly affected. Or maybe similarly afflicted.

The cold truth was that in situations like this one—in the
cockpit, with all the needles in the green, in the last few
instants before he would shove the throttle forward and then
touch his mike button and announce to the tower, with
studied savoir faire, "Five Niner Niner rolling"—he was
afraid.

He could tell himself that it was irrational, that he was a
better pilot than most people he knew, that the aircraft he
was about to fly was perfectly safe, that he had so many hours
total time; and he could even remind himself that a study by
the University of California had proved beyond reasonable
doubt that a cretin (defined as the next step above morons)
could be taught to fly; but it didn't work. At that moment—
and all those other times—he had a very clear image of the
airplane going out of control, smashing into the ground,
rolling over, exploding. And it scared him. Sometimes his
knees actually trembled. And more than once he had taken

his hand from the stick so he could try to hold his shaking knees still.

Today, as he sat there waiting, he reminded himself of the command decision he had made vis-à-vis himself and Lieutenant Bill Dunn: who would fly what and why. Dunn was a good pilot, and he had done something Galloway had not done. He had met the enemy in aerial combat and shot down two airplanes. Galloway believed that there was no way to vicariously experience what it was like to have someone shooting at you.

That did not change, however, his belief that good pilots were a product of two qualities: natural ability and experience. He really believed that he was a better natural pilot than Dunn, and there was no question that he had much more experience.

The mission of VMF-229 at the moment was to become operational, which is to say its eighteen F4F-4 Wildcats and their pilots had to be made ready to go where the squadron was ordered to go, and to do what the squadron was ordered to do.

All his pilots were of course rated as Naval Aviators. Someone in authority had decreed that they were qualified to fly. But with Galloway's certain and Bill Dunn's possible exception, the pilots VMF-229 had so far were for all practical purposes novices. They were highly intelligent young men in superb physical condition who had passed through a prescribed course of training. But none of them had been flying for more than a year; and none of them, so far as Galloway had been able to determine, had ever been in trouble in the air.

And they were all impressed with Lieutenant Bill Dunn— understandably . . . if, in Galloway's judgment, rather naively. Dunn had *been in combat,* and he'd been *hit* and *wounded,* and he'd returned alive and *with two kills.*

All the same, just as soon as Big Steve Oblensky was able to make flyable two of the Wildcats they had trucked to Ewa from the docks at Pearl Harbor, Galloway flew against Dunn in half a dozen mock dogfights. He had no trouble outmaneuvering him the first time out, or the second, or the third; and he was starting to wonder if he should, so to speak, throw a dogfight, because consistently whipping Dunn was likely to humiliate him.

Then he thought that through and realized that humiliating Dunn was precisely the thing he *should* do. As the privates in a rifle squad should think, *believe,* that their sergeant was the best fucking rifle shot in the company, so should the lieutenant pilots of a fighter squadron *believe* that The Skipper was the best fucking airplane driver in Marine Aviation.

That policy seemed to have worked out well, even better than Galloway foresaw. For one thing, Dunn wasn't impressed with his own heroic accomplishment at Midway. So he was not humiliated when he was bested by a pilot who'd been flying when he was trying out for the junior varsity football team in high school.

For another, as the other pilots drifted into the squadron, Dunn let each of them know that The Skipper was really one hell of a pilot. Coming as it did from a pilot who had been wounded and scored two kills at Midway, Dunn's opinion was taken as Gospel.

And Galloway didn't let either himself or Dunn sit and rest on their accomplishments. He believed the simple old Marine Corps adage that the best way to learn something was to teach it. So he had Dunn up all the time teaching techniques of aerial combat and gunnery to the kids, honing his own skills in the process, and picking up time, which meant experience.

As for Galloway, whenever possible he did the test flying himself—simply because he was the best qualified pilot to do it. Most test flights were simply routine. If everything worked, they could be flown by one of the University of California's cretins. It was only when something went wrong that experience became important. An experienced pilot often sensed when something was about to go wrong, and so he could act to reduce the risk to the airplane before things went seriously bad. Even when some major system failed unexpectedly, an experienced pilot could often recover, and put the airplane back on the ground in one piece, while a pilot without his experience was likely not only to get himself killed, but to send the airplane to the junkyard, as well.

No aircraft assigned to VMF-229 had been lost—or even

seriously damaged—during test flights. In Galloway's view this was a pretty good record . . . especially when you considered that three times the test pilot—C. M. Galloway— had lost power on take-off: When the fan of a Wildcat stopped spinning, the Wildcat didn't want to fly anymore; as soon as the power quit, the nose got heavy, and it started to stall. (Although the manual usually read like a sales brochure for Grumman, it nevertheless warned—in small print—that the aircraft became "excessively nose heavy in a power loss situation.") And then, even if you could keep it from stalling by getting it into a glide, the Wildcat sank like a rock.

Despite all that, Galloway somehow managed to bring each of those three aircraft down without cracking up the aircraft or the test pilot.

And so as Galloway sat there in the cockpit of the Wildcat he was testing that afternoon, cleared by the tower as Number One for take-off, and with all the needles in the green, it started to hit him that his anxious feelings, viewed objectively, just might be pretty goddamned ridiculous.

Captain Galloway pressed his mike button.

"Ewa," he said confidently, "Five Niner Niner. I'm experiencing a little roughness and low oil pressure. I want to check it out a moment."

"Roger, Five Niner Niner. Do you wish to leave the threshold at this time?"

"Five Niner Niner, negative. I think I'll be all right in a minute."

It would be a mistake I would regret all my life, correction, for all eternity, *however the fuck long that is, if I took this bird off and crashed in flames with a letter from my girlfriend I hadn't read in my pocket.*

He put his finger in his mouth, caught the index finger of the pigskin glove on his right hand between his teeth, and pulled the glove off. Then he repeated the process with the glove on his left hand. He took the envelope from his pocket and sniffed it.

I am probably fooling myself, but I think I can smell her perfume.

The envelope contained what Charley thought of as "ladies' stationery," a squarish, folded, rather stiff piece of paper. The outside bore a monogram. Scotch-taped to the inside was a small piece of jewelry, a round gold disc on a chain.

Jenkintown, June 30 '42

My Darling,

This is an Episcopal serviceman's cross. I know you're not an Episcopalian; and now that I'm divorced (and for other reasons), I am a fallen Episcopalian woman. But I wish you would wear it anyway, to know that I am praying for you constantly.

It has occurred to me that the only time you will ever notice it is when it gets in your way when you're taking a shower. But perhaps that will remind you of the showers you have shared with someone who loves you and lives for the moment when she can feel your arms around her again.

All my love, now and forever,
Caroline

Charley Galloway reached up and shoved his goggles up on his forehead. For some reason, his eyes were watering. He pried the medallion loose from the Scotch tape and looked at it. He tried to open the clasp on the gold chain, but couldn't manage it. There was no way he could get that fragile gold chain over his head. So he leaned forward and looped it around the adjustment knob of the altimeter on the control panel, then tugged on it to make sure vibration wouldn't shake it off.

He wiped his eyes with his knuckles, put his goggles back in place, worked his hands back into his gloves, and put them on the throttle and the stick. He inched the throttle forward and turned onto the runway. Then he moved the throttle to full take-off power, and pushed his mike button.

"Ewa," he said, with practiced savoir faire, "Five Niner Niner rolling."

Four hundred yards down the runway, he spoke to the engine.

"Don't you dare crap out on me now, you sonofabitch!"

A moment after that, F4F-4 tail number 40599 of VMF-229 lifted off into the air.

(Three)
HEADQUARTERS, MAG-21
EWA USMC AIR STATION
OAHU, TERRITORY OF HAWAII
1445 HOURS 7 JULY 1942

Lieutenant Colonel Clyde D. Dawkins, USMC, commanding, MAG-21, was by no means unhappy with First Lieutenant James G. Ward, USMCR. He would have been happier, of course, if Ward had another five hundred hours of flight time, all of it in F4F-4s; but compared to the other replacement pilots they were getting fresh from Pensacola, Ward was a grizzled veteran.

He liked his attitude, too, which was not surprising, since Charley Galloway had recruited him. Galloway would not recruit a fool or a troublemaker.

"Captain Galloway until recently was a flying sergeant. Is that going to pose any problems for you?"

"Yes, Sir," Ward replied. "I mean I knew he was a flying sergeant. He was a sergeant when he taught me to fly the R4D, Sir." The question had obviously surprised him. "I don't know what you mean about problems, Sir."

"Well, Mr. Ward, there are some officers, generally very stupid officers, who resent Mustangs. I'm pleased to see that you're not one of them."

"No, Sir. I consider myself very fortunate to have a squadron commander who knows what he's doing."

Dawkins restrained a smile at the honest naïveté of the remark.

"Mr. Ward," he said sternly, "you are not suggesting, I trust, that there are squadron commanders who do not know what they are doing?"

Ward flushed.

"Sir," he began lamely.

"I know what you mean, Mr. Ward," Dawkins laughed. "That works both ways. I'm glad to have Charley Galloway as one of my squadron commanders. I share your opinion that he knows what he's doing. I will refrain from comment on my other squadron commanders."

"Yes, Sir," Ward said. His relief was evident on his face.

"I thought there were two of you?" Dawkins said.

"Yes, Sir. Lieutenant Schneider is outside."

Dawkins stood up and offered his hand. "Welcome aboard, Mr. Ward. We're glad to have you. I'm available to my officers for any reason, around the clock."

"Thank you, Sir."

"Would you send Mister—what did you say, 'Schneider'?—in please?"

"Yes, Sir."

Lieutenant Colonel Dawkins was initially very favorably impressed with First Lieutenant David F. Schneider, USMC. He was a well-set-up young man; he looked remarkably crisp for someone who had just flown from the States to Hawaii. And he wore an Annapolis ring. Colonel Dawkins had been commissioned from Annapolis.

There were very few officers in the pre-war Navy who were not Annapolis graduates.

There was a theory . . . it was soon to be tested in the crucible of war . . . that the real value of Annapolis graduates to the country did not derive from their experience manning the ships of the peacetime Navy, but from the fact that they would now serve as the firm skeleton for the flesh and musculature of the enormous Navy that would be required to win the war.

Some of this would come from the presumed professionalism and Naval expertise that could be expected of a man who had spent his life, from the age of seventeen or eighteen, in Naval uniform. The rest would come because the Annapolis graduates—from ensigns, to first lieutenants, USMC, to admirals—would serve as role models for an officer corps that would be seventy or eighty percent civilian Marines and sailors. Dawkins privately thought that this was the more important of the two.

Even if they had difficulty admitting this in person to a graduate of Hudson High, virtually all Annapolis graduates both admired and tried hard to adhere to the code West Point put in words, *Duty, Honor, Country.*

And so Dawkins felt at first that Galloway was fortunate to have someone like Schneider in his squadron. He even imagined, somewhat wryly, that Schneider might be able to temper Charley Galloway's policy that he had greater right to any government property that was not chained to the ground or under armed guard than whoever it was issued to.

He was so impressed with Schneider that he almost passed over the question he had asked Lieutenant Ward, and in fact every other officer newly assigned to VMF-229. But in the end, he did ask him:

"Captain Galloway until recently was a flying sergeant. Is that going to pose any problems for you?"

"No, Sir. Not for me, Sir."

Why don't I like that response? What did he say? "Not for me"?

"Not for you? Is that what you said, Mr. Schneider? Are you suggesting that it might be a problem for Captain Galloway?"

"Sir," Schneider said, with a disarming smile, "I'm a regular. I know that before Captain Galloway was commissioned, a good deal of thought went into it. I certainly don't mean to suggest that Captain Galloway is not a first rate squadron commander."

"But?"

"Sir, what I'm saying, badly I'm afraid, is that I really wish I hadn't served with Captain Galloway when he was an enlisted man."

What bothers me about that? Dawkins wondered, and then he understood: *You didn't serve with Charley Galloway, Lieutenant, with him on your wing, or vice versa. He was your IP. By definition, IPs are superior to their students. I'm getting the idea, you presumptuous puppy, that you think an officer of suitable grade should have been assigned to instruct an officer and a gentleman and an Annapolis graduate such as yourself.*

"Because you will always think of him as a sergeant, you mean?"

"No, Sir. Because I think he may remember that I was one of his officers. And that might be a little awkward for him."

So you're a fucking liar, too, Mr. Schneider? I'll be goddam-

ned! *And an arrogant sonofabitch, too, if you really thought you were going to take* me *in with that bullshit.*

"I think I take your point," Dawkins said. "Well, let me give it a little thought. Perhaps we could quietly arrange a transfer for you to one of the other squadrons."

"I wouldn't want any special treatment, Sir."

"I understand," Dawkins said. "We're talking about the good of the service, aren't we?"

"I think so, Sir."

What I don't understand is how this asshole fooled Charley Galloway. Maybe there's something here I'm missing. But if Galloway hasn't figured this self-serving prick out, I will transfer him for the good of the service. Charley has enough on his mind without worrying about this back-stabbing prick. He'll spend the rest of this fucking war test-flying Piper Cubs in Kansas.

"Well, that seems to be about it, Mr. Schneider," Dawkins said. "Unless there's something on your mind?"

"I hate . . . "

"Let's hear it?"

"My Uncle Dan is over at Pearl, Sir. On the CINCPAC staff. I wonder if there's any chance that I could get over to see him for a couple of hours before I begin my duties here?"

"Your Uncle Dan? I know a *Karl* Schneider . . . "

"This is my mother's brother, Sir. Daniel Wagam. Admiral Wagam."

You didn't lose any time letting me know that, did you?

Dawkins looked over Schneider's head at the clock on the wall. It was twenty after three. Certainly, Galloway wasn't going to put Schneider in a cockpit today. For one thing, it was too late. For another, Schneider was just off a long plane ride from the States. What Galloway probably had in mind was taking this prick and the nice kid over to the club so they could meet the other squadron officers. That could wait.

"Why don't you call and see if Admiral Wagam has time for you?" Dawkins said. "If he does, we'll get you a ride over there. I'm sure the admiral could arrange to get you back here by 0500 tomorrow, don't you think?"

"Yes, Sir. I'm sure he'd be able to do that."

Dawkins pointed to his telephone.

"Help yourself, Mr. Schneider."

(Four)
HEADQUARTERS, VMF-229
EWA USMC AIR STATION
OAHU, TERRITORY OF HAWAII
1640 HOURS 7 JULY 1942

When Captain Charles M. Galloway walked into his headquarters, two people were waiting for him, Lieutenant Jim
Ward and PFC Alfred B. Hastings. Both rose to their feet.

Galloway was starting to wonder where Schneider was
when he noticed that PFC Hastings was holding something
in his hand. It was a piece of cardboard, a laundry shirt stiff-
ener, on which he had drawn a rather nicely done skull and
crossbones, the international symbol of danger; an oak leaf,
the insignia of majors and lieutenant colonels; and an arrow
pointing to Galloway's office.

"Stand at ease," Galloway said sternly. He smiled at Ward,
winked at PFC Hastings, and walked into his office.

"Good afternoon, Sir," he said.

Lieutenant Colonel Clyde W. Dawkins was sitting in Charley's chair with his feet on Charley's desk. "You look like
shit, Charley," he replied. "How many hours were you up
today?"

"Six, I guess. Maybe a little more."

"Well, cut it down," Dawkins said. "I don't want to find
myself writing 'pilot fatigue' as the probable cause of your
fatal accident."

"Aye, aye, Sir."

"Close the door," Dawkins said.

Charley did so.

Dawkins was not through with him.

"What the hell is the matter with you?" he demanded.
"You didn't start flying last week. You know better."

"Big Steve had a bunch of airplanes that needed test flying.
I flew them," Galloway answered.

"How many have you got operational?"

"Eighteen, Sir. All of them," Galloway said, not without
a hint of pride in his voice. "I have more operational aircraft
than I do pilots."

"Christ, that was quick," Dawkins said.

"Big Steve's as good as they come."

"Yeah, but he's got a commanding officer who takes dumb chances test-flying them when he should know better."

"Yes, Sir," Galloway said.

"OK. Tomorrow you don't fly. Tonight, go get drunk. Consider that an order."

"Aye, aye, Sir. Actually, Sir, that thought had gone through my mind."

"I'm serious about this, goddamn you. I want *you* commanding VMF-229, not some kid six months out of Pensacola."

"Yes, Sir."

"But that's not the reason I am here, instead of inside a cold martini," Dawkins said. "I have interviewed your two new officers, Captain. The one outside seems to be a nice enough kid. Maybe too nice. Tell me about the other one."

Galloway hesitated.

"Out of school, Charley. Consider me your friendly parish priest. Bare your soul."

"The miserable sonofabitch knows how to fly," Galloway said.

"Really?" Dawkins asked doubtfully.

"He's really good," Charley said. "I need pilots like that. And I can handle the sonofabitch part."

"Did you know his uncle is an admiral? Admiral Wagam at CINCPAC?"

"No, but it doesn't surprise me. He's trade-school," Charley said, and then heard what he had said. "Sorry, Sir."

"Some of us trade-school graduates are sterling fellows," Dawkins said. "But—and I wouldn't want this to get around—a very small percentage are genuine pricks. I think your man Schneider is one of them."

"I can handle him, Sir," Charley said.

"Well, that's what I came to find out. If he starts giving you trouble, let me know."

"Aye, aye, Sir."

"He's over at Pearl with his uncle the admiral," Dawkins said. "I'm not sure if that's because they have a close-knit family or because he wanted me to know that his uncle is an admiral. But I told him he could go, and to be back at 0500. Will that cause any problems for you?"

"No, Sir."

Dawkins looked into Galloway's eyes for a moment, and then snorted. He swung his feet off the desk.

"You know what will cause a real problem for you, Captain?"

"Sir?"

"If I don't see you at the club tonight, really spiffy in your whites, having trouble with slurred speech and the other effects of alcohol."

"Well, Sir, that will cause a problem," Charley said. "While I'm sure my speech will probably get a little slurred as the night progresses, I hadn't planned to go to the club. I would really much rather not go to the club."

"I don't want to hear about it, Captain. Neither do I want to hear that, clear-eyed and bushy-tailed, you went anywhere near an airplane tomorrow."

"Aye, Aye, Sir."

"You've done a good job here, Charley," Dawkins said. "Christ, I didn't think you'd have eighteen operational aircraft for another two weeks."

"That's Big Steve, Sir, not me."

"Bullshit. But it raises a question. How much flying are you giving your people?"

"Sir?"

"How many hours a day are they flying?"

"No more than four, Sir."

"Do as I say, not as I do, right? Cut down your flying hours, Charley. I mean that."

"Aye, aye, Sir."

"I've enjoyed our little chat, Captain," Dawkins said. "We must have another, real soon."

He walked to the door, opened it, and walked through. Lieutenant Ward and PFC Hastings came to attention. He walked past them, then stopped and turned, and went back to Hastings.

"Captain Galloway's been telling me of your good work, Son," he said. "Keep it up!"

"Yes, Sir," Hastings said. He glowed with pride.

What the fuck was that all about? Charley wondered. *I didn't say a word to him about Hastings. Was that just apply-anywhere bullshit? Or was it Lesson Three in how to be a good commander?*

He saw Jim Ward looking into the office.

What the hell do I do with him tonight?

He waved him into the office.

"Dave went to Pearl Harbor," Jim Ward said. "He got permission from the colonel."

"So I hear. Did you get settled in the BOQ?"

Ward nodded. Somewhat uneasily, he said, "Did you know his uncle is an admiral?"

"No. Not until just now."

"This is going to sound ridiculous," Jim Ward said. "But I promised Aunt Caroline I would ask. Six hours after I got here. Are you wearing your necklace?"

Charley pulled the zipper of his flying suit down and pointed to the medallion.

"Oh," Ward said, smiling. "I thought it might be something like that. Are you Episcopal?"

"No. But do you think God really gives a damn?"

Jim Ward looked startled for a moment, then replied, "Hell, no."

Galloway made up his mind what he was going to do with Jim Ward.

"You can meet the rest of the guys tomorrow," he said. "Tonight we're going to go have dinner with some friends of mine."

"Won't I be in the way?"

"No. I don't think so," Charley said. "Come on, let's get out of here."

PFC Hastings rose once again from behind his typewriter as they walked into the outer office.

"Two things, Hastings," Charley said.

"Yes, Sir?"

"I don't want to hear that you've been here after 1730."

"Sir, I've got a lot to do."

"It'll wait."

"Aye, aye, Sir. And the second thing?"

"Cut a promotion order for the colonel's signature," Galloway said. "Make yourself a corporal."

"Aye, aye, Sir."

(Five)
NEAR WAIALUA, OAHU
TERRITORY OF HAWAII
1800 HOURS 7 JULY 1942

Greeting her dinner guests, Lieutenant Commander Florence Kocharski, Nurse Corps, USN, was attired in sandals and a shapeless, loose fitting cotton dress printed with brightly colored flowers, called a *Muumuu*. Over her ear she had a gardenia stuck through her silver hair.

"Hi, Charley," she said and let him kiss her cheek.

He handed her a brown paper sack which obviously contained bottles.

"Flo, this is Jim Ward," Charley Galloway said. "He's a friend of mine. I didn't think you would mind if I brought him along."

"No, of course not," Flo said, not very convincingly. "There's enough food to feed an army. How are you, Lieutenant?"

"I said 'friend,' Flo," Charley said. "His aunt is my girl. He introduced us."

Technical Sergeant Stefan Oblensky, USMC, attired in sandals, short pants, and a gaily flowered loose fitting cotton shirt, appeared behind her.

"Jesus, Charley!" he said, his tone torn between hurt and anger.

"I'm going to say this again," Galloway said. "Jim is a friend. More than a friend. Damned near family. My girl is his aunt."

"Yeah, sure," Big Steve said, far from mollified.

"And I told him what's going on here," Charley said. "He knows how to keep his mouth shut."

"What the hell," Flo said. "What's done is done. Come on and we'll open the jug." She put her arm around Jim Ward. "I know more about your aunt than I really want to know," she said. "He doesn't talk about her much, but once he gets started, you can't shut him up."

Jim smiled at her shyly.

"He told me about you, too," he said.

"He did? What?"

"About you being on the *West Virginia* on Pearl Harbor Day and getting the Silver Star."

"Like I say, sometimes you can't shut him up," Flo said.

With her arm still around his shoulders—she was just as tall as he was, and outweighed him by twenty pounds—Flo marched Jim Ward across the small living room of the frame cottage and into the kitchen.

She took the two bottles of scotch from the bag, opened one, and set out glasses. Then she reached under the sink and opened an insulated gray steel container, labeled MEDICAL CORPS USN, and took ice from it.

"No refrigerator," she said, as she dropped ice cubes in the glasses, "and the head is that small wooden building out there. But what the hell, what do they say, 'Be It Ever So Humble'?"

"It's very nice," Jim said.

"It belongs to a guy, retired Marine, who lets us use it," she said.

"Charley told me you were up here on Pearl Harbor Day," Jim said.

"He told you that, too, did he? He say who he was with?"

Jim shook his head "no."

Flo laughed. "Then I won't."

"Then you won't what?" Charley said, coming into the kitchen.

"I won't tell him who you was with on Sunday, December seven."

Galloway chuckled. "I was hoping you would," he said. "I was hoping you would have a motherly word to him about the dangers of getting involved with certain members of the Navy Nurse Corps."

"Don't play Mr. Innocent with me, Charley. The way I remember that, nobody had to drag you up here."

"This was all, Jim, pre-Caroline, when I was a footloose and carefree flying sergeant, like skinhead here."

"I told you, Charley," Flo said, "I don't like you to call Stefan that."

"Well, 'Curly' sure doesn't fit," Galloway said, unabashed.

"Who are you talking about?" Jim asked.

"One of Flo's angels of mercy," Charley said.

"Angel, my ass," Flo said. "I'm always wondering if she

won't say something to somebody about Stefan and me, out of pure bitchiness."

"Does she know about you?" Charley asked.

"Not that we're married," Flo said. "But I have to let them know where I am. I'm assistant chief nurse. She knows damned well that I'm not coming up here alone to count the pineapples; she knows I'm still 'dating' Stefan. She's always making some sweet little crack, you know, 'give my regards to Sergeant Oblensky,' like that."

"I don't think she'll say anything," Charley said. "You know too much about her."

"I know more about her than you think I do," Flo said, "but now that she's running around with that lieutenant of yours, no telling what she's liable to do."

By then, she had finished making the drinks. She handed them out.

"Well, welcome to our happy home," she said.

"Thank you," Jim said.

"I'm getting really sick of the whole goddamned thing," Big Steve said, "hiding out like we're doing something wrong. I'm pretty close to telling them. 'We're married. Fuck you, what are you going to do about it?' "

"Watch your mouth, Honeybun!" Flo snapped.

"They wouldn't court-martial us," Big Steve went on. "That's bullshit."

"Maybe not. You can never tell," Charley said. "But they'd sure as hell transfer one of you. Probably you. You'd spend the war changing Yellow Peril engines at Quantico or Pensacola. You could kiss these weekends up here good-bye."

"What the hell's the difference? Here or Pee-Cola? The fuckers won't let me fly anymore anyway."

"You're too goddamned old to fly, you old fart," Charley said, laughing. "The Corps's not flying Spads any more."

"I don't know what the hell is with you two," Flo said, angrily. "Watch your mouths, there's a lady present!"

"Sorry," Big Steve said, contritely.

"Just watch it!" she said. Then, "Charley's right, Honey-bun. Be grateful for what we have. Don't do something dumb."

"Just because he's an officer now don't make him smart," Big Steve said.

"The hell it doesn't!" Charley protested, jokingly. "We officers have to know how to read and write and how to tie our own shoes. Don't we, Flo?"

"You tell him, Charley," Flo said, laughing.

"If you're so fu—smart, Captain, Sir," Big Steve said, "tell me about Guadacanal."

"About what?"

"Guadacanal," Big Steve said, triumphantly.

"Never heard of it," Charley confessed.

"Well, for your general information, Captain, Sir, it's an island. The Japs are building a fighter base on it, and the First Marine Division is going to take it away from them."

This scuttlebutt has the ring of truth to it, Charley decided.

"Where is this island?" Charley asked.

Big Steve shrugged his massive shoulders.

"It's in the Solomon Islands, Charley," Flo said, softly. "Down by Australia. And it's *Guadalcanal,* with an 'L.' I heard the same thing. They've been levying us for doctors and corpsmen. I heard they're going to invade this place right after the first of the month."

"You heard that too, huh, Honey?" Big Steve asked.

Charley looked at Jim Ward.

"Jim, do I have to tell you not to repeat this scuttlebutt?"

"No, Sir. Of course not."

"I don't even know where the Solomon Islands are," Charley said, as much to himself as to the others.

"Wait a minute," Big Steve said. "I brung some maps. I was going to ask Flo."

He left the kitchen. They heard him a moment later walking across the living room, and then they heard the screen door screeching.

"Straight poop, would you say, Flo?" Charley asked softly.

She nodded. "I don't know where he heard it, but I'd bet on my information."

The screen door slammed again, and then Big Steve called for them to come into the living room. They went in, to find him fastening the corners of a large map to the floor with ashtrays and a bottle.

They all got on their knees and examined the map.

"There it is," Flo said, pointing. "And those itsy-bitsy little islands near it. Tulagi and Gavutu. I heard that, too."

"God," Charley said thoughtfully. "It's a long way from nowhere, isn't it?"

There was no reply, except a grunt from Big Steve. And then Charley asked for a sheet of paper and a pencil. When Flo produced both, he laid the paper on the map and copied the scale from it.

Then he began moving the paper around on the map.

"What the *hell* are you doing?" Big Steve asked, taking the words from Jim's mouth.

"Ssssh, Honeybun," Flo said.

Finally, Charley sat back on his heels.

"Well, if this is the place the First Marine Division is going, they're going without VMF-229," he said.

"How can you tell that?" Jim asked, curiously, not as a challenge.

"Because it's out of fighter range from any land airbase we control," Charley said. "Which means they're going to have to use carrier-based aviation. And VMF-229 is not carrier qualified. I think only Dunn and me ever were."

Big Steve grunted again.

"And, if your date is anywhere near close, Flo, there's no way we could qualify in time."

"Why not?" Big Steve asked. "All you'd need is, what? Two, three days to shoot some landings."

"We'd need a carrier to shoot them on," Charley said. "There's no carrier here right now. And even if there was, there's no way we could be qualified, and put aboard, and still steam that far in time to make the invasion."

"Huh!" Big Steve said, disappointed.

"But I tell you what *could* happen," Charley said thoughtfully. "They are going to need fighters on that island when they take it."

"Why, if we take it?" Jim asked.

"Because all of those islands are within fighter range of each other. They will be within range of land-based Japanese aircraft. And they're not about to leave aircraft carriers in the area; they'd be too vulnerable to the Japs."

"OK," Big Steve said. "So what? What are you driving at?"

"They could load us on one of those escort carriers, and then catapult us off that onto this island when they have captured the airfield."

"I thought you said nobody but you and Dunn was carrier qualified," Flo asked.

"Nobody else is, but that wouldn't matter. If they were to catapult us off one of the escort carriers, we wouldn't go back to it. The hard part of carrier operation is landing—the approach and the arrested landing. Getting catapulted off a carrier is something else. It's scary, especially the first time. You go from zero to ninety knots in a second. But then you're flying."

Big Steve snorted.

Galloway looked at him and shrugged.

"I was just thinking out loud."

"I was just thinking," Big Steve said, "that you may not be so dumb after all—for an officer, that is."

"You have just been complimented," Flo chuckled. "Enjoy it, Charley."

"I'll drink to that," Charley said, and then looked at Jim Ward. "But you will not. You are flying tomorrow. You will be practicing the technique of taking off short. And you will be as baffled as any of your peers when they start wondering out loud what that crap is supposed to be all about—as opposed to mock dogfights, which are a lot more fun."

"Aye, aye, Sir."

"Let's eat," Flo said. "We've having a Hawaiian Luau. Except it's a pork loin. I can't stand the sight of one of those poor baby pigs with apples in their mouths."

(Six)
OFFICER'S CLUB
U.S. NAVY BASE, PEARL HARBOR
OAHU, TERRITORY OF HAWAII
2130 HOURS 7 JULY 1942

Although he was of course delighted to see his sister's son, Rear Admiral Daniel J. Wagam was also a little annoyed at the way the kid popped up unannounced out of nowhere, expecting to be entertained.

The Admiral had been working his ass off since the Eyes Only EXECUTE OPERATIONAL PESTILENCE radio had come in five days before, and it seemed obvious that the work days were going to grow longer rather than shorter as things finally started to mesh.

The truth of the matter was that the Pacific Fleet and attached Marine Forces were not prepared—in any way—to stage an amphibious assault on an island in the Hawaiian chain, much less on three islands a quarter of the world away in the Solomons.

There was not enough of anything that would be needed. About the only thing that was not in short supply was senior officers. A whole flock of commanders and captains and even a dozen or so flag officers had been called back from retirement. They had come back into uniform willingly, even eagerly, and their expertise was most welcome. But at times, Admiral Wagam had reluctantly concluded, they were like a bunch of goddamned old maids.

By his own actual calculation, Admiral Wagam was spending two-thirds of his time establishing shipping priorities and scheduling convoys and the other third settling disputes over Naval protocol between the retreads, who were exquisitely sensitive to the prerogatives of rank and time in grade.

Most often, the disputes had to do with the assignment of creature comforts—who had a permanently assigned staff car with driver, and who didn't, that sort of thing. But the worst fights were over quarters—where the most desirable rooms in the Bachelor Officer's Quarters were assigned, or in cottages, in the case of captains and flag officers. These assignments were ordinarily made on the basis of rank, and within rank, on the basis of time in grade. Now and again, however, some of the retreads came to believe that the assignment they had been given was beneath their dignity and inappropriate to their rank and seniority.

As Admiral Wagam knew only too well, "seniority" was not as simple a concept as it might at first appear to be. For instance, seniority could not be established solely by date of promotion; for this would have made virtually all of the retreads senior to virtually all of the officers in a particular grade who had not retired. Some of the retreads had retired as early as 1935.

Thus it had been necessary to make up a seniority list for the retreads. Clerks had dug into the records to see how much time in grade Captain So-and-so had at the time of his retirement. This would be added to the time he now had on active duty since being recalled. This produced a seniority list based on time in grade, not date of promotion.

It had not been possible, however, to merge this list with a similar list prepared for nonretired officers, and announce that Captain A, who had never retired, and who had five years, nine months, and *eleven* days of service as a captain, therefore outranked Captain B, a retread, who had five years, nine months and *one* day of service as a four striper. When this happened, Captain B would very often make it known that the list be damned, when he retired, Captain A was a lowly lieutenant commander, a none-too-bright one, as he recalled; and he had no intention of taking orders from the young pup now.

And it wasn't a question of simply reminding Captain B that he was back in the Navy and expected to take orders, although Dapper Dan Wagam had done just that several times. Even when there was no question of seniority, a good many of the retreads seemed to have an uncontrollable urge to question the orders they had been given. Even when he himself was giving the orders, he'd come to expect from these guys a moment of smug hesitation, then something like, "Well, in my experience, we did . . . or did not . . ." Or, "In the *Old* Navy, they . . ." When they believed that they were being forced by an unappreciative Navy to take orders from some young pup still wet behind the ears, their obedience ceased being cheerful and willing. "After all," they were quick to point out, "we were *asked* to return to duty."

It often lent an entirely new meaning, Wagam had concluded, to the word "grudging."

And since he was on the bridge of a desk, rather than at sea, Admiral Wagam had, he believed, more than his fair share of the retreads. Indeed, very few of *them* were actually being sent to sea, although virtually all of them had volunteered—often two or three times a week—to take a command.

When his sister's son, First Lieutenant David F. Schneider, USMC, showed up, Admiral Wagam was trying to recover from yet another bad day. For one thing, he was frustrated that he'd failed to solve logistical problems there was no satisfactory solution for—there was simply not enough available tonnage for OPERATION PESTILENCE; and consequently, the First Marine Division was going to assault a hostile shore inadequately supplied. And for another, he'd been forced to handle no less than three retreads who truly believed that their professional reputations were being demeaned by the duties he had assigned them.

But Admiral Wagam was as gracious to David Schneider as he could be under the circumstances. He realized his problems were certainly not David's fault; but more to the point, his sister was hell on wheels when she felt one of her children had been slighted. . . .

So he personally showed David around the office, to give the boy some understanding of what he was up to.

He did not, of course, mention OPERATION PESTILENCE, which was classified TOP SECRET.

And then he took him to dinner in the Flag Officer's Mess and introduced him around. It would have been nice if David could have written his mother that he had been introduced to Admiral Nimitz, but Nimitz apparently had elected to eat in his quarters.

Nimitz was probably eating alone, or as alone as the CINC-PAC ever got to be, Admiral Wagam thought, *as opposed to having a working dinner. If it had been a working dinner, he probably would have been invited.*

And then he sent him on his way:

"David, I'd like to send you back to Ewa in my car, but I'm going to need it."

"I understand."

"There's a bus that runs between here and Ewa. Among other places, it stops at the Main Club."

"I can manage, Uncle Dan."

"I would suppose there will be a number of officers from MAG-11 at the club. Ask around. The odds are you can find a ride back with one of them."

"Thank you."

"Give your mother my love when you write."

"Yes, Sir, I'll do that."

XIII

(One)

First Lieutenant William C. Dunn, Executive Officer, VMF-229, was sitting at the bar with Lieutenant (j.g.) Mary Agnes O'Malley, Nurse Corps, USN, having an after-dinner cognac. Dunn had learned that an after-dinner cognac—for that matter, any kind of alcohol at any time—seemed to trigger in Mary Agnes lewd and carnal desires. As they sipped their cognacs, her arm was resting on his upper leg, and her hand was gently stroking his inner thigh. She was fully aware what this did to him. And he knew that once there was proof positive, so to speak, that she had flipped his HORNY ON switch, and the mechanism had been activated, she would look into his eyes with pleasure and understanding, and purse her lips in promise of what was to come. And probably even give it a friendly little pat on the head. *Good doggie.*

Dunn had recently been giving a good deal of thought to his relationship with Mary Agnes O'Malley.

For starters, he was the envy of most of his peers, even the noble minded who chose to believe she wasn't really giving him any. The ratio of young bachelor officers in the Naval

Establishment around Pearl Harbor to good-looking, socially acceptable females—or for that matter, to any kind of females—was probably two-hundred-fifty to one. Phrased another way, the odds against a first lieutenant hooking up with a good-looking, firm-breasted, blonde-headed nurse who fucked like a mink were probably on the order of a thousand to one.

What did every red-blooded Marine Aviator want? A nymphomaniac whose father owned a liquor store. Mary Agnes's father didn't own a liquor store, but there didn't seem to be any question that if she wasn't really a nympho, she was pretty damned close.

But Bill Dunn kept remembering from college some great philosophical truth—he forgot who said it—to the effect that the only thing worse than not realizing one's dreams was to realize them: Here he was with a good-looking woman who couldn't wait to get him in bed every night. There she would eagerly perform sexual acts he had seen before only in stag movies. And he was unhappy with the situation.

Even the sex, once the novelty wore off, was becoming a chore. He was regarding it lately as his duty, his more and more reluctant holding up of his end of the bargain.

The sad truth was that Mary Agnes O'Malley was dumber than dog shit. It was a realization he'd come to somewhat belatedly, probably because intellectual attainment was not high on his original list of priorities. But it didn't take him long to begin to think that it was entirely within the realm of possibility that an original idea and a cold drink of water *would* actually kill her.

Mary Agnes O'Malley read *Photoplay* and *Screen Life* magazines for intellectual stimulation; she was a veritable fountain of information regarding the private life of movie stars. She had read somewhere, for instance, that actor Tyrone Power had entered the Corps and was in flight training. Her dream was that Power would be assigned to Hawaii and Dunn would introduce them. She spoke of this often.

If that happened, Lieutenant Power—or Captain Power, whatever he was—would probably set the minimum time record for the Marine Aviator getting his ashes hauled after arrival in the Territory of Hawaii.

But in the meantime, Mary Agnes made it plain that Lieutenant Bill Dunn was all that her heart—and other anatomical parts—desired. This was not because she found him a charming companion, or even an outstanding lover, but because he looked, as she often told him, just like an actor named Alan Ladd.

Dunn knew that if he really wanted to break it off with Mary Agnes, he could do it relatively easily. He could just call her and say that he had the duty and could not make it over to Pearl. She was dumb, but she was capable of understanding that. He was convinced that if he did this five nights in a row, say, no matter how determined she was not "to cheat" on him, she would have a snifter or two of Hennessey VSOP, her blood would start to boil, and some other soul would find himself sneaking up the back stairs to Room Eleven, Female Officer's Quarters Fourteen.

But in his own eyes he had no character. Or phrased less delicately, he was letting his dick do his thinking for him. He made "Sorry, I have the duty" telephone calls at least four times—for two nights in a row, twice. But that was as far as logic could go, vis-à-vis overwhelming the sinful lusts of the flesh.

No matter how high his original resolve and how firm his original intentions, by the third day, he was unable to refute the whispers in his ear, *Billy-Boy, they are* not *pulling your chain with that "Live Today For Tomorrow We Die" shit. The piece of ass you are so casually rejecting may well be the last piece you are ever offered. Tomorrow morning, you may crash in flames. Or they may tell you to get your ass aboard a carrier; and away you will sail to your hero's death. With that in mind, does it really make any sense to spend your last night alive or ashore in your room with a portable radio for company, when you can play Hide the Salami and other games in Mary Agnes's perfumed bed?*

Dunn noticed First Lieutenant David Schneider within sixty seconds or so of the moment Schneider walked into the bar of the Main Club. Schneider caught Dunn's attention because he was wearing a white uniform. Officers wearing white uniforms outnumbered officers wearing greens about ten to one, but Schneider's white uniform was the only one—

Marine or Navy—with gold Naval Aviator's wings pinned to it.

I wonder who that horse's ass is? was Bill Dunn's first thought. If you were an aviator, you could get away with not wearing whites.

His second thought immediately followed the first: *He probably just got here. He's probably, as a matter-of-fact, one of the two we got today.*

When Dunn had signed out in the squadron office for the Main Club at Pearl Harbor, PFC Hastings told him VMF-229 had two new officer pilots.

"If you don't stop that, I'm going to bust my zipper," First Lieutenant Dunn said quietly to Lieutenant (j.g.) O'Malley, removing her hand from his crotch.

"Promises, promises," she replied and pursed her lips at him.

"Excuse me," he said, getting up.

"Where are you going?"

"I think the guy in whites down at the end of the bar is one of ours," he said. "I'll be right back."

Mary Agnes looked toward the end of the bar and saw First Lieutenant David Schneider.

"Oh, he's cute!" she exclaimed, "He looks just like John Garfield."

Dunn reached Schneider in time to see the bartender fill the lieutenant's glass with ginger ale. He was a little surprised, because there was no darker liquid already in the glass.

"Good evening," Dunn said.

Schneider nodded an acknowledgment, but did not speak.

"Is your name John Garfield, by any chance?"

"No, it is not."

"Just get in? To VMF-229 by any chance?"

Dunn saw that the question made the lieutenant uncomfortable.

Obviously, he can't answer that question. Japanese ears are everywhere. Loose lips sink ships. And I probably look like a Jap spy in disguise.

"My name is Dunn. I'm Exec of VMF-229."

"Oh," Schneider said, straightening. "Yes, Sir. My name is Schneider, Sir. I reported aboard today, Sir."

Dunn gave him his hand.

"How do you do, Sir?"

"I heard there were two of you?"

"Yes, Sir. Lieutenant Jim Ward was on the same set of orders."

"He here with you?"

"No, Sir. I believe he stayed aboard Ewa."

"Oh, now I know who you are. The Skipper stole you from Quantico, right?"

"We were stationed at Quantico, yes, Sir."

"Now, don't misunderstand this. This is a simple suggestion. I'm about to return to Ewa. I have a car. If you need a ride?"

"Yes, Sir, thank you very much. Actually, I came in here hoping to get a ride."

"Well, then, come on down the bar while I finish my drink."

"Won't I be in the way, Sir? Two's company, and so on?"

"Not at all," Bill Dunn said. "The lady and I are just friends."

This is despicable of you, Billy Dunn. But on the other hand, what a clever sonofabitch you are sometimes.

"Lieutenant O'Malley, may I present Lieutenant Schneider, who joined the squadron today?"

"Pleased to meet you, I'm sure," Mary Agnes said. "Did anyone ever tell you you look just like John Garfield?"

Dave Schneider flushed. "No, I can't say that anyone has."

"Don't you think he does, Bill?"

"Spitting image," Bill Dunn said. He was pleased to see that Lieutenant Schneider did not seem to be able to keep his eyes away from Mary Agnes's tunic, where her bosom placed quite a strain against the material; it sort of made her gold buttons stand to attention.

He beckoned to the bartender.

"We'll have a round," he said.

"Sir," Dave Schneider said uncomfortably, "I was led to believe we'd be flying tomorrow."

"One cognac won't hurt you," Bill Dunn said. "And we can't welcome you aboard with ginger ale."

"Yes, Sir," Dave Schneider said.

"And another part of the welcome aboard ritual is a dance

with Lieutenant O'Malley," Dunn said. "Mary Agnes is
something like the squadron mascot, isn't that so, Mary
Agnes?"

"Oh, it is not," she said. "You make me sound like a cocker
spaniel. But I do like to dance."

How about a bitch in heat?

(Two)
HEADQUARTERS, RAN COASTWATCHER
ESTABLISHMENT
TOWNESVILLE, QUEENSLAND
1945 HOURS 15 JULY 1942

Both Major Ed Banning, commanding officer of U.S. Marine
Corps Special Detachment 14, and Lieutenant Commander
Eric Feldt, Officer Commanding, Royal Australian Navy
Coast Watcher Establishment, were waiting at the small
Townesville air strip when the Royal Australian Air Force
Lockheed Hudson came in low over the sea and touched
down.

As the twin engine bomber-transport taxied to a parking
place, Banning put the Studebaker President in gear and
bounced over the grass to it.

By the time the rear door opened, and Captain Fleming
Pickering, USNR, was emerging from it, Banning and Feldt
were standing on either side of the spot where his feet would
alight. After Feldt saluted elaborately, in the British palm-
out manner, the hand quivering, he barked, "Sir!"

Banning extended a towel-wrapped bottle in an ice-filled
cooler. The cooler had begun life as a tomato can.

"It's beer," he said. "But you can't fault our good
intentions."

"I expected at least a band," Pickering said, taking the
bottle from the can and removing the towel. "What am I
supposed to do, bite the cap off?"

"Sir!" Feldt barked again, and bowing deeply handed him
a bottle opener.

Pickering opened the beer bottle, took a pull from the neck,
and offered the bottle to Feldt.

"Very good of you, Sir," Feldt said, taking a pull at the

beer and handing it to Banning. "And may I say how honored we all feel that you could find time in your busy schedule to honor us with a visit."

Pickering appeared to be thoughtfully considering the remark. Finally, smiling, he said, "Yes, I think you may."

Feldt laughed with delight.

The pilot, a silver-haired Wing Commander, the co-pilot, a Squadron Commander, and the crew chief, a sergeant, came out of the airplane. Banning introduced them, and then said, "I think, Wing Commander, that you may unload the emergency rations for these starving savages."

"Very good, Sir," the Wing Commander said.

The sergeant went back in the Hudson and started handing boxes out. There was a case of scotch, a case of bourbon, six cases of beer, and a wooden case marked Moet & Chandon.

"Do you sodding Americans do everything backward? Christmas is in *December,*" Feldt said.

"A small contribution to the *enlisted* mess," Pickering said. "Knowing as I do that a fine Christian officer such as yourself would never allow alcohol to touch his lips."

"I can get it down without it coming near my lips," Feldt said. "Anyone who comes between me and the bubbly does so at his peril."

"What's up, Boss?" Major Ed Banning asked.

"Never treat with the natives until you've plied them with alcohol," Pickering said. "And always hope that no one has warned them to beware of Americans bearing gifts."

"Why don't I like the sound of that?" Feldt asked.

"Because you're prescient," Pickering said. "You intuit that I am here to tell you how to do your job."

Feldt continued to smile, but the warmth was gone from his eyes.

"Will it wait until after dinner? Or should I more or less politely tell you to climb back on the sodding airplane and bugger off now?"

"That would depend on dinner," Pickering said. "What are we having?"

"Probably very little," Banning said. "I told them to go ahead and eat if we weren't back by 1830."

"We ran against a forty-knot headwind all the bloody

way," the Wing Commander said. "We had to set down and refuel."

"Then I suppose we'll have to drink our dinner," Pickering said. "How are we going to get all that in the car?"

"We'll take the booze, naturally, and leave you and Banning here," Feldt said. "There's such a thing as going too sodding far with this international cooperation crap."

"Why don't you and the Wing Commander and Captain Pickering take half of the booze, and then send the car back to pick up the rest of us and the rest of the booze?" Ed Banning suggested.

"Why don't we leave the Wing Commander, too?" Feldt said. "That way there would be no witnesses when I remind the Captain that the understanding was that he would keep his sodding nose the hell out of my business?"

"That," Pickering said, after a moment, "as you suggested, can wait until after dinner."

"It's a pity, really," Feldt said. "I was on the edge of almost liking you, Pickering. A man, even a sodding American, can't be all bad if he brings me Moet & Chandon."

"Into each life," Pickering intoned sonorously, "some rain must fall."

"Get in the car, you sodding bastard," Feldt said. "You drive. The sodding steering wheel is on the wrong side."

Lieutenant Commander Eric Feldt rose somewhat unsteadily to his feet.

"If you will excuse us, gentlemen," he said, "the time has come for me to tell Captain Pickering to bugger off before I am too pissed to do so."

"Ed," Pickering said, as he stood up from the dinner table, "you and Wing Commander Foster, too."

Feldt looked, not at all friendly, at Wing Commander Foster.

"You, too, Wing Commander?" he asked. "I wondered what the hell a Wing Commander was doing chauffeuring Pickering around."

Wing Commander Foster was aware of Lieutenant Commander Feldt's reputation even before Air Vice-Marshal Devon-Jaynes and Captain Fleming Pickering warned him that Feldt was difficult. As they all ate dinner, while Feldt bitterly criticized everyone involved in the war except the Japanese, Foster had managed to keep his mouth shut—though with an effort.

But now, momentarily, he lost control.

"One does what one is ordered to, Commander," he said icily. "In this instance, I am here at the direction of Air Vice-Marshal Devon-Jaynes."

"Air Vice-Marshal Devon-Jaynes?" Feldt replied. "Well, sod him, too."

He turned and marched out of the room. Pickering shook his head and made a gesture with his hand to Wing Commander Foster, signifying both an apology for Feldt and an order to say nothing more.

"Sorry, Sir," Foster said.

"Commander Feldt," Pickering said, touching Foster's arm, "is both a remarkable man, and a man whose contributions to this goddamn war cannot be overstated."

"Yes, Sir," Foster said, and then followed Pickering into Feldt's office. Banning brought up the rear.

Feldt was standing behind his desk, pouring scotch into a glass.

"I presume," he said nastily, "that since the Wing Commander is here at the direction of Air-Vice Marshal Whatsisname that he has the sodding Need to Know whatever it is we're going to talk about?"

"Wing Commander Foster has a TOP SECRET OPERATION PESTILENCE clearance," Pickering said evenly. He took a business-sized envelope from his inner jacket pocket and handed it to Feldt. "That's an authorization from Admiral Boyer to give Wing Commander Foster access to Coastwatcher classified information through TOP SECRET."

Feldt looked at the envelope, and then tossed it unopened on his desk.

"I'll take your word for it," he said. "Ok. Let's get to it."

"Why don't we uncover the map?" Pickering said.

"Why don't we?" Feldt said. He turned around and faced the wall behind his desk. A four-by-six-foot sheet of plywood, hinged at the top, lay against the wall. With some difficulty, Feldt raised it, then attached a length of chain which held it horizontally, exposing the map beneath.

The map displayed the Solomon Islands area from New

Britain and New Ireland in the North, through Santa Isabel and Guadalcanal in the Southeast, and the upper tip of Australia to the Southwest. It was covered with a sheet of celluloid, on which had been marked in grease pencil the location of the thirty or more Coastwatchers, together with their radio call signs.

"Why don't you have a look at that, Wing Commander?" Pickering said.

Foster went to the map and studied it carefully in silence for more than a minute.

"This is the first time I've seen this . . ." he said.

"We don't publish it in the sodding *Times,* for Christ's sake," Feldt said.

". . . and I had no idea how many stations you have," Foster concluded, ignoring him.

"Not as many as we would like. Or had," Feldt said. "Note the red Xs."

There were a dozen or more locations which had red grease pencil Xs drawn through them.

"No longer operational, I gather?" Foster said.

"No longer operational, for one reason or another," Feldt said. "Betrayed by natives. Or felled by one sodding tropical disease or another. Or equipment failure. Or the sodding Japs just got lucky and found them."

"We are going to land on Guadalcanal, Tulagi, and Gavutu on August first," Pickering said. He stopped and then went on. "Actually, I don't think there is any way they can make that schedule. There's going to be a rehearsal in the Fiji Islands first. And then they'll probably land on Guadalcanal on seven August or eight August."

"If then," Ed Banning said, a little bitterly. "I heard what a mess things are in in New Zealand."

"It'll have to be by then," Pickering replied. "If the Japanese get that airfield near Lunga Point on Guadalcanal operational—even for Zeroes, not to mention bombers—I hate to think what they could do to an invasion fleet."

"The point of all this?" Feldt asked.

"At the moment, the bulk of Japanese aerial assets are in— or around—Rabaul. When they attack the invasion fleet, or the islands themselves after we land, they will use planes based at Rabaul. The more warning we have, obviously, the better. I am concerned with Buka."

"Buka is up and running," Feldt said.

Foster searched on the map and found Buka, a small island at the tip of Bougainville.

"Here?" he said, but it was more of a statement than a question.

"Buka is the only Coastwatcher station, Wing Commander," Feldt said, "manned by U.S. Marine Corps personnel. Do you suppose that has anything to do with Captain Pickering's concern?"

Banning looked at Pickering and actually saw the blood drain from his face.

"There is a point, Eric," Pickering said icily, "when you cross the line from colorful curmudgeon to offensive horse's ass. At that point I will not tolerate any more of your drunken, caustic bullshit. You have passed that point. Do you take my meaning?"

"Not really," Feldt said, unrepentant. "Explain it to me."

"Let me put it this way: How would you like to spend the rest of this war counting life preservers in Melbourne?"

"Don't you threaten me!"

"If I don't have an apology in thirty seconds, I'm going to pick up that telephone and call Admiral Boyer and tell him that I have reluctantly come to agree with him about the necessity of relieving you."

"Sod you, Pickering."

"We're not going to need the thirty seconds, I see," Pickering said. He walked to the desk and reached for the telephone.

He had it halfway to his ear when Feldt stayed his hand.

"It's the booze, for Christ's sake."

"Then leave the goddamned booze alone!"

"I have this terrible tendency to lubricate myself when I find myself writing letters that go, 'Dear Mrs. Keller, I very much regret having to inform you that information has come to me indicating that your husband has been captured and executed by the Japanese . . .' "

Pickering put the telephone back in its cradle, but did not take his hand off it, nor take his eyes off Feldt.

Feldt avoided Pickering's eyes and looked at Wing Commander Foster.

"When they catch one of our lads, Wing Commander, what the Nips do—after interrogation, of course—is put him down ceremonially. First, they make him dig his own grave; and then they behead him, after making sure their chap with the sword is of equal or superior grade. After that, they pray over the grave. Did you know that?"

"No," Foster said quietly, "I did not."

Feldt looked at Pickering.

"Letting the side down, in my cups, I look for someone, a friend, against whom I can vent my 'caustic bullshit.' Ed Banning usually gets it. I don't know how or why he puts up with it. And I certainly can understand why you won't, Pickering. But for the record, I am fully aware that Buka would not be up and running if it weren't for your two lads. They have balls at least as big as any of my lads, and the one thing I was not suggesting was that they don't."

Pickering looked into his eyes for a moment, then took his hand from the telephone and straightened up.

"Let's talk about Buka," he said.

"I gather you accept my apology?"

"Oh, was that an apology?" Pickering asked lightly.

"As close as I know how to come to one."

"In that case, yes," Pickering said.

"Let's talk about Buka," Feldt said.

"We can't afford to lose it," Pickering said. "Worse possible case, we can't afford to lose it in the last few days before and the first few days following the invasion of Guadalcanal. Every plane the Japanese launch from Rabaul to attack the invasion force will pass over Buka. If we know the type of aircraft, how many, and when they're coming, we can have our fighters in the air to repel them. If we don't have that intelligence from Buka, a lot of people are going to be killed, and ships we can't afford to lose will be sunk."

"So?"

"I want to reinforce it," Pickering said. "I've discussed this with Admiral Boyer and he agrees. Wing Commander Foster has been directed to provide aircraft to drop another team, or teams, in."

"Sod Admiral Boyer," Feldt said. "No."

"You have reasons?" Pickering asked. Banning saw his face pale again.

"If there is anybody in Australia or New Zealand who knows his way around Buka, I haven't been able to find him," Feldt said. "And Christ knows, it's not for want of trying."

"What's your point?"

"There is only one spot on Buka where we could parachute a team in with any chance of them surviving the landing. We already used it to put your lads in there. The Nips know we used it. They are now watching it. So we can't use that again. The sodding island is covered with dense jungle, except where the Nips are. You jump a team in there, what you're going to have is three skeletons in trees. And even if by some miracle that didn't happen, and they got to the ground in one piece, they still wouldn't know the island, would they? They'd never be able to get from where they were dropped to where they could do any good. Either the jungle would get them, or the natives—you understand that the natives are still reliably reported to be cannibals?—or the sodding Nips, of course."

Pickering nodded, and then said softly, "It might become necessary to send in one team after another until one made it."

"You are a cold-blooded bastard, aren't you, Pickering?" Feldt asked softly.

"A lot of lives are at stake," Pickering replied. "We simply can't afford to lose that early intelligence."

"Are you looking for advice? Or did you come here to tell me when we are going to start dropping parachutists?"

"Advice."

"OK. Form your teams. Banning's already done that, anyway. Lay on an airplane, have it ready around the clock. For that matter, if you have the clout, lay on a submarine, or maybe a PT boat, in case we decide the best thing is to put them ashore and not parachute them in. If Buka goes down, then we start sending people. Not before. This isn't the Imperial sodding Japanese Navy; our lads don't want to die for their emperor, and I will be damned if I'll ask them to."

Pickering pursed his lips for just a moment.

"OK," he said. "We'll do it your way. And pray that Buka doesn't go down."

Feldt nodded.

"Since you've been so sodding agreeable, I'm going to offer you some of my bubbly. You understand I wouldn't do that for just anybody, Pickering."

(Three)
COMPANY GRADE BACHELOR'S OFFICER'S
QUARTERS #2
SUPREME HEADQUARTERS, SOUTH WEST PACIFIC
AREA
(FORMERLY, COMMERCE HOTEL)
BRISBANE, AUSTRALIA
0430 HOURS 22 JULY 1942

As often happened when the telephone rang in the middle of the night, and he made a grab for it, Lieutenant Pluto Hon, BS, MS, PhD (*summa cum laude*, Mathematics), Massachusetts Institute of Technology, knocked the unstable fucking museum piece off the bedside table and had to retrieve it from under the bed before he could answer it. The unstable fucking museum piece held its cone-shaped mouthpiece atop a ten-inch Corinthian column, and the ear piece hung from a life boat davit on the side.

"Lieutenant Hon, Sir."

"What the hell was that noise?" Captain Fleming Pickering asked.

"I knocked the phone over, Sir."

"Pluto, I'm really sorry to wake you at this ungodly hour, but something has come up, and I really want to have a word with you before I go."

"No problem, Sir. Where?"

"Here. On the way to the airport. Is that going to be a problem?"

"No, Sir. I'll catch a ride out there as soon as I can."

"No. I called Moore and told him to pick you up on his way out here. He should be at the hotel in ten, fifteen minutes."

"I'll be waiting for him, Sir."

"Thank you, Pluto. I am really sorry to have to do this to you. But I think it's important."

"No problem, Sir."

I have just spoken to the only officer in the grade of Army captain or above at the Emperor's Court who would dream of apologizing for waking a lowly lieutenant up. I am really going to miss Captain Pickering.

Pickering was leaving Brisbane to join the Guadalcanal invasion fleet in time for the rehearsal in the Fiji Islands. Hon suspected he would not be back for a long time, if ever.

Pickering hadn't come right out and said so, but there was little doubt in Hon's mind that when the rehearsal was over, Pickering was going with the invasion fleet to Guadalcanal instead of resuming his duties as the Secretary of the Navy's personal representative to the Emperor. Hon thought it was entirely likely that Pickering wouldn't stop there—watching the landing from the bridge of the command ship USS *McCawley*—but would actually go ashore with the Marines.

Pickering's contempt for the brass hats—at least for their petty bickering—at SHSWPA and CINCPAC had been made clear in the reports he had written (and Hon had read in the process of transmission) to Secretary of the Navy Frank Knox. And Pickering had also taught Hon that there was still life in the old saw, "Once A Marine, Always A Marine." Pickering thought of himself as a Marine. He felt a tie of brotherhood with the men who were actually invading Guadalcanal and Tulagi. The notion of returning to the cocktail party circuit in Australia while they were going in harm's way was repugnant to him.

In Hon's opinion, it would not be at all hard for Pickering to convince himself that he could best discharge his duty by going ashore with the Marines. If he was actually on the scene, he'd be in a better position to keep Frank Knox informed than if he were back in Australia—or at least so he would rationalize. Hon half expected that Pickering would actually suggest this plan to Knox in one of his reports. When he didn't, Hon suspected it was because he knew Knox would immediately forbid him to go anywhere near Guadalcanal.

If he decided to go ashore with the invasion force, there was nobody in the Pacific with the authority to stop him. His orders made it absolutely clear that he was subordinate only to Frank Knox.

Lieutenant Pluto Hon got out of the narrow iron bed, with its lumpy mattress, and took a very quick shave over the tiny sink in his room. The toilet and bath, in separate rooms, were down the corridor. About the only good thing Hon could think to say about the Commerce Hotel was that it was only a block and a half from the new Supreme Headquarters, South West Pacific Area. After the move from Melbourne, that was established in an eight-story building from which an insurance company had been evicted for the duration.

Before the war, the Commerce Hotel had apparently catered to traveling salesmen on very limited expense accounts. It was, of course, good enough for company grade officers assigned to the Emperor's Court.

He dressed quickly, ran down the stairs rather than wait for the small, creaking elevator (which often did not answer the button, anyway), and was standing outside on the sidewalk when Sergeant John Marston Moore pulled up in the Studebaker President sedan Banning's sergeant had scrounged for them.

Hon got in the front seat beside him.

Moore had really been screwed by the move from Melbourne, he thought. In Melbourne, he'd lived in a large room at The Elms. In Brisbane, the only property Pickering could find was a small house, called Water Lily Cottage, out by the racetrack. There was not only no room for Moore there, but when Pickering had ordered Hon to find someplace decent for Moore to live in and give him the bill, Hon had been unable to find any kind of a room at all.

So Moore lived outside of town with the other headquarters enlisted men in an old Australian barracks. When he didn't have the Studebaker, he had to ride back and forth to work on Army buses, when they were running. Worse, in the barracks, a headquarters company commander and a first sergeant, who could not be told what Moore was doing, saw in him just one more sergeant who could be put to work doing what sergeants are supposed to do, like supervising linoleum waxing and serving as sergeant of the guard.

Captain Pickering spoke several times with the

headquarters commandant about his needing Moore around the clock, which meant he would not be available for company duties. The last time he made such a call, he told the headquarters commandant he would register his next complaint with General Sutherland. And that worked. But with Pickering gone, it would happen again. Lieutenant Hon could not register complaints with MacArthur's Chief of Staff, "Dick, I'm having a little trouble with your headquarters commandant."

"I think we're going to miss Captain Pickering, Lieutenant," Moore said as they pulled away.

"Don't read my mind, please. Lowly sergeants should not be privy to the thoughts of officers and gentlemen."

"I went by the shop," Moore said, chuckling. "To see if there was anything for the boss. Nothing."

"Nothing?"

"Two more of Feldt's Coastwatchers are—'no longer operational.' "

"Buka?"

"Buka's all right. Should I tell the boss?"

"Not unless he asks. What can he do anyway?"

There were lights on all over Water Lily Cottage when Moore turned off Manchester Avenue into the driveway. Pickering's borrowed Jaguar drophead coupe was parked in the driveway ahead of them.

Pickering came out onto the porch in his shirt-sleeves as Hon got out of the car.

"Come on in, the both of you," he said. "There's time for coffee, and I want you to meet someone."

There was a woman in Water Lily Cottage. She had apparently spent the night, for she was wearing a bathrobe. It covered her from her neck to her ankles. She was, Hon quickly judged, in her thirties. Her dark hair was parted in the middle, brushed tightly against her scalp, and drawn up in a bun at the back. She wore no makeup.

Jesus, what's the boss been up to? I can't believe he's been screwing this dame.

"Gentlemen," Pickering said, "I'd like you to meet Mrs. Ellen Feller. She got in last night from Pearl Harbor."

I would never have thought she was an American, Hon thought, and then revised his opinion of her sexual desirability. Even the padded bathrobe could not conceal an attractive breastworks, which was apparently unrestrained by a brassiere.

I still don't think he's been screwing her. But on the other hand, I was twenty before I was willing to admit that my parents hadn't had me via immaculate conception.

Ellen Feller's smile, which accompanied the hand she gave Hon, was somewhat the wrong side of being friendly and inviting.

"Ellen and I go back pretty far," Pickering said. "She was my secretary in Washington."

"We're old friends," Ellen Feller added, quietly demure. Then she turned to Moore. "I believe I know your father," she said. "The Reverend John Wesley Moore, isn't it? Of Missions?"

"Yes, Ma'am," Moore said, visibly surprised.

"Of what?" Pickering asked.

"Missions, Sir," Moore furnished. "The William Barton Harris Methodist Episcopal Special Missions to the Unchurched Foundation."

"My husband and I were in China before the war," Mrs. Feller said, "with the Christian and Missionary Alliance. I met your father, and your mother, too, I believe, in Hong Kong."

"Ellen will be working with you," Pickering said, obviously impatient with missionary auld lang syne. "She's a damned good linguist, and a damned good analyst, and more to the point, she's MAGIC cleared."

I'll be damned.

But then another thought struck him, *It makes a lot of sense though.*

The high-ups in the intermingled and confusing multiservice command structure of communications intelligence had to send someone else with a MAGIC clearance to MacArthur's headquarters. They didn't know that Pickering had brought Sergeant John Marston Moore in on the most important secret of the war in the Pacific, which meant they believed only two underlings, Hon himself and Major Ed Banning, even knew what MAGIC was.

That made a total of four people in the Emperor's Court who were cleared to read intercepted messages between the

Japanese Imperial General Staff and Japanese Naval Headquarters and units at sea: The American Emperor himself, of course; MacArthur's G-2, newly promoted Brigadier General Charles M. Willoughby (who to Hon's private amusement spoke with an unmistakable German accent); and Banning and Hon.

Even taking very seriously the cliche that the more people in on a secret, the greater the chance the secret will soon be out, it just didn't make sense not to send at least one other person to Brisbane. For the most basic of reasons: If a Brisbane bus ran over Lieutenant Hon while Banning was up at Townesville, as he was most of the time, and a hot MAGIC came in, it would not reach MacArthur or Willoughby until Banning could fly down from Townesville to decrypt it for them.

As a practical matter, of course, Sergeant Moore would have filled in. Hon had given him a crash course in operation of the cryptographic equipment, and he knew what to do with MAGIC messages. But *they* didn't know that.

And so they sent someone else in; and not the kind of person Hon might have expected—a Navy Lieutenant Commander or an Army Signal Corps Lieutenant Colonel, the rank a sop to the rank consciousness of MacArthur's headquarters, where daily Hon was made to realize that a lowly lieutenant was of no consequence whatsoever. Instead, they sent a civilian, and even more incredibly, a female civilian.

"There was a chance for Ellen and me to talk last night," Pickering continued. "So it was fortunate that she came in when she did. I'm sure everybody would have been confused had she come in this afternoon." He stopped for a time to gather his thoughts. "Her coming," he went on after a moment, "might cause us a few minor problems. But let's deal with who's in charge first. Pluto, that's you. You're doing a fine job, and there's no one better qualified. Unfortunately, you're a lowly first lieutenant. I've been— punching pillows is what it feels like—trying to get you promoted to at least captain. For reasons that escape me, that has so far proven impossible. I left word with Ed Banning that he is to continue trying."

"That's very good of you, Sir, but . . ."

"Oh, bullshit . . . sorry, Ellen. *Nonsense,* Pluto. You're well deserving of promotion, and we all know it. But anyway, you are outranked not only by Ed Banning, obviously, but by Ellen as well."

"Sir?"

"What is it they said you are, Ellen?"

"An assimilated Oh Four, Captain."

"You know what that means, Pluto?" Pickering asked.

"Yes, Sir. Mrs. Feller is entitled to the privileges of a major, Sir. Or a Navy lieutenant commander."

"OK. That may come in handy for billeting, or whatever. And I don't give a damn who anyone at the Palace thinks is running things. But between you and Ellen, so far as MAGIC is concerned, you're in charge, Pluto. I have also left word with Ed Banning making that clear."

"Yes, Sir."

"You remain, Sergeant Moore," Pickering said, "low man on the totem pole, outranked by everybody."

"Yes, Sir. I understand."

"But since I suspect that moron at Headquarters Company will have you on a guard roster the moment he hears I've left, I want you to clear your things out of that barracks and move in here. I had to take a six month's lease on this place, and there's no sense letting it go to waste."

"Yes, Sir."

"Mrs. Feller will also be living here. I have assured her that you are a well-bred gentleman who will not be bringing any wild Australian lasses home for drinking parties late at night."

"No, Sir."

"There's only two bedrooms, Pluto," Pickering said. "I'm afraid you're stuck with the Commerce Hotel. The important thing, I think, is to keep Moore out of the hands of Headquarters Company—without calling attention to him."

"Absolutely, Sir," Hon said.

"Take Mrs. Feller to the bank later today or tomorrow and see that she is authorized to draw on our account," Pickering said. "And on that subject, Banning has been spending a lot of money. I have asked for more, and it should be coming quickly. If, however, one of the officer couriers does not bring you a check within the next week, radio Haughton. The one thing I do not want to do is run out of money for Banning and Feldt."

"Yes, Sir."

"Can you think of anything, Pluto? Or you, John?"

"No, Sir," Moore replied immediately.

"No, Sir," Hon said, a moment later.

"Ellen?"

"Credentials for me, Captain."

"Oh, yeah. There's a Major Tourtillott who handles that sort of thing. Ellen needs what you and Banning and Moore have. Anywhere in the building, at any time. If Tourtillott gives you any trouble, see Colonel Scott, who works for Sutherland. If he gives you trouble, radio Haughton."

"Yes, Sir," Hon said.

"The liaison officer, Captain," Ellen Feller said.

"Oh, yeah. Thank you. That's important. I suggested to Frank Knox that he send a liaison officer between here and CINCPAC. Ellen tells me that Colonel Rickabee found one. He should be coming in soon. He is not, repeat, not, to be made a member of your happy circle. He's not cleared for MAGIC, or for what Banning is doing. I mention that solely because Rickabee's name may come up. Or because I'm afraid the poor bastard may be another orphan around here and may seek company in his misery."

"I understand, Sir," Hon said. He looked at his watch. "Captain, what time is your plane?"

Pickering looked at his watch.

"Christ," he said. "And I didn't give you the coffee I promised."

"No problem, Sir."

"Moore can drive me to the airport, Pluto. You don't have to go."

"I'd like to see you off, Sir, if that would be all right."

"Why thank you, Pluto," Pickering said. He looked at Ellen. "Sorry to have to leave you in the lurch like this."

"Take care of yourself, Fleming," Ellen Feller said.

Why does the way she said that make me suddenly think that they have been making the beast with two backs? . . . Even after the modest declaration she just gave about how my-husband-and-I-were-missionaries-in-China and Fleming-and-I-are-just-old-friends?

Because you're a dirty-minded young man, Pluto Hon, who hasn't had his own ashes hauled in so long you probably wouldn't know what to do with an erection.

"Where's your bags, Sir?" Hon asked.

"I'll get them," Moore said.

"I'll carry my own damned bags, thank you," Captain Pickering said.

(Four)
HEADQUARTERS, VMF-229
EWA USMC AIR STATION
OAHU, TERRITORY OF HAWAII
1555 HOURS 25 JULY 1942

Corporal Alfred B. Hastings, USMC, followed Captain Charles M. Galloway, USMCR, into his office.

"Whatever it is, Corporal Hastings, fuck it," Captain Galloway said. "Your beloved commanding officer has had it for today."

Galloway's cotton flight suit was sweat soaked. His hair was matted on his skull, and his hands and face were covered with a film of oil. He looked exhausted. He settled himself like an old man in the chair behind his desk.

"It's the colonel, Sir," Hastings said. "He said for you to phone him the minute you got in."

"Did he say what he wanted?"

"No, Sir, but he's called three times."

Galloway pointed to the telephone on his desk. Hastings took the handset from the cradle, listened for a dial tone, handed the handset to Galloway, and then dialed a number.

"This is Captain Galloway, Sergeant. I understand the colonel wants to speak at me."

Hastings left the room. He returned a moment later with a bottle of Coke, which he set on Galloway's desk. Galloway covered the microphone with his hand.

"Bless you, my son," he intoned solemnly.

"Yes, Sir," Hastings said, smiling.

"Galloway, Sir," Charley said to the telephone. "I just got in."

"And how many hours is that today, Captain Galloway?" Lieutenant Colonel Clyde W. Dawkins asked, innocently.

"I haven't checked my log book, Sir."

"But you can tell time and count, right? Up to say five hours and forty-five minutes?"

What the hell has he done? Gone and checked the goddamned board?

"Was it that much, Sir?"

"You know goddamned well it was," Dawkins said. "On the other hand, if you're dumb enough not to believe me when I say I don't want you flying more than four hours, maybe you *are* too dumb to count."

"Yes, Sir."

"But that is not the reason, at least the main reason, I wanted this little chat with you, Captain Galloway."

"Sir?"

"Knowing as I do your penchant for obeying only those orders you find it convenient to obey, I suppose it's hoping too much to expect you to have a white uniform for formal occasions?"

"Sir, I have a set of whites."

"Just in passing, I believe the regulation says you are required to have *two* sets. Is the one set you have suitably starched and pressed for wear at a formal occasion, for example, taking cocktails and dinner with an admiral?"

Charley took a quick mental inventory of his closet in the BOQ. His whites, never worn, were there, still in the bag they'd come in. If they weren't pressed, he had an iron.

"Yes, Sir," he said.

"Good. The admiral will be pleased. He is sending his car for us at 1830. Try not to spill tomato juice on your whites between now and then. With you owning only one set, that would pose a problem."

"What admiral is that, Sir?"

"Take a guess."

Since Charley was reasonably convinced that for reasons he could not imagine, Dawkins was pulling his chain about dinner with some admiral, he could not resist the temptation:

"Admiral Nimitz?"

"No. Close, but no. Guess again."

Christ, he's serious!

"I have no idea," he confessed.

"I'll give you a hint: How many officers do you have with uncles who are admirals?"

"Oh, Christ! What's he want?"

"I don't know. What I do know is that his aide was over here around noon—in his whites by the way, with the golden rope and everything—bearing an invitation for you and me to take cocktails and dinner with the admiral at his quarters. The admiral is sending his car for us, and the uniform is whites."

"Jesus!" Charley said.

"Have you been saying unkind things to Lieutenant Schneider, Charley?"

"No. I was just flying with him, as a matter-of-fact. He's doing very well, and I just told him so. He's going to be all right, Colonel."

"Well, he is not, repeat not, to be informed of where you and I are going tonight. The way the aide put it was, 'the admiral thinks that it would be best if Lieutenant Schneider didn't hear of this.' "

"I wonder what the hell is going on?"

"Considering how you ignore me when I tell you I don't want you flying more than four hours a day, *I* wonder if you will be able to keep our dinner plans a secret from Lieutenant Schneider."

That won't be a problem. Schneider at this very moment is probably already showered, shaved, shined, and doused with cologne, and breathing through flared nostrils as he arranges tonight's rendezvous with Mary Agnes O'Malley; he won't surface until tomorrow morning, looking wan, exhausted, and visibly satiated.

"That won't be a problem, Sir."

"You told me that keeping your flying under four hours a day wasn't going to be a problem, either, as I recall," Colonel Dawkins said. "My quarters, not a second after six-thirty. We don't want to keep the admiral waiting, do we, Charley?"

Colonel Dawkins hung up while Charley was on the "No" of "No, Sir."

* * *

At 1825 Admiral Daniel J. Wagam's aide-de-camp arrived at Lieutenant Colonel Dawkins's BOQ in the Admiral's Navy gray Plymouth staff car. Captain Charles M. Galloway arrived a moment later in his nine-year-old yellow Ford roadster. By the time Charley found a place to park the Ford, Colonel Dawkins had emerged from the building and was standing by the Plymouth.

The admiral's aide, a Lieutenant (j.g.), got in the front seat beside the driver, affording Captain Galloway, in deference to his rank, the privilege of riding in the back. Charley had often wondered why in military protocol the back seat represented privilege and prestige. If he were the brass hat, he would have chosen to ride in front, where there was often more room and you could see better.

After considerable idle thought, he'd finally figured out an answer that made sense: It went way back, to horse-drawn carriages. The front seat then had been less comfortable, and often out in the rain.

The services were very reluctant to change tradition. Charley knew that chances of his ever having to take a swipe at somebody with a sword were pretty goddamned remote. But a sword, in the pattern prescribed for Marine officers, was like his white uniform, yet one more thing he had had to buy when he took the commission.

The crown of his white brimmed hat cover had embroidered loops sewn to it. These were not the gold embroidered loops ("scrambled eggs") worn by senior officers on their caps. So anyone could tell at a glance whether or not he was looking at some lowly company grade officer. The loops went back to the days when Marines were posted as sharpshooters in the rigging of sailing ships. The officers then had fixed knotted rope to their headgear so the sharpshooters would not shoot them by mistake. Charley somewhat irreverently wondered if that now sacred tradition had come into existence after too many officer pricks had been popped "by mistake" by their men in the rigging.

"You should not have shot Lieutenant Smith in the head, Private Jones. You could see that he was an officer. He had rope on his hat."

How come, Charley wondered, *only the officers wore rope*

loops? Why not all Marines? Or in those days, was it considered OK to shoot enlisted Marines by mistake?

Admiral Wagam's aide turned around on the front seat.

"Colonel, by any chance do you know Commander C.J. Greyson?"

"Yes, I do," Colonel Dawkins replied. "He was a classmate."

"Yes, Sir. I knew that. I didn't know if you knew Charley."

"Knew him well. We were both cheerleaders."

You were what? Cheerleaders? *Jesus! Siss Boom Bah! Go Navy!*

"Charley's my brother, Sir."

"Oh, really?"

"He's on the staff of COMDESFORATL now, Sir. I had a letter last week." (Commander, Destroyer Force, Atlantic.)

"Well, when you write him, please give him my best regards," Dawkins said.

Back in Central High School, those of us who played varsity ball thought the male cheerleaders were mostly pansies. But I guess things are different at the United States Naval Academy, huh?

"Yes, Sir, I'll be happy to."

"You went to the Academy?"

"Yes, Sir. '40."

Lieutenant (j.g.) Greyson smiled at Charley.

"I understand you were directly commissioned, Sir."

"Well, the Commandant had to make a choice," Charley said. "It was either commission me, or send me to Portsmouth."

Lieutenant (j.g.) Greyson looked uncomfortable and turned to the front again.

"Watch it, Charley," Dawkins said, softly and sternly; but he was unable to suppress a smile.

In 1937–39, when he was still a Captain, Rear Admiral (upper half) Daniel J. Wagam and his family occupied the quarters he shared now with Rear Admiral (lower half) Matthew H. Oliver.

(Rear Admirals, upper half, are equivalent to Army and Marine Corps Major Generals. Rear Admirals, lower half, are equivalent to Army and Marine Corps Brigadier Generals. Army and Marine Corps Major Generals wear two

silver stars as the insignia of their rank, while Army and
Marine Corps Brigadier Generals wear just one star. All Rear
Admirals, however, wear the same two stars that Major
Generals wear. This practice is said to annoy many Army
and Marine Corps Brigadier Generals, particularly when
they learn that they actually outrank the Rear Admiral,
lower half, whom they have just saluted crisply.)

Though the Pearl Harbor officer corps had tripled or
quadrupled in size since 1939, there were now very few
dependents. That meant that many former family quarters
were now occupied by "unaccompanied" officers. It had
worked out remarkably well.

Placing "unaccompanied officers" in family quarters
afforded senior officers with quarters appropriate to their
rank. This was valuable not only because these provided
greater creature comforts—such as privacy and luxury—
than can be found in Bachelor Officer quarters, but because
these also gave them a place where they could hold private
meetings over drinks, or drinks and dinner.

Admiral Wagam's quarters were a four-bedroom house.
He occupied the master bedroom, Admiral Oliver the guest
room, and their aides-de-camp occupied what he still thought
of as Danny's and Joan's rooms. The admiral's children were
now waiting out the war with their mother, near Norfolk,
Virginia.

Three Filipino messboys took care of the housekeeping and
cooking. (Two of them were assigned as a prerogative of rank
to Admiral Wagam and one to Admiral Oliver.) The loyalty
and discretion of Filipino messboys was legendary. Admiral
Oliver was not senior enough to have a permanently assigned
staff car and driver. Admiral Wagam's driver lived over the
garage.

Admirals Wagam and Oliver got along splendidly. When
one or the other of them wished to hold a meeting in the
house, he simply asked the other if it would be possible for
him to eat in the Flag Mess that night. Neither, both being
gentlemen, ever asked who was being entertained. It might
be CINCPAC himself, for example; or it could be an old
family friend—female—with whom the admiral had a
platonic relationship but did not wish to wine and dine at the

mess because of the way people talked. No matter who it was, each admiral could count on the discretion of the other.

A white-jacketed, smiling Filipino messboy had the front door of Admiral Wagam's quarters open even before Lieutenant Greyson could put his finger on the highly polished brass door bell.

Greyson waved Dawkins and Galloway through the door.

"I'll tell the Admiral you're here, gentlemen," he said, and went to the closed door to the study and knocked.

In a moment, Admiral Wagam emerged, carrying a leather briefcase.

"Lock that up, will you please, Dick?" he said, as he handed the briefcase to his aide-de-camp.

"Aye, aye, Sir."

"Gentlemen," Admiral Wagam said, smiling at Dawkins and Charley. "Welcome. I'm glad you were able to come tonight."

"Very good of you to have us, Sir," Dawkins said.

"Dick's been telling me, Colonel, that you and his brother are classmates."

"Yes, Sir. '32."

"I'm '22," the admiral said, and turned to Galloway.

"And the famous—or is it infamous—Captain Galloway. I've been looking forward to meeting you, Captain. I was present, Captain, for the famous 'Q.E.D.' remark."

"Sir?" Galloway asked, wholly confused.

"I was in Admiral Shaughn's office when word came that you were flying that F4F out to the *Saratoga*. Captain Anderson of BUAIR [Bureau of Aeronautics] was there, sputtering with rage. He said, 'Admiral, this simply can't be. My people have certified all of VMF-211's aircraft as totally destroyed.' And Admiral Shaughn replied, '*Quod erat demonstrandum,* Captain, *Quod erat demonstrandum.*' What made it even more hilarious was that Anderson didn't have any Latin, and it had to be translated for him."

"Yes, Sir," Charley said, still wholly confused.

"He didn't know that '*Quod erat demonstrandum*' meant 'the facts speak for themselves'?" Dawkins asked. "Really?"

You made that translation for me, Charley realized. *Thank you, Skipper.*

"He hadn't the foggiest idea what it meant," Admiral

Wagam said, chuckling. "And he gave an entirely new meaning to the word 'ambivalent.' Like everybody else . . . Anderson is really a nice fellow, personally . . . he was hoping that Galloway would make it onto *Sara*. But on the other hand, if he *did,* in an airplane Anderson's BUAIR experts had certified was damaged beyond any possibility of repair, he was going to look like a fool."

Admiral Wagam laughed out loud. "Which Galloway did, of course, making him look like a fool. No wonder BUAIR was so angry with you, Galloway. Well, it turned out all right in the end, didn't it? All's well that ends well, as they say."

"Yes, Sir," Charley said.

"Let's go in the living room and have a drink," Admiral Wagam said. "I've been looking for an excuse since three o'clock."

A small, pudgy Filipino messboy in a starched white jacket was waiting for them behind a small, well-stocked bar. Through an open door, Charley saw a dining room table set with crystal and silver. A silver bowl filled with gardenias was in the center of the table.

"We've got just about anything you might want," the Admiral said, "but Carlos makes a splendid martini, and I've always felt that a martini is just the thing to whet the appetite before roast beef."

"A martini seems a splendid notion, Admiral," Dawkins said.

"Yes, Sir," Charley said.

"Four of your best, Carlos, please," the admiral ordered. "And I suggest you have a reinforcement readily available."

I could learn to like living like this, Charley thought. But this was instantly followed by two somewhat disturbing second thoughts: *Jesus, Caroline's house in Jenkintown is bigger than this. And so is Jim Ward's parents' house. And compared to the apartment on the top floor—the* penthouse*— of the Andrew Foster Hotel, this place—this* Admiral's Quarters*—is a dump.*

Carlos filled four martini glasses from a silver shaker, and the Admiral passed them around.

The Admiral raised his glass, and looking right at Charley, said, "To youth, gentlemen. To the foolish things young men do with the best of intentions."

"Admiral," Colonel Dawkins said, "with respect, I would prefer to drink to the wise elders who keep foolish, well-intentioned young men out of trouble."

"Colonel, I normally dislike having my toasts altered, especially by a Marine, but by God, I'll drink to *that,*" Admiral Wagam said, taking a sip and beaming at Dawkins.

Charley and Lieutenant (j.g.) Greyson dutifully sipped at their martinis.

"So you have the feeling, do you, Colonel . . ." Admiral Wagam said, interrupting himself to turn to the messboy: "Splendid, Carlos. Splendid."

"Thank you, Admiral," Carlos beamed.

". . . that senior officers rarely get the appreciation they should," Admiral Wagam went on, "for—how should I put this?—*tempering the enthusiasm* of the young men for whom they are responsible?"

"Yes, Sir," Dawkins beamed. "I was just this afternoon having a conversation with Captain Galloway about his excessive enthusiasm for flying."

"At the expense of his duties as commanding officer, you mean?"

"No, Sir. I can't fault Captain Galloway's command. What I was trying to do was point out that all work and no play makes good squadron commanders lousy squadron commanders."

The Admiral grunted. "There was a study, a couple of years back, Medical Corps did it on the quiet. They found out that a newly appointed destroyer captain on his first voyage as skipper averaged five point three hours sleep at night. A man, especially an officer in command, can't function without a decent night's sleep. There's such a thing as too much devotion to duty, Galloway. You listen to Colonel Dawkins."

"Yes, Sir."

"That sleep requirement apparently doesn't apply to aides, Admiral?" Lieutenant (j.g.) Greyson asked.

"Aides have very little to do," the Admiral replied. "They can get their necessary sleep while standing around with their mouths shut." He put his arm around Greyson's shoulders. "I learned that from a distinguished sailor, Mr. Greyson. Your father. I was his aide when he told me that."

A second messboy appeared in the door to the dining room.

"Excuse me," he said. "Admiral, dinner is served."

"Hold it just a moment, Enrique," Admiral Wagam said. "I need another one of Carlos's martinis."

Charley glanced at Dawkins. Dawkins, just barely perceptibly, shrugged his shoulders, signifying that he had no idea what the hell this was all about, either.

The admiral passed out four fresh martinis.

"Let me offer another toast," he said. "Prefacing it with the observation that, obviously, it is not for dissemination outside this room. To the officers and men of VMF-229, who will sail from Pearl Harbor aboard the escort carrier *Long Island* two August. May God give you a smooth voyage and good hunting."

"Hear, hear," Colonel Dawkins and Lieutenant (j.g.) Greyson said, almost in unison.

"Thank you," Charley said.

"Although I am afraid he sometimes qualifies as one of the foolish, overly enthusiastic young men we were talking about a moment ago, my nephew tells me that VMF-229 is the best fighter squadron in Marine Aviation. Do you think I should believe him, Captain?"

"Sometimes even foolish young men have it right, Admiral," Charley said.

"Is that another example of that famous Marine modesty, Captain?" Admiral Wagam asked, as he put his hand on Charley's arm and led him into the dining room.

"A simple statement of facts, Sir," Charley said.

The admiral took his seat at the head of the table and pointed to the chair where Charley was to sit. Dawkins went to the far end of the table. Greyson sat across from Charley.

"I'm a little surprised you haven't asked where you're going," Admiral Wagam said.

"Sir, I thought that would be classified," Charley said.

"It is, of course," Wagam said. "And I suppose that disqualifies you as a foolish young man. Only a foolish young man would ask, right?"

"Yes, Sir."

"But let me put you on the spot, Galloway. Where do you think you'll be going? What's the scuttlebutt?"

Wagam saw Galloway's discomfiture.

"I will neither confirm nor deny, Galloway. But sometimes it is of value to know what people think, what they are guessing."

Galloway looked at Dawkins for help. Dawkins shrugged again, barely perceptibly. Galloway interpreted this to mean, "Tell him what you think."

"Sir, I think that once the 1st Marine Division has secured the airfield on Guadalcanal, we'll be flown off the *Long Island* onto the island."

Admiral Wagam audibly sucked in his breath.

"And when does the scuttlebutt have it that the 1st Marines are going to invade, what did you say, Guadalcanal?"

"Yes, Sir. Guadalcanal. Shortly after the first of the month, Sir."

"Goddamn it, I'd love to know where you got that!" Admiral Wagam exclaimed, and then immediately regained control of himself. He held out his hand in a stop gesture. "If you were about to answer me, belay it. We will now change the subject."

"Yes, Sir," Charley said, and put a fork to the shrimp cocktail the messboy had set in front of him.

There was no question in his mind now that Big Steve's scuttlebutt, and his own studied guesses, were right on the mark. VMF-229 was going to Guadalcanal to operate off a captured Japanese airfield. Presuming, of course, that the 1st Marine Division could capture it.

"You're a bachelor, I understand, Galloway," the admiral said.

"Yes, Sir."

"In wartime, there are a number of advantages to being a bachelor," the admiral said.

"And in peacetime, there are a number of advantages to being a bachelor," Dawkins said.

The admiral gave him a frosty look.

"Spoken like a longtime married man, Colonel," he said. "I share that opinion, to a degree. But what I had in mind was that a bachelor can devote his full attention to his duties, where a married man is always concerned with the welfare of his family. Wouldn't you agree?"

"Yes, Sir. I take your point."

"But what you said just made me think of something else," the admiral said. "My wife would probably kill me if she heard me say this, but I would say—how can I phrase this delicately?—Would you agree, Colonel, that the pain of separation from one's wife is less for people like you and me, who have been married for a long time, than it would be for someone who has recently married and then is almost immediately separated from his bride?"

"Yes, Sir. I agree. And I think you phrased that very delicately, Admiral."

"Yes," the admiral agreed.

The messboys appeared, removed the silver shrimp cocktail bowls, and served the roast beef, roasted potatoes, and broccoli with hollandaise. A bottle of wine was introduced, opened, sipped by the admiral, and then poured.

The admiral raised his glass.

"To marriage, gentlemen. A noble institution. But one into which, I don't think, speaking of foolish young men with the best of intentions, Lieutenant David Schneider should enter at this point in his life and career."

Jesus Christ, what's this?

"I wasn't aware he was contemplating marriage." Colonel Dawkins said.

"He is," the admiral said, sawing at his roast beef. "He is now experiencing the ecstasy of what he really believes is true love. True love at first sight, to put a point on it."

"I'll be damned," Dawkins said.

Not Mary Agnes, for Christ's sake!

"The young lady in question is a Navy Nurse," the admiral said. "Lieutenant (junior grade) Mary Alice O'Malley."

Holy Christ!

"Mary *Agnes,* Sir," Lieutenant Greyson corrected him.

"Mary *Agnes,* then," the admiral said, a trifle petulantly. "David came to me last night and told me that he intended to apply for permission to marry. He tells me that he has stolen the affections of this young woman away from your executive officer, Captain Galloway; and for that reason, and others, he fears that his application will be delayed by you. He therefore sought my good offices to overcome your objections." He looked at Galloway. "Was he correct? Would you have, by fair means or foul, put obstacles in his path?"

"Yes, Sir, I would have."

"Good. Then we are all on the same wavelength," the admiral said. "What we have to do now is come up with a plan that will both keep him from making a fool of himself and keep both of us out of the line of fire. Just between us, gentlemen, I don't intend to spend the rest of my life explaining to my sister why I stood idly by and watched her precious Davey-boy marry a peroxide blonde floozie who is seven years older than he is, and who has been satisfying the sexual desires of every other junior officer in Pearl Harbor." The admiral paused and looked at Captain Charles M. Galloway, USMCR. "Including some squadron commanders who should have known better, even when they were in enlisted status."

XIV

(One)
MARINE CORPS LIAISON OFFICE
PRINCETON UNIVERSITY
PRINCETON, NEW JERSEY
27 JULY 1942

When his sergeant major loudly bellowed, "telephone for you, Major, Sir," Major George F. Dailey, USMC, a curly haired, slightly plump man six months shy of his thirtieth birthday, was sitting at his desk in shirt-sleeves in surrender to the heat.

Sergeant Major Martin was more than a little deaf. He was an Old Breed Marine recalled from the Fleet Reserve. He originally retired, after twenty-five years of service, the year before Dailey was commissioned.

"Thank you, Sergeant Major," Dailey said, and picked up the telephone.

"Major Dailey speaking."

"Major George Frederick Dailey?"

"Yes."

"What was your mother's maiden name?"

"I beg your pardon?"

"I asked what was your mother's maiden name?"

"Who is this, please?"

"My name is Rickabee. I'm a lieutenant colonel on the headquarters staff."

He means, Daily realized, genuinely surprised, *Headquarters, United States Marine Corps staff*. The Director, Central North East Region, Officer Procurement—Dailey—had never before heard directly from Headquarters, USMC.

"Cavendish, Sir," Dailey said.

"OK," his caller said. "I want you to catch a train as soon as you can, Major, and come down here. We're in Temporary Building T-2032 on the Mall. Take a cab from the station. Write that down. T-2032. My name is Rickabee." Rickabee obligingly spelled his name.

"Sir, would . . . day after tomorrow be all right?"

"I'm talking about this afternoon."

"Sir, that would be difficult. I have a . . ."

"Get your ass on a train and get down here this afternoon, Major," Colonel Rickabee said, and then hung up.

Dailey held the telephone in his hand for a moment before replacing it in the cradle. Then, for another minute, he looked out his window at the Princeton campus. Then he called for Sergeant Major Martin. He had to call three times before the old Marine appeared at his door.

"They want me to come to Washington," he said. "You'll have to reschedule whatever's on the schedule for this afternoon."

Major Dailey was himself a Princetonian, and he supposed that had more than a little bit to do with his first assignment in wartime. He understood the importance of officer procurement, of course, and why it made a good deal of sense to have a professional, such as himself, deciding which eager young man had the stuff required of a Marine officer and which did not. All the same, he would have much preferred to be in the Pacific as a fighter pilot, but that was out of the question.

At one time Major Dailey was a fighter pilot. He had gone from Princeton to Quantico, after which he'd done two years duty with troops. And then, just after he had been promoted to first lieutenant, he was sent to flight school at Pensacola. He flew for not quite four years, and loved every moment of it. But then he was called in after his annual flight physical and told that he had a heart murmur, and he had better give serious thought to what he wanted to do in the Corps now that he was no longer physically fit to fly.

He seriously considered resigning—he had no interest in the infantry or artillery, which seemed his other options. If he no longer could fly, what good to the Corps could he be? But a full bull colonel he had a lot of respect for told him the Corps needed unusually bright, well-educated officers in procurement, logistics, or intelligence even more than it needed yet one more aviator. So he decided to put off resigning for a couple of years to see what happened.

The Corps sent him back to college for six months for a crash course in the German language, and then sent him to the U.S. Embassy in Berlin as an Assistant Naval Attache. His promotion to captain came along when it was due, and he was not blind to the fact that a six-room apartment on Onkle Tomallee in Berlin-Zehlendorf was considerably more comfortable than a BOQ in Quantico.

He came home in 1940 and did an eighteen-month tour in Headquarters, USMC, essentially studying German tactics for review by G-3. And in November, 1941, he was promoted to Major (in the reserve; he was still only a Captain on the numerical list of regular Marine Corps Officers). When war came, he expected to be assigned some sort of duties which would take advantage of his European experience, but that didn't happen.

They sent him to Princeton to serve as President of the Officer Selection Board for the area, and to modify (that is to say, condense) the Platoon Leader's Training Program at the university. He was led to believe that the decisions he made about what could be cut from the pre-war program would set the pattern for other programs across the country.

He didn't like the prospect of sitting out the war in Princeton, but he was able to resign himself to it, particularly in the belief that his assignment probably would not last long. The projected growth of the Corps boggled the mind . . . they were now talking of hundreds of thousands of Marines—*divisions* of Marines. And certainly, they would need an officer of his rank and experience doing something besides selecting potential officers.

He expected to be reassigned, in other words. But the suddenness of the event, and the assignment itself, were startling.

At 1615 that afternoon, Lieutenant Colonel Rickabee ushered Major Dailey into the office of Brigadier General Horace W.T. Forrest, USMC, Assistant Chief of Staff for Intelligence. To Dailey's surprise, Rickabee was not only not in uniform, he had a large revolver "concealed" in the small of his back under his seersucker jacket.

Dailey noticed on General Forrest's desk both his Officer's Service Record and another file, marked SECRET, and DAILEY, GEORGE F.

He could not remember afterward what questions General Forrest put to him, and thus not his answers, but he remembered clearly how the interview ended:

"He'll do," General Forrest announced. "You brief him. I'm too busy, and I don't want him contaminated by those bastards in G-1."

"Aye, aye, Sir," Colonel Rickabee said, smiling, and then signaled for Dailey to leave. When he came out of General Forrest's office, Dailey saw that he was carrying both the files that the General had apparently been reading.

In the unmarked (but obviously government owned) car they drove back from Eighth and "I" Streets to Rickabee's office on the Mall, Rickabee gave him the first inkling of the billet that General Forrest had now officially given him.

"You know the good news–bad news routine?" Rickabee asked.

"Yes, Sir."

"The good news is that you are, effective today, a lieutenant colonel and on leave. The bad news is that when you come off your leave you will be in San Diego, about to board an airplane for Pearl Harbor. Your ultimate destination is Brisbane, Australia, where you will be the Marine liaison officer between CINCPAC—Admiral Nimitz—and The Supreme Commander, Southwest Pacific Area—General MacArthur."

"Why is that bad news, Sir?"

"Haven't you ever heard that primitive cultures always shoot the bearers of bad news?" Rickabee said.

Despite what General Forrest said about contamination, Lieutenant Colonel Dailey was briefed by a team of officers of the Office of the Assistant Chief of Staff for Personnel. The lieutenant colonel in charge told him (and Dailey believed him, and could not help but be flattered by the statement) that G-1 had been looking all along for a suitable assignment for him . . . God knew the Corps needed experienced officers; but, until the day before, there had been "a G-2 Hold" on his records; and as long as that was there, he could not be reassigned without G-2 concurrence; and that had not been given.

"We didn't even propose you for this billet, frankly," the lieutenant colonel said. "We thought it would be a waste of time with the G-2 Hold. So, wouldn't you know, G-2 proposed you to us. We're delighted, of course. And I suppose I will have to take back all the unpleasant things I've been saying about G-2."

The G-1 lieutenant colonel went on to describe the bad feeling between General MacArthur's and Admiral Nimitz's headquarters. This was recently brought to a head when SHSWPA (Supreme Headquarters, South West Pacific Area) formally charged that CINCPAC had been denying MacArthur information he was entitled to have; or at least was delaying it until it was too late to act upon.

"That brought the Secretary of the Navy in on this, Dailey," the lieutenant colonel said. "He sent word down that he didn't want MacArthur to have grounds to even suspect that anything was being kept from him; he ordered that an officer be assigned to Brisbane to do nothing but pass information between CINCPAC and SHSWPA; and he specified a Marine. We thought of you right away, of course, with your diplomatic experience . . . but with that G-2 Hold?" he shrugged. "Anyway, here you are."

Lieutenant Colonel Dailey took a seven-day leave, spending it with his mother in Greenwich, Connecticut. And then returned to Washington, where Colonel Rickabee informed him that he would travel at least as far as Pearl Harbor with a briefcase chained to his wrist.

"Two birds with one stone," Rickabee explained. "And it will free the seat the officer courier would normally occupy."

At Anacostia Naval Air Station, Dailey asked Rickabee about the G-2 Hold. He did that just before he got on the plane to San Diego, reasoning that it was too late for Rickabee to do anything about it, even if he did make him mad.

"I presume the G-2 Hold situation has been resolved, Colonel," he said. "May I ask what it was, specifically?"

"I see that our friends in personnel have diarrhea of the mouth again," Rickabee said.

"What I'm asking, Colonel, is whether there is some sort of cloud over me."

"No. I assure you there is not."

"Then may I ask why there was a hold?"

"Am I to suspect, *Colonel*," Rickabee replied, "that your conscience is bothering you vis-à-vis your relationship with Fraulein Ute Schellberger?"

"I wondered if that was a matter of official record," Dailey confessed. For an instant it all seemed perfectly clear. That's why he was sent to Princeton. If there was anything worse for a young officer on attache duty than getting drunk and pissing in the Embassy's potted palms, it was getting involved with a German blonde.

"Well, it bothered the FBI some, frankly," Rickabee said. "But then I told them that so far as the Corps was concerned, we would have been worried if a red-blooded young bachelor Marine officer far from home had *not* been fucking the natives, and that we were convinced you had not become a National Socialist."

"Christ!" Dailey had said.

Rickabee smiled at him.

"I can't tell you how relieved I am to hear that," Dailey said.

"You didn't hear anything from me, Colonel," Rickabee said. "Understood?"

"Understood."

"And now you are wondering, naturally, how come you were given this assignment? And are too polite, or too discreet, to ask?"

"Yes, Sir."

"There are several things going on over there in which we have an interest. Since you have no need to know what they are . . ."

"I understand, Sir."

"We may need replacements for the incumbents. An ideal replacement would be an officer of appropriate grade, who had already gone through the FBI's screening and been declared ninety-nine and forty-four one-hundredths percent pure on the morals scale—like Ivory soap. And who was not only over there, but in a position to know more of what's going on than, say, a battalion commander. Or for that matter, a division G-2. A liaison officer, for example."

"I think I understand, Sir," Dailey replied, very seriously.

"Think of yourself as a spare tire, Colonel. I devoutly hope we never have to take you out of the trunk."

"Yes, Sir."

(Two)
CAPE ESPERANCE
GUADALCANAL, SOLOMON ISLANDS
7 AUGUST 1942

At 0200, the Amphibious Force of OPERATION PESTILENCE, Transport Groups X and Y, reached Savo Island, which lies between Guadalcanal and Florida islands. The skies were clear, and there was enough light from a quarter moon to make out both the land masses and the other ships.

The fifteen transports of Transport Group X carried aboard the major elements of the 1st Marine Division and were headed for the beaches of Guadalcanal. These turned and entered Sealark Channel, which runs between Savo and Guadalcanal.

Meanwhile, Transport Group Y sailed along the other side of Savo Island, that is, between Savo and Florida Island, and headed toward their destinations, Florida, Tulagi and Gavutu islands. Transport Group Y consisted of four transports carrying the 2nd Battalion, 5th Marines, and other troops, and four destroyer transports carrying the 1st Raider Battalion. These were World War I destroyers that had been converted for use by Marine Raiders by removing two of their four engines and converting the space to troop berthing.

The Guadalcanal Invasion Force was headed for what the Operations Plan called "Beach Red." This was a spot about 6,000 yards East of Lunga Point, more or less directly across Sealark Channel from where the Tulagi-Gavutu landings were to take place. The distance across Sealark Channel was approximately twenty-five miles.

Three U.S. Navy cruisers and four destroyers began to shell the Guadalcanal landing area at 0614. It had already been bombed daily for a week by U.S. Army Air Corps B-17s. At 0616, one cruiser and two destroyers opened fire on Tulagi and Gavutu.

By 0651 the transports of both groups dropped anchor 9,000 yards off their respective landing beaches. Landing boats were put over the side into the calm water, and Marines began to climb down rope nets into them.

Mine sweepers working the water between the ships and their landing beaches encountered no mines, but a small Japanese schooner carrying gasoline wandered into Sealark Channel. It was set afire and quickly sunk by Naval gunfire and machine gun fire from Navy fighter aircraft and dive bombers These were operating from carriers maneuvering seventy-five miles away from the invasion beaches.

The Navy sent forty-three carrier aircraft to attack the Guadalcanal invasion beach, and forty-one to attack Tulagi and Gavutu. Eighteen Japanese seaplanes at Tulagi were destroyed.

At 0740, B Company, 1st Battalion, 2nd Marines, went ashore near the small village of Haleta, on Florida Island. They encountered no resistance.

At 0800, the First Wave of the Tulagi Force, Landing Craft carrying Baker and Dog Companies of the 1st Raider Battalion, touched ashore on Blue Beach. A Marine was killed almost immediately by a single rifle shot, but there was no other resistance on the beach. The enemy had elected to defend Tulagi from caves and earthen bunkers in the hills inland and to the South.

The Landing Craft returned to the transports, loaded the Second Wave (Able and Charley Companies, 1st Raiders), and put them ashore. Then a steady stream of Landing Craft put 2nd Battalion, 5th Marines on shore.

Once on Tulagi, the 2nd Battalion, 5th Marines crossed the narrow island to their left (Northwest), to clear out the enemy, while the Raiders turned to their right (Southeast) and headed toward the Southern tip of Tulagi. About thirty-five hundred yards separated the Southern tip of Tulagi from the tiny island of Gavutu (515 by 255 yards) and the even smaller (290 by 310) island of Tanambogo, which was connected to Gavutu by a concrete causeway.

The Raiders encountered no serious opposition until after noon. And 2nd Battalion, 5th Marines, encountered no serious opposition moving in the opposite direction until about the same time.

Off Guadalcanal, at 0840, the destroyers of the Guadalcanal Fire Support Group took up positions to mark the line of departure for the Landing Craft, 5000 yards North of Beach Red. Simultaneously, small liaison aircraft (Piper Cubs) appeared over Beach Red, and marked its 3200 yard width with smoke grenades.

At exactly 0900, all the cruisers and destroyers of the Guadalcanal Fire Support Group began to bombard Beach Red and the area extending 200 yards inshore.

The Landing Craft carrying the first wave of the Beach Red invasion force (the 5th Marines, less their 2nd Battalion, which was at that moment in the process of landing on Tulagi) left the departure line on schedule. When the Landing Craft were 1300 yards off Beach Red, the covering bombardment was lifted.

At 0910, on a 1600 yard front, the 5th Marines began to land on the beach, the 1st Battalion on the right (West) and the 3rd Battalion on the left (East). Regimental Headquarters came ashore at 0938, and minutes later it was joined by the Heavy Weapons elements of the regiment.

Again, there was virtually no resistance on the beach.

As the Landing Craft returned to the transports to bring the 1st Marines ashore, the 5th Marines moved inland, setting up a defense perimeter 600 yards off Beach Red, along the Tenaru River on the West, the Tenavatu River on the East, and a branch of the Tenaru on the South.

Once it had become apparent that they would not be in

danger from Japanese artillery on or near the beach, the transports began to move closer to shore, dropping anchor again 7000 yards away.

At about this point, serious problems began with the off-loading process, in many ways duplicating the disastrous trial run in the Fiji Islands.

The small and relatively easy to manhandle 75mm pack howitzers (originally designed to be carried by mules) of the 11th Marines (the artillery regiment) had come ashore with the assault elements of the 5th Marines.

The 105mm howitzers now came ashore. But their emplacement was hindered because there were not enough drop-ramp Landing Craft to handle their "prime-movers," the trucks which tow the cannon. The "prime mover" for the 105mm howitzer was supposed to be a 2½-ton, 6×6 truck. The 11th Marines had been issued instead a truck commonly referred to as a "one-ton." Instead of the six (actually ten) powered wheels of the "deuce and a half," it had only four powered wheels to drive it through mud, sand, or slippery terrain.

It was this much smaller, inadequate, one-ton "prime mover" for which there were insufficient drop-bow Landing Craft to move immediately onto Beach Red.

So when the 105mm howitzers arrived on the beach, the only vehicles capable of towing them inland to firing positions were the few, overworked, Amphibious Tractors. These had a tank-like track and could negotiate sand and mud.

They were pressed into service to move the 105mm howitzers. In doing that, however, their metal tracks chewed up the primitive roads and whatever field telephone wires they crossed, effectively cutting communication between the advanced positions, the beach, and the several headquarters.

Within an hour or so of landing on the beach, moreover, the Marines were physically exhausted. For one thing, because of the long time they had spent aboard the troop transports, they had lost much of the physical toughness they'd acquired in training.

For another, as they moved through sand and jungle and up hills carrying heavy loads of rifles, machine guns, mortars

and the ammunition for them, Guadalcanal's temperature
and high humidity quickly sapped the strength they had left.

And there was not enough water. Although Medical
Officers had strongly insisted that each man be provided with
two canteens (two quarts) of drinking water, there were not
enough canteens in the Pacific to issue a second canteen to
each man.

The Navy was asked to provide beach labor details of
sailors to assist in unloading the supplies coming ashore from
the Landing Craft, and then to move the supplies off the
beach to make room for more supplies. The Navy refused to
do this.

Marines exhausted by the very act of going ashore were
thus pressed into service unloading supplies from Landing
Craft.

But first there were no trucks to move the supplies off the
beach, and then when the "one-ton" trucks finally began to
come ashore, these proved incapable of negotiating the sand
and roads chewed up by amphibious tractors.

The result was a mess. Landing Craft loaded with supplies
were stacked up off the beach. They were unable even to
reach the beach, much less rapidly discharge their cargoes.

Meanwhile, starting at 1145, Navy SBD dive-bombers
attacked Gavutu across the channel. Ten minutes later, the
Navy started a five minute barrage of the island, creating
huge clouds of smoke and dust.

By 1500, both Tulagi and Gavutu were "secured."

On Guadalcanal itself, the main invasion force spent the
rest of the afternoon and the night trying—with little
success—to clear up the mess on the beach itself, and to set
up a perimeter defense around the beach and the six hundred
yards the Marines had moved inshore.

There was no question that the Japanese would try to
throw the Marines back into the sea. The only question was
when.

(Three)
BUKA, SOLOMON ISLANDS
0745 HOURS 8 AUGUST 1942

"I rather think that's more than one, wouldn't you agree?" Sub-Lieutenant Jacob Reeves, Royal Australian Navy Volunteer Reserve, said, turning to Miss Patience Witherspoon and nodding vaguely toward the far off sound of aircraft engines to the North.

Reeves was a bit old—forty-one—to be a Sub-Lieutenant, the lowest commissioned rank in the Royal Australian Navy; and his uniform fell far below the standards usually expected of an officer on duty. He was wearing a battered and torn, brimmed uniform cap; an equally soiled khaki uniform tunic with cut off sleeves; and khaki shorts and shoes whose uppers were spotted with green mold. His hair tumbled down his neck; and he was wearing a beard. A 9mm Sten submachine gun and a large pair of Ernst Leitz Wetzlar binoculars hung from his neck on web straps.

He and Miss Witherspoon were standing beneath an enormous tree, down from which hung a knotted rope.

"Oh, yes, Sir," Miss Witherspoon replied. "That's certainly more than one. A great many, I wouldn't be surprised."

"Well, then, I suppose I'd better go have a look, and you had better wake up the sodding Yanks, don't you think?"

"Yes, of course," Miss Witherspoon said. "I'll fetch them."

Lieutenant Reeves reached for the knotted rope. And then hanging onto it, he agilely climbed the trunk of the enormous tree, disappearing in a moment into the foliage.

Miss Witherspoon, who was eighteen, ran quickly and gracefully to Sergeant Stephen M. Koffler's hut down a narrow dirt path cut through lush vegetation. She ducked through the low entrance and knelt by his bed.

She giggled. Sergeant Koffler was also eighteen, and Miss Witherspoon was more than a little attracted to him. He was on his back, asleep. He was wearing only his U.S. Marine Corps issue skivvie shorts. The anatomical symbol of his gender, gloriously erect, poked through the flap in his skivvie shorts.

Miss Witherspoon, tittering, put one hand to her mouth, and with the other gave Sergeant Koffler's erection a friendly little pat. Sergeant Koffler gave a pleasant little grunt. Miss Witherspoon patted him again, just a little harder, but enough to waken him. He reached down and caught her wrist.

"God*damn* it, Patience!" Sergeant Koffler said, sounding more exasperated than angry.

"Lieutenant Reeves sent me to fetch you," Miss Witherspoon said, pronouncing the rank title in the British manner—Lef-ten-ant. "There's a large number of aircraft."

"Be right there," Koffler said. "Make sure Lieutenant Howard is up."

"Right you are," Miss Patience Witherspoon said cheerfully. Smiling, she backed out of the hut.

Steve sat on the edge of his bed. Miss Patience Witherspoon herself had constructed it of narrow tree trunks driven into the ground; a sort of "spring" of woven strips of bark supported a thin mattress. The mattress was covered with a surprisingly clean white sheet. The mattress and the sheet had also been made by Miss Witherspoon, who also washed them regularly.

Sergeant Koffler pulled on a pair of shorts that had once been a pair of "Trousers, Utility, Summer Service"; and then a pair of socks. He jammed his feet into his just-about-rotted through ankle high shoes, once a pair of "Shoes, Service, Dress." When he graduated from Parris Island these had worn a shine he could actually see his reflection in. Last he picked up his weapon where it lay under his bed.

The truly astonishing thing about Miss Patience Witherspoon, Sergeant Koffler thought for perhaps the hundredth time, was not her teeth, which were stained blue-black and filed into points; or even her breasts, which she made no effort to conceal, and which were elaborately decorated with scar tissue; or even that she lusted absolutely shamelessly after him. The truly astonishing thing about her was the way she talked.

Miss Witherspoon sounded almost exactly like Miss Daphne Farnsworth, who was the only other female subject of his Most Britannic Majesty Steve Koffler had come to know intimately. Miss (actually Yeoman, Royal Australian Navy Volunteer Reserve) Farnsworth had neat, pure white, intact teeth, and her breasts, which she modestly concealed virtually all of the time, were not only unscarred, but in Steve's opinion, they were an absolute work of art.

Without really being aware that he was doing it, Steve removed the magazine from his Thompson .45 ACP caliber submachine gun, worked the action, and then replaced the magazine. If necessary, it would fire.

The moment he ducked through the entrance to his hut, he heard the sound of aircraft engines. The hut was constructed of narrow tree trunks, covered with a thatch of enormous leaves. The sound had not penetrated the thick leaves of the hut.

He started to trot toward the Tree House, slinging the Thompson over his shoulder on its web strap as he ran. A hundred yards up the path, he encountered First Lieutenant Joseph L. Howard, USMCR, commanding the Marine Garrison on Buka Island.

Sergeant Koffler saluted crisply, and his salute was as impeccably returned.

"Good morning, Sergeant," Lieutenant Howard said. "You are to be commended on your shipshape appearance."

"Thank you, Sir. I try to set an example for the men."

Lieutenant Howard was dressed and shaved and coiffured exactly as Sergeant Koffler was. That is to say, he was wearing rotting shoes; cut off utility pants; and no shirt. A Thompson was slung over his shoulder. The last time either of them had a haircut or a shave was two months before in Australia, on June 6, the night before they jumped into Buka. And there were in fact no other men to set an example for. What was carried on the books as "Detachment A of USMC Special Detachment 14" consisted of Lieutenant Howard and Sergeant Koffler.

But at least once a day, they went through a little routine like this one. It was ostensibly a joke, but there was more to it than that. It reminded them that they were in fact Marines, part of a fellowship greater than two individuals living in the jungle on an island neither of them had heard of three months before; dodging the Japs; and with chances of getting home alive ranging from slim to none.

Two days before, after supper, Lieutenant Howard had told both Reeves and Koffler that in the very early hours of 7 August, OPERATION PESTILENCE, the invasion of the Solomon Islands of Tulagi, Gavutu, and Guadalcanal by the 1st Marine Division, would begin.

The great majority of Japanese bombers intending to strike at the invasion force would come from their major base at Rabaul or from its satellite installations; the flight path of these bombers would take them over Buka. Thus the importance of the Coastwatcher station on Buka could hardly be overstated. If the Americans in the invasion fleet knew when the Japanese could be expected, they could launch their aircraft in time to intercept them. This early warning would be of even greater importance once the Americans got the Japanese-started airfield on Guadalcanal completed and operational.

"How come you never said anything about this before?" Sergeant Koffler had inquired.

"In case either of you were captured by the Japs," Howard had explained, "you couldn't have told them because you didn't know."

"You knew," Koffler pursued. "What if you got caught?"

"I couldn't let myself get caught, Steve," Howard said, softly.

"What were you going to do, shoot yourself?"

"Let it go, Steve," Howard had said.

The sound of aircraft engines was now quite definite, Howard thought, but it was still sort of fuzzy, suggesting that there were a large number of aircraft some distance off, rather than one or two aircraft somewhat closer.

When they reached the tree, Howard gestured for Koffler to go ahead of him, and Koffler scurried quickly up the knotted rope and out of sight. Since the arm he'd broken when they first landed was now pretty well healed, Howard was able to follow him.

A platform had been built in the tree a hundred feet off the ground. It was large enough for three or four people to stand or sit comfortably. Reeves was sitting with his back against the trunk, when Steve Koffler stepped from a limb onto the platform.

He handed Koffler his binoculars and pointed north. Steve followed the directions and thought he could pick out, far off and not very high in the air, specks that almost certainly were aircraft. He leaned his shoulder against the trunk to steady himself, and with some difficulty found the specks through the binoculars. They were still too far away to see clearly, but he could now see that they were flying in formation, a series of Vs.

Lieutenant Howard touched his arm; he wanted the binoculars. Steve handed them to him.

Howard hooked the eyepieces under the bones above his eyes, took a breath, let half of it out, and held the rest, much the same technique that a skilled rifle marksman uses to steady his sight picture before firing.

"There's a bunch," he said. "What do you think they are, Steve?"

"Too far away to tell," Steve replied.

"If they were Bettys, for example, how could you tell?" Howard asked innocently.

"Shit," Koffler chuckled, realizing that he was being tested. Since they had been on Buka, they had been training each other—not just because there wasn't much else to do. Koffler had rigged up a simple buzzer and taught Howard Morse code, and Howard had not only sketched various Japanese aircraft, but had called forth their characteristics from memory and passed them on to both Koffler and Reeves.

"Well?" Howard went on.

Koffler pushed himself away from the tree and came to attention—except for a broad, unmilitary smile.

"Sir," he barked. "The Japanese Mitsubishi G4M1 Type 1 aircraft, commonly called the Betty, is a twin-engine, land-based bomber aircraft with a normal complement of seven. It has an empty weight of 9.5 tons and is capable of carrying 2200 pounds of bombs, or two 1700 pound torpedoes, over a nominal range of 2250 miles at a cruising speed of 195 miles per hour. Its maximum speed is 250 miles per hour at 14,000 feet. It is armed with a 20mm cannon in the tail, and four 7.7mm machine guns, one in the nose, one on top, and two in beam positions." He paused just perceptibly, and barked "Sir!" again.

Lieutenant Reeves applauded.

"Very good, Sergeant," he chuckled. "You win the prize."

"I'm afraid to ask what the prize is," Steve said, leaning against the tree again.

"How about Patience?" Howard asked innocently. "I've noticed the way she looks at you."

"Shit!" Steve said. "You know what she did to me just now?"

"Tell me," Howard said.

"No. Shit!"

"You might as well let her," Howard said. "You're going to have to sooner or later. And besides, you're a Marine sergeant now. It's time you lost your cherry."

Reeves laughed. Steve Koffler glowered at Howard.

Pretending not to notice, Howard put the binoculars back to his eyes. He studied the sky intently for thirty seconds, and then handed the binoculars to Reeves.

"I make it Betty," he said. "Large Force. I count forty-five."

"That's a bit, isn't it?" Reeves said, and put the binoculars to his eyes. Thirty seconds later, he took them away. "Vs," he said. "Five to a V. Nine Vs. Forty-five Bettys. Looks like they're climbing slowly."

He handed the binoculars to Koffler, who waved them away.

"You better see who you can raise, Steve," Howard said.

"Aye, aye, Sir," Steve said, and left the platform for the limbs of the tree, and then started climbing down.

"Why don't you go along with him?" Reeves said. "I'll stay and see if anything else shows up. Send Patience up."

"All right," Howard said.

"We can't have her distracting our operator, can we?" Reeves chuckled. "And if there's anything I don't recognize, I'll send her after you."

Howard climbed out of the tree and walked quickly to the village. He saw two men tying the long wire antenna for the Hallicrafters radio in place in two trees on opposite sides of the cleared area. The antenna lead wire rose from the center of one hut.

The antenna was erected only when they intended to use the radio. Otherwise, like the other parts of the radio, it was neatly stored and packed, ready to be carried into the jungle if the Japanese should send a patrol into the area.

When he entered the hut, Howard saw that Koffler had the radio just about set up. A muscular native, named Ian

Bruce, was already in place at the generator, which looked something like the pedals of a bicycle, waiting for orders to start grinding. Koffler was carefully checking his connections for corrosion. He glanced up at Howard when he sensed his presence, but said nothing.

Howard walked to the set itself and glanced down at the message pad. There was nothing Koffler had written on it that needed correction. All the message consisted of was the time, the type and number of aircraft, and their relative course. In Australia, or if the connection to Australia could not be completed, in Pearl Harbor, there were experts who would understand this information and relay it.

Koffler screwed a final connection in place, went outside to quickly check on the antenna, and then squatted on the floor by a packing case which held the transceiver, the key, and two sets of headphones. He picked up one set of headphones (which Howard now thought of as "cans," which is what Koffler called them) and handed them to Howard. He put the second set on and made a winding motion with his finger. Ian Bruce smiled and began to pedal the generator; there was a faint, not unpleasant whine.

In a moment, the dials on the Hallicrafter lit up and their needles came to life.

Koffler put his fingers on the key.

The dots and dashes went out, repeated three times, spelling, simply, FRD6. FRD6. FRD6.

The code name for the Coastwatchers Organization was Ferdinand. It was a fey title, chosen, Howard suspected, by Lieutenant Commander Eric Feldt himself. Ferdinand was the bull who would rather sniff flowers than fight. The Coastwatchers were not supposed to fight either.

There was no response to the first call. Koffler's finger went back to the key.

FRD6. FRD6. FRD6.

This time there was a reply. Howard had learned enough code to be able to read the simple groups.

FRD6.KCY.FRD6.KCY.FRD6.KCY.

KCY, the United States Pacific Fleet Radio Station at Pearl Harbor, Territory of Hawaii, was responding to Ferdinand Six.

That radio room leapt into Joe Howard's mind. Before the

war, as a staff sergeant, he had been stationed at Pearl
Harbor; and he had been sergeant of the guard at CINCPAC,
Commander in Chief, Pacific. He saw the immaculate officers
and the even more immaculate swabbies at their elaborate
shiny equipment in a shiny, air-conditioned room with
polished linoleum floors. Air-conditioned!

Now Koffler's hand came to life. Howard could not read
what was going out over the air. Koffler was proud of his
hand. He could transmit fifty words a minute. He was doing
so now. Even repeated three times, the message didn't take
long.

Then there was a reply, slow enough for Howard to
understand it.

FRD6, KCY. AKN. SB.

*Ferdinand Six, this is CINCPAC Radio. Receipt of your last
transmission is acknowledged. Standing By.*

Koffler's fingers flew over the keys for a second or two.

FRD6 CLR.

*Detachment A of Special Marine Corps Detachment 14 has
no further traffic for the Commander in Chief Pacific Fleet
and thus clears this communications link.*

Koffler put his fingers in his mouth and whistled shrilly.
When he had Ian Bruce's attention, he signed to him to stop
cranking the generator. Then he looked at Howard.

"No traffic for us, I guess," he said.

Howard shrugged.

"I mean, I guess if there was bad news at home or
something, they'd let us know, right?"

"Yeah, sure they would, Steve," Howard said.

(Four)
RADIO ROOM
USS *MCCAWLEY*
1033 HOURS 8 AUGUST 1942

"Sir," the Radio Operator 2nd Class sitting at the console
called out, "I've got a TOP SECRET Operational Immediate
from CINCPAC." Operational Immediate is the highest
priority message, taking precedence over all others.

A tall Lieutenant Junior Grade went to his position and

stood over him as the radio operator typed out the rest of the message. The moment the radio operator tore it from the typewriter, he snatched it from his fingers and took it to the cryptographic compartment.

Five minutes later, a Marine corporal in stiffly starched khakis stepped onto the bridge of the *McCawley*. He was armed with a .45 pistol, its holster suspended from a white web belt with glistening brass accoutrements.

He walked to Rear Admiral Richmond K. Turner, Commander, Amphibious Forces, South Pacific.

"Sir, a message, Sir," he said.

"Thank you," Admiral Turner said, and took it and read it.

OPERATIONAL IMMEDIATE
TOP SECRET
FROM CINCPAC
TO COMAMPHIBFORSOPAC
INTELSOURCE 1 INDICATES YOU MAY EXPECT ATTACK BY FORTY FIVE BETTY AIRCRAFT AT APPROXIMATELY 1200 YOUR TIME. END

Admiral Turner handed the sheet of paper to his aide-de-camp.

"See that the word is passed to the fleet," he said. "Tell the carriers I want to know when they launch their fighters. Tell them I think this is reliable, and I want to go with it."

"Aye, aye, Sir."

(Five)
USS *MCCAWLEY*
OFF BEACH RED
GUADALCANAL, SOLOMON ISLANDS
8 AUGUST 1942

At 1600 Admiral Fletcher received word from General Vandergrift that the 1st Battalion, First Marines had captured the Japanese airfield on Guadalcanal, relatively intact. The field was renamed Henderson Field in honor of Major Lofton R. Henderson, USMC, who had died at Midway. In

Vandergrift's opinion, the airfield could be repaired enough to accept fighter aircraft within forty-eight hours.

At 1807, Admiral Fletcher radioed Admiral Ghormley stating that in repelling the Japanese aerial attack at noon, he had lost twenty-one of his ninety-nine aircraft. He stated further that the necessary maneuvering of the ships of the invasion fleet during the invasions had reduced his fuel supply to a level he considered inadequate. He further stated that there was a strong probability that a second Japanese attack by air or sea would be made against his fleet. Unless permission to withdraw the invasion fleet was immediately granted, this attack would result in unacceptable losses to his Task Force.

At 2325 hours, General Vandergrift, having been ordered to report to Admiral Fletcher, came aboard the *McCawley*. There Admiral Fletcher informed General Vandergrift that he had received permission from Admiral Ghormley to withdraw from the Guadalcanal area. At 1500 9 August (the next day), he went on to say, ten transports, escorted by a cruiser and ten destroyers, would depart from the beachhead. The balance of the invasion fleet would sail at 1830.

General Vandergrift is known to have protested that the off-loading of the 1st Marine Division and its supporting troops—including the heavy (155mm) artillery, along with considerable quantities of ammunition and supplies, including rations—had not been completed. Admiral Fletcher's reply to the protest has not been recorded.

General Vandergrift returned to the invasion beach on Guadalcanal shortly after midnight.

(Six)
HEADQUARTERS, FIRST MARINE DIVISION
BEACH RED
GUADALCANAL, SOLOMON ISLANDS
1830 HOURS 9 AUGUST 1942

Division Sergeants Major have far more important things to do than escort individual replacements to their assigned place of duty. But in the Marine Corps, as elsewhere, there is an exception to every rule, and this was an exceptional circumstance.

For one thing, Major General A.A. Vandergrift had personally told his sergeant major to "take this gentleman down to Colonel Goettge and tell him I sent him."

The gentleman in question was more than a little out of the ordinary, too. He was in his forties, silver-haired, tall, erect, and with a certain aura of authority about him that the sergeant major's long military service had taught him came to men only after a lifetime of giving orders in the absolute expectation that they would be obeyed.

The gentleman was wearing Marine utilities, loosely fitting cotton twill jacket, and trousers already sweat stained. The outline of a Colt .45 automatic pistol and two spare magazines for it pressed against one of the baggy pockets of the utilities. The outlines of two "Grenades, Hand, Fragmentation" bulged the other trousers pocket. A Springfield Model 1903A3 .30-06 caliber rifle hung with practiced ease from his shoulder on a leather strap. And the outline of a half dozen five-round stripper clips of rifle cartridges pressed against the material of the right breast pocket of his utility jacket.

There was a small silver eagle pinned to each of the utility jacket's collar points. Fleming Pickering looked for all the world like a Marine Colonel engaged in ground combat against the enemy. Considering his age and rank and his casual familiarity with the Springfield, other Marines would probably guess that he was a regimental commander, rather than a staff officer.

But the Sergeant Major had learned that he was not a Marine. The silver eagles on his collar points were intended to identify him as a Navy Captain. And the Sergeant Major had also heard that Captain Fleming Pickering was the only man in the United States Naval Service on Guadalcanal, sailor or Marine, who had not been ordered there. He was on Guadalcanal because he wanted to be. According to the General's orderly, who overheard a great deal, and who was a reliable source of information for the Sergeant Major, no one—not General Vandergrift, not even Admiral Chester W. Nimitz, the overall Pacific Ocean Areas (POA) Commander-in-Chief back in Pearl Harbor—could order him off, or for that matter, order him to do anything.

The Sergeant Major was just about convinced that he liked this Navy VIP. This was unusual for him. His normal reaction to Naval officers generally, and to Naval VIPs specifically, was to avoid the sonsofbitches as much as possible.

One reason he sort of liked this one was because he was here on the beach, in Utilities, carrying a Springfield over his shoulder, and a couple of grenades in his pocket. The rest of the fucking Navy was already over the horizon and headed for Noumea . . . after leaving Marines on the beach, less their heavy artillery and most of their rations and ammunition.

But the primary reason that the Sergeant Major decided that this Navy captain was the exception to the general rule that Navy captains are bad fucking news was that this captain enjoyed the friendship and respect of one of the sergeant major's few heroes, Major Jack NMI (for "No Middle Initial") Stecker.

Major Stecker, who had commanded the 2nd Battalion, 5th Marines, in the invasion of Tulagi the day before, came into the Division Command Post on Guadalcanal a few minutes after Captain Pickering showed up on the island.

There is, of course, by both regulation and custom, a certain formality required in conversation between Sergeants Major and Majors, but the Sergeant Major and Jack NMI Stecker had been Sergeants Major together longer than Jack Stecker had been an officer. When the Sergeant Major inquired of Major Stecker vis-à-vis Captain Fleming W. Pickering, he was perhaps less formal than Marine regulations and custom required.

"Jack," the Sergeant Major inquired, "just who the fuck is that swabbie trying to pass himself off as a Marine?"

Stecker's voice and eyes were icy: "He's someone an asshole like you, *Sergeant,* better not let me hear calling a swabbie."

"Sorry, Sir," the Sergeant Major replied, coming to attention. Stecker's temper was a legend. It was always spectacular when aroused, and it usually lasted a long time.

This time it began to pass almost immediately.

"Captain Pickering, Steve," Major Stecker went on, "won the Croix de Guerre at Belleau Wood. Everybody in his squad was dead, and he had an 8mm round through each leg when we got to him, and twenty-four German Grenadiers needing burying."

"He was a Marine?" the Sergeant Major asked, so surprised that there was a perceptible pause before he remembered to append, "Sir?"

Stecker nodded. "You ever hear what they say, Steve, 'Once a Marine, always a Marine'?" he asked, now conversationally.

"Yes, Sir."

"Captain Pickering is one of the good guys, Steve. Don't forget that."

"I won't, Sir."

"If you had taken a commission when they offered you one, you stupid sonofabitch, you wouldn't have to call me 'Sir.' "

"Calling *you* 'Sir' doesn't bother me, Major."

"Do what you can for Captain Pickering, Steve," Stecker said. "Like I said, he's one of the good guys."

The G-2 (Intelligence) General Staff Section of Headquarters, 1st Marine Division was set up in its own tent fifty yards from the Division Command Post, which had been established in a frame building that had survived both the prelanding bombardment and the invasion itself.

A labor detail, bare chested, sweat soaked, looking exhausted, had just about completed a sandbag wall around the tent. In Captain Pickering's opinion, the wall would provide some protection from small arms fire, and from shrapnel from incoming mortar or artillery rounds landing nearby, but that was about all. A direct hit from an artillery shell would be devastating. What was needed, he thought, based on his World War I experience, was a hole in the ground, timbered over, and with a four- or five-foot-thick layer of sandbags on top.

Colonel Frank B. Goettge, the G-2, was standing before a large, celluloid covered map mounted on a sheet of plywood. He was watching one of his sergeants mark on it with a grease pencil, when the Sergeant Major and Captain Pickering came in.

"The General, Sir," the Sergeant Major said when Goettge looked at him, "asked me to bring this gentleman to you. Captain Pickering, this is Colonel . . ."

"I have the pleasure of Captain Pickering's acquaintance," Goettge said, walking to Pickering, smiling, and offering his hand. "Good to see you, Sir. And a little surprised."

"I'm a little surprised myself," Pickering said, shifting his shoulder to indicate the Springfield. "I would have given odds I'd never carry one of these things again."

"I don't mean to sound facetious, Sir," Goettge said, "but what did you do, miss the boat?"

"Something like that," Pickering said. "I just couldn't bring myself to sail off into the sunset with the goddamned Navy."

"Is there anything I can do for you, Sir?" Goettge asked, in some confusion.

"Tell me how I can make myself useful to you," Fleming Pickering said, "and stop calling me 'Sir.' "

"I don't understand . . ."

"I asked General Vandergrift where he thought I could be helpful, and he sent me to you," Pickering said.

"For 'duty,' so to speak?"

"Anywhere where I can earn my rations—I understand, by the way, there are goddamn few of those. I'm a little long in the tooth to go on patrol, but if that's all you've got for me . . ."

Colonel Goettge looked at Pickering intently. He had not had time to digest the presence of Captain Fleming Pickering, much less the reason for his presence, whatever that may be. He knew Pickering was wrapped in the mantle of the Secretary of the Navy and that he personally owned the Pacific & Far East Shipping Corporation. And yet, here he was in Goettge's bunker with a rifle slung over his shoulder.

I'll be damned, he's dead serious about going out into the boondocks of this goddamned island with that rifle, as if he was still an eighteen-year-old Marine corporal.

"Even if I couldn't think of half a dozen ways where you can really be of help around here, Captain," Goettge said, "I think we're both a little too long in the teeth to go running around in the boondocks."

Pickering nodded.

"Thank you, Sergeant Major," Goettge went on. "Please tell the General 'thank you' for Captain Pickering."

"Aye, aye, Sir," the sergeant major said, and then he added: "If I can help in any way, Captain, you just tell me what and how."

XV

(One)
THE FOSTER LAFAYETTE HOTEL
WASHINGTON, D.C.
10 AUGUST 1942

As the 1940 Packard limousine passed out of the gates of the White House onto Pennsylvania Avenue, The Honorable Frank Knox, Secretary of the Navy, pulled a handkerchief from the cuff of his rumpled seersucker suit jacket, removed his Panama hat, and mopped at his forehead. Since the handkerchief was already damp with sweat, he did little but rearrange beads of sweat.

As he did now and again in such weather, Knox let his mind dwell on Thomas Jefferson and George Washington. *They must have really been marvelous practical politicians,* he thought, *right up there with Franklin Delano Roosevelt in their ability to talk people into doing foolish things against their better judgment.*

There was no other reason he could think of why the fledgling nation established its capital in a steaming swamp on the Potomac River. Certainly, Adams and Stockton and the other founding fathers must have known that the logical place for the capital was Philadelphia. Or New York. Or Boston. Or Richmond, for that matter. Anywhere but where they agreed to put it.

It was a thought that kept popping into Secretary Knox's mind over the last week, during which the temperature in Washington had rarely dipped below ninety-five degrees Fahrenheit and ninety-five percent humidity.

"Mr. Secretary?"

Knox turned to look at Captain David Haughton, USN, his administrative assistant, a tall, slender officer in a mussed, sweat-soaked khaki uniform. Haughton extended a fresh handkerchief to him.

"Thank you," Knox said. As he mopped at his forehead again, he saw that Haughton had half a dozen handkerchiefs in the open briefcase he held on his lap, in addition to the probably five pounds of paper, all stamped TOP SECRET, and the snub-nosed .38 Colt revolver. In the summer, he carried the revolver in the briefcase, because the shoulder holster was too visible under khaki and white uniforms.

Knox spoke aloud what came into his mind: "What the hell would I do without you, David?"

"Probably a lot better, Mr. Secretary," Haughton said. "May I respectfully suggest that you get someone who could really take care of you, and perhaps arrange to send me to sea?"

"You can suggest it all you want, but you're stuck with me."

"Yes, Sir."

"Where now?" Knox asked.

"Across the street, Sir," Haughton said, and pointed toward the elegant brick facade of the Foster Lafayette Hotel. "Senator Fowler."

"I'd forgotten," Knox confessed.

"He didn't offer to come to your office, Mr. Secretary," Haughton said. "He usually does."

"No problem. We're here," Knox said, and then added, chuckling, "He has a nicer office than I do, anyway."

Senator Richmond K. Fowler, Republican of California, maintained a suite in the Foster Lafayette. Not an ordinary suite—though God knew suites in the Lafayette were as large and elegant as they came—but an apartment made up of a pair of suites. It was furnished with antiques that were the personal property of old Andrew Foster himself.

Fowler was quite wealthy, and unlike some of his peers in the Senate, he made no effort at all to conceal it. In many ways he was like Knox: He considered public service a privilege; living in Washington, D.C., even as well as he did, was the terrible price he had to pay for that privilege.

Fowler was also, in Knox's opinion, one of the better senators. He was enormously influential, but rarely used his influence like a club, or a baton of power. For example, he did not make telephone calls to the Secretary of the Navy— or to other senior executive department officials—just to hear the sound of own voice, to remind himself of his own importance, or as a fishing expedition. He called only when he had something to say, or wanted specific information he could not get elsewhere. Consequently, his calls were put through to Knox—and to others—when other senators would be told the Secretary had just left for a meeting.

Even more rarely, he requested a personal audience with Knox. He understood his time was precious, and that he could usually accomplish in ninety seconds on the telephone business that would take thirty minutes or an hour from the Secretary's available time if they met face to face.

So when he did ask to see Knox personally, the Secretary of the Navy was usually willing to give him the time he needed, if at all possible. There was some business that should not be discussed on the telephone. Fowler had proven over the years that he knew what that was.

The limousine pulled up before the marquee of the hotel, and a doorman, sweating in his uniform coat, opened the door.

"Welcome to the Lafayette, Mr. Secretary," he said.

"Thank you," Knox said and offered his hand. "How are you? Hot enough for you?"

"I didn't think I'd be this hot until after Saint Peter pointed toward the basement," the doorman said. He waited until Captain Haughton was out, and then spoke to the chauffeur: "Pull it up there where it says DIPLOMATIC CORPS ONLY."

A bellman spun the revolving glass door for Knox as he approached, and then smiled at him as he came through.

Knox walked across the quiet, heavily carpeted lobby to the bank of elevators.

"Eight," Captain Haughton ordered.

By the time the elevator reached the eighth floor, there had been a telephone call from the doorman. A large, very black man wearing a gray cotton jacket and a wide smile was standing by the open door of Senator Fowler's suite when the elevator door opened.

"Hello, Mr. Secretary Knox, Sir. Nice to see you again, Sir. And you too, Captain Haughton. The Senator's waiting for you."

"Hello, Franklin," Knox said. "How do you manage to look so cool on a day like this?"

"I just don't go outside in the heat, Sir," Fowler's butler chuckled.

Senator Richmond K. Fowler was in the sitting room. He was not alone. A tall, shapely, aristocratic woman was with him. She had silver hair, simply but elegantly coiffured, and she was wearing a cotton suit, with a high-necked white linen blouse under it. For jewelry, she wore a simple wedding band, a single strand of pearls, and a small, cheap pin on the lapel of her jacket. It held two blue stars on a white background and signified that two members of her immediate family were serving their country in uniform. Secretary Knox had not previously had the honor of the lady's acquaintance, but he knew who she was.

Her father owned the Foster Lafayette Hotel (and forty others), and her husband owned the Pacific & Far Eastern Shipping Corporation. She was, *pro tempore,* in her husband's absence, Chairman of the Board of P&FE. Her name was Patricia Foster (Mrs. Fleming) Pickering.

She stood up as Knox and Haughton entered the room, and the Secretary liked what he saw. Nice-*looking woman,* he thought. This was immediately followed by, *Her presence here is not coincidental. I wonder what she wants?*

"Hello, Frank," Senator Fowler said, walking up to him and offering his hand. "Thank you for finding time for me." He looked at Captain Haughton, nodded, and said, "Haughton."

"Senator," Haughton replied.

"I was right across the street," Knox said. "And anytime, Richmond."

"I don't believe you know each other, do you?"

"I know who the lady is," Knox said. "How do you do, Mrs. Pickering? I'm pleased that I'm being given the chance to meet you."

"How do you do, Mr. Knox?" Patricia Pickering said, giving him her hand.

She's striking now, Knox thought. *She must have been a real beauty when she was twenty.*

She turned to Haughton. "My husband has often spoken of you, Captain Haughton. How do you do?"

"Very well, thank you," Haughton said.

"Would you do any better if we got you something cold to drink?"

"Oh, yes, Ma'am," he said.

"Franklin?" Patricia Pickering said, and the butler appeared.

"I hope that offer includes me," Knox said.

"Oh, yes. We intend to ply you with liquor and anything else that might please you," she said.

"Do you really?" Knox said, taken a little aback.

"I've been drinking—what is this, Franklin?"

"An Orange Special, Miss Patricia."

"Orange juice, club soda, and a hooker of rum," she said. "I can't handle gin, for some reason."

"That sounds wonderful," Knox said.

"Make a pitcherful, please," she ordered.

"Patricia is in town for a meeting of the War Shipping Board," Senator Fowler said.

"That's not quite true," she said. "What I did, Mr. Knox, was take one of the three airline ticket priorities they gave P&FE to send people to the WSB meeting, so that I could come here and see Senator Fowler."

"But you are a member of the War Shipping Board," Fowler protested.

"Yes, I am. In the same way that I am chairman of P&FE," she said. "But I don't like sailing under false colors."

"I don't think I know quite what you mean, Mrs. Pickering," Knox said. There was something about this woman, beyond her grace and her beauty, that he instinctively liked.

"I am not foolish enough to think that I can run P&FE, Mr. Knox," she said evenly. "And only fools think I do. Despite the title. My position, I've come to think, is analogous to that of the King. I understand that every day they bring him a red box containing important state documents. They make sure he knows what's going on. But they don't let him run the British Empire."

"Well, then, may I say that you make a lovely queen?" Knox said.

She smiled at him, a genuine smile. "Richmond is supposed to be the politician," she said. "Saying, as a reflex action, what he thinks people want to hear."

"She was a sweet child when I first met her, Frank," Fowler said. "And then she married Flem Pickering, who has poisoned her against public servants."

"That's not true," she said. "Flem Pickering proposed because my father had already told me about public servants."

"I'm afraid to ask what he told you," Knox said.

"He started by saying that one should regard them as used car salesmen in one-tone shoes," she said. "And then, I'm afraid, he became somewhat cynical."

Knox laughed.

"But here you are, seeing Senator Fowler," he said.

"My father and my husband feel he's the exception to the rule," she said. "And he tells me you are, too."

Franklin, the butler, appeared with a pitcher and glasses on a tray. It occurred to Knox that since there hadn't been time to make it, obviously Franklin had prepared it beforehand, probably on orders from Patricia Pickering.

Knox took one of the glasses and raised it. "Your health, Ma'am."

"Thank you," she said. "Would that include my peace of mind?"

"Certainly," Knox said, smiling.

"You can do something about that," she said. "You can tell me where he is and what he's doing."

"He's in the Pacific, as you know," Knox said. "As my personal representative."

"A week ago, I had a message from him saying that he was going to sea for a while and would be out of touch," Patricia Pickering said. "And now the radio tells me that we have invaded Guadalcanal in the Solomons. And I have learned that my husband is no longer in Australia. I want to know where he is and what he's doing. And Richmond tells me that you're the only man who knows."

"Are you sure he's no longer in Australia?" Knox replied. "I'm curious. How could you know that?"

"The *Pacific Endeavor* is now in Melbourne. I radioed a message there to be relayed to my husband; and her master replied that his whereabouts are unknown to our agent there. And that MacArthur's headquarters denied any knowledge of him."

Use of Maritime Radio for transmission of personal messages had been forbidden since the United States had entered the war, but Knox was not surprised to hear what she just told him. The master of the *Pacific Endeavor* was not going to ignore a message from her owner, or refuse to do whatever the message ordered him to do, whether or not the U.S. Navy liked it.

Patricia Pickering read his mind. "Please don't tell me I wasn't supposed to do that."

"I have the feeling, Mrs. Pickering," Knox said, "that anything I say wouldn't make very much difference to you."

"I would take your word if you tell me there were good reasons why my husband disappeared from the face of the earth," she said. "Is that what it is?"

"David," Knox said, turning to Captain Haughton, "would you show Mrs. Pickering our last message from Captain Pickering?"

Haughton opened his briefcase, took out a two-inch thick sheaf of papers, looked through it, and pulled a file from it. The file cover sheet was marked with diagonal red stripes across its face and TOP SECRET was stamped at the top and bottom. He handed it to Patricia Pickering.

Eyes Only--The Secretary of the Navy

DUPLICATION FORBIDDEN
ORIGINAL TO BE DESTROYED AFTER ENCRYPTION AND
TRANSMITTAL TO SECNAVY

Aboard USS McCawley
Off Guadalcanal
1430 Hours 9 August 1942

Dear Frank:
  This is written rather in haste, and will be
brief because I know of the volume of radio
traffic that's being sent, most of it unnecessarily.
  As far as I am concerned the Battle of Guadalcanal began on 31 July when the first Army Air
Corps B-17 raid was conducted. They have
bombed steadily for a week. I mention this because I suspect the Navy might forget the bombing in their reports. They were MacA's B-17s
and he supplied them willingly. That might be
forgotten, too.
  The same day, 31 July, the Amphibious Force
left Koro in the Fijis, after the rehearsal. On
2 August, the long awaited and desperately
needed Marine Observation Squadron (VMO-251,
sixteen F4F3-Photo recon versions of the Wildcat) landed on the new airbase at Espiritu
Santo. Without the required wing tanks. They
are essentially useless until they get wing
tanks. A head should roll over that one.
  The day before yesterday, Friday, Aug 7, the
invasion began. The Amphibious Force was off
Savo Island, on schedule at 0200.

The 1st Marine Raider Bn under Lt Col Red Mike
Merritt landed on Tulagi and have done well.

The 1st Parachute Bn (fighting as infantry-
men) landed on Gavutu, a tiny island two miles
away. So far they have been decimated, and will
almost certainly suffer worse losses than this
before it's over for them.

The 1st and 3rd Bns, 5th Marines, landed on
the Northern Coast of Guadalcanal, west of
Lunga Point, to not very much initial resistance. They were attacked by Japanese twenty-
five to thirty twin-engine bombers from Rabaul, at half past eleven.

I can't really tell you what happened the
first afternoon and through the first night,
except to say the Marines were on the beach and
more were landing.

Just before eleven in the morning yesterday
(8 Aug), we were alerted (by the Coastwatchers
on Buka, where Banning sent the radio) to a 45-
bomber force launched from Kavieng, New Ireland (across the channel from Rabaul). They
arrived just before noon and caused some damage. Our carriers of course sent fighters
aloft to attack them, and some of our fighters
were shot down.

At six o'clock last night Admiral Fletcher
radioed Ghormley that he had lost 21 of 99
planes, was low on fuel, and wants to leave.

I am so angry I don't dare write what I would
like to write. Let me say that in my humble
opinion the Admiral's estimates of his losses
are over generous, and his estimates of his
fuel supply rather miserly.

Ghormley, not knowing of this departure from

the facts, gave him the necessary permission.
General Vandergrift càme aboard the <u>McCawley</u>
a little before midnight last night and was informed by Admiral Fletcher that the Navy is
turning chicken and pulling out.

This is before, I want you to understand, in
case this becomes a bit obfuscated in the official Navy reports--<u>before</u> we took such a whipping this morning at Savo Island. As I
understand it we lost two US Cruisers (<u>Vin-
cennes</u> and <u>Quincy</u>) within an hour, and the Australian cruiser <u>Canberra</u> was set on fire. The
<u>Astoria</u> was sunk about two hours ago, just
after noon.

In thirty minutes, most of the invasion fleet
is pulling out. Ten transports, four destroyers, and a cruiser are going to run first, and
what's left will be gone by 1830.

The ships are taking with them rations, food,
ammunition, and Marines desperately needed on
the beach at Guadalcanal. There is no telling
what the Marines will use to fight with; and
there's not even a promise from Fletcher about
a date when he will feel safe to resupply the
Marines. If the decision to return is left up to
Admiral Fletcher, I suppose that we can expect
resupply by sometime in 1945 or 1950.

I say "we" because I find it impossible to
sail off into the sunset on a Navy ship, leaving
Marines stranded on the beach.

I remember what I said to you about the Admirals when we first met. I was right, Frank.

Best Personal Regards,

Fleming Pickering,
Captain, USNR

Patricia Pickering looked at Frank Knox.

"I didn't know that we lost three cruisers. My God!"

She may not consider herself qualified to run Pacific & Far East Shipping, Knox thought, *but she knows what a cruiser is, and what the loss of those three cruisers means to the Pacific Fleet.*

"That was very bad news," Knox said.

"And they had to leave, to avoid the risk of losing even more ships?"

"Your husband doesn't think so," Knox said. "I don't want to sit here in Washington and judge the decisions made on the scene of battle by an experienced admiral whose personal courage is beyond question."

"And my husband? Do I correctly infer that he went ashore on Guadalcanal and is there now?"

"I'm afraid so."

"God *damn* him!" Patricia Pickering said furiously. "The old fool!"

"Apparently, there *is* someone more annoyed with Captain Pickering than I am," Knox said. "I didn't send him over there to shoulder a rifle."

She smiled at him.

"They're mad, you know. Anyone who is, or who ever was, a Marine is mad. And I am blessed—or cursed—with two of them."

"Blessed, I would say," Knox said. "Wouldn't you, really?"

She smiled at him again. "What happens now?"

"That message came in just as Haughton and I were leaving for the White House. As soon as we get back to the office, Captain Haughton is going to radio orders for Captain Pickering to be withdrawn from Guadalcanal as soon as possible. How long would you say it's been, Mrs. Pickering, since someone read the riot act to your husband?"

"Much too long, Mr. Knox," Patricia Pickering said.

"My heart won't be in it, frankly," he said. "But under the circumstances—I used to be a sergeant myself, you know— I don't think I've forgotten how to chew somebody out."

Mrs. Fleming Pickering surprised the Secretary of the Navy. She moved her head quickly to his and kissed him on the cheek.

(Two)
NEAR LUNGA POINT
GUADALCANAL, SOLOMON ISLANDS
1440 HOURS 12 AUGUST 1942

Captain Fleming Pickering, USNR, stood on the bed of a
Japanese Navy Ford truck and watched as Marines worked
to put the finishing touches on the airfield the Japanese had
begun. He was wearing sweat-streaked utilities; on his head
was a soft utility cap (instead of the steel helmet he was supposed to wear). A Springfield 1903 .30-06 rifle was cradled
like a hunting rifle in his arms.

This airfield, in his judgment, was the reason for OPERA-
TION PESTILENCE. Even before it was ready to handle aircraft it was named "Henderson Field" by General
Vandergrift in order to honor Major Lofton Henderson,
USMC, who had been killed after some spectacularly heroic
airmanship at Midway. Whoever controlled this airfield was
going to be able to control the Solomons, and thus New
Guinea and Australia, and very likely the outcome of the
war.

There was no doubt in Pickering's mind that the Japanese
Imperial General Staff was at least as aware of the importance of this airfield as Frank Knox's personal snoop. And
thus there was no question in his mind that they were going
to make a valiant effort to take it back. Soon they would try
to throw the First Marine Division back into the sea. He was
surprised that there had not already been a violent counterat-
tack, if not by the Japanese actually on Guadalcanal, then
by Japanese naval and air forces.

So far, OPERATION PESTILENCE had gone much better
than Pickering had expected, particularly after the Navy had
sailed off to protect its precious aircraft carriers, taking with
them a long list of material and equipment that was desperately needed on the island.

The area held by the Marines was now about 3,600 yards
wide and 2,000 yards deep. Not all of the perimeter was occupied, however; that is, not every part of the perimeter was
protected by trenches and foxholes. The entire beach line was
so defended; but at the ends of the beach, the foxholes and
machine gun emplacements extended only 500 yards or so

away from the water. The cannon of the 11th Marines, in fortified positions, were in place on the forward line; and there were fortified positions scattered among the artillery emplacements.

Facing inland, the Marines held positions from 700 yards to the right of the mouth of the Kukum River to the right bank of Alligator Creek (also called "The Tenaru River") on the left. "Henderson Field" was within this area, roughly in the middle, and about 1200 yards from the beach. Division Headquarters had been set up about equidistant between Lunga Point on the beach and Henderson Field.

The invasion of Guadalcanal had taken the Japanese by surprise. Their major troop units there had been the 11th and 12th Naval Rikusentai companies, about 450 men in all. The nearest American equivalent of these units would be Naval Construction Battalions. But the Rikusentai were neither trained nor equipped the way the American Sea-Bee's were— to fight as infantry as well as to build. Thus when the invasion began, the Japanese Rikusentai units on Guadalcanal had scattered to the boondocks—specifically to somewhere near Kukum.

Fortunately for the Marines, whose own engineer equipment had never been off-loaded from the invasion fleet, they left behind all of their engineer equipment, as well as large quantities of food and other equipment, and even cannon. That wasn't the end of the bounty, though: A Japanese communications radio, far superior to anything the Marines had, had been captured intact and converted to American use. And Marines of Lieutenant Jim Barrett's machine-gun platoon, M Company, 5th Marines, had captured two Japanese 3-inch Naval cannon, found ammunition for them, and pointed their ad hoc coast artillery battery seaward from the beach. They would be used against the Japanese warships everyone knew would soon appear offshore.

The large stocks of food the Rikusentai left behind would probably keep the 1st Marine Division from starving, Pickering thought. The departing fleet had carried away with it most of the rations it was supposed to have put ashore for the Marines.

Though the Rikusentai had rendered unusable the truck Pickering was standing on—the tires had been slashed and sand poured into the gas tank and engine oil filter—they didn't have time to sabotage most of the other trucks they left behind. So these were either intact or repairable. And so were several small bulldozers and other engineer equipment. Without the Japanese equipment, completing the airfield would have been impossible.

The Japanese plan for constructing the field involved starting from both ends and working toward a natural depression in the middle. Since the Japanese had not yet filled in the depression by the time the invasion came, when the Marines started work, that was their first order of business. One of the officers told Pickering that the job required moving 100,000 cubic yards of dirt. After that, the Marines extended the runway to 2600 feet, which was the minimum length required for operation by American airplanes.

But all that was now just about completed—*with more help from the Japanese than the U.S. Navy,* Pickering thought bitterly. The proof seemed to be that a Navy Catalina amphibious long range reconnaissance airplane was overhead, acting as if it wanted to come in for a landing.

Pickering jumped off the bed of the derelict Japanese truck, and walked to the Henderson Field control tower—obligingly built by the Rikusentai. They neglected to destroy it before heading for the boondocks.

Antennae had already been erected and strung. And when Pickering entered the building, a ground-to-air voice radio was in operation, manned by a Marine aviator who had obviously come ashore with the invasion force.

He looked at Pickering curiously, even with annoyance; but Lieutenants do not casually ask officers wearing silver eagles on their caps what the hell they want. So he returned his attention to the Catalina overhead, holding his microphone to his mouth.

"Navy two oh seven, I repeat the airfield is not, repeat not, ready to accept aircraft at this time."

"It looks fine to me," a metallic voice replied. "I repeat, I am exceedingly reluctant to land this aircraft on the water."

"Oh, shit!" the Marine Lieutenant said, and then pressed the TRANSMIT button on his microphone. "Navy two oh seven, the winds are negligible, the altimeter is two niner niner niner. Be advised that the runway may be soft, may be obstructed, and has vehicular and personnel traffic all over it. That said, you are cleared as number one to land, to the north, at your own risk. I say again, at your own risk."

"Henderson," the metallic voice replied cheerfully, "Navy two oh seven, turning on final."

Pickering went to the window of the control tower and noticed that some glass panes were missing. This was not due to any kind of bombing or shelling of the field, however. There was a jar of putty on the floor. The Rikusentai had not completed installing the glass when the Americans arrived.

Once its gear unfolded from the boat-shaped fuselage, the Catalina banked, lined up with the runway, lowered its flaps, and dropped toward the ground. It touched down, bounced back into the air, and then touched down again and stayed down. When it completed its landing roll, stopped, and began to turn, there was shouting and applause; and any vehicles with horns blew them.

Henderson Field was now in operation, and the men who made it so were delighted with themselves, with Naval Aviation, and with the world in general.

In fact, everyone in sight seemed pleased—with the exception of the Marine Aviator who had been on the radio. He started down from the tower as the Catalina taxied toward it. Pickering followed him.

The pilot parked the Catalina and shut the engines down. A moment later, he emerged from a door in the fuselage, wearing a large grin.

He was a Lieutenant, one grade senior in rank to the Marine Aviator First Lieutenant who greeted him, "What's wrong with it? I want to get you out of here as soon as I can. Before the Japs start throwing artillery at us."

"Nothing's wrong with it, Lieutenant," the Naval Aviator said.

"You said you couldn't land it on water."

"I said, I was *'exceedingly reluctant'* to land it on water," the Navy pilot said. "My name is Sampson, Lieutenant William Sampson, USN, in case you might want to write that down in some kind of log. I believe this is the first aircraft to land here."

"You sonofabitch!" the Marine Aviator said.

If it was Lieutenant Sampson's notion to remind the Marine Lieutenant that it was a violation of Naval protocol to suggest to a senior Naval officer that his parents were unmarried, he abandoned it when he saw Pickering . . . when he saw specifically the silver eagle on Pickering's cap.

He saluted. "Good afternoon, Colonel."

Pickering returned the salute. He did not correct Lieutenant Sampson's mistake.

"Welcome to Guadalcanal," Pickering said. "Do you have business here? Or was your primary motive turning yourself into a footnote when the official history is written?"

"I'm Admiral McCain's aide, Sir. I have a bag of mail for General Vandergrift."

"I've got a Jeep," Pickering said. "I'll take you to him."

"That's very good of you, Sir."

A Jeep bounced up to them, and an officer in Marine utilities, wearing a Red Cross brassard on his arm got out from behind the wheel.

"Have you got any space on that airplane to take critically wounded men out of here?"

"I can take two, Sir," Sampson replied. "That's all."

"When are you leaving?"

"Just as soon as I can deliver something to General Vandergrift."

"I can have them aboard in ten minutes," the doctor said.

"My crew will help you, Sir," Sampson said, and then looked at Pickering, who gestured toward the derelict Japanese Ford truck and his Jeep.

(Three)
G-2 SECTION
HEADQUARTERS, 1ST MARINE DIVISION
NEAR LUNGA POINT, GUADALCANAL
1710 HOURS 12 AUGUST 1942

Captain Fleming Pickering, USNR, did not hear Major General Alexander A. Vandergrift enter the map room of the G-2 section.

The title "map room" was somewhat grandiose: A piece of canvas (originally one of the sides of an eight-man squad

tent) had been hung from a length of communications wire,
dividing the G-2 Section "building" in two. The G-2 building
was another eight-man squad tent, around which had been
built a wall of sandbags. When there was time, it was planned
to find some timbers somewhere and build a roof structure
strong enough to support several layers of sandbags. At the
moment, the roof was the tent canvas. Because of the sandbag
walls, an artillery or mortar shell landing outside the tent
would probably not do very much damage. But the canvas
tenting would offer no protection if an artillery or mortar
shell hit the roof.

Pickering was on his knees, working on the Situation Map.
Specifically, he was writing symbols on the celluloid sheet
that covered the Situation Map. This in turn was mounted
to a sheet of plywood leaning against the sandbag walls.
When there was time, it was planned to find some wood and
make some sort of frame, so that the Situation Map would
not have to sit on the ground.

In his hand, Pickering held a black grease pencil. He was
marking friendly positions and units on the map. In his
mouth, like a cigar, was a red grease pencil, which he used
to mark enemy positions. A handkerchief, used to erase
marks on the map, stuck out of the hip pocket of his utility
trousers. He was not wearing his utility jacket. The Map
Room of the G-2 Section was like a steam bath, and Captain
Pickering had elected to work in his undershirt.

General Vandergrift walked to a spot just behind Pickering
so that he could examine the map over Pickering's shoulders.
Vandergrift's face, just starting to jowl, showed signs of fatigue. He stood there for more than a minute before his presence broke through Pickering's concentration. And then,
startled, Pickering looked over his shoulder. A split second
later, he realized who was standing behind him.

He rose quickly to his feet and came to attention.

"I beg your pardon, Sir."

Vandergrift made an "it doesn't matter" wave of his hand.

"Is that about it?" he asked, with another gesture at the
map.

"Yes, Sir."

"Where's Colonel Goettge?" Vandergrift asked. "For that

matter, where's the sergeant who normally keeps the Situation Map up to date?"

"Colonel Goettge is out with a patrol, Sir. I suppose I'm in charge."

"Say again?"

"Colonel Goettge is out with a patrol, Sir. He and the sergeant and some others."

Vandergrift's eyes tightened.

"I thought that's what you said," he said. "Tell me about it."

If I knew him better, I could answer that question without beating around the bush: "I think Goettge's gone off the deep end, General."

But that's not the way it is. He doesn't know me. All he knows is that I am a rich man, highly connected politically, who was sent over here to serve as Frank Knox's eyes and ears, and didn't even do that somewhat ethically questionable task well. A wiser man than I am would not take advantage of his position—no one had the authority to tell me to stay on the McCawley—to make a gesture of contempt for Navy Brass by staying with the Marines here.

What standing I have in his eyes, if any, is because Jack NMI Stecker told him that I was a pretty good Marine Corporal a generation ago.

I would not tolerate criticism of one of my officers from an ordinary seaman; why should General Vandergrift tolerate my unpleasant, and very likely uninformed opinion of one of his colonels?

Christ! I wish I knew this man better!

Although he had had only brief contact with General Vandergrift, Fleming Pickering had already formed strong opinions about him. The first was that he was competent, experienced, and level-headed. The second was that if the opportunity came, they could become friends.

Vandergrift reminded Pickering of a number of powerful commanders he had known and respected. The first of these was his own father, whose first command, at twenty-one, had been of a four-master Brigantine. And there was the master of the Pacific *Emerald*, on which Fleming Pickering, also at twenty-one, had made his first voyage with his brand-new third mate's ticket; this man had taught Pickering just about all there was to know about the responsibility that went with authority. Pickering had himself earned his any-tonnage, any-ocean Coast Guard Master Mariner's ticket at twenty-six. Since then, he'd come to know well maybe a half dozen other masters in command of Pacific & Far East Shipping Corporation vessels whom he held in serious respect. (Most of the others he employed were better than competent, but not up to the level of the six.)

And Vandergrift reminded Pickering of Pickering himself. Pickering had long believed that there were only very few men who were born to accept responsibility and discharge it well. Such men had a strange ability to recognize similar characteristics in others; they formed a kind of fraternity without membership cards and titles. Thus he had the strong conviction that he and General Vandergrift were brothers.

"Sir," Pickering said, "two days ago, a Japanese warrant officer, a *Navy* warrant officer, was captured by 1st Battalion, 5th Marines. During his interrogation, he said there were a large number of Rikusentai . . ."

"What?"

"Rikusentai, Sir. They're Naval Base troops. Sort of soldiers. Not Marines, Sir. They take care of housekeeping, construction. That sort of thing. They're in the Navy, but not sailors."

Vandergrift nodded.

"The warrant officer said there were a number of Rikusentai, and at least as many civilian laborers, wandering around in the bush near Matinikau. Here, Sir," Pickering said, pointing to the map. "In this general area. And he felt they could be induced to surrender. He said they were starving."

"He was unusually cooperative for a Japanese Naval officer, wasn't he?" Vandergrift said.

"He was originally pretty surly, as I understand it, Sir. But he was in bad shape. What used to be known as shell-shocked."

"You saw him, Pickering?"

"Yes, Sir. The 5th sent him up here."

"And?"

"What the warrant officer said was corroborated, Sir, by another prisoner. A Navy rating. Not captured at the same place. And not one of the warrant officer's men. He said there were both Rikusentai and civilian laborers in the area here," he pointed at the map with the red grease pencil, "at the mouth of the Matanikau River, in the vicinity of Point Cruz."

"And Colonel Goettge apparently believed both of them?"

"Yes, Sir. I assume that he did."

"Tell me about the patrol," Vandergrift said.

"Colonel Goettge had previously ordered a patrol under First Sergeant Custer. As originally set up, Custer was to take about twenty-five men into the Point Cruz-Mouth of the Matanikau River area. But then Colonel Goettge decided to lead the patrol himself."

"Did he offer any explanation for his decision?" Vandergrift asked, evenly.

"He apparently felt that the mission was too important to be entrusted to First Sergeant Custer, Sir."

What he did was act like an ass. He had no business going on patrol himself.

"Twenty-five men, you say? All from the 1st of the 5th?"

"No, Sir. He took several men from here, clerks and scouts. And Lieutenant Cory, our linguist. And Dr. Pratt, the 5th's surgeon."

"In other words, Captain Pickering, instead of a patrol of scouts and riflemen under a First Sergeant, we now have a patrol substantially made up of technicians of one kind or another, under the personal command of the Division Intelligence Officer?"

Pickering didn't reply.

Vandergrift met his eyes.

"And he left you in charge?" Vandergrift asked.

"Not in so many words, Sir."

"You just decided to fill the void left by Colonel Goettge when he went on this patrol of his?"

"I'm trying to make myself useful, Sir."

"Yes, of course you are. Actually, I came here to see you."

"Sir?"

Vandergrift reached in the cavernous pocket of his utility jacket and handed Pickering a crumpled sheet of paper.

URGENT
CONFIDENTIAL
NAVY DEPARTMENT WASHDC 10AUG42

TO: COMMANDING GENERAL
    FIRST MARINE DIVISION

INFORMATION; CINCPAC

1. BY DIRECTION OF THE SECRETARY OF THE NAVY CAPTAIN
FLEMING PICKERING USNR IS RELIEVED OF TEMPORARY AT-
TACHMENT 1ST MARINE DIVISION AND WILL PROCEED BY
FIRST AVAILABLE AIR TRANSPORTATION TO WASHINGTON
DC REPORTING UPON ARRIVAL THEREAT TO THE SECRE-
TARY.
2. THE OFFICE OF THE SECRETARY OF THE NAVY WILL BE
ADVISED BY RADIO OF RECEIPT OF THESE ORDERS BY CINC-
PAC, COMMGEN FIRST MARINE DIVISION AND CAPTAIN
PICKERING. OFC SECNAV WILL BE SIMILARLY ADVISED OF
DATE AND TIME OF CAPTAIN PICKERING'S DEPARTURE
FROM 1ST MARDIV AND ARRIVAL AND DEPARTURE FROM
INTERMEDIATE STOPS EN ROUTE TO WASHINGTON.
DAVID HAUGHTON, CAPT, USN, ADMINISTRATIVE ASST TO
SECNAV

"It may be some time before you go home, Pickering,"
General Vandergrift said. "I have no idea when the field will
be able to take anything but fighters. That Catalina coming
in here was an aberration."

"Yes, Sir."

"In the meantime, I am sure that you will continue to make
yourself useful," Vandergrift said. "When Colonel Goettge
and his . . . what did you call them, Pickering?"

"Rikusentai, Sir."

". . . Rikusentai. When he returns, would you tell him I
would like to see him, please?"

"Aye, aye, Sir."

Their eyes met briefly, but long enough for Pickering to
understand that Vandergrift shared his opinion that Division
Intelligence Officers should not shoulder rifles and go off into
the boondocks like second lieutenants. And there was confir-

mation, too, of Pickering's conviction that if there was only the opportunity, he and Vandergrift could become friends.

(Four)
G-2 SECTION
HEADQUARTERS, 1ST MARINE DIVISION
GUADALCANAL
2250 HOURS 13 AUGUST 1942

Major Jake Dillon, USMCR, a Leica 35mm camera suspended around his neck, a Thompson .45 caliber submachine gun cradled in his arm, pushed aside the canvas black-out flap and stepped into the G-2 section.

"Where can I find Captain Pickering?" he demanded of the Marine buck sergeant sitting by the three field telephones on a folding wooden desk.

A very tall, very thin Marine with sergeant's stripes painted on the sleeve of his utility jacket followed Dillon into the room. He was unarmed, and looked haggard and shaken, shading his eyes against the sudden brightness of the hissing Coleman lanterns.

The Marine sergeant started to rise to his feet. Dillon waved him back in his chair.

"The Captain's in there, Sir," he said, pointing to the map room. "I think he's asleep."

Dillon motioned for the sergeant who had come with him to follow him. Then he pushed the canvas flap aside.

Captain Fleming Pickering, USNR, was not only asleep, he was snoring. He was fully dressed, except for his boondockers, which were on the floor beside him. Next to the boondockers was a .45 Colt automatic pistol, the hammer cocked. His Springfield rifle hung from its sling on a length of steel pipe near his head.

His bed was two shelter halves laid on communications wire laced between more steel piping. A Coleman lantern hissed in the corner of the room.

Jake Dillon looked quickly around the room, walked quickly to the "bed," and placed his foot on Pickering's pistol.

"Flem!" he called. He immediately had proof that stepping

on the pistol had been the prudent thing to do. It was the
first thing Pickering reached for.

"It's me. Jake Dillon."

"What the hell do you want?" Pickering asked, a long way
from graciously. He stretched a moment, and then sat up,
swinging his feet to the floor and reaching for his boondockers. "What time is it?"

"Nearly eleven," Dillon replied, then checked his watch
and corrected himself. "Ten-fifty."

Pickering looked at the sergeant.

"This is Sergeant Sellers, Flem," Dillon said. "He's one
of mine."

Pickering nodded at the sergeant curtly.

"He was with Goettge," Dillon added.

Pickering's face lit up with interest.

"You were with Colonel Goettge, Sergeant? Where is he?"

"He's dead, Sir. Just about everybody is dead," the sergeant said.

"Christ!" Pickering said softly. "Everybody?"

The sergeant nodded dazedly.

"Just about everybody," he said.

"I thought you had better hear this, Flem, right away,"
Dillon said.

Pickering looked at Sergeant Sellers and saw in his face—
especially in his eyes—the absent look that comes into men's
eyes when they have seen something horrifying.

This guy is right on the edge of shock!

Pickering reached under his commo wire and shelter
halves bed and came out with a musette bag. He opened the
straps and took from it a bottle of Old Grouse scotch, thickly
padded with bath towels. He took the top off and extended
it wordlessly to Sergeant Sellers.

Sellers looked at it for a moment before somewhat dream-
ily reaching for it and putting it to his lips. He took a healthy
pull and then coughed and then handed the bottle back to
Pickering.

"You need some of this, Jake?" Pickering asked.

Resisting the temptation to reach for the bottle, Dillon
shook his head no. Liquor, like everything else, was in short
supply on the island.

"Sure?"

Dillon reached for the bottle and took a sip.

Pickering took the bottle from him, and began to wrap it in the towels again.

"You were with Colonel Goettge's patrol, Sergeant?" he asked, gently.

"Yes, Sir."

"How did that happen, Jake?"

"I heard about the patrol and told Goettge I'd like to send one of my people along. He said, 'sure.' "

Pickering had a sudden, furious thought: *Was that simple stupidity, or did Goettge want to make sure his Errol Flynn-John Wayne heroics were properly photographed for posterity?*

He immediately regretted the snap decision: *There you go again, Pickering, from all your vast experience as a corporal twenty-odd years ago, judging a man who spent that much time learning his profession. Who the* hell *do you think you are?*

"Can you tell me about the patrol, Sergeant? You say you're just back?"

"Yes, Sir," Sergeant Sellers replied, and then fell silent.

"Start from the beginning, why don't you? You went with Colonel Goettge on the ramp boat from Kukum?"

That much Pickering already knew. When the Navy sailed away from Guadalcanal, they did so in such haste that a number of the landing boats normally carried aboard the transports were left behind. Before the Naval bombardment, there had been a small village called Kukum. The village was almost totally destroyed, but it remained a good spot for keeping the boats the Navy left behind. So Vandergrift formed there an ad hoc unit, "The Lunga Boat Pool," made up of the boats and their mixed Navy and Coast Guard crews.

"That was about eighteen hundred?" Pickering pried gently. He knew what time Goettge left.

Fucking around with one thing and another, including taking his own combat correspondent with him, Goettge's ramp boat left at least two hours too late to do any good once he got where they were headed.

"That's about all we know, Sergeant," Pickering said, gently. "Could you fill me in from there?"

"Well, it was dark when we got there, Sir."

"You mean at the Matanikau River?"

Pickering knew that too. Following First Sergeant Custer's original plan at least that far, Goettge had told him he planned to go ashore about two hundred yards west of the mouth of the Matanikau.

"Yes, Sir. That's probably why we ran aground. It was dark and we couldn't see."

"Where did you run aground?"

"About fifty yards offshore, Colonel," Sergeant Sellers said. Pickering did not correct him. "The . . . watchacallem? The guy who runs the boat?"

"The coxswain," Pickering furnished.

"The coxswain said it was a sandbar."

"What happened then?"

"Some of the guys went over the sides and tried to rock it free, but when that didn't work, we all went into the water and waded ashore."

"What happened to the ramp boat?"

"A couple of guys stayed behind and kept rocking it. I guess they finally got it loose. We could hear it after a while; we couldn't see it, it was too dark. We could hear it going away."

"So there you were on the beach?"

"So they talked it over."

" 'They'?"

"Colonel Goettge and the officers," Sellers said. "I was there with them."

"And?"

"They decided it was too late, too dark, too, to do anything. Except find some place to spend the night. And then go on patrol in the morning. So Colonel Goettge and Sergeant Custer started walking toward the coconut trees . . ."

"What coconut trees?"

"There was a grove of coconut trees. It was dark on the ground, Colonel, but we could see the tops of the trees . . . You know what I mean?"

"Yes, I think so. Then what happened?"

"That's when the Japs started shooting," Sellers said, very quietly, barely audibly.

"Was anyone hit?"

"Colonel Goettge. He got it first. Then Sergeant Custer," Sellers said. "They went down right away. Christ! Then the Doc ran out to help them . . ."

"That would be Captain Pratt, the surgeon?"

"I think that was his name," Sellers said. "And then Sergeant Caltrider shot the Jap."

"What Jap was that?"

"The one we brought with us. The Jap warrant officer."

"Sergeant Caltrider shot him?"

"Blew the cocksucker's head off," Sellers said. "The bastard led us into a trap. That's what it was, a trap. He deserved it, the cocksucker."

"Was Colonel Goettge badly wounded?"

"Killed. Had half of his face shot away. Sergeant Custer, too. He was hit four, five times. Killed him right away."

"And Doctor Pratt?"

"Him, too."

"And what were the rest of you doing?"

"One of the guys ran back in the water and fired his rifle, to get the ramp boat to come back. The rest of us just laid there. Jesus, there was no place to get out of the line of fire. It was like they were waiting for us, knew where we would be, and when we got where they wanted us, they opened up with everything they had."

"Did the boat come back?"

"No, Sir. Either he didn't know we wanted him to, or he could see what was going on and figured we were all dead."

"Then what?"

"We just laid there. Christ, we couldn't even see where they were to shoot back at them. I mean, we knew where they were, but we couldn't see them."

"But they knew where you were?"

"The only reason I'm alive is because of the way the beach sloped. There was just enough sand to hide behind."

"Where was Captain Ringer? Did you see him?"

Ringer was the S-2 of the 5th Marines. In Pickering's judgment, if any staff Intelligence officer should have gone out on this patrol—and he didn't think any should have—it should have been under the command of an infantry platoon leader. It should have been Ringer. And now he thought, unkindly, that since Goettge had insisted on going himself, Ringer should have stayed behind.

"Yes, Sir. He sort of took over after the colonel was killed. Him and Lieutenant Cory."

"What were they doing at this time?"

"Well, the first thing he did was send a corporal down the beach for help. And then, I guess it was about an hour later, Sergeant Arndt volunteered to swim back for help. I went with him."

"You swam back?"

"Yes, Sir. We ran into a Jap—I think he was as lost as we were—and Arndt killed him. And then we found a boat and paddled most of the way back."

"Most of the way?"

"Sergeant Arndt thought we would probably get shot by our own guys, so we paddled out to one of the landing boats we knew was anchored off shore, and then we got them to start it up and take us in."

"Where is Sergeant Arndt now?"

"They took him to the 5th Marines Command Post, Sir."

"I was there, Flem," Jake Dillon said. "I thought you had better hear this, so I brought him here."

"Yeah," Pickering said.

He looked at Sergeant Sellers.

"Is that about it, Sergeant? Is there anything else?"

Sellers met his eyes but didn't speak for a moment.

"Sir, as we were swimming away," he said finally, hollow voiced, "we could make out . . . the Japs came out of the boondocks, Sir, from the coconut trees and the other side of them. They . . . They went after the people on the beach, Sir. Not only with rifles and pistols. I mean, they were using swords. We could see the swords, reflections from them, I mean. And we could hear our guys screaming."

From a remote portion of his brain, dimmed by more than two decades, and intentionally hidden on top of that, Pickering's memory brought forth the sound of the screams men made when their bodies were violated by sharpened steel. Some of the Marines at Belleau Wood, Corporal Fleming Pickering among them, had armed themselves with intrenching shovels. They sharpened the sides with sharpening stones.

These had been more effective than the issue bayonets and trench knives.

"Sergeant," Pickering said after a moment, "I'm going to leave you here for a while. Lie down on my bed. Help yourself to some of the whiskey, if you want. But I think that some other officers will want to talk to you, so go easy with the whiskey."

That's so much bullshit. Debriefing should be performed by Intelligence Officers. All of ours are now dead.

"Jake, you stay with him. I'm going to see General Vandergrift."

"Aye, aye, Sir."

XVI

"I'd like to see the General, please," Captain Fleming
Pickering said to the sergeant in the Division Command Post.

"He's in there, Sir," the sergeant said, pointing, "with
Colonel Hunt. I'll see if he can see you."

Colonel Guy Hunt was the regimental commander of the
5th Marines.

*If he's here, Pickering reasoned, he knows what has
happened.*

"Keep your seat, Sergeant," Pickering said, and walked
into Vandergrift's office.

Both Hunt and Vandergrift looked with annoyance at
Pickering when he walked in. Officers, even Navy Captains,
do not enter the "office" of the commanding general of the
1st Marine Division without permission.

Vandergrift met Pickering's eyes.

"For reasons I suspect you already know, Captain,"

Vandergrift said after a moment, "please consider yourself the acting G-2 of this division."

Oh, shit! I am no more qualified to be the Division G-2 than I am to flap my wings and fly.

"Aye, aye, Sir."

"I know you know Colonel Hunt, Pickering. Do you know Marine Gunner Rust?" (Marine Gunners were almost always veteran Master Gunnery Sergeants promoted to warrant officer rank.)

"No, Sir."

"Rust, this is Captain Pickering. He and Jack NMI Stecker were at Belleau Wood together."

"I know the captain by reputation," Rust said and gave Pickering his hand.

"How much do you know about what's happened to Goettge's patrol, Pickering?" Vandergrift asked.

"I just finished talking to Sergeant Sellers, Sir. He swam back with Sergeant Arndt."

"Sellers?" Master Gunner Rust asked.

"He's one of Major Dillon's combat correspondents," Pickering explained.

"Christ, another feather merchant who went along!" Rust exploded.

"A technician, maybe," Pickering heard himself say, angrily. "Or a specialist. But feather merchants, in my book, are those who head in the other direction from the sound of the guns."

Rust glowered at Pickering for a moment, and then shrugged.

"I beg the captain's pardon," Rust said.

"Not mine," Pickering said. "I know I'm a feather merchant. But that Four-Months-in-the-Corps Hollywood photographer has no apologies to make for his behavior on this patrol."

Pickering glanced at Vandergrift and found the general's serious eyes on his.

"Speaking of this patrol, Pickering," Vandergrift said, "we were just discussing the possibility of sending a patrol out to look for survivors. What's your feeling about that?"

"Sir, I don't feel qualified to . . ."

"I make the decisions about who is and who is not qualified to offer an opinion, Captain. I asked for yours."

"Based on what Sergeant Sellers told me, I don't think there will be many survivors, if any," Pickering said. "And I would presume the Japanese will be waiting for us to do something. At night, Sir, in my opinion, it would be suicidal. I think we could, should, send a strong patrol over there at first light."

"I agree," Vandergrift said. "I appreciate the offer, Rust, but that makes it three to one against your idea."

"Yes, Sir," Rust said.

"You can head it up yourself, Rust, if you like," Vandergrift said. He turned to Colonel Hunt. "All right with you, Guy?"

"Yes, Sir. A *strong* patrol, Rust. They'll be expecting you."

"Aye, aye, Sir."

"Guy, why don't you and Rust go set it up?" Vandergrift said. "Let me know before you take off. I want a word with Captain Pickering."

Hunt and Rust left the room. Then Colonel Hunt returned. He offered his hand to Pickering.

"Good luck, Captain," he said. "Thank God we have somebody like you to step into the breach."

"Thank you, Sir," Pickering said.

Hunt left again. Pickering looked at Vandergrift.

"That was gracious and flattering," Pickering said. "But I am not qualified to step into Goettge's shoes."

"You weren't listening carefully, Captain," Vandergrift said. "The operative words were 'somebody like you to step into the breach.' I don't have anyone else. You don't expect to lose your division G-2 like this. Nor the 5th Marines' G-2, who would have been my choice for a temporary replacement."

"I'll do my best, Sir. But you need a professional."

"I'll send a radio asking for one, of course," Vandergrift said. "But until he arrives, or until I have to order you off the island, you're it."

"I'll need some help, Sir."

"Jack Stecker? Am I reading your mind?"

"Yes, Sir."

Major Jack NMI Stecker had commanded 2nd Battalion,

5th Marines, when they invaded Tulagi. During the battle, Stecker had personally taken out a sniper-in-a-bunker who had been holding up the 2nd Battalion's advance by standing in the open and shooting him, offhand, in the head from a distance of 200 yards. The story had not surprised Pickering when he heard it.

"General Harris won't like losing Stecker, but he'll have to live with it. Tulagi is secure, and Stecker will be of more value to the division working with you here. I'll send a boat to Tulagi at first light to fetch him. He's not going to be happy about it, either, but that's the way it's going to have to be."

"What he really won't like is working for me," Pickering chuckled. "In France, in 1918, he was my sergeant when I was a corporal."

Vandergrift looked at Pickering, and then smiled. "I think they call that the fortunes of war, Captain," he said, in mock solemnity, and then went on, changing the subject, "There's something I feel I should tell you: How well do you—perhaps that should be, 'did you'—know Lieutenant Cory?"

"You're speaking of the 5th Marines Japanese language officer?" Vandergrift nodded. "Not well, Sir."

"He is another of your Four-Months-in-the-Corps Marines, Pickering. He came in April. Direct commission. He was previously employed by the Navy. In Washington. Something to do with communications intelligence. Something hush-hush. I received a special message about him. I was directed to take whatever action was necessary to keep him from falling into Japanese hands."

"Jesus!" Pickering said, not aware he had spoken.

My God, he might have known about MAGIC! What idiot assigned him to an infantry regiment here?

"From your reaction, I gather you might know what that's all about," Vandergrift said. " 'Whatever action' was not defined. Did it mean that I should make an effort to see that he did not go on patrols like this one? Or was more unpleasant action on my part suggested?"

"Sir, there are some classified matters which would justify any action to keep people privy to them out of enemy hands."

"Are you in that category, Captain?"

"Yes, Sir."

"Then it won't be necessary for me to tell you not to put

yourself in a position where you might fall into enemy hands, will it?"

"No, Sir."

"Unless there's something else going on that I don't know about, I think the thing for you and me to do is try to get some sleep. There's nothing else that can be done about Goettge and his people tonight."

"Yes, Sir," Pickering said. "Sir, is our communications in to Pearl Harbor?"

"As far as I know."

"I have a message to send," Pickering said. "I have authority, Sir . . ."

"I know all about your authority, Pickering: You don't have to ask my permission to radio the Secretary of the Navy, and I don't have the authority to ask what you're saying to him."

He thinks, Pickering thought, *that I am going to radio Washington that Cory may have been captured by the Japanese. I hadn't even thought about that. But I'll do that, too.*

"With your permission, Sir?" Pickering said.

Vandergrift smiled, nodded, and waved his hand in a gesture of dismissal.

"For what it's worth, I share Colonel Hunt's sentiments about you, Pickering," Vandergrift said.

(Two)

The duty officer in the communications section of Headquarters, 1st Marine Division was a second lieutenant. He was dozing, but woke up when Pickering entered the small, sandbag walled room.

"May I help you, Colonel?" he asked, getting to his feet.

"I'm Captain Pickering. I need to send a radio, classified TOP SECRET. Are you a crypto officer?"

"Yes, Sir, I am, but . . . Captain, what's your authority?"

Pickering took his orders, wrapped in waterproof paper, from his pocket and showed them to the young officer.

"If that won't do it for you, Lieutenant, call General Vandergrift."

"This will do, Sir. Where's the message?"

"I haven't written it yet," Pickering said. "Sergeant, you want to get up and let me at that typewriter?"

The sergeant, who had been monitoring his radio, waiting for traffic, looked at the lieutenant for guidance. The lieutenant nodded. The sergeant got up, and Pickering sat down at the typewriter. There was a blank sheet of paper in it.

Pickering looked at the lieutenant.

"The priority immediately below 'Operational Immediate' is 'Urgent,' right?"

"Yes, Sir."

Pickering tapped the balls of his fingers together impatiently as he mentally composed the message, and then he began to type. He typed with skill. He had taken up typing to pass time as a junior officer at sea. It wasn't too much later than that when he learned that doing the typing himself was much faster than dictating to a secretary.

URGENT

FROM: HQ FIRST MARINE DIVISION

TO: CINCPAC

0045 13AUG42

FOLLOWING CLASSIFIED TOP SECRET FROM CAPTAIN FLEMING PICKERING USNR FOR EYES ONLY SECNAVY WASHINGTON DC

1. LOSS IN COMBAT OF COLONEL FRANK GOETTGE 1ST MARDIV G2, CAPTAIN WILLIAM RINGER 5TH MARINES S2 AND 1STLT RALPH CORY 5TH MARINES LANGUAGE OFFICER REQUIRES IMMEDIATE ACTION TO AIRSHIP QUALIFIED REPLACEMENT PERSONNEL.

2. DESPITE URGENT NECESSITY TO FURNISH 1ST MARDIV WITH QUALIFIED PERSONNEL I URGE IN STRONGEST POSSIBLE TERMS THAT EXISTING POLICIES PROHIBITING ASSIGNMENT OF PERSONNEL WHO HAVE HAD ACCESS TO HIGHLY CLASSIFIED INFORMATION TO DUTIES WHERE THEY MAY FALL INTO ENEMY HANDS BE STRICTLY OBSERVED.

3. PENDING ARRIVAL OF QUALIFIED REPLACEMENT, THE UNDERSIGNED HAS TEMPORARILY ASSUMED DUTIES OF 1ST MARDIV G2.

SIGNED FLEMING PICKERING CAPTAIN USNR

END TOP SECRET EYES ONLY SECNAV FROM PICKERING CAPT USN G2 1ST MARDIV

He tore the paper from the typewriter and read it.

If that second paragraph doesn't tell Haughton that some damned fool assigned Cory, who almost certainly knew about MAGIC, *to an infantry battalion, he's not as smart as I think he is.*

He handed the sheet of paper to the lieutenant.

"Encrypt it and get it out as soon as you can," he said.

"Yes, Sir," the lieutenant said. He read the message.

"My God, they're all dead? What the hell happened?"

"It's a long, sad story, Lieutenant," Pickering said and walked out of the commo bunker.

(Three)
SUPREME HEADQUARTERS SOUTHWEST PACIFIC AREA
BRISBANE, AUSTRALIA
13 AUGUST 1942

On the plane from Pearl Harbor, Lieutenant Colonel George F. Dailey, USMC, seriously considered doing something about the pristine newness of his silver oak leaves. The problem was that he didn't know what would do the job . . . He didn't think that rubbing them—on a carpet, say—would effectively dim their gloss. And working on them with, say, a nail file, would probably produce a silver lieutenant colonel's leaf that looked like somebody had worked it over with a nail file.

Before he fell asleep, he thought that when he got to his new billet in Australia, *before* he actually reported in, he would find some sand and rub it into his insignia with his Blitz cloth. The idea was amusing. After eight years in the Corps, he'd worn out probably twenty Blitz cloths in practically daily use putting a high shine on his insignia. He would now use one to dull it.

Lieutenant Colonel Dailey's concern was based less on personal vanity than on his belief that he could function better in new duties if it was not immediately apparent that he had been promoted so recently. After all, he reasoned, he had been a lieutenant colonel only thirteen days. And he wanted to do well in his new billet.

When he actually reached Brisbane, so many things happened so quickly that he forgot about taking the shine off his new silver oak leaves.

For one thing, there was a general's aide-de-camp, a lieutenant, waiting for him at the airport, with a 1940 Packard Clipper staff car, a driver, and an orderly.

"Colonel," the lieutenant said, "on behalf of Supreme Headquarters, SWPA, and General Willoughby specifically, welcome to Australia. The General asked me to express his regret that he couldn't meet you here himself, but he's tied up with the Supreme Commander at the moment."

The Supreme Commander, of course, was General Douglas MacArthur. General MacArthur was a full, four-star general. Dailey had never seen a four-star general. There were no four-star generals in the Marine Corps. The Commandant of the Corps was only a three-star lieutenant general. And until recently, his title had been Major General Commandant, and he had had but two stars.

"It's very good of you to meet me," Dailey said.

"I'll have the sergeant get your luggage, Sir," the aide said, "and then we'll try to get you settled. General Willoughby hopes we can do that by sixteen hundred, so there will be a chance for him to have a quick word with you before you see the Supreme Commander—he'll take you to see him—which we have penciled in for sixteen forty-five."

My God, I'm going to meet MacArthur!

"If I'm to see the General," Dailey said, "either general, I really am going to have to have a uniform pressed."

"No problem, Sir," the aide said. "There's a valet service in Lennon's. I'll have a word with the manager and explain the situation."

"Lennon's?"

"Lennon's Hotel, Sir. Sometimes irreverently known as 'The Lemon.' It's the senior staff officer's quarters, Sir."

"Splendid," Dailey said. He was human. He was not yet really accustomed to being addressed as "colonel," and liked the sound of it; and the phrase "senior staff officer" had a nice ring to it, too, especially since it had been made clear that he was regarded as such by at least one general officer of General Douglas MacArthur's general staff.

Lennon's Hotel turned out to be very nice. It was a rambling, turn-of-the-century structure with high ceilings and a good deal of polished brass and gleaming wood. As General Willoughby's aide led him across the lobby, Dailey saw a bar, and then smiled when he saw the brass sign above its door: GENTLEMEN'S SALOON.

It was well patronized in the middle of the afternoon, Dailey saw, by men wearing a wide variety of uniforms. He did not see a Marine uniform, however, and wondered how many—if any—other Marines were assigned here. The subject had not been mentioned in the briefings he had been given in Washington and at CINCPAC in Pearl Harbor.

At 1555 hours, General Willoughby's Packard Clipper deposited Lieutenant Colonel Dailey at the main entrance to Supreme Headquarters, South West Pacific. It was a modern office building. Dailey wondered what it had originally been, but a new sign, reading SUPREME HEADQUARTERS, SOUTH WEST PACIFIC AREA, had been placed on the building wall over the spot where he was sure the building's name had been chiseled into the marble.

General Willoughby's aide read his mind: "It used to be an insurance company, Colonel. The Aussie military does things right. When they need a building, they just tell the occupants to get out."

"I see," Dailey said.

He saw one more thing of interest before an Army Military Policeman in a white cap cover pushed open the door for them. He saw a Studebaker President pull into a parking spot marked RESERVED FOR SENIOR OFFICERS. A Marine Corps emblem was on its door, and the letters USMC were painted on the hood. A Marine sergeant, carrying a briefcase, got out and headed for the entrance. Obviously, there was at least one other Marine officer assigned here, one senior enough to have his own staff car and driver.

"I see that I am not alone," he said to the aide. "There's a Marine."

"He's one of the cave-dwellers, Colonel."

"I beg pardon?"

"Classified documents and cryptography are two floors underground. They call the people who work down there in the dark 'cave-dwellers.' "

"I see."

"I think I heard someone say that that sergeant is a Japanese-language linguist."

"I see," Dailey said. He was about to ask how come a sergeant had a staff car when the obvious answer came to him. It belonged to a Marine officer of appropriate rank. He wished they'd gotten into that in the briefings. He would have liked to know if he was junior to or senior to the other Marine officer. Or officers.

The elevator took them to the eighth floor.

Brigadier General Charles Willoughby greeted Dailey cordially, offered him coffee, quite unnecessarily apologized for not having met him personally at the airport, and asked if he found his quarters satisfactory.

And he asked an odd question:

"Does the phrase MAGIC mean anything to you, Colonel?"

"No, Sir. I can't say that it does."

"It's of no importance," Willoughby said.

Dailey was no fool. He knew that General Willoughby had not asked him about MAGIC, whatever the hell that was, because it was "of no importance," but very probably because it *was* important, and he expected Dailey to know what it was.

I wonder what the hell MAGIC is, and why haven't I been told about it?

At 1643, they were in General Douglas MacArthur's outer office. General Willoughby introduced Dailey to Lieutenant Colonel Sidney Huff, MacArthur's aide-de-camp. Dailey was reminded again what august company he was now keeping. A *lieutenant colonel* for an aide-de-camp!

At 1645 exactly, Colonel Huff formally announced, "The Supreme Commander will see you now, gentlemen."

General Douglas MacArthur looked exactly like the picture of him that had been on the cover of *Life* magazine. When he rose from behind his huge, mahogany desk, he was wearing a khaki shirt open at the neck and pleated khaki trousers. The famous, battered, heavily gold embroidered cap was sitting in MacArthur's IN basket. Dailey looked for but did not see MacArthur's famous corncob pipe.

"General, may I present Lieutenant Colonel Dailey? Colonel, the Supreme Commander."

Dailey remembered that it was the Army's odd custom to salute indoors, and did so. MacArthur returned it with a vague gesture toward his forehead and then offered that hand to Dailey.

"We are very pleased to have you here, Colonel," he said.

"I am honored to be here, Sir."

"To clear the air between us, Colonel . . ." MacArthur said, interrupting himself to say, "Please, be seated. There's coffee of course, but it's nearly seventeen hundred—what is it you sailors say? Time to sink the main brace?—and at that hour I always like a little pick-me-up."

"Thank you, Sir."

"There is no naval officer for whom I have higher professional or personal regard than Admiral Chester Nimitz," MacArthur said, coming very quickly to the reason why Dailey was there. "I regard him as a brother."

"Yes, Sir."

"There has been some unfortunate talk of friction between us. That's absolute rot. We *have* had some frank interchanges of thought, where we both approached problems from our different perspectives. Which is as it should be. We have resolved our differences without an iota of rancor. Isn't that so, Willoughby?"

"Absolutely, General."

"I don't know how that sort of thing gets started," MacArthur said. "All I know is that it does, and that it's circulated so quickly that the Signal Corps should find out how and adapt the technique for themselves."

Dailey understood in a moment that the General had been witty, and he was expected to at least chuckle and smile. He did so.

"General Willoughby's got you settled all right, I presume. Decent quarters, a car, that sort of thing? Is there anything I can do to make Admiral Nimitz's representative here feel more welcome than General Willoughby has?"

"My quarters are fine, Sir. General Willoughby has been most gracious."

"No car, General," Willoughby said. "I didn't think about that."

"Sid, get on the phone and tell the headquarters commandant to arrange for a car for Colonel Bailey . . ."

"It's 'Dailey,' General," General Willoughby said.

"Dailey then," MacArthur said, his tone making it clear
that he did not like to be either interrupted or corrected. "Effective immediately."

"Yes, Sir," Huff said, and started to leave the room.

"Sid," MacArthur called after him, "Tell Sergeant Gomez
that I have just decreed that it is seventeen hundred. He has
his orders to be executed at that hour."

A moment later, a stocky Filipino Master Sergeant rolled
in a tray loaded with liquor bottles, glasses, and a silver bowl
full of ice.

Five minutes or so later, one of the four telephones on
MacArthur's desk rang.

Huff grabbed it on the second ring.

"Office of the Supreme Commander, Colonel Huff."

He listened, then covered the mouthpiece with his hand.

"General, it's Lieutenant Hon. He has two MAGICs."

There's that word MAGIC *again. And it's obviously important, or they wouldn't be telling General MacArthur about it.*
Them. *He said* MAGICs. *Plural. What the hell does it mean?*

"Ask him to bring them up," MacArthur ordered. "Tell
him General Willoughby is here."

Huff nodded.

"Come up, Hon. General Willoughby is here."

MacArthur looked at Dailey.

"Take your time, Bailey. Finish your drink. But when
Pluto—Lieutenant Hon. Unusual fellow. He has a PhD in
Mathematics from MIT; splendid bridge player—gets here,
I'll have to ask you to excuse me."

"Yes, of course, Sir."

"Do you play bridge, by chance, Bailey?"

"Yes, Sir. I do."

"Well, Mrs. MacArthur and I like to think we play well.
We'll have to try that some evening."

"I would be honored, Sir."

"Make a note, Sid, to ask Colonel Bailey, when he's had
time to settle in, for bridge."

"Yes, Sir."

A minute later, there was a knock at the door. A very large

Asiatic of some sort wearing the insignia of an Army Signal Corps First Lieutenant walked in the room. He held two TOP SECRET cover sheets in his hand.

"Nothing startling, I hope, Pluto?" General MacArthur said.

"I would say 'interesting' rather than 'startling,' Sir."

"Well, let's see them," MacArthur said. "Sid, you make sure Bailey here gets a car."

"Yes, Sir."

"Glad to have you here, Bailey," MacArthur said.

"Thank you, Sir," Dailey said. Huff ushered him out of the room.

(Four)

Sergeant John Marston Moore, USMCR, noticed Lieutenant Colonel George F. Dailey outside the building and wondered idly who he was. But then he put him out of his mind. The only thing really unusual about him was that he had aviator's wings on his blouse. There were Marine officers commonly in and out of SWPA, for one reason or another, but this was the first aviator that Moore could remember seeing.

He got into the elevator and rode it down to the basement. He showed his identity badge to the MP buck sergeant on guard in the passageway outside the elevator. Although they knew each other, he examined it carefully. And then Moore signed himself into the commo center.

"They were looking all over for you last night and this morning," the MP sergeant said. "You were supposed to be charge-of-quarters."

"I was moved out of the barracks," Moore said.

"I guess nobody told them. They were pissed."

"Fuck 'em," Moore said.

"They were pissed, you better watch out," the MP sergeant said. "The whole fucking war will be lost because you weren't there to answer their fucking phone."

Moore chuckled, nodded at him, and went down the corridor. There was a steel door at the entrance to the cryptographic section. It was guarded by another MP, this one a corporal. He had another IN/OUT log.

Moore went through that security check, and then unlocked the steel door where he, Pluto Hon, and, at least in theory, Mrs. Ellen Feller plied their trade.

When he turned and locked himself inside, Pluto said, "I gather the Deaconess didn't come with you? Prayer meeting, no doubt?"

"She's playing tennis," Moore said. "She said that if it was anything interesting, I should bring it out to the house."

For what Moore thought were obvious reasons, Mrs. Feller did not like to spend any more time than she had to in their cubicle.

"Tennis? That's new."

"There's half a dozen courts at the racetrack. She asked around, and they let her join."

"War is hell, isn't it, Moore?"

"She has nice legs," Moore said, and immediately wondered why he had volunteered that. It was sure to result in a crack from Pluto. It came immediately.

"It's not nice to notice married women's legs, Moore," Pluto said, mockingly stern. "And how did you get to see them? Is something that I don't know about going on at Water Lily Cottage between you and the Deaconess?"

"She bought tennis clothes. You know. And she asked me if I thought they were too daring."

"And were they?"

"Come on. No, of course not. They were hardly shorter than a regular dress."

"But short enough for you to notice her legs, right?"

"I knew I made a mistake the minute I said that," Moore said. "What came in?"

I hope that gets him off the subject.

Hon pushed a TOP SECRET cover sheet off a thin sheaf of papers fresh from the crypto machine. He handed these to Moore.

"The Nips may finally be getting off the dime," he said.

Moore read the intercepts.

The most significant one was on top. It was from the Imperial General Staff in Tokyo, addressed to Vice Admiral Nishizo Tsukahara, commander of the 11th Air Fleet; and to Lieutenant General Harukichi Hyakutake, who commanded the 17th Army, whose headquarters were in Rabaul.

It relieved the Navy of responsibility for dealing with the Americans on Guadalcanal, Tulagi, and Gavutu, and gave it to the 17th Army.

"What does Pearl Harbor make of this? I mean, wasn't it expected?" Moore asked. "The Navy doesn't have any troops they could use on Guadalcanal. If anyone is going to be able to throw us off, it will have to be the Jap Army."

"Pearl Harbor expected it," Hon said. "Read the other ones."

The next intercepted message, also from the Imperial General Staff, was to a convoy of ships at sea. It directed the convoy commander to divert to Truk and off-load the Ichiki Butai.

"That's the 28th Infantry, 7th Division, right?" Moore asked. "The ones that were on Guam?"

"Right. First class troops. Colonel Kiyano Ichiki. Two thousand of them."

The Japanese Army, Moore had learned, had the interesting habit of officially referring to outstanding units by the name of the commanding officer.

The next intercepts, two of them, were an offer from the Japanese Navy to General Hyakutake of a battalion of Rikusentai "for use in connection with your new responsibility"; and his acceptance.

The last two intercepts placed an infantry brigade in the Palau Islands under Hyakutake's command and assigned the Ichiki Butai to him as soon as they reached "their next destination," which of course a previous intercept had identified as Truk.

"OK," Moore said. "What are we looking for?"

"You tell me. You're the one always noticing things you shouldn't, like missionary ladies' legs."

"Ah, come on, Lieutenant!"

"I'll give you a hint," Hon said. "Numbers. Ratios. That's two hints."

"I don't know what you mean?"

"What do we have on Guadalcanal?"

"I don't know," Moore replied, then thought about it and came up with an answer: "Less than a division, since they didn't all get to land. Is that what you're driving at?"

"Plus the Raider Battalion, plus the Parachute Battalion,

less the troops that didn't make it onto the beach. A Division, about. Ten, twelve thousand troops."

"OK."

"I personally thought the estimate of Japanese on Guadalcanal at the time of the invasion was high, but let's say it really was six thousand. For the sake of argument, let's say there are four thousand effectives—I don't think there are . . ."

"OK," Moore said, grasping Hon's line of thought.

"OK, what?"

"How many Japs in a brigade?"

"For the sake of argument, three thousand. It's like one of our regimental combat teams. Basically an infantry regiment that they've augmented with artillery, and maybe some tanks, and some service troops."

"Three thousand in the brigade in the Palau Islands, plus two thousand in the Ichiki Butai on Truk, plus what? Five, six hundred in the Rikusentai battalion? Five thousand five hundred people. Plus the four thousand you say may be left on Guadalcanal. Ninety-five hundred, ten thousand."

"At the most optimistic," Hon said, "they would have as many people there as we do. Much more likely, a couple of thousand less."

"And you can't push an Army back in the sea unless you outnumber them—what? Two to one?"

"Question," Hon said. "Are we missing intercepts that authorize more troops than these? Probable answer, probably not. We know about the two divisions they intend to stage through Rabaul to use in New Guinea. So again, probably not."

"Question," Moore picked up, "Do they not know how many men we have on Guadalcanal? Probable answer, they know damned well."

"So?"

"Question, do they really think they are so much better soldiers than we are that they can kick us off Guadalcanal with the troops they have and the ones they're sending? Answer: I don't know. They are not stupid, but when they get their pride going, all bets are off."

"How about this? Question, are they only sending five thousand troops because they don't have shipping to transport any more than that? Probable answer, I haven't the faintest idea. Maybe there are enough ships and they intend to use them to move those two divisions from Rabaul to New Guinea with them, leaving Guadalcanal until later."

"So what we're looking for is shipping information?" Moore asked.

"One other thing. I have seen nothing in any of these intercepts that suggests the Japs are worried about our getting that airfield up and running. Does that mean they don't think we can do it? Or they don't understand what it will mean?"

"How much more is there to go through?"

"I've got another thirty intercepts."

"I'll get on them," Moore said.

"The reason I was hoping you would bring the Deaconess with you was so that she could help. Why should we do all the work? She's making all the money."

"Lieutenant," Moore said, in mock shock and outrage, "that's very ungentlemanly of you."

"*I* haven't been admiring her legs. *I* don't have to be gentlemanly."

"I'll take the intercepts out to the cottage."

"I thought you said she was playing tennis?"

"You don't play tennis all afternoon."

"OK," Hon said. "Now listen to me, John. I'm not pulling your leg. I don't trust that woman. She looks to me like she has taken post graduate courses in how to take credit for what other people have done, while simultaneously keeping her own ass out of the line of fire."

"You better go deeper into that," Moore said.

"So far, she has not put her ass on the line with any analysis we've taken to the Emperor. Think about it. So far we have been right. She's getting credit for that, because they think she's in charge. But if we had been wrong, I think she would have said, 'Lieutenant Hon never discussed that with me.' "

"You really think she's that much of a bitch?"

"Yeah."

"Well, there's something damned cold about her, I'll admit that."

"I want to make sure she reads every goddamned thing that comes through here. I don't want her to be able to say she never saw something."

"What are you going to do about the Emperor?"

"I'm going to call Sid Huff and tell him I have some MAGIC. What you read. Before we offer an analysis, I want the Deaconess's two cents."

"I'm on my way," Moore said.

"Take a pistol and use the chain on the briefcase. Do it by the book, Sergeant."

"OK."

"Do I have to tell you that making a pass at the Deaconess would earn you a prize for Stupid Action of the Century?"

"Jesus Christ, that never entered my mind."

"Bullshit. That leg crack didn't just pop into your head."

"Believe what you want. But rest assured, the lady's virtue is in no danger from me."

"OK. One final thing. Did you know that you're on the AWOL report this morning?"

"I heard they were looking for me."

"Well, you are. I think I fixed it. But you better not go anywhere near the headquarters company barracks until I know for sure."

"Don't worry about that either," Moore said.

He picked the briefcase off the floor, opened it, and set it on the table. Hon put the intercepts into it—it looked more like fifty or sixty than thirty, Moore thought. And then Moore closed the briefcase and snapped the handcuff around his wrist. Hon took a .45 Colt automatic from a file cabinet. Moore hoisted the skirt of his tunic and put the pistol in the small of his back under his trouser waistband.

"You're going to shoot yourself in the ass one day doing that," Hon said.

Then he picked up the telephone and dialed a number.

"Colonel Huff? Sir, this is Lieutenant Hon. I have several MAGIC messages that I believe should be brought to the Supreme Commander's attention."

Moore unlocked the steel door and let himself out. When he reached the security post by the elevator, an Army technical sergeant from headquarters company was waiting for him.

"Sergeant Moore, you went AWOL last night."

"There's been a mistake, Sergeant," Moore said. "I don't

live in the barracks any more. I'm not supposed to be on your duty rosters."

"You tell that to the first sergeant, Sergeant. He told me to find your ass and bring you home."

"I'm sorry," Moore said. "I can't do that." He held up the briefcase.

"I don't give a shit about any fucking briefcase," the sergeant said. "You come with me."

"I'll have to tell my officer where I'm going," Moore said and went back to the office. Hon was locking the steel door when he got there.

"There's a tech sergeant out there who wants to haul me off to headquarters company," he said.

"Oh, shit!" Hon said. "Come on."

The tech sergeant was waiting at the outer security point with his arms folded.

"All right, Sergeant, what's this all about?"

"Sir, I'm here to return Sergeant Moore to Headquarters Company. We're carrying him as AWOL."

"That's in error. Sergeant Moore is not attached to Headquarters Company."

"Sir, I got my orders."

"And I have mine, Sergeant. Mine are to dispatch Sergeant Moore, with a briefcase full of classified documents, to—to who is none of your business. But to someone who ranks much higher around here than the first sergeant of Headquarters Company. For that matter, than the Headquarters Company commander. You will not interfere with that. If necessary, I will have this MP place you under arrest. Do you understand me, Sergeant?"

"Yes, Sir."

"All right, Moore, get going," Hon said.

"Yes, Sir."

"Sergeant, you will return to Headquarters Company. You will tell your first sergeant that (a) Sergeant Moore is no longer his responsibility and (b) if he ever does something like this again around here, I will be forced to bring the matter to the attention of Captain Pickering—that's Navy Captain Pickering—and I think he would speak to General Sutherland about it. You understand that?"

"Yes, Sir."

"You may go, Sergeant."

"Yes, Sir."

That may work, Hon thought. *If it doesn't,* fuck *it, I'll go to Sutherland.*

As Moore was unlocking the door of the Studebaker, the Marine Aviator lieutenant colonel he had seen before walked up to him.

"Good afternoon, Sergeant," he said.

Moore straightened and saluted.

"Good afternoon, Sir."

"I'm delighted to see a familiar uniform around here," Dailey said. "I'm Colonel Dailey. I've just been assigned here as the CINCPAC liaison officer."

"Yes, Sir," Moore said. He remembered the radio Captain Pickering had sent SECNAV asking that a liaison officer be assigned.

"What have they got you doing around here, Sergeant?"

"I work for Major Banning, Sir."

"Major Banning is assigned to this headquarters?"

"No, Sir. I mean, he works with SWPA, Sir. But he's not assigned here."

"Oh?"

"He commands Special Detachment 14, Sir."

"I see," Dailey said. "Do you happen to know, Sergeant, who is the ranking Marine officer here?"

"I suppose that would be Major Banning, Sir."

Well, that's nice to know, too, Dailey thought. *Since this man Banning is only a major, that makes me the senior Marine officer present.*

"When you see Major Banning, Sergeant, would you please tell him we bumped into each other, and that I'd like to meet him?"

"Yes, Sir, I'll do that."

"Thank you, Sergeant."

Dailey smiled at Moore and went back to the front door to wait for the car and driver that had been assigned to the CINCPAC liaison officer by General Douglas MacArthur's personal order.

He wondered what Special Detachment 14 was and what it did around here.

(Five)
WATER LILY COTTAGE
MANCHESTER AVENUE
BRISBANE, AUSTRALIA
1730 HOURS 13 AUGUST 1942

Ellen Feller was annoyed when she returned from the Doom-ben Tennis Club to see that the Studebaker was not there. She parked the Jaguar drophead coupe Fleming Pickering had left for her to use and went into the house.

She wondered why it should annoy her that the car—and thus, Sergeant John Marston Moore—was not there. She concluded that it was because it left her with the choice of either driving to the Lennon Hotel for dinner, which she did not like to do alone, or making herself something to eat, alone, here. Neither option was appealing.

She was desperately thirsty. The water at the tennis courts tasted as if it had been stored for a decade in a rusty barrel; and of course the Turf Club was closed for the duration, so there was no place to get even a soft drink.

She found a bottle of water in the refrigerator. And beer. She shrugged and reached for a beer bottle and opened it. And since there was no one around to see her, she drank from the neck. It was good beer, more bitter than American beer, and reminded her somewhat of the beer she'd grown to like in China.

On the sly, of course, she thought. *The wife of the Reverend Glen T. Feller of the Christian & Missionary Alliance could not afford to have the recent heathen see her sucking on a bottle of beer.*

I wonder what that bastard is up to these days?

The Reverend Feller had elected to go about The Lord's Work during the war years by bringing the Gospel to the Indians in Arizona.

Which is probably where he has the jade he smuggled out of China when we left. I know it's nowhere around Baltimore or Washington. If it was, I would have found it.

He's probably waking up right about now in bed with some well-muscled, smooth-skinned young Indian lad in whom he was taking a special interest.

Well, what's wrong with that? There is a lot to be said for being in bed with well-muscled, smooth-skinned lads. Like Sergeant John Marston Moore, for example.

Oh, God, is that why I was so annoyed when I found out he wasn't here? Am I in that dangerous condition again? That's absurd. I know better. Only a stupid ladybird dirties her own nest, to coin a phrase.

She finished the bottle of beer and was surprised at how quickly she did it.

It was the lousy undrinkable water at Doomben. I'm dehydrated. I'm not even very sweaty.

She tested this theory by raising her arm and sniffing her armpit. There was an unpleasant odor, but not what she expected after an hour and a half on the court with an Australian woman who was built like a boxcar but who moved around the court with really amazing speed and grace.

Ellen opened the refrigerator door again and started to reach for another bottle of beer, and then changed her mind.

It will make me flatulent and probably keep me up all night.

There was a quart can of Dole's pineapple juice in the refrigerator.

Moore's, she thought. *Lieutenant Hon got it for him somewhere.*

Well, fuck him, I'm thirsty.

There you go again, Dear. Thinking dangerous thoughts.

She took the can of pineapple juice from the refrigerator, punched a hole in the top with a beer can opener, and then poured it in a glass and added ice cubes.

After that she walked into the living room, to the array of bottles on a table, and went through them. She could find neither gin nor vodka, but there was a bottle of rum. She carried that back into the kitchen.

I wonder what that will do to pineapple juice? For that matter, what does straight rum taste like?

She took a pull from the neck of the rum bottle.

God! That's awful! It burns like cheap whiskey!

She poured rum into the pineapple juice, stirred it with her finger, and then licked her finger.

Not bad!

She took a tiny sip from the glass, then a much larger one. She was pleased with the taste.

She put the glass on the table and went into the refrigerator again, looking for something she could make for dinner after she had her shower. She saw the remnants of a leg of lamb.

Nothing in the world tastes worse than cold lamb!

In the pantry, she found a dozen cans of chicken and dumplings, furnished, she supposed, by Lieutenant Hon.

I wonder what he does about his sinful lusts of the flesh? God knows, no respectable Australian girl would dare to be seen with an Oriental, even one wearing an American officer's uniform.

I wouldn't mind trying a few relatively hairless muscular young male bodies again; but that would be even more stupid than doing something with John Marston Moore.

She took one of the cans of chicken and dumplings from the pantry, carried it into the kitchen, and set it on the sink. Then she picked up her drink and finished it.

She could feel the warmth spread through her body.

You have another one of those, Dear, you'll have trouble finding the bathroom. And God knows how you'll manage to get in and out of the tub.

She put more ice, pineapple juice, and rum into the glass, stirred it with her finger, licked her finger, took one little sip, added another little drop of rum, stirred, licked, and tasted again. Satisfied, she carried it with her out of the kitchen and into the master bedroom, where she would have it when she finished her bath.

She undressed, and put the soiled tennis dress and her underclothes in the hamper. When she turned, she saw her reflection in the mirror over the chest of drawers. She remembered what Fleming Pickering said the night he saw the same thing, the night she arrived in Australia: "I wondered what they would really look like."

She smiled to herself. Making love to Fleming Pickering had been a wise move. He regarded their sex together as far more important than she ever dreamed he would. It was the first time he had been unfaithful to his wife, he told her, and she believed him. But Ellen was truly surprised to hear it. Someone as good looking and as rich and prominent as Fleming Pickering should have had women jumping into his bed the moment word got out that Mrs. Pickering wasn't in it.

Anyway, doing it had accomplished her intentions. It put Fleming Pickering permanently in her corner. It was sort of a living, breathing insurance policy. And she needed that. There was still a chance—more and more remote as time passed, to be sure—that the smuggled jade would become a matter of official attention. If it did, she would need a bit of insurance.

Back in China before the war, Ken McCoy told her that the Marines knew all about the jade. McCoy was a member of the 4th Marine's escort detachment then. They were guarding the missionaries from the mission to Shanghai when they had to get out.

But she didn't know exactly what he meant: The junior officers of the guard detachment? Or just the other enlisted men? Or Captain Ed Banning, who had been the 4th Marines Intelligence Officer? She hadn't thought to ask until it was too late.

For a while, Ellen Feller thought the whole matter of the jade was water under the bridge. So far as getting in trouble for smuggling it out of China was concerned, at least. Getting her fair share of the money from her husband would have to wait until the war was over.

But then she'd taken a job as a Japanese language translator with Naval Intelligence in Washington, and both McCoy and Banning had turned up again. McCoy by then had been commissioned, and Banning had been promoted to major.

She hadn't thought that McCoy would be a problem. She could buy his silence in Washington the same way she had bought it in China . . .

Here come those smooth, muscular young male body thoughts again, Dear . . .

But Banning was one of those moral, highly principled men who would have loved to blow the whistle on her. His sense of right and wrong would have been offended if he ever found out that his Marines had risked their lives to protect jade that missionaries were illegally removing from China to line their own pockets.

But nothing was ever said about that. Ken McCoy kept his mouth shut, apparently. And just as apparently, Major Ed Banning did not know about the jade. Otherwise he *would* have blown the whistle.

Now, Ellen thought, as she walked into the bath and turned on the water, *the whole affair is almost certainly buried for-*

ever. Even if something happens—and as stupid as the Reverend Glen T. Feller can sometimes be, that is a real possibility—and the smuggled jade comes to light, it probably won't touch me. I am now a respected, responsible senior civilian employee of Naval Intelligence, and if I say I don't know a thing about any jade, I will be believed. Especially if Captain Fleming Pickering comes to my aid, as he would probably do in any case. But he certainly will do that now that he's been in my bed.

As she adjusted the temperature of the water, she decided to shower rather than have a bath. So she pulled the thingamabob on the faucet. At that moment her lovemaking with Fleming Pickering flashed again into her mind. And it brought with it another one of those dangerous thoughts about smooth young muscular male bodies generally and Sergeant John Marston Moore specifically.

In bed, Fleming Pickering was everything that she hoped he would be, and more. He held his age well. Even his body had been firmer and more youthful than she expected.

It wasn't that he left me unsatisfied, but that he whetted my appetite; opened the floodgates, so to speak.

But I am not a fool. I am not going to risk what I have so carefully built up for so long by behaving like a bitch in heat. While it would be very nice to actually have John Marston Moore's smooth and muscular young body in my bed, I am going to have to do that in fantasy.

She turned the shower head so that it produced a strong, narrow stream of water, rather than a spray; and then she directed the stream where she thought it should go.

Sometimes, under the right circumstances, the fantasy is better than the actuality.

She sat down in the tub, slid against the sloping back side, and spread her legs. The stream of water struck the tub eight inches from the right spot.

"Damn!"

She stood up and moved toward the shower head again.

The screen door slammed, and a moment later, the front door. Sergeant John Marston Moore did that every time he came home. Thus every time he came home, the whole damned house shook.

She inhaled deeply. After that, she changed the shower

flow back into a spray, and shifted the head again, so that it flowed onto her hair, instead of halfway down the tub. Then she picked up the soap and went ahead with her shower.

Fate, she thought. *Kismet. I really didn't want to do it that way, anyway.*

XVII

Three or four hairs popped up from the aureola of Sergeant John Marston Moore's nipples. Ellen Feller thought they were adorable. She toyed with them with her fingernail, watching them spring back into little coils when she turned them loose.

"Baby," she said, "if we're going to do this again, you're going to have to use something."

"I beg your pardon?"

"I don't want to find myself in the family way," Ellen said.

I should have thought of that before. God, was it the rum? Or how excited his shyness made me? For a while there, I was beginning to think that he was either a fairy or a virgin.

"Oh," he said. "I see what you mean. Are we going to do it again?"

408

"You don't sound very enthusiastic. You did a minute or two ago."

"I mean, is it smart? What if we got caught?"

"Who's going to catch us? Or *didn't* you like it?"

"It was great," Moore said.

And fuck you, Mrs. Howard P. Hawthorne. You are not the only fish in the sea. And your teats aren't as nice, either.

"It was great for me, too," she said. "I can't believe it happened."

"Me, either."

"You must think me terrible, giving in to you the way . . ."

"No. Not at all."

"I didn't have any idea you . . . were thinking of me in that way."

"It was the tennis dress," he said. "When you showed me your tennis dress."

"What about my tennis dress?"

"I thought your legs were great," he said.

I'll be damned. He's blushing again. How sweet!

"You really think so?" she asked, and threw the sheet off them.

"They're beautiful," he pronounced.

"Yours aren't so bad, either," she said, and ran her hand over his hip and then down his leg.

"There's a pro station at the barracks," he said. "But, Christ, I hate to go out there."

"What?"

"There's a pro station. When they give out the you-know-whats, at the barracks. But I hate to go out there."

"Maybe you could buy some at a drug store. What do they call them here, 'chemists'?"

"Yeah."

"Is there any chance that Hon is going to show up here?" she asked.

"I don't think so. He's going to play bridge with General MacArthur."

Thank God for small blessings!

"But he's going to want to know what we thought of the intercepts in the morning," Moore added.

"We'll have time," she said. "We have plenty of time. For everything. But what are we going to do about that?"

"About what?"

"You know very well what I mean," she said.

She moved her hand to his stirring erection and felt it stiffen to her touch.

"I don't know," he said, and blushing again, which pleased her very much, he added: "I could get dressed and go look for a chemist's."

"We don't know if chemists even sell them," she said.

"That's right."

"There is one thing I could do," she said. "But I'm afraid you'd think I was terrible."

"I would never think that."

"Oh, you're just saying that. You probably already think I'm really terrible."

"No."

"Close your eyes, then," she ordered.

He closed his eyes.

A moment later, she said, "Open them."

He opened them.

"Did you like that?"

"Oh, yes."

"You want to watch me do it?"

"Yes."

After a moment she stopped.

"Some women like to do that," she said. "I love it."

"I love it when you do it."

"And some men like to do it to women."

"Do they?"

"Do you want to do it to me?"

"Do you want me to?"

"Oh, yes, Baby."

"Then, OK."

"Close your eyes again."

He felt her shifting around on the bed.

What the hell, guys are always talking about it. It probably won't kill me.

(Two)
**THE OFFICE OF THE SECRETARY OF THE NAVY
WASHINGTON, D.C.
1605 HOURS 15 AUGUST 1942**

Captain David Haughton, USN, signed the receipt for the
TOP SECRET Eyes Only SecNav radio, smiled at the messenger, said "Thank you," and waited until the messenger
had left before lifting the cover sheet and reading the
document.

"Jesus Christ," he muttered, frowning and shaking his
head.

Then he stood up, went to the door to the Secretary's
office, opened it, and stood there until the Secretary of the
Navy sensed his presence and raised his eyes to him.

"Something important, David?"

"Guadalcanal has been heard from, Mr. Secretary."

"Do you mean Pickering's received the 'come home, all
is more or less forgiven' radio? Or something else?"

Haughton handed him the Eyes Only.

Knox's face tightened as he read it. He looked up at
Haughton.

"What is this, David, do you think? A blatant defiance of
the radio? Who the hell does he think he is? 'The undersigned
has temporarily assumed duties of First Marine Division
G-2.' By what authority?"

"Sir, I don't know. But I would be inclined to give Captain
Pickering the benefit of the doubt. The second paragraph
caught my eye."

Knox read the Eyes Only again.

"Good Christ, do think he's trying to tell us that Goettge
or one of the other officers had a MAGIC clearance?"

"Mr. Secretary, he didn't say 'Killed in Action,' he said
'lost in combat.' That suggests the possibility that they may
have been captured. If you go with that line of reasoning,
paragraph two makes some sense."

"How quickly can you find out if any of these people had
access to MAGIC?"

"They're not on the list I'm familiar with. Maybe Naval
Intelligence has added some others—cryptographers—that
sort of thing. And I think, Sir, that we may have to consider

the possibility that Captain Pickering brought Colonel Goettge, officially or otherwise, in on it."

It was a moment before Knox replied.

"That's one of your 'worst possible scenarios,' David, right?"

"Yes, Sir."

"Well, I thank you for it. I appreciate why you had to bring that up. I am unable to believe that he would do that. He knows what's at stake."

"Yes, Sir."

"Find out from Naval Intelligence . . . you had better check with the Army, too, while you're at it. And in person. Stay off the phone. See if any of these names ring a bell."

"Yes, Sir."

"Let me know the minute you find out, one way or the other."

"Yes, Sir."

"I just thought of another worst possible case scenario, David," Knox said. "Pickering gets himself captured."

"I think we have to consider that possibility, Sir."

"Send an urgent radio to Admiral Nimitz. Tell him to get Pickering off Guadalcanal now. I don't care if he has to send a PT boat for him. I want him off of Guadalcanal as soon as possible."

"Yes, Sir."

"Sir," Captain David Haughton, USN, reported to the Secretary of the Navy not quite two hours later, "I think I've come up with something."

"Let's have it. I'm due at the White House in fifteen minutes."

"Neither Colonel Goettge nor Captain Ringer was cleared for MAGIC. And it is my opinion, and that of the Chief of Naval Intelligence, Sir, that it is unlikely that either of them ever heard more than the name."

"Unless, of course, Pickering talked too much to Goettge."

"I think we can discount that, too, Sir. Colonel Goettge visited Captain Pickering in Australia. While he was there, he apparently picked up on the word. MAGIC, I mean. He sent a back channel communication to General Forrest—the Marine Corps G-2—"

"I know who he is," Knox said impatiently.

"Yes, Sir. He said that he had heard the word MAGIC and wanted to know what it was. He and General Forrest are old friends, Sir."

"I know how it works. Get on with it."

"Forrest is MAGIC cleared. He replied to Goettge that he had never heard of MAGIC, and then reported the message to the Chief of Naval Intelligence."

"What you're suggesting is that if Pickering had told Goettge, there would have been no back channel message to General Forrest?"

"Yes, Sir."

Knox considered that a moment.

"OK," he said finally. "But what the hell was Pickering driving at? If, indeed, he was suggesting anything at all?"

"Lieutenant Cory, Sir, was a civilian employee of Naval Communications Intelligence, here in Washington."

"So I *am* going to have to tell the President that MAGIC has been compromised?"

"I don't think so, Sir. What's happened, Sir, I think, is that if anything Naval Intelligence erred on the side of caution to preserve the integrity of MAGIC."

"I don't understand a thing you just said."

"Lieutenant Cory did *not* have a MAGIC clearance."

"Thank God!"

"But the crypto people, the intelligence people, the intelligence *community*, I guess is what I'm trying to say, being the way they are, it occurred to somebody that he might have heard the name at least, and possibly had guessed what it was all about."

"So?"

"So a special radio was sent to General Vandergrift directing him to make sure that Lieutenant Cory did not fall into enemy hands."

"How was he supposed to do that?" Knox asked.

"I didn't get into that, Sir."

"Well, he didn't, did he? Cory may well indeed be a prisoner of the Japanese?"

"I think we have to consider that possibility, Sir."

Knox snorted.

"You're suggesting that Vandergrift told Pickering about

the message vis-à-vis Cory? And *that's* what Pickering was driving at?"

"Yes, Sir, that's what I think."

"This is not enough to take to the President," Knox decided aloud. "But I want Nimitz radioed tonight, Dave, telling him to get Pickering off Guadalcanal."

"I took care of that, Sir," Haughton said, and handed him an onion skin.

URGENT
WASHINGTON DC 1710 15AUG42
SECRET
FROM: NAVY DEPARTMENT
TO: CINCPAC PEARL HARBOR TH
FOR THE PERSONAL, IMMEDIATE ATTENTION OF ADMIRAL NIMITZ
INASMUCH AS THE PRESENCE OF CAPTAIN FLEMING PICKERING USNR, PRESENTLY ATTACHED TO HEADQUARTERS 1ST MARINE DIVISION, IS URGENTLY REQUIRED IN WASHINGTON, THE SECRETARY OF THE NAVY DIRECTS THAT EXTRAORDINARY EFFORT CONSISTENT WITH CAPTAIN PICKERING PERSONAL SAFETY BE MADE TO WITHDRAW THIS OFFICER FROM GUADALCANAL BY AIR OR SEA, AND THAT HE BE ADVISED OF PROGRESS MADE IN COMPLIANCE WITH THIS ORDER.
DAVID HAUGHTON, CAPT USN, ADMIN ASST TO SECNAV

(Three)
TEMPORARY BUILDING T-2032
THE MALL
WASHINGTON, D.C.
1750 HOURS 15 AUGUST 1942

Lieutenant Colonel F.L. Rickabee, USMC, was in his shirt-sleeves, his tie was pulled down, and he was visibly feeling the heat and humidity, when Brigadier General Horace W. T. Forrest, Assistant Chief of Staff, Intelligence, Headquarters, USMC, walked into his office.

"Good evening, Sir," he said, standing up. "I hope the General will pardon my appearance, Sir."

"Don't be silly, Rickabee," Forrest said. "Christ, I hate Washington in the summer."

"I don't put any modifiers on the basic sentiment, Sir," Rickabee said dryly.

Forrest looked at him and chuckled.

"There's ice tea, Sir, and lemonade, and I wouldn't be at all surprised if someone defied my strict orders and hid a bottle of spirits or two in one of these filing cabinets."

"I'd like a beer, if that's possible."

"Aye, aye, Sir," Rickabee said. "Excuse me."

He went through a wooden door and came back in a moment with two bottles of beer and a glass.

"Keep the glass, thank you," General Forrest said. He raised the beer bottle.

"Frank Goettge," he said and took a pull.

"Frank Goettge," Rickabee parroted and took a sip. "Was there any special reason for that, Sir?"

"Frank's dead. Or at least missing and presumed dead."

"Jesus Christ! What happened, Sir?"

"I don't know. I know only that. I got it from the Commandant thirty minutes ago. He got it from the Secretary of the Navy. There have been no after-action reports, casualty reports, anything else. I can only presume that Frank Knox got it directly from that commissioned civilian he sent over there . . . what's his name?"

"Pickering, Sir."

". . . as his personal snoop. Pickering is on Guadalcanal. Did you know that?"

"No, Sir. I did not."

"The Secretary of the Navy has directed the Commandant to replace Colonel Goettge immediately with a suitably qualified officer. Don't waste our time suggesting yourself. You're cleared for MAGIC. You can't go."

"Yes, Sir."

"What about Major Ed Banning? He was S-2 of the Fourth Marines. He could handle it, and he's in Australia."

"Banning's cleared for MAGIC, too, Sir."

"I didn't know that."

"Captain Pickering had him added to the list."

"Damn that man!"

"I don't think the Secretary would want us to send Banning in any event, Sir. He sent him over there."

"That's right, isn't it? I'd forgotten."

"Sir, isn't there someone in the First Division who could take over?"

"I asked the same question. Do you know Captain Ringer, Bill Ringer?"

"Yes. That's right. He's there, too, isn't he? S-2 of the 5th."

"He's dead, or missing, too. And a Lieutenant named Cory. You know Cory?"

"He was a civilian here. Navy communications. He was commissioned only a couple of months ago."

"Knox's aide—Haughton. He's not his aide. What do they call him?"

"Administrative Assistant, Sir."

"Haughton was all exercised that Cory might have had access to MAGIC."

"Did he?"

"No. What I would really like to know is what the hell went on over there to take out the Division Two, the 5th Marines Two, and a Japanese linguist all at once. The last after-action report I saw didn't show a hell of a lot going on over there."

"And the Commandant didn't know?"

"You mean did he know and wouldn't say? I don't think he knew a thing more than he told me. We were talking about Major Banning."

"Banning is out, Sir."

"Yes, of course," Forrest said. "I must be getting senile. Suggestions, Rickabee?"

"We have a man in Brisbane. His name is Dailey. Lieutenant Colonel. Ex-aviator. He was in Berlin before the war as an assistant Naval attache."

"What's he doing in Brisbane?"

"He's liaison officer between MacArthur and Nimitz."

"How do you know about him?" Forrest asked, and when Rickabee hesitated, snapped, "Come on. I've got to get back to the Commandant tonight with a name."

"Sir, I sort of stashed him over there."

"Stashed?"

"As a replacement, Sir, a supernumerary, in place. In case anything happened to Ed Banning. Or some other people. He has gone through the FBI background check."

"MAGIC?"

"No, Sir. I would be surprised if he ever heard the term. But, if it came to that, I would feel easy about clearing him for access to MAGIC."

"Could he handle being a division two?"

"I think so, Sir. He wouldn't be a Frank Goettge . . ."

"You just lost your supernumerary, Rickabee. Now, what about a regimental two to replace Captain Ringer?"

"Sir, I have no idea what to do about that."

"Don't try to tell me you don't have any linguists you can spare."

"I *don't* have any linguists I can spare, General," Rickabee said. "Wait a minute . . ."

"Well?"

"I found a kid at Parris Island. He was supposed to go to Quantico for a commission. But Banning wanted a linguist, so we put sergeant's stripes on him and sent him to Australia."

"He's a linguist?"

"Yes, Sir. Fluent Japanese. Reads and writes."

"How critically does Banning need a linguist?"

"I'm sure he would say he needs one desperately, Sir."

"I'm asking you."

"I think if Banning doesn't have this kid, General, and needs a linguist, he will either do it himself or he'll find someone in Australia. Secretary Knox sent Pickering's secretary over there, now that I think about it. She's a Japanese-language linguist. She's cleared for MAGIC, too."

"I presume the sergeant has had no access to MAGIC?"

"I'm sure he hasn't, Sir."

"I want his name and serial number, and the supernumerary's name and serial number. You have them, I presume?"

"Yes, Sir. Sir, the order to appoint a liaison officer between CINCPAC and MacArthur came from the Secretary. He might not like having him reassigned."

"Let him make that decision. I'll make a note of what this

officer is doing on the buck slip I give to the Commandant.
Is there someone around here who can type it up for me? It
would save me a trip to Eighth and 'I.' "

"Yes, Sir. That'll be no problem."

(Four)
HEADQUARTERS, FIRST MARINE DIVISION
GUADALCANAL, SOLOMON ISLANDS
17 AUGUST 1942

Both Major General Alexander Archer Vandergrift, the division commander, and Captain Fleming Pickering, USNR
(acting) Division G-2, went down to the beach when the destroyers appeared on the horizon.

Vandergrift was wearing sweat-streaked, soiled khakis and
a steel helmet; and he was armed with a .45 Colt automatic
pistol suspended from a web pistol belt. Pickering was wearing utilities, a utility cap, and carried a Springfield rifle in the
crook of his arm.

There were four destroyers.

"They're older than most of the boys, Fleming, do you realize that?" Vandergrift said to Pickering.

"I thought they looked familiar," Pickering said. "I remember seeing them."

"In France?"

"No. They had some tied up in Washington state. And
somewhere on the East Coast. Virginia. I remember thinking
that it was a stupid idea, they'd never get them ready for sea
again after tying them up for twenty years. I'm glad to see
I was wrong."

Vandergrift snorted.

The destroyers came in in a line. The first in line slowed;
water was churning at its stern as the engines were put in
reverse.

One, and then another, and finally a line of landing craft
from the Lunga Boat Pool headed away from the beach toward the destroyers.

Pickering handed a pair of binoculars to General Vandergrift.

The General examined them before he put them to his eyes.

"Leitz 8×50s," he said. "Why do I suspect these aren't issue?"

"My father gave those to me when I got my first officer's license. They don't wear out. I thought they might come in useful."

Vandergrift took the binoculars from his eyes and handed them back to Pickering.

"If the Japanese know about those destroyers, they're in trouble," he said.

Pickering looked through them at the landing craft. Each carried a half dozen Marines, most of them wearing only their undershirts. They were a work party, men taken from their units to function as stevedores.

During the planning process for this operation, the Marines had asked for sailors to manhandle supplies; but the Navy had refused. That question, he thought, would have to be resolved before the next Marine amphibious landing.

As they handed the binoculars back and forth, Pickering and Vandergrift watched sailors on the deck of the nearest destroyer unlashing 55-gallon barrels and then manhandling them to the rail. Life boat davits had been jury-rigged to lower the barrels into the landing craft.

Five minutes later, the first landing barge started for the beach.

"There's an officer standing next to the coxswain," Vandergrift said, handing the binoculars back to Pickering.

"And for the rest of his career, he can command attention in the officer's club by beginning a sentence, 'When I was on the beach at Guadalcanal . . .' " Pickering said.

"Fleming, have you ever heard that old saw about people who live in glass houses?" Vandergrift said.

Pickering looked at him in surprise and saw Vandergrift smiling at him.

"Touché, General," Pickering said.

We have become friends, Pickering thought. *It didn't take long.*

When the landing barge touched on the beach and dropped its ramp, a dozen Marines who had been waiting on shore went up the ramp and began rolling the 55-gallon barrels onto the beach.

The officer who had been standing next to the coxswain

came ashore. When he arrived, he spoke to another officer, who looked around and then pointed to Vandergrift and Pickering.

The officer made his way up the beach to them. He was wearing a steel helmet, and he carried a pistol on a web belt. He even wore canvas puttees. His khaki uniform was starched. There was a crease in his trousers.

"Natty, wouldn't you say?" Vandergrift said softly.

The officer saluted. Vandergrift and Pickering returned it.

"Sir, I'm Lieutenant Goldberg. I'm executive officer of the *Gregory.*"

"We're very glad to see you, Mr. Goldberg," Vandergrift said. "Welcome to Guadalcanal. I really regret the division band is otherwise occupied. You really deserve a serenade."

"Thank you, Sir."

"What have you got for us, Mr. Goldberg?"

"Each of us is carrying 100 drums of AvGas, Sir, and eight drums of Aviation lubricants. We also have some aircraft bombs, one hundred pounders, and linked .50 caliber ammo. And there's some tools."

"Chamois? I especially asked for chamois."

"Yes, Sir, there are several cartons of chamois."

"Thank God, for that. The AvGas wouldn't have done us any good without a means to filter it."

"There's chamois, Sir," Goldberg said. "And we're carrying some tools. The *Little* and the *Calhoun* have some ground crewmen aboard, too."

"At the risk of repeating myself, Mr. Goldberg, you are very welcome indeed."

"And I have this for you, General," Goldberg said and handed Vandergrift an unsealed envelope.

Vandergrift took a sheet of paper from the envelope, glanced at it, and handed it to Pickering.

"I got my copy of this last night," he said. "I don't think you've seen it."

Pickering took it. It was a radio message, all typed in capital letters.

URGENT
SECRET
FROM: CINCPAC

TO: COMMANDER DESTROYER FORCE TWENTY
INFORMATION: COMMANDING GENERAL FIRST MARINE DIVISION
1. BY DIRECTION OF THE SECRETARY OF THE NAVY YOU WILL TRANSPORT FROM YOUR DESTINATION TO SUCH PLACE AS WILL BE LATER DIRECTED CAPTAIN FLEMING PICKERING, USNR, PRESENTLY ATTACHED HQ FIRST MARDIV.
2. YOU WILL ADVISE CINCPAC, ATTENTION: IMMEDIATE AND PERSONAL ATTENTION OF CINCPAC, WHEN YOU HAVE SAILED FROM YOUR DESTINATION WITH CAPTAIN PICKERING ABOARD.
BY DIRECTION: D.J. WAGAM, REARADM USN

Pickering looked at Vandergrift, who smiled.

"Lieutenant Goldberg, may I present Captain Pickering?" Vandergrift said.

"How do you do, Sir?" Goldberg said. His surprise was evident. He had not expected to see a Navy Captain in Marine Corps utilities, carrying a Springfield rifle like a hunter.

"I think I've just been sandbagged, as a matter of fact," Pickering said.

"That boat is about ready to go back out to the *Gregory*, Captain Pickering. Don't you think you had better get on it? I'm sure her captain wants to get underway as soon as possible."

Pickering didn't reply.

"Major Stecker was good enough to pack your gear, Captain," Vandergrift said, and pointed to the landing barge.

Pickering saw Jack NMI Stecker handing a bag to one of the Marines on the barge. It was the bag he brought with him from the command ship USS *McCawley* when he'd come ashore.

"I know I've been sandbagged," Pickering said. "I gather there is no room for discussion?"

"Thank you for your services, Captain Pickering," Vandergrift said. "They have been appreciated by all hands."

Vandergrift handed Pickering the Ernest Leitz binoculars.

"General, I would be honored if you would hang onto those," Pickering said.

Vandergrift looked at the binoculars and then met Pickering's eyes.

"That's very kind of you, Fleming, thank you," he said. He put out his hand to Pickering.

Pickering had to grab the Springfield rifle with his left hand in order to take Vandergrift's hand with his right.

Then he held the rifle up.

"I won't need this any more, will I?"

"Why don't you take it with you?" Vandergrift said. "If nothing else, you could hang it on your wall. Then for the rest of your life, you could command attention by pointing to it and beginning a sentence, 'when I was on the beach at Guadalcanal . . .' "

"Touché, again, General."

"Bon voyage, Fleming," Vandergrift said. "I look forward to seeing you again."

He touched Pickering's arm and then walked away.

(Five)
WATER LILY COTTAGE
MANCHESTER AVENUE
BRISBANE, AUSTRALIA
0815 HOURS 17 AUGUST 1942

Mrs. Ellen Feller had just about finished dressing when she heard the crunch of tires on the driveway. A few seconds later, the double slamming of the front doors told her that Sergeant John Marston Moore had returned to the cottage.

The slamming doors annoyed her. She was already annoyed. Lieutenant Pluto Hon had been summoned to Townesville by Major Ed Banning—for reasons Banning had not elected to tell her. And that meant she was going to have to spend all day in the dark, damp cell two floors underground at SHSWPA. And probably do the same thing all day tomorrow, too. Someone had to be available to deliver MAGIC intercepts to Generals MacArthur and Willoughby, and since Banning and Hon were in Townesville, and Moore was officially not supposed to know even what MAGIC meant, that left her.

When she looked at her watch and saw that it was only

a quarter after eight, she was even more annoyed. She had told him to pick Hon up at the Commerce Hotel and deliver him to the airport; then to stop at the Cryptographic Facility, pick up what had come in, and run it through the machine; and then, 'about nine, Baby, come pick me up.' "

She decided she knew what was in his mind, the horny little devil, and while that was flattering, now was not the time. She had just spent an hour washing and doing her hair, and if *that* happened, as appealing as it was, she would have to go through the whole process again, starting with the shower.

The door to her bedroom was flung open.

"You ever think of knocking?"

"Sorry," he said, visibly unrepentant. "Take a look at these."

There was something important in the overnights, she thought. *He doesn't have that delightfully shyly naughty look in his eyes.*

She took the two sheets of onion skin from him, and read them.

URGENT
SECRET
HQ USMC WASHDC 2205 15AUG42
VIA: SUPREME HEADQUARTERS
       SOUTHWEST PACIFIC AREA
TO: COMMANDING OFFICER
       USMC SPECIAL DETACHMENT 14
1. ON RECEIPT OF THIS MESSAGE SGT JOHN M. MOORE IS DE-
TACHED FROM USMC SPECDET 14, ATTACHED HQ FIRST
MARDIV, AND WILL PROCEED THERETO IMMEDIATELY.
2. YOU ARE AUTHORIZED TO INFORM SHSWPA THAT AN UR-
GENT REQUIREMENT FOR JAPANESE-LANGUAGE LINGUISTS
EXISTS WITHIN FIRST MARDIV AND REQUEST OF THEM
HIGHEST POSSIBLE AIR TRANSPORTATION PRIORITY FOR
SERGEANT MOORE.
BY DIRECTION: H.W.T.FORREST, BRIGGEN USMC
                    ACOFSG-2
URGENT
CONFIDENTIAL
HQ USMC WASHDC 2207 15 AUG42
TO: LT COL GEORGE F. DAILEY

CINCPAC LIAISON OFFICER

SUPREME HEADQUARTERS SOUTHWEST PACIFIC AREA
INFORMATION: CINCPAC ATTN: CHIEF OF STAFF
             COMMANDING GENERAL 1ST MARINE DIVISION

1. ON RECEIPT OF THIS MESSAGE YOU ARE DETACHED FROM PRESENT DUTIES AND WILL PROCEED IMMEDIATELY TO HEADQUARTERS FIRST MARDIV FOR DUTY AS ASSISTANT CHIEF OF STAFF, G-2. THIS MESSAGE CONSTITUTES AUTHORITY FOR AAAA AIR TRAVEL PRIORITY.

2. YOU ARE AUTHORIZED TO INFORM SHSWPA THAT THE EXIGENCIES OF THE SERVICE MAKE THIS TRANSFER NECESSARY AND THAT A LIAISON OFFICER TO REPLACE YOU WILL BE ASSIGNED AT THE EARLIEST POSSIBLE TIME.

3. IF POSSIBLE, AND TO THE DEGREE THAT IT WILL NOT REPEAT NOT INTERFERE WITH YOUR MOVEMENT TO FIRST MARDIV, YOU ARE DIRECTED TO FACILITATE THE MOVEMENT TO FIRST MAR DIV OF SERGEANT J.M.MOORE, PRESENTLY ASSIGNED USMC SPECIAL DETACHMENT 14.

BY DIRECTION OF BRIG GEN FORREST:

F L RICKABEE, LTCOL, USMC

"I called Townesville," Moore said. "They either don't know where Banning is, or he doesn't want it known."

"I wonder why Rickabee signed the one to Dailey?" Ellen said, thoughtfully, "and General Forrest the one about you? And the one about you is classified Secret, and the one to Dailey only Confidential?"

"What the hell difference does it make?" Moore asked, but he took the onion skins from her hand. "Probably because everything about the detachment is classified Secret but the name," he said.

"Obviously, you don't want to go," Ellen said. "Is that why you tried to call Banning?"

"I *can't* go, for Christ's sake," Moore said. "I'm privy to MAGIC."

"Not officially," she thought out loud.

"That's not the point," he said. "I *know* about MAGIC."

"The point is, they—Rickabee and Forrest—don't know that. That's why they're sending you to Guadalcanal."

She thought: *And if it comes out that Fleming Pickering*

compromised MAGIC *by letting you in on it, he's in trouble. I don't want to see that happen.*

Banning is supposed to be clever. Let him see if he can find a solution to this.

"I think the thing for you to do is make yourself scarce until we can get in contact with Major Banning," Ellen said.

"Too late. That was the first thing I thought of. But Dailey's caught me."

"How?"

"His orders didn't have to go through crypto. So as soon as they came in, the message center gave them to him . . . Christ, *that's* why they classified them Confidential, so they wouldn't have to go through crypto . . ."

Ellen thought about that quickly, and said, "Yes. Probably."

"I had just run the radio to Banning through the crypto machine and was trying to get him on the telephone, when an MP came to the cell and said I had a visitor at Outer Security."

"Dailey?"

"Yeah. Pumped full of his own importance. You could practically hear the Marine Corps Drum and Bugle Corps playing the Marine Hymn in the background."

She smiled, and their eyes met.

I'm going to miss him.

"What did he say?" she asked.

" 'Sergeant Moore,' Moore quoted sonorously, *'I have been ordered to Guadalcanal by Headquarters, USMC. You are to accompany me. We leave immediately.' "*

She smiled at him again.

"I didn't tell him I had just decrypted my own orders; I told him I worked for Banning, and he would have to talk to him."

"And?"

" 'Sergeant, I am the ranking Marine officer present. I will see that Major Banning is informed of what has transpired,' or bullshit to that effect."

"My God!"

"I tried refusing," Moore said. "Politely. I told him that Major Banning had told me to take orders from nobody else."

"And?"

Moore pointed toward the window. Ellen went and pushed the curtain aside. There was a 1941 Ford staff car in the drive. It had MILITARY POLICE painted on the doors. An MP wearing a white helmet liner was sitting on it. Another rested his rear end on the front fender.

"They're going to take me to the airport," Moore said. "Dailey apparently rushed to tell Willoughby, or maybe Sutherland, of his orders . . . for all I know, The Emperor himself may have gotten into the act by now. Anyway, a B-25 is going to fly us to Espíritu Santo. The field at Guadalcanal won't take a B-25 yet. So from Espíritu Santo, we'll go by Catalina."

"He didn't put you under arrest?" Ellen asked.

"No. Except by inference. The MPs are to 'help me gather' my gear and get me to the airport."

"I don't see what else you can do," Ellen said.

"I've got to go, there's no question about that. And what you have to do is one of two things: Call Willoughby now, tell him you have just heard about this, and that I'm into MAGIC."

"I don't think that's smart," Ellen said. "I think a decision like that should be made by Major Banning."

"That's 'B,' " Moore said. "Get on the phone and keep trying to get through to Banning."

"I will," she said. "That's the way to handle this."

The horn on the MP car blew.

"Shit," he said.

He walked out of her bedroom and across the living room to his bedroom and began stuffing his belongings into his seabag.

Ellen stood in his doorway and watched.

"Is there anything I can do to help?"

"I can handle it," he said.

Inasmuch as she was unaware how many times Private John Marston Moore had, under the skilled eye of a Parris Island Drill Instructor, packed and unpacked, packed and unpacked a seabag until he had it right, Ellen was genuinely surprised to see how quickly and efficiently he packed his gear.

He finally picked up the seabag and bounced it three or four times on the floor. This caused the contents to compact.

He reached inside, removed a precisely folded pair of pants, reached under the skirt of his blouse, and came out with a Colt .45 and four extra magazines. He put these in the bag, replaced the pants on top, and closed the bag.

"I decided I needed that pistol more than one of the classified documents messengers," he said. "So I signed it out before I left the basement. If they come looking for it, send them to Guadalcanal."

My God, he really is going to the war! He is too beautiful to be killed!

She stepped into the room and closed the door after her. She walked up to him and put her hand on his cheek, then raised her head and kissed him lightly on the mouth.

"Do you think they'll wait another five minutes, Baby?" she asked, dropping her hand down his body, pushing aside the skirt of his blouse, and finding the buttons of his fly. "Or will they break the door down?"

When he was gone, she decided calmly that it was probably a good thing. Their relationship could easily have gotten out of hand.

If only Fleming Pickering hadn't been such a damned fool and brought him into MAGIC!

The thing to do about that, she decided, *is nothing. The chances that John Moore will fall alive into Japanese hands are negligible to begin with. And even if he does, he is only a sergeant. Sergeants are not expected to be privy to important secrets.*

She would have to make that point to Banning. Hon would argue against it, but Hon was a lieutenant and Banning a major. The important thing to do was to protect Fleming Pickering. Banning, for his own reasons, would understand that, and he almost certainly would be able to convince Pluto Hon as well.

That *was* going to be possible, she decided. Fleming Pickering would be protected . . . and it followed that he would be available to protect her, if need be.

She had—years ago, she couldn't remember where—heard someone described as "being able to walk around raindrops." She was a little uneasy about thinking that she was one of these people, but the facts seemed to bear it out. Just when things started to get out of hand, something happened that put them in order again.

XVIII

(One)
ABOARD USS *GREGORY* (APD-44)
CORAL SEA
0735 HOURS 18 AUGUST 1942

Captain Fleming Pickering stood in the port leading from the Chart Room to the bridge until the captain turned, saw him, and motioned him to come in.

"Permission to come onto the bridge, Sir?" Pickering asked. He was wearing borrowed khakis that were just a bit too tight for him.

"Captain, aboard this tin can, you have the privilege of the bridge at any time."

"That's very kind of you, Captain," Pickering said, coming onto the bridge. "But—in the olden days—when I was a master and carrying supercargo, I always wanted the bastard to ask."

The USS *Gregory*'s Captain, a Lieutenant Commander, laughed.

"I appreciate the sentiment, Sir, but I repeat: You have the privilege of this bridge whenever you wish. Can I offer you some coffee?"

"No, thank you. I just had a potful for breakfast."

"And you slept well, Sir?"

"Like a log. Despite the fact that I felt like an interloper in your cabin."

"My pleasure, Sir. I rarely use it at sea, anyway."

"You're very gracious."

"We seldom have a chance to show our party manners to a VIP, Sir."

Christ, is that what I am?

"Beautiful day," Pickering said.

"We're making good time, too, Sir. Did you check the chart?"

"We're making, if I haven't forgotten how to read a chart, better than twenty knots?"

"We are making 'best speed consistent with available fuel,' Sir," the captain said, then took a sheet from his shirt pocket and handed it to Pickering.

URGENT
SECRET
FROM: CINCPAC
TO: COMMANDER DESTROYER FORCE TWENTY
1. GREGORY IS DETACHED FROM DESFORCE TWENTY. GREGORY IS TO STEAM FOR BAKER XRAY MIKE AT BEST SPEED CONSISTENT WITH AVAILABLE FUEL.
2. DESFORCE TWENTY WILL PROCEED TO BAKER XRAY MIKE IN COMPLIANCE WITH PRESENT ORDERS.
3. PASS TO CAPTAIN PICKERING ARRANGEMENTS FOR HIS FURTHER MOVEMENT BY AIR HAVE BEEN MADE.
BY DIRECTION: D.J. WAGAM, REARADM USN

Pickering went to the heavy plate glass windows of the bridge and looked out. There was no other vessel in sight on the smooth, blue swells of the sea.

"Where, or what, is Baker XRay Mike?"

"Espíritu Santo, Sir. They've got a pretty decent airfield up and running there."

"Is this what the Navy calls 'flank speed'?" Pickering asked.

"She'll go a bit faster than this, Captain. But the ride gets a little rough, and the fuel consumption goes way up. I dislike not having enough fuel in the bunkers."

"That was a question, not a criticism. I've never been on one of these before."

"You know what they are?"

"High speed transport," Pickering said. "Right?"

"That's something of a misnomer, Sir. They removed half the boilers and converted that space to troop berthing. It's high speed relative to a troop transport, not compared to anything else. She's considerably slower than she was before they removed half her boilers."

"Well, whoever's idea it was, it seems to be a good one. They couldn't start landing aircraft on Henderson until they got some fuel in there, and they couldn't risk sending a transport."

"The original idea, as I understand it, Sir, was that the APDs would be used to transport the Marine Raiders. We even trained with them for a while. You familiar with the Raiders, Sir?"

"Yes," Pickering said. "A little."

Franklin Roosevelt copying—or trying to best—the British again. They almost wound up being called The Marine Commandos.

"What happened to the idea of using these ships to transport Raiders?" Pickering asked.

"Well of course, in a sense, we did. We are. We put the Raiders ashore on Tulagi. But that was a conventional amphibious assault. What I meant, Sir, was that I think the idea for the conversion of these ships was to transport the Raiders on raids."

"That isn't going to happen?"

"There is some scuttlebutt, Sir, that the Second Raider Battalion was to be landed yesterday on Makin Island from submarines. I emphasize, Sir, that it's scuttlebutt, and probably shouldn't be repeated."

Meaning, of course, that you know goddamn well the Second Raider Battalion was landed yesterday on Makin by submarine, but are afraid that when your VIP supercargo has a few drinks with the brass, he will report that you told him.

"I know an officer with the Second Raiders," Pickering

thought aloud, and then corrected himself. "I have a friend who is an officer with the Second Raiders."

I know Colonel Evans Carlson and Captain Roosevelt, whose father is our Commander-in-Chief, and a dozen other Raider officers. But I'm not sure—I frankly doubt—if they would appreciate me going around announcing that I'm a friend of theirs. Killer McCoy, on the other hand . . .

"And actually, he's more my son's friend—they went through officer candidate school at Quantico together—than mine. Very interesting young man. He was an enlisted man with the Fourth Marines in China before the war. They call him 'Killer' McCoy."

"Your son is a Marine, Sir?"

"Yes, he is."

"With the First Division?"

"No. Thank God. He's just finished flying school. Actually, the last I heard, he'd just finished F4F training. I expect he's on his way over here, or will be shortly."

"The F4F is supposed to be quite an airplane," the captain said.

Thank you, Captain, for your—failed but noble—attempt to reassure the father of a brand-new Marine Corps fighter pilot that all is right with the world.

"Bridge, Lookout," the loudspeaker above Pickering's head blared suddenly. "Aircraft, to port. On the deck."

The captain ran to the port to the open portion of the bridge, rested his hands on the steel surrounding it, and looked out.

Aware that his function as supercargo was to stay the hell out of people's way, Pickering successfully resisted the temptation to look for himself. He backed up until his back touched the aft bulkhead of the bridge.

The captain turned around. "Sound General Quarters," he ordered. "All ahead full. All weapons to fire when ready." He looked at Pickering, and over the clamor of the General Quarters bell, said, "It's an Emily. Obviously on a torpedo run."

Then he turned to look at the aircraft again.

The Emily, Pickering knew, was the Kawanishi H8K2, a four-engine flying boat which had obviously borrowed much of its design from Igor Sikorski's Pan American Airways flying boats. It was fast—he recalled that it cruised at 290 mph—had a range of 4000 miles, and could carry either two of the large, excellent, 1780-pound Japanese torpedoes, or just over two tons of bombs.

It's spotted the Gregory, *Pickering realized, and has decided an American destroyer all alone on the wide sea is just what she is looking for.*

With the element of surprise on the side of the bomber, a destroyer made an excellent torpedo target. On the other hand, hitting an aircraft with the 40mm Bofors and .50 Caliber Brownings on a destroyer was very difficult, even if they could be brought to bear in time. An aircraft slowed to a speed that allowed it to safely and accurately launch a torpedo was a little more vulnerable, but not much.

Thirty seconds later—it seemed like much, much longer—there was a sudden, violent eruption of noise and sound on the bridge. Explosions followed, and smoke, and shattering glass. And before Pickering regained his senses, there was another explosion and then a water spout thirty feet off the port rail; and a moment later a hundred feet off the starboard rail, another.

The captain was wrong, Pickering decided, even as he looked down at his body and saw with surprise that his upper chest and right arm were bloody, *the sonofabitch was not on a torpedo run. Her pilot opted for a bomb run. Maybe he didn't have any torpedoes. So he came in far faster than he would have if he were dropping a torpedo.*

He looked for the captain and found him almost immediately. He was on his back on the deck, his eyes and mouth open in astonishment, his shirt a bloody mess. He was very obviously dead.

There had been six, seven, eight people on the bridge a moment before. Now Pickering saw only two others on their feet. The talker, his earphones and microphone harness in place, leaned against the aft bulkhead not far from Pickering, a look of shock and horror on his face. A sailor, whose function Pickering did not know, stood with his back to the forward bulkhead, his face blackened, his arms wrapped tightly around his chest.

The helmsman was crumpled on the deck by the wheel,

and the others were scattered all over the rest of the bridge. One sailor was crawling toward the chartroom port.

A bomb didn't do this, Pickering thought. These were small, explosive shells. He remembered then that the Emily carried five 20mm cannon and four 7.7mm machine guns. The Emily had strafed the *Gregory* before, during, and after the bombing run.

He tried to push himself off the bulkhead, and heard himself moan with pain. He looked again at his arm, and saw that it was hanging uselessly.

I am about to go into shock.

There was confirmation of that. He felt light-headed and was chilled.

He finally managed to stand erect and went to the talker, who looked at him but did not see him.

"Get the executive officer to the bridge," he ordered. When there was no response, when the talker's eyes looked at him but did not see him, Pickering slapped him hard across the face. The talker looked at him like a kicked puppy, but life came back in his eyes.

"Get the executive officer to the bridge," Pickering repeated. The talker nodded, and Pickering saw his hand rise to the microphone switch.

As Pickering went to the other sailor, he slipped and nearly fell in a puddle of blood.

"Take the wheel," Pickering ordered.

"I'm the ship's writer, Sir."

"Take the goddamned wheel!"

"Aye, aye, Sir."

Pickering went to the window of the bridge. Only shards remained of the thick glass. Dead ahead, he could see the Emily, still close to the sea, making a tight turn. He was about to make another bomb run.

An officer, a nice-looking kid in a helmet, appeared on the bridge.

"Mother of Christ!" he said, looking around in horror.

"Get the executive officer up here!" Pickering shouted at him.

"Sir, I . . . Mr. Goldberg's dead, Sir. I came up here to report."

"Can you conn this vessel?"

"No, Sir. I'm the communications officer."

"Get someone up here who can," Pickering ordered. "Get people up here. I need someone on the telegraph, someone on the wheel."

"Aye, aye, Sir," the communications officer said, then turned and left the bridge. Pickering saw that he stopped just outside and became nauseous.

He returned his attention to the Emily, which was now in level flight, low on the water, making another bombing run to port.

"Prepare to come hard to port," Pickering said.

"Damage report, Captain," the talker said.

"What?"

"Damage control officer reports no damage, Sir."

"Tell him to get up here!" Pickering said, then: "Hard to port."

"Hard to port it is, Sir."

The *Gregory* began to turn, heeling over. It was now pointing directly at the Emily.

Pickering saw four dark objects drop from the airplane, and watched in fascination as they arced toward the ship.

And then he saw something else: Red tracers from a Bofors 40mm cannon splashing into the sea, and then picking up, moving toward the Emily. When she was just about overhead, the line of tracers moved into the Emily's fuselage, and then to her right wing. The wing buckled as the airplane flashed over.

Pickering ran to the exposed portion of the bridge, his feet slipping in the pool of blood now spreading from under her captain's body. He looked aft. The Emily had already crashed. As he watched, what was left of it slipped below the water, and the dense cloud of blue-black smoke that had been rising from her wreckage was cut off. For a moment, there were patches of burning fuel on the water, but they started to flicker out.

He returned to the bridge. A lieutenant whom he remembered seeing in the wardroom at dinner the night before came onto the bridge.

"I'm the damage control officer, Sir."

"Can you conn this vessel?"

"Yes, Sir."

"Sir, you have the conn," Pickering said, and then put his hand out to steady himself. He really felt faint.

"I have the conn, Sir," the lieutenant said, ritually, and then Pickering heard him say, "Help the Captain, Doc. Stop that bleeding."

(Two)
ABOARD USS *GREGORY* (APD-44)
CORAL SEA
1425 HOURS 18 AUGUST 1942

Pickering was in the Captain's cabin, in the Captain's bunk, his back resting on pillows against the bulkhead. He was naked above the waist. His arm, in a cast, was taped to his chest. He appeared to be dozing.

The lieutenant walked to the bunk and looked down at him.

"How do you feel, Sir?"

Pickering looked at him for a moment without recognition, and then, with an effort, forced himself awake.

"Oh, it's you," he said cheerfully. "Mr. 'No Damage to Report, Sir.' "

"Sir," the Lieutenant said, obviously hurt. "I didn't know what had happened on the bridge, Sir. Except that Mr. Goldberg had been killed on the ladder."

"I shouldn't have said that," Pickering said. "I'm sorry. I had a tube of morphine; I must still be feeling it."

"Are you still in pain, Sir?"

"Every time I breathe. That's a hell of a place to be stitched up." He changed the subject: "What shape are we in?"

"We're about five hours out, Sir, from Espíritu Santo. There's some things that have to be decided."

"Are you the senior officer?"

"No, Sir. You are."

"I'm supercargo."

"Sir, I checked the manual. Command passes—in a situation like this—to the senior officer of the line. Captain, that's you, Captain."

"What is it?"

"The bodies, Sir. I have them prepared, Sir."

"Where are they?"

"The captain and three others are in sick bay, Sir. The others are in the Chief's quarters."

"If you're suggesting a burial at sea . . ."

"That's your decision, Captain."

"If we're only five hours out, I think we should take them to Espíritu Santo," Pickering said. "I have no intention of conducting a burial at sea."

"Aye, aye, Sir," the lieutenant said. "And we seem to have forgotten the report, Sir."

"I don't know what you're talking about."

"Mr. Norwood, the communications officer, has prepared it, Sir," the lieutenant said, and handed it to him.

OPERATIONAL IMMEDIATE
SECRET
FROM USS GREGORY
TO: CINCPAC
1. GREGORY ATTACKED 0750 HOURS 18AUG42 POSITION WHISKEY ABLE OBOE SLASH NAN NAN CHARLEY BY ONE REPEAT ONE EMILY. MODERATE TO SEVERE DAMAGE TO BRIDGE. EMILY SHOT DOWN.
2. CASUALTIES: CAPTAIN, EXECUTIVE OFFICER, TWO ENLISTED KIA. THREE OFFICERS AND SEVEN ENLISTED WIA.
3. GREGORY PROCEEDING BAKER XRAY MIKE.
PICKERING, CAPTAIN, USN, COMMANDING

"It's 'USNR,' not 'USN,' " Pickering said. "I'm not a regular."

"Yes, Sir. I'll have that changed."

"What about the wounded?"

"One of them is in pretty bad shape, I'm afraid. We're hoping he makes it. There's medical facilities at Espíritu. The others will be all right, Captain."

"*Captain,*" Pickering said thoughtfully, sadly, and paused, and then went on: "The captain died quickly. I don't think he knew what hit him."

"Mr. Goldberg, too, Sir. He was . . . whatever got him, got him in the head."

"Jesus Christ!" Pickering said.

"Captain, can I get you something to eat? A tray, maybe. A sandwich? You really should have something."

"What I really would like is a drink," Pickering replied.

"I wish I could help you, Sir."

"Is there any medicinal bourbon aboard?"

"Yes, Sir."

"How much?"

"There's four cartons, Sir. I think they pack them forty-eight of those little bottles to a carton."

"Enough for one per man?"

"Yes, Sir. More than enough, Captain."

"Issue one bottle per man. If there is any left over, bring me a couple."

"Aye, aye, Sir."

(Three)
WATER LILY COTTAGE
MANCHESTER AVENUE
BRISBANE, AUSTRALIA
1925 HOURS 18 AUGUST 1942

There was the sound of tires crunching on the driveway. Major Ed Banning went to the window, pushed the curtain aside, and saw the Studebaker President stopping in the drive.

"Pluto," Banning said, turning to Mrs. Ellen Feller. She was sitting on the couch, holding a tea cup and saucer in her hand.

"I presumed he would come here to discuss this situation with you," Ellen Feller said. "Didn't you?"

Banning didn't reply. He went to the door and opened it as Hon bounded onto the porch.

"I gather you've heard about Moore?" Banning greeted him.

"Yeah," Pluto said. "Take a look at this."

He handed Banning a sheet of onion skin, walked into the room, and nodded at Ellen Feller.

"Major Banning and I have been talking about what to do about Sergeant Moore," she said.

"And?"

"We've decided the best thing is to do nothing," Ellen said.

"What is this thing?" Banning asked, confused.

"The Signal Corps monitors the Navy frequencies when they can," Hon explained, "and they copy what they think might be interesting. Operational Immediates, for example. The crypto officer handed me that the moment I walked in. *Before* he told me that he had to fill in for the missing Sergeant Moore."

"But what the hell *is* this?"

"Read the signature," Pluto Hon said.

Banning did so.

"I'll be damned," he said.

"May I see that?" Ellen Feller asked, rising to her feet and walking to Banning. Banning handed her the Operational Immediate message radioed from the USS *Gregory* to CINCPAC after the Emily attack.

"Well, we knew that Mr. Knox told CINCPAC to take him off Guadalcanal," Ellen Feller said. "He was apparently on this ship, and I suppose that as the senior officer aboard, he would naturally take command if the captain was killed."

Banning ignored her.

"I don't suppose you know off-hand what Baker XRay Mike is. Or where?"

"Espíritu Santo," Hon said. "With great reluctance, the Navy Liaison Officer told me."

"Well, thank God, Captain Pickering is all right," Ellen said.

Banning looked at her but said nothing.

"Lieutenant Hon," Ellen said. "As I was saying, Major Banning and I have been discussing Sergeant Moore."

"What do you mean by that?" Hon asked.

"We can't let it get out that Moore knew . . . more than a sergeant should have been permitted to know . . . can we? I mean, the greater priority is to protect Captain Pickering, isn't it?"

He looked at her for a moment before replying. Then he asked, "Are you suggesting that we should not do whatever the hell has to be done to get Moore the hell off Guadalcanal?"

He looked at Banning, who met his eyes, but said nothing. Hon looked back at Ellen Feller.

"The only way," she said, "we can, as you put it, get Moore the hell off Guadalcanal is to make it known that he has had access to MAGIC. That will get Captain Pickering—for that matter, all of us—in a great deal of trouble."

"Your discussion, I'm afraid, Mrs. Feller," Pluto Hon said, coldly, "is academic."

"What does that mean?" Banning asked.

Hon handed him a sheet of paper.

URGENT

TOP SECRET

SERVICE MESSAGE

FROM: OFFICER IN CHARGE SPECIAL COMMUNICATIONS FA-CILITY JKS-3 SHSWPA BRISBANE

TO: OFFICER IN CHARGE SPECIAL COMMUNICATIONS FACIL-ITY JKS-1 CINCPAC PEARL HARBOR

1. FOLLOWING TOP SECRET EYES ONLY TO BE RELAYED UR-GENT TO CAPTAIN FLEMING PICKERING USNR SOMEWHERE ENROUTE VIA BAKER XRAY MIKE TO OFFICE SECNAV WASH-INGTON: BEGIN MSG ONLY ENLISTED MEMBER JKS-3 EN ROUTE VIA AIR GUADALCANAL ON ORDERS ACOFS G2 HQ USMC SIGNATURE PLUTO END MSG.

2. IMPORTANCE OF DELIVERY AS SOON AS POSSIBLE CANNOT BE OVEREMPHASIZED. HON 1STLT SIGC USA

Ellen Feller stepped behind Banning and read the message over his shoulder.

"You had no authority to do that!" she flared.

"This has gone out, Pluto?" Banning asked.

"Yes, Sir."

"If you did so in the presumption that I would agree with it, you were absolutely right, Lieutenant," Banning said.

"It's insane," Ellen said. "The people in Hawaii aren't stu-pid. They are going to know exactly what this means."

"I hope so," Pluto said. "MAGIC is too important to risk being compromised."

"I can't imagine what Captain Pickering is going to think when he gets that," she said.

"He's probably going to wonder why we let it happen," Banning said.

"What could we do? How could we stop it?" she snapped.

"Since Pluto and I were gone, obviously, we couldn't."

"You're not suggesting that I could have stopped him from going?"

Banning didn't answer.

"You tell me, Banning," she flared, "how I could have stopped him from going."

"You could have hid him under your bed, if nothing else, until Colonel Dailey was gone."

She snorted contemptuously.

"Or in it," Banning added, nastily.

"How dare you talk to me like that?"

"For your general information, Mrs. Feller," Banning said evenly, turning to meet her eyes, "at my request, the Army Counterintelligence Corps has been providing security for this house since Captain Pickering rented it. He's a splendid fellow, but he's a little lax about classified document security. They kept it up after Captain Pickering left and turned the house over to you and Sergeant Moore. The CIC people go through the house every time it's left empty, to make sure there's nothing classified lying about. They're very thorough in their surveillance. They even write down which bedrooms are used by whom, and they've been furnishing me a daily report."

(Four)
HENDERSON FIELD
GUADALCANAL, SOLOMON ISLANDS
1045 HOURS 19 AUGUST 1942

A bag of official mail and six insulated metal boxes marked with red crosses and the legend, HUMAN BLOOD RUSH, were aboard the PBY-5 Catalina from Espíritu Santo. There were also three passengers.

One of the passengers was wearing a steel helmet and a Red Cross brassard on the sleeve of his obviously brand-new USMC utilities.

The Navy Medical Corps, Lieutenant Colonel George F.

Dailey thought approvingly, was just about as efficient in sending replacements for lost-in-action physicians as Marine Corps intelligence had been in getting him and Sergeant Moore to the scene of battle.

Sergeant Moore did not favorably impress Lieutenant Colonel Dailey. When he was told that he was going to be given the opportunity to serve the Corps and the nation doing something far more important than shuffling classified documents, Moore's behavior in Brisbane was really distressing, not at all that expected of a Marine sergeant. He didn't want to go. And while Dailey was not prepared to go so far as to suggest cowardice, he was convinced that if he hadn't sent the Army Military Policemen to "help him collect his gear" there was more than a slight chance that Moore would not have shown up at the airport. At least until after the plane to Espíritu Santo had left.

As the Catalina landed, Dailey saw that there were no other airplanes on the field, and wondered why. If the Catalina could land, why not fighters?

The pilot taxied up to the control tower and shut down the engines. A crewman opened the door and made a gesture for the passengers to get out.

"Welcome to Guadalcanal," he said. "Cactus Airlines hopes you have enjoyed your flight."

There were two Jeeps sitting by the control tower. A medical officer wearing a Red Cross brassard sat on the hood of one of them. Surprising Dailey, he had a .30 caliber carbine slung over his shoulder. A major leaned against the other Jeep. A 35-mm camera was hanging around his neck, and a Thompson .45 caliber submachine gun was cradled in his arm.

The major smiled and pushed himself erect.

"Well, I'll be damned, look who's here! I warned you not to screw up, Sergeant."

Moore saluted.

"Hello, Major Dillon," he said.

"Major," Dailey said. "My name is Dailey."

Dillon did not salute. He offered his hand, and announced, "Jake Dillon, Colonel."

The medical officer, and a Corpsman who appeared from inside the control tower building, went to the Catalina. The refrigerated blood containers were handed out and put into the medical Jeep. The doctor who had been on the plane from Espíritu Santo climbed out.

He shook hands with the doctor who had been waiting with the Jeep, then he stepped up to the front seat. The corpsman climbed over the rear and sat down precariously on one of the blood containers. The Jeep drove off.

The pilot came out the door.

"Just the man I'm looking for," Dillon said, and took an insulated Human Blood container from the back of his Jeep. A failed attempt to cross off HUMAN BLOOD with what appeared to be grease pencil had been made.

When he looked closer, Dailey saw that the grease pencil had also been used to write, EXPOSED PHOTOGRAPHIC FILM. FOR PUBLIC RELATIONS SECTION, HQ USMC, WASHINGTON DC on several sides of the container.

"Hello, Major," the pilot said.

"You don't have any film for me, by any chance, do you?"

"There's four boxes for you at Espíritu, but I didn't have the weight left."

"Christ, I'm running low."

"I had the medic and those two to carry. They had the priority. Next time, I hope."

"If you can't bring all of it, bring at least one. Or open one. Bring what you can. I'm really running low. And film doesn't weigh that much."

"I'll do what I can, Jake."

"Thank you," Dillon said, and walked back to Dailey and Moore.

"I think I know where Sergeant Moore is going," Dillon said. "Is there any place I can carry you, Colonel?"

"I'm reporting for duty as Division G-2," Dailey said.

"I thought that might be it," Dillon said. "Hop in, I'll give you a ride."

"Thank you," Dailey said. "What's your function around here, Major?"

"I'm your friendly neighborhood Hollywood press agent," Dillon said, as he got behind the wheel.

"I'm afraid I don't understand?"

"I've got a crew of combat correspondents recording this operation for posterity," Dillon said.

"How is it you know Sergeant Moore?"

"I was in Melbourne—with Frank Goettge, the man you're replacing—a while back. At Fleming Pickering's place. Moore worked for him." He turned to look at Moore in the back seat. "You knew he was gone from here, didn't you?"

"I knew he was going, Sir," Moore said. "I didn't know he was gone."

"Well, don't worry, they'll find a lot for you to do here. You heard what happened to Colonel Goettge and the others?"

"No, Sir."

Dillon told them.

When they reached the G-2 Section, Dillon got out of the Jeep.

"Major Jack NMI Stecker is acting G-2," he said. "I'll introduce you. He'll be damned glad to see you."

"Why do you say that?"

"Because they took him away from his battalion to put him in G-2 when Goettge got himself killed, and he's very unhappy about that."

Dillon entered the G-2 section. It was dark inside, and it took a moment for his eyes to adjust. Before they did, before he could make out more than shadowy bodies, he called out: "Christmas present, Jack. Your replacement."

There was silence for a moment, and then a dry voice said, "At least he didn't go 'Ho, Ho, Ho.' I suppose we should be grateful for that."

Major Dillon's eyes had by then become acclimated to the lower light. He could now make out a familiar face.

"I beg your pardon, General. I didn't know you were in here."

"I wonder if that would have made any difference?" General Vandergrift asked, and then advanced on Dailey.

"I'm General Vandergrift, Colonel," he said offering his hand. "I hope that wasn't more of Major Dillon's Hollywood hyperbole, and you are indeed the intelligence officer we've been promised."

"Sir," Dailey said, coming to attention, "Lieutenant Colonel Dailey, Sir. Reporting for duty as G-2."

"I'm very pleased to meet you, Colonel," Vandergrift said.

"Welcome aboard. This is Major Stecker, who has been filling in."

Stecker offered his hand. Vandergrift spotted Moore, and offered him his hand.

"You came in with Colonel Dailey, Sergeant?"

"Yes, Sir."

"He was Flem Pickering's—I don't know what, *orderly,* I guess—in Australia," Dillon volunteered.

"Is that what you've been doing, Son?" Vandergrift asked. "Orderly?"

"No, Sir. I'm a Japanese-language linguist, Sir."

"In that case, I'm sure Major Stecker is even more glad to see you than he is to see Colonel Dailey," Vandergrift said. He looked at Major Jake Dillon and shook his head.

"Think about it, Jake," he said. "Did you really think they would airship an orderly in here?"

Stecker walked over to Moore and examined him closely.

"Give me a straight answer, Sergeant. How well do you speak—more important, how well do you read—Japanese?"

"Fluently, Sir."

"Sergeant!" Stecker said, raising his voice.

A head appeared from behind the canvas that separated the outer "office" from "the map room."

"Sir?"

"Take the sergeant here up to the First Marines. He's a Japanese-language linguist."

"Belay that, Sergeant," General Vandergrift said. "I'm sure you have more important things to do, and Major Dillon has just kindly offered to take the sergeant, haven't you, Major?"

"Yes, Sir," Dillon said. "I'd be happy to."

"Sergeant," Jack Stecker said, "there's several boxes of stuff at the First, taken from the bodies of Japanese. We haven't had anybody who can read it. I want anything that looks official, anything that can help us identify enemy units, anything that would be useful to know about those units. Do you understand what I'm talking about?"

"Yes, Sir. I think I do."

"If you come across something, give it to Captain Feincamp. He's the S-2. I'll get on the horn and tell him you're coming."

"Aye, aye, Sir."

"Anything that *looks* to you like it might be interesting. Don't bother with actually translating it. Just make a note of what it is. I'll decide whether or not you should make a translation."

"Aye, aye, Sir."

"Have you got a weapon?"

If I tell him about the .45, he's probably going to take it away from me.

Sergeant John Marston Moore, surprised with how easily it came, lied.

"No, Sir."

"Sergeant!" Stecker raised his voice again, and again the head appeared at the canvas flap.

"Sir?"

"Give the sergeant that extra Thompson."

"Aye, aye, Sir."

"You *can* use a Thompson?" Stecker asked Moore.

"Yes, Sir."

"I think that probably I'll have you—Colonel Dailey will have you—work here. But right now, we need to go through the stuff the First has collected."

"Yes, Sir."

The sergeant appeared and handed Moore a Thompson submachine gun and two extra magazines.

"Thank you."

"Drive slow, Jake," Stecker said. "Sergeant Moore is a very valuable man. We can't afford to lose him."

"Right," Dillon said. "OK, Sergeant. Let's go."

An alarm went off in the back of General Vandergrift's head. Something was wrong, but he couldn't put a handle on it.

Stecker's words, he finally realized. *"We can't afford to lose him."*

It was that, and the reference to Flem Pickering. And what Flem had said about Lieutenant Cory, whose place this young sergeant was taking.

The morning he left, Pickering had told him about MAGIC, and about his concern that Cory might have known about it. If Cory had that knowledge, he should never have been sent to Guadalcanal.

The sergeant, obviously, does not know about MAGIC. *For one thing, that sort of secret is not made known to junior enlisted men. For another, he worked for Fleming Pickering. Therefore, if he knew, Pickering would have made sure he would not be sent to Guadalcanal.*

But this lieutenant colonel: He was an intelligence officer, he's senior enough to have had responsibilities which would have given him the Need to Know. And they rushed him here to replace Goettge. Since so few people actually knew about MAGIC, *it was possible that whoever had rushed him over here hadn't even considered that possibility.*

And this fellow—General Vandergrift had made a snap, and perhaps unfair, judgment that Lieutenant Colonel Dailey was not too smart; otherwise he would not have been assigned as a liaison officer to SHSWPA—*if he was privy to* MAGIC, *it might well have been decided to send him to Guadalcanal anyway.*

"Colonel," General Vandergrift asked. "Does the phrase MAGIC mean anything to you?"

"No, Sir," Lieutenant Colonel Dailey replied. "I've heard the word, Sir, but . . ."

"It's not important," General Vandergrift said.

(Five)
S-2 SECTION, FIRST MARINES
GUADALCANAL, SOLOMON ISLANDS
2005 HOURS 19 AUGUST 1942

Sergeant John Marston Moore, USMCR, sat on the dirt floor of the S-2 bunker in the brilliant light of a hissing Coleman gasoline lamp. His legs were crossed under him, and his undershirt was sweat soaked. He had long before removed his utility jacket. The Thompson submachine gun Major Stecker had given him now rested on it.

He was about two-thirds of the way, he judged, through the foot-and-a-half-tall pile of personal effects removed from Japanese bodies; and he had been at it steadily since shortly after eleven, less time out for "dinner"—a messkit full of rice, courtesy of the Japanese; a spoonful of meat and gravy, courtesy Quartermaster Corps, U.S. Army; and two small cans of really delicious smoked oysters, again courtesy of the Japanese.

He had found virtually nothing that Major Stecker could possibly use. He had learned that the Marines already knew the identity of the Rikusentai engineers—the 11th and 23rd Pioneers—who had been building the airfield.

He had been able to augment this by finding, in written-but-not-mailed letters home, references to the names of the commanding officers. He had written them down. He couldn't see how the names of three or four junior Japanese officers would be of much use, except perhaps as a psychological tool for prisoner interrogation.

That seemed to be a moot point. For one thing, Moore had learned there were damn few prisoners. The story of the Japanese warrant officer who led Colonel Goettge and the others into the trap had quickly spread through the division. The Marines had decided that discretion—*don't take a chance, shoot the fucker!*—overwhelmed the odd and abstract notion that prisoners had an intelligence value.

Tell that to Colonel Goettge!

For another, there seemed to be very few people around capable of interrogating prisoners at all, unless they happened to speak English, much less of outwitting them with psychological tricks.

He had spent long hours reading letters from home. It had been emotionally unnerving. He had lived in Japan. Tokyo was really as much home to him as Philadelphia. When he found an envelope bearing a Denenchofu return address, he knew it was entirely possible that he and the writer, somebody's mother, had met and bowed to each other at the door of a shop.

Much of the stuff was stained with a dark and sticky substance, now beginning to give off a sickly sweet smell, that he could not pretend was mud or oil or plum preserves.

Moore heard someone coming into the sandbagged tent. He turned and looked over his shoulder. It was Captain Feincamp, the First Marine's S-2, and he had with him a lieutenant and a technical sergeant, a balding, lean man in his late thirties.

"How you coming, Sergeant?" Feincamp asked.

"I haven't found anything interesting so far, Sir," Moore replied.

"He's a linguist," Captain Feincamp explained to the lieutenant. "They just flew him in. There's a replacement for Colonel Goettge, too."

And then he explained to Moore the reason why the lieutenant and the technical sergeant were there.

"They just came off patrol, Sergeant," he said. "They ran into some Japs and had themselves a little firefight. I think maybe you'd better listen in on this."

"Yes, Sir," Moore said, grateful for the chance to stop rummaging through personal effects.

He spun around on the dirt floor.

The lieutenant and then the technical sergeant handed him several wallets and some more personal mail.

"We're the first ones back, I suppose," the lieutenant said. "Maybe you can make something out of this shit."

Moore took it, glanced through it, and quickly decided it was more of the same sort of thing he'd been looking at for hours.

Feincamp produced a map. The lieutenant looked at it for a moment, and then pointed.

"Right about here on the beach, Captain," he said. "Captain Brush called a lunch break. I told him that I'd been there before, and twenty, thirty minutes inland was an orange farm . . ."

"A what?"

"Orange trees."

"Orange *grove*," Feincamp provided.

"Yes, Sir. Well, the captain said we could walk another half hour if it meant fresh fruit, so we started inland. Ten, fifteen minutes later, right about here . . ." he pointed, "all hell broke loose. We lost Corporal DeLayne right away. He took a round in the head."

"The big blond kid?"

"Yes, Sir."

"Damn."

"So Captain Brush told me to take a squad around here, on the right flank, and the rest started for where the fire was coming from. Straight ahead. When we started that, they started withdrawing, and we started after them."

Moore saw that the technical sergeant was admiring a Japanese helmet he had taken as a souvenir.

"So then it was sort of like the wild west for maybe twenty minutes. But we whipped their ass!"

"Casualties?"

"A pisspot full of them. We counted thirty-one Japs, and I'm sure we missed some."

"I was speaking of Marines," Feincamp said coldly.

"Three KIA, Sir. Three wounded."

"Sergeant," Moore suddenly interrupted, "let me see that helmet, please?"

The technical sergeant looked at him doubtfully.

"Huh?"

"May I please see the helmet?" Moore asked.

"You want a helmet, Sergeant, you just take a walk up the beach."

"Give him the helmet, Sergeant," Captain Feincamp ordered softly.

The technical sergeant reluctantly handed it over.

"What is it, Sergeant?" Feincamp asked, after a moment.

"This isn't a Rikusentai helmet, Captain," Moore said.

"It isn't a what?" the lieutenant asked.

Moore ignored the question.

"Were the Japanese all wearing helmets like this?" he asked.

"They was—the ones that *was* wearing helmets—were wearing helmets like that," the technical sergeant said.

"With this insignia?" Moore pursued, pointing to a small, red enamel star on the front of the helmet.

"I don't know," the lieutenant said. "What was that you said before?"

"The Rikusentai, the construction troops who were building the airfield, are in the Japanese Navy. The Navy insignia is an anchor and a chrysanthemum. This is an Army helmet."

"Meaning what?"

"Meaning, possibly," Moore thought aloud and immediately regretted it, "that the Ichiki Butai is already ashore."

"What the fuck is whatever you said?" the technical sergeant asked.

"The Ichiki Butai is an infantry regiment—the 28th—of the 7th Division. First class troops under Colonel Kiyano

Ichiki. The Japanese are going to send them here from Truk. If I'm right, and they're already here, that *would* be important."

"How the hell do you know that?" Captain Feincamp asked. "What units the Japs intend to send?"

"I know, Sir. I can't tell you how I know."

"The captain," the technical sergeant said furiously, "asked you a question. You answer it!"

Captain Feincamp raised his hand to shut off the technical sergeant.

"How do we know the Japs didn't issue Army helmets to— what was it you called them?" Captain Feincamp asked.

"The Rikusentai, Sir," Moore furnished. "It's possible, of course. But that Major in G-2 . . ."

"Major Stecker?"

"Yes, Sir, I think so. He told me to look for anything out of the ordinary."

"Captain," the lieutenant said thoughtfully. "I have something . . . I mean, out of the ordinary. The Japs we killed seemed to be heavy on officers. Maybe half of them were."

"You just forgot to mention that, right?" Feincamp said, sarcastically.

"Sorry, Sir. I didn't think it was important."

"What I think you had better do, Lieutenant," Feincamp said, "is get down to Division G-2, and tell Major Stecker what happened . . . No, tell the new G-2; I forgot about him. I'm going to send your sergeant and Sergeant Moore back down the beach to see what else Moore can come up with."

"Aye, aye, Sir."

"I don't think I have to tell you, Moore, do I, what to look for?"

"No, Sir."

(Six)

Aside from perhaps four hours familiarization at Parris Island, the only experience Sergeant John Marston Moore, USMCR, had with the U.S. Submachine Gun, Caliber .45 (Thompson) was vicarious. He had watched half a dozen movie heroes—most notably Alan Ladd—and as many movie gangsters—most notably Edward G. Robinson—use the weapon against their enemies with great skill, elan, and ease.

They were now forty minutes down the beach toward the site of the encounter between Able Company, First Marines, and the Japanese; and he really had had no idea until that moment how heavy the sonofabitch was.

He had opted to leave his utility jacket in the S-2 Section of the First Marines, which he now recognized to be an error of the first magnitude. The canvas strap of the Thompson had worn one shoulder and then the other raw. And as they made their way down the sandy beach, the two spare 20-round Thompson magazines he carried, plus the .45 pistol and its two spare magazines, had both banged against him, in the process wearing raw and badly bruising the skin and muscles of his legs and buttocks.

He had also quickly learned that the good life he had been living in Melbourne and Brisbane had not only softened the calluses he had won at Parris Island—the balls of his feet and the backs of his ankles had quickly blistered, and the blisters had broken—but it had softened him generally.

To the technical sergeant's great and wholly unconcealed annoyance and contempt, he had absolutely had to stop every five minutes or so to regain his breath. His heart pounded so heavily he wondered if it would burst through his rib cage.

Twenty minutes down the beach, they began to encounter other members of Captain Brush's patrol. Five minutes after that, they encountered Captain Brush himself, bringing up the rear.

When the technical sergeant responded to, "Sergeant Ropke, where the *hell* do you think you're going?" by informing him of their mission, Captain Brush assigned a Corporal and a PFC to go with them.

Fifteen minutes after that, they reached the site of the action. It was marked by Japanese bodies scattered over the beach in various obscene postures of death. Even more obscene, in Moore's judgment, were the three-quarters-buried bodies of the three Marines who had been killed.

They had been buried with one boondocker shod foot sticking out of the ground so that their bodies could be more easily found later.

In the clothing of the third body Moore examined, that of a Japanese Army Captain, he found positive proof that the Ichiki Butai had indeed been landed on Guadalcanal. He also found in the calf of the Captain's boot a map which looked to him like a Japanese assessment of the Marine defense positions on the beachhead.

He gave this to the technical sergeant, and oriented the map for him.

"Jesus Christ!" the technical sergeant said, after carefully examining the map. "They did a good fucking job with this!"

Moore spent another twenty minutes searching for the bodies of Japanese officers, and then searching the bodies for materials he thought would be important. Finally he had a Japanese knapsack full of documents, maps, and wallets.

They started back. Five minutes down the beach, after the first time he stopped to catch his breath, the technical sergeant relieved him of the Thompson.

"Let me carry the Thompson," he said, not unkindly. "That shit you picked up is slowing us all down."

I should be embarrassed, ashamed, humiliated. I am not. I am simply grateful that I don't have to carry that sonofabitch anymore!

Ninety seconds after that, there was a faint suggestion of something—some *things*—flying through the air in high arcs. And a moment after that, there were two almost simultaneous flashes of light, and then a moment later, a third.

And then something like a swung baseball bat hit Sergeant John Marston Moore twice, once in the calf of his left leg and once high, almost at the hip joint of his right leg.

This was followed immediately by a loud roar, and the sensation of flying through the air. He landed on his back, and the wind was knocked out of him.

After a moment, while he was still trying to figure out what was happening, he became aware of people running out from the woods onto the beach. Two of them had rifles, and the third a pistol.

He rose on his elbow for a closer look.

He saw that the Corporal and the PFC who had been sent with them were down on the beach, crumpled up, and that the technical sergeant was trying, without much success, to get to his feet.

Moore rolled over onto his stomach and took the .45 Colt automatic from where it had been bruising his buttocks raw and sore and worked the action and held it in two hands and shot at the three men running onto the beach. He shot until two of them fell, and until the slide locked in the rear position indicating that the last of the seven rounds in the magazine had been expended.

He searched desperately for a spare magazine.

There was a short, staccato burst of .45 fire, accompanied by orange flashes of light, and then another. The technical sergeant had gotten the Thompson into action.

By the time Moore found a fresh magazine, ejected the empty magazine, inserted the fresh magazine, let the slide slam forward, and then looked for a target, there was none.

What he saw was the technical sergeant, bleeding profusely from cuts or wounds on the neck and face, crawling over to him.

"You all right?" the technical sergeant said.

"I think I broke both legs."

"It'll be all right. They probably heard the fire, they'll send somebody back for us."

"Bullshit," Sergeant John Marston Moore said.

"Yeah, probably," the technical sergeant said. "But maybe when it gets light in the morning, they will."

One of the two Marines who had been sent with them— Moore couldn't tell which—moaned and then began to whimper.

They will find my body on this fucking beach in the morning, Sergeant John Marston Moore thought, *unless the tide comes in and washes it out to sea for the sharks to eat.*

Two minutes after that, there was the unmistakable sound of a Jeep in four-wheel drive making its way through soft sand.

When the Corpsmen loaded Sergeant John Marston Moore onto the litter, he screamed with pain.

They loaded the technical sergeant in the other litter. And then, because they didn't know what else to do with them, they laid the bodies of the PFC and the Corporal on the Jeep hood. The PFC's body started whimpering again.

"Jesus," Moore heard one of the Corpsmen say, "I thought he was dead."

(Seven)

"The Doc tells me you took grenade fragments in your legs," Major Jack NMI Stecker said to Sergeant John Marston Moore. "That's better than getting shot."

"What?" Moore asked incredulously. His legs were now one great sea of dull aching pain, with crashing wavelets of intense, flashing, toothache-like agony.

"There's often less tissue damage; and they can repair a jagged wound easier than a smooth one. The worst is a slice."

"I hurt," Moore said. "Why won't they give me something for the pain?"

"I told them not to, until I could get here and talk to you," Stecker confessed. "I want to hear more about Ichiki Butai."

"You *sonofabitch!*" Moore flared. The moment the words were out of his mouth, he realized with horror what he had said. Marine Sergeants do not call Marine Second Lieutenants, much less Marine Majors, sonsofbitches. Moore realized that he was horror stricken, but not repentant. Under the circumstances, if Jesus Christ himself was responsible for the withholding of pain killers, he would have questioned the parentage of the Son of God.

Major Jack NMI Stecker did not seem to take offense.

"Yeah," he said. "Are they or aren't they?"

"They were all Ichiki Butai," Moore said. "I think it was a headquarters team or something. I saw two lieutenant colonels, three majors, five or six captains. A bunch of senior NCOs."

"OK, Sergeant. I've got what linguists I could scrounge up working on those documents."

"How did you know about Ichiki Butai?" Moore asked.

"I've seen the Order of Battle," Stecker said. "What interests me is how you knew what you told Captain Feincamp."

"I want something for this fucking pain!"

"Son," a vaguely familiar voice asked. "Does the word MAGIC mean anything to you?"

"I *hurt!* God*damn* it, doesn't anybody care?"

"I'm General Vandergrift, Son. You can tell me. Do you know what MAGIC means?"

"Yes, Sir, General, I know what MAGIC is."

"All right, Doctor. Do what you can for this boy," General Vandergrift said.

Moore felt a surprisingly cool rubber mask being clamped over his mouth. Then there was a rush of cool air. It felt good. He took a deep breath.

"Well done, Lad," he heard General Vandergrift say. "Well do . . ."

XIX

Captain Charles M. Galloway slid open the canopy of his
Wildcat, then lowered the left wing just a little, just enough
to give him a good look at Henderson Field.

A Douglas SBD-3 Dauntless was just about to touch down.
Another Dauntless—the last of a dozen—was just turning
on final.

Galloway turned to his right, saw Jim Ward looking at
him, and gestured to him to go on down. Ward nodded and
peeled off. The other three Wildcats in the first five-plane V
followed Ward.

As the first planes of VMF-229 landed, Galloway flew two
wide three-sixties, mostly over the water (there was no
reported anti-aircraft fire, but why take a chance?). And then
Bill Dunn, leading the second five-plane V, pulled up
alongside him. Galloway signaled for him to land. Dunn
nodded, and gave the signal to his wing man. He peeled off

456

and made his approach, followed by the others. Dunn remained on Galloway's wing tip.

Soon it was the two of them alone above the field.

Two mother hens, Galloway thought, *making sure the little chickies get home safe.*

Except this isn't home and it isn't safe.

Charley reached his left hand down beside his seat, found the charging handle for the outboard .50 Caliber Browning in the left wing, and turned it ninety degrees, putting the weapon on SAFE. Then he found the inboard handle, and rotated that. He put his left hand on the stick, put his right hand down beside his seat, and repeated the action, putting the guns in the right wing on SAFE.

Then he looked over at Dunn, held up his index finger, and then pointed it at himself.

Me First.

He could see Dunn smiling.

Charley peeled off and put the Wildcat into a dive.

There are two ways to lower the landing gear of a Grumman F4F. The means specified in *AN 01-190FB-1 Pilot's Handbook of Flight Operating Instructions for Navy Model FM-2 Airplanes (As Amended)* specifies that the pilot will turn the landing gear handcrank located on the right side of the cockpit approximately twenty-eight times until the crank handle hits a stop indicating the landing gear has been fully extended.

The second way was not listed in any pilot's manual. The technique was not only not recommended, it was forbidden. It was the technique Charley Galloway used—and, he was sure, most of the pilots of VMF-229. Charley had explained it to them back at Ewa, so they would know what they were forbidden to do . . .

He released the landing gear handcrank brake just before he came out of the dive. Following Newton's Law that a body in motion tends to remain in motion, when he pulled out of the dive to make his final approach, the forces of gravity pulled the landing gear out of the retracted position.

You had to be very careful that the rapidly spinning handle didn't get your arm, which would probably break it, but on the other hand, you didn't have to turn the damned crank twenty-eight times with your right hand while flying the airplane with your left.

Charley touched down; and twenty seconds later, Bill Dunn touched down behind him. Before he finished the landing roll, the humid heat began to get to him. He felt his back break out in sweat.

He was not very impressed with the airfield. It looked to him like a half inch of rain would turn it into a sea of mud. And he understood that a half inch of rain a day was not at all uncommon on Guadalcanal.

The entire runway was lined with spectators. Not solidly, but every couple of yards there seemed to be a Marine. They were smiling, and a few of them even waved.

Charley waved back, and even forced a smile.

The Marines looked like hell. They looked exhausted and underfed and filthy. And they regarded the arrival of the first combat aircraft as something more important than it really was.

It was actually a desperate attempt to stop a major Japanese effort to throw the Marines off Guadalcanal and reclaim the airbase.

That effort was about to get underway. Charley Galloway had private personal doubts that nineteen F4Fs and a dozen SBD-3s were going to be able to do much to stop it. Not to mention anything else they scraped off the bottom of the barrel.

Just before they'd left the *Long Island,* he heard that the Army Air Corps was sending a squadron of Bell P-400s to Guadalcanal. The reaction of the group was that the goddamned Army Air Corps was butting in on the Marine Corps' business.

Galloway's reaction was that the Marines, and maybe especially MAG-21 in particular, could use all the help they could get; but they weren't going to get very much from a squadron of P-400s. He knew the story of the P-400.

Technical Sergeant Charley Galloway first heard about the aircraft in 1939. Curious about it, he managed to have a little engine trouble over Buffalo, New York, which gave him a chance to sit down at the Bell plant and have a look at the plane that began life as the Bell P-39 Aircobra.

He had not been impressed. It was a weird bird, sitting on

what looked to Charley like a very fragile tricycle landing gear. It had a liquid cooled Allison engine, mounted amidships, *behind* the pilot. The prop was driven by a shaft. The shaft was hollow, and carried a 37mm cannon barrel. There was no turbocharger, giving it, consequently, low to lousy performance at high altitudes.

All of which, in the final analysis, meant that nobody wanted the damned things.

The English wouldn't have anything to do with them. So the Aircobras that were supposed to go to them were sent to the Russians. Though Charley couldn't say for sure, it was entirely possible that the Russians, as desperate as they were for anything that would fly, didn't want them either. And so somebody had turned them over to the Army Air Corps.

Their reputation was so bad they'd even changed the name from P-39 to P-400. The only thing that surprised Charley was that the Marines hadn't wound up with them. The Marines normally got what the Army and the Navy didn't want.

It was not the sort of thing you talked to your men about, to bolster their morale, so Charley kept his mouth shut.

A familiar bald head and naked barrel chest appeared on the side of the runway, directing Charley to taxi to a sandbag revetment.

Tech Sergeant Big Steve Oblensky climbed up on the wing root before Charley stopped the engine.

"Well, I see you all got here," he said.

"There was some doubt in your mind?"

"Only about you," Big Steve said.

"What shape are we in?"

"Great. We have to pump fuel—the fuel there is—by hand through chamois. That runway's going to be a fucking muddy . . ."

" 'The fuel there is'?" Charley quoted, interrupting him.

Big Steve waited until Charley hauled himself out of the cockpit before replying.

"Those converted tin cans that brung us here," he said, "carried 400 barrels of Avgas. That's not much. Some of it they already used to refuel the Catalinas that have been coming in."

"You're telling me we have less than 22,000 gallons of gas?"

"Maybe a little more. They're bringing in a little all the time, but when we start using it . . ." Oblensky gestured at the aircraft that had just flown in. "And I just heard that the Army is sending in a half dozen P-400s tomorrow."

"Jesus Christ," Charley said.

There was the sound of aircraft engines, a different pitch than a Dauntless or Wildcat made. Charley looked up at the sky and saw a Catalina making its approach.

We make fun of them, he thought. *Aerial bus drivers. But it has to take more balls to fly that slow and ungainly sonofabitch in and out of here than it does to fly a Wildcat.*

"And there's no fucking chow," Oblensky said, almost triumphantly. "We're eating captured Japanese shit."

"Well then, I guess we better hurry up and win the war," Charley said. "I wouldn't want you writing Flo that we officers are starving your fat ass."

(Two)
U.S. NAVY HOSPITAL
SAN DIEGO, CALIFORNIA
0905 HOURS 24 AUGUST 1942

The nurse bending over the chest of Captain Fleming Pickering, USNR, was a full lieutenant who had been in the Navy for six years. She was competent, aware of this, and had a well-deserved reputation among her peers as being both hard nosed and unable to suffer fools.

She looked over her shoulder when she sensed movement behind her, and barked, "You'll have to leave. Who let you in here, anyhow? Visiting hours start at oh nine thirty."

Pickering laughed, and it hurt.

"Lieutenant," he said, "may I present the Secretary of the Navy?"

"Bullshit," the lieutenant said and chuckled, then looked, and said, "Oh, my God!"

"Please carry on," Frank Knox said. "How are you, Fleming?"

"I'm all right," Pickering said, and then, "Jesus Christ, take it easy, will you?"

"You want an infection? I'll stop."

"I thought they had some new kind of miracle drug—Sulfa?—you could just sprinkle on it," Pickering said, looking down at his chest.

"It's bullshit," she said. "What I'm doing works."

"It should, it hurts like hell."

"Be a big boy, Captain, I'm just about finished."

"So, I suspect, am I. Finished, I mean," Pickering said, looking at Knox.

"No," Frank Knox said. "I checked with the hospital commander. Despite your *grievous and extremely painful wounds,* you'll live. You should be out of the hospital in two weeks."

"That's not what I meant," Pickering said.

"I know what you meant," Knox said.

"I'm not finished?"

"I bring the personal greetings of the President of the United States," Knox said. "That sound like you're finished?"

"It sounds suspicious."

"Take a look at this," Knox said, and walked to the bed and handed Pickering a sheet of paper.

URGENT
CINCPAC 0915 22AUG1942
SECRET
PERSONAL FOR SEC NAVY
INFORMATION: CHIEF OF NAVAL OPERATIONS
1. CAPTAIN FLEMING PICKERING, USNR, DEPARTED PEARL HARBOR VIA MARINER AIRCRAFT FOR SANDIEGO NAVAL HOSPITAL 0815 22AUG1942. THE PROGNOSIS FOR HIS RECOVERY FROM WOUNDS TO THE CHEST AND FRACTURED ARM IS QUOTE GOOD TO EXCELLENT END QUOTE.
2. IN VIEW OF CAPTAIN PICKERINGS UNIQUE ASSIGNMENT THERE IS SOME QUESTION OF THE AUTHORITY OF THE UNDERSIGNED TO DECORATE THIS OFFICER, AND THE MATTER IS THEREFORE REFERRED FOR DETERMINATION.
3. IF CAPTAIN PICKERING WERE SUBORDINATE TO CINCPAC, THE UNDERSIGNED WOULD AWARD HIM THE SILVER STAR

MEDAL WITH THE FOLLOWING CITATION: CITATION: CAP-
TAIN FLEMING PICKERING, USNR, WHILE ABOARD THE USS
GREGORY IN THE CORAL SEA ON 18 AUGUST 1942 WAS ON
THE BRIDGE WHEN THE GREGORY WAS ATTACKED BY
ENEMY BOMBER AIRCRAFT. WHEN THE CAPTAIN AND THE
EXECUTIVE OFFICER OF THE GREGORY WERE KILLED IN
THE ENEMY ATTACK, AND DESPITE HIS GRIEVOUS AND EX-
TREMELY PAINFUL WOUNDS, INCLUDING A COMPOUND
FRACTURE OF HIS ARM CAPTAIN PICKERING ASSUMED COM-
MAND OF THE VESSEL. REFUSING MEDICAL ATTENTION
UNTIL HE COLLAPSED FROM LOSS OF BLOOD, CAPTAIN PICK-
ERING MANEUVERED THE SHIP DURING THE CONTINUING
ATTACK WITH CONSUMMATE MASTERY, WHICH NOT ONLY
SAVED THE SHIP FROM FURTHER ENEMY DAMAGE BUT RE-
SULTED IN THE DESTRUCTION OF THE ENEMY AIRCRAFT,
A FOUR-ENGINED JAPANESE HEAVY BOMBER. HIS CALM
COURAGE, ABOVE AND BEYOND THE CALL OF DUTY IN THE
FACE OF ADVERSITY INSPIRED HIS CREW AND REFLECTED
GREAT CREDIT UPON THE OFFICER CORPS OF THE UNITED
STATES NAVAL SERVICE. ENTERED THE FEDERAL SERVICE
FROM CALIFORNIA
NIMITZ, ADMIRAL, USN, CINCPAC

Pickering handed the message back to Knox.

"Before you start handing out any medals, you better look
at this," Pickering said. It was handed to me a few minutes
ago, just before Florence Nightingale came in here."

"Will you hold still, please?" the nurse snapped.

Pickering handed Knox the radio message Lieutenant
Pluto Hon had sent to MAGIC headquarters in Pearl Harbor.

Knox glanced at it and handed it back.

"I've seen it," Knox said. "How do you think they knew
where to deliver it?"

"You don't know what it means," Pickering said.

"I've got a damned good idea," Knox said. "I also have
this."

He handed Pickering another radio message.

URGENT
SECRET
HQ FIRST MARDIV 0845 20AUGUST 1942

SECNAV WASHINGTON DC
PLEASE PASS URGENTLY TO CAPTAIN FLEMING PICKERING
USNR SERGEANT J M MOORE USMCR HAS BEEN AIRLIFTED
ON MY AUTHORITY TO USNAVAL HOSPITAL PEARL HARBOR
FOR TREATMENT OF WOUNDS SUFFERED IN COMBAT 19 AU-
GUST 1942. THE RABBIT DID NOT GET OUT OF THE HAT.
BEST PERSONAL REGARDS SIGNED VANDERGRIFT MAJGEN
USMC
BY DIRECTION: HARRIS BRIGGEN USMC

"I wonder what he means about the rabbit in the hat," Knox said. "That sounds like MAGIC."

"It never entered my mind that boy would be sent to Guadalcanal," Pickering said. "How the *hell* did that happen?"

"No one knew any reason he should not have been sent. Not even me."

"I thought it was necessary that Hon have some help."

"So did I. That's why I sent your secretary over there."

"I didn't know she was coming," Pickering said.

"I told myself that," Knox said.

"I think you should know that I would do the same thing again, under the same circumstances."

"Except that next time, you might bring me in on it?"

"Yes. I am sorry about that. If it had been compromised, it would have been my fault."

"Who else knows?"

"Just Vandergrift."

"OK," Knox said.

The nurse finished cleaning the wounds on Pickering's chest.

"I'm going to send a nurse in to give you a sponge bath," she said. "And this time, you will not run her off."

"Yes, Ma'am," Pickering said.

"You're on the way to recovery. Don't screw it up by getting yourself infected," the nurse said.

"No, Ma'am," Pickering said, and then to Knox: "I don't suppose you know how badly Moore was hurt?"

"He's well enough to be flown home; I ordered that."

"That kid should be an officer," Pickering said.

"Why don't you make up a list of things you think the Secretary of the Navy should do?" Knox said, and then called after the nurse, "Lieutenant, there's a Captain Haughton and a lady out there. Would you send them in, please?"

"Yes, Sir."

Captain David Haughton held the door open for Patricia Pickering to enter her husband's hospital room.

She looked at him. Tears welled in her eyes.

"You goddamned old fool, you!" she said, and walked to the bed and kissed him.

"Haughton," the Secretary of the Navy ordered. "Give him the medal. I think we can dispense with the reading of the citation."

(Three)
BUKA, SOLOMON ISLANDS
1105 HOURS 24 AUGUST 1942

"Here you go, Steve," First Lieutenant Joseph L. Howard, USMCR, said to Sergeant Stephen M. Koffler, USMC, handing him a limp, humidity-soaked piece of paper. He had had to be very careful as he encrypted the message so that his pencil would not tear through the paper.

Koffler smiled at him and laid the paper on the crude table. Koffler, Howard thought, looked like hell. There were signs of malnutrition and fatigue. There was a good chance that Koffler had malaria. There was no question that he had a tape worm, and probably a half dozen other intestinal parasites.

Koffler thought much the same thing about Joe Howard, who was down to probably one hundred thirty pounds, and whose eyes were deeply sunken and unnaturally bright.

But, like Howard, he kept his thoughts to himself. Talking about it wasn't going to fix anything.

"Hey!" Koffler called. Ian Bruce was sitting on the generator. He smiled, exposing his black, filed to a point teeth, and began to pump slowly but forcefully.

There was a whine; and after a moment, the dials on Koffler's radio began to glow a dull yellow. The yellow turned almost white, and the needles came off their pegs.

Koffler put earphones on his head and arranged his own pad of paper on the table. He had attempted to dry out his paper on a heated rock. The result was that the paper had shrunk and twisted.

Koffler reached for the key.

The dots and dashes went out, repeated three times, spelling out simply, FRD6. FRD6. FRD6.

Detachment A of Special Marine Corps Detachment 14 is attempting to establish contact with any station on this communications network.

This time, for a change, there was an immediate reply.

FRD6.FRD1.FRD6.FRD1.FRD6.FRD1.

Hello, Detachment A, this is Headquarters Royal Australian Navy Coastwatcher Establishment, Townesville, Australia, responding to your call.

As Koffler reached for the RECEIVE/XMIT switch, there was another reply.

FRD6.KCY.FRD6.KCY.FRD6.KCY.

Hello, Detachment A, this is the United States Pacific Fleet Radio Station at Pearl Harbor, Territory of Hawaii responding to your call.

"What's that?" Joe Howard asked.

"We got both Townesville and Pearl Harbor," Koffler said. Meanwhile his fingers were on the key.

FRD1.FRD1.SB CODE. KCY.KCY.PLS COPY.

Townesville, stand by to copy encrypted message. CINCPAC Radio, please copy my transmission to FRD1.

FRD6.FRD1. GA.

Townesville to Detachment A: Go ahead.

KCY.FRD6.WILL COPY YRS FRD1.GA.

CINCPAC to Detachment A. As requested we will copy your transmission to FRD1. Go ahead.

Koffler put the sheet of damp paper Howard had given him under his left hand, then pointed his index finger at the first block of five characters.

As his right hand worked the telegrapher's key, his index finger swept across the coded message. It is more difficult to transmit code than plain English, for the simple reason that code doesn't make any sense.

It took him not quite sixty seconds before he sent, in the clear, END.

FRD6.FRD1.VRF.

Detachment A, this is Townesville. I am about to send to

you the material you just transmitted to me for purposes of verification.

FRD1.FRD6.GA

Townesville, this is Detachment A. Go ahead.

Koffler picked up a stubby pencil carefully.

We're running out of pencils, too. If something doesn't happen, if they don't send us some supplies, I'll be taking traffic from the Townesville and the Commander-in-Chief, Pacific by writing it with a sharp stick in the dirt floor.

After the message was received, Koffler handed it to Howard, who checked it against his original. Then Koffler began to write down the verification from Pearl Harbor.

The message informed both the Royal Australian Navy Coastwatcher Establishment and the Commander-in-Chief, Pacific, that Detachment A had observed, beginning at 1025 hours, a fleet of approximately ninety-six Japanese aircraft, consisting of approximately thirty Aichi D3A1 "Val" aircraft; ten Mitsubishi G4M1 Type 1 "Betty" Aircraft; fifteen Nakajima B5N1 "Kate" aircraft and approximately forty-one Mitsubishi A6M2 Model 21 "Zero" aircraft, flying at altitudes ranging from 5,000 to 15,000 feet, on a course which would probably lead them to Guadalcanal.

Howard wanted to make sure the message had been correctly transmitted. It took a little time.

FRD6.KCY ?????????

Detachment A. This is CINCPAC Radio. What's going on? We haven't heard from you in ninety seconds.

KCY.FRD6. FU FU.

CINCPAC Radio. This is Detachment A. Fuck You Twice.

"OK, Steve," Howard said. "Tell them we verify."

FRD6.FRD1.KCY. OK VRF. SB.

Detachment A to Townesville and Pearl Harbor. Verification is acknowledged. Detachment A is standing by.

FRD1.FDR6. SB TO COPY CODE.

FDR6. GA.

A minute later, Sergeant Stephen Koffler asked rhetorically, as he scribbled furiously, "what the hell are they sending us, the goddamned Bible?"

The message took three minutes to take down.

FDR1.FDR6. CLR.

Townesville to Detachment A. We have no further traffic for you at this time and are clearing this channel.

FDR6.FDR1. CLR.

Detachment A to Townesville. OK, Townesville, Good-bye.

KCY.FD6. FOLLOWING FOR COMMANDING OFFICER. PASS TO ALL HANDS. WELL DONE. NIMITZ. ADMIRAL.KCY CLR.

FRD6.KCY. GRBL. RPT.

Detachment A to CINCPAC Radio. Your last transmission was received garbled. Please repeat it.

KCY.FD6. FOLLOWING FOR COMMANDING OFFICER. PASS TO ALL HANDS. WELL DONE. NIMITZ. ADMIRAL.KCY CLR.

"I'll be goddamned," Sergeant Koffler said, and sent: FRD.6.KCY.CLR.

"Ian!" he called to the now completely sweat-soaked man pumping the generator. When he had his attention, he made a cutting motion across his throat.

"About fucking time!" Ian Bruce replied.

Steve handed the sheet of paper to Joe Howard.

"You think that's for real?" he asked.

"I can't imagine CINCPAC Radio fucking around," Howard said, seriously. "I'll be damned."

"What was the long code?" Steve asked.

Howard handed it to him.

Deeply regret am unable to relieve or reinforce at this time. Cannot overstate importance of what you are doing. Hang in there. Semper Fi. Banning.

"That's all there was?" Koffler asked.

"That's not enough?" Howard asked.

"You know what I meant," Koffler said. "I thought he was sending the goddamned Bible."

"That was all, Steve."

"Are we going to get out of here?"

"Until we got that 'Well Done' from the Commander-in-Chief Pacific, I thought so," Howard said. But when he saw the look on Koffler's face, he quickly added, "Just kidding, for Christ's sake."

"I was thinking of Daphne this morning," Koffler said. "I can't remember what she looks like. Ain't that a bitch?"

"When you see her, you'll know who she is," Howard said seriously. "Let's go get something to eat."

(Four)
HEADQUARTERS MAG-21
HENDERSON FIELD
GUADALCANAL, SOLOMON ISLANDS
1215 HOURS 24 AUGUST 1942

First Lieutenant Henry P. Steadman, USMC, reminded Lieutenant Colonel Clyde W. Dawkins, USMC, Commanding, Marine Air Group 21, of First Lieutenant David F. Schneider, USMC. Like Lieutenant Schneider, Steadman was a graduate of the United States Naval Academy and a brand-new replacement from the States; and the similarity did not please him.

When he saw Steadman with apparently nothing to do sitting on a folding chair just outside the sandbagged frame building which was serving as his headquarters, Lieutenant Colonel Dawkins ordered, "Steadman, pass the word to the pilots there'll be a briefing in ten minutes, will you?"

Lieutenant Steadman rose to his feet, looked baffled, and inquired, "The enlisted men, too, Sir?"

Dawkins's temper escaped.

"No, *of course* not," he said, with withering sarcasm. "I certainly have *no* intention of letting any of *my* flying *sergeants* in on *officer type* secrets like who and where we are going to fight."

Steadman's face colored.

"Sorry, Sir."

"You stupid little sonofabitch," Dawkins went on, his anger not a whit diminished, "if you don't know it yet, I'll spell it out for you: There's not a flying sergeant around here who can't fly rings around you. I would cheerfully trade two of your kind for one flying sergeant. You better write that on your goddamned forehead, I don't want you to forget it."

"Yes, Sir. I mean, No, Sir. I won't forget that, Sir."

"Go!" Dawkins ordered, extending a pointed finger at arm's length.

Lieutenant Steadman took off at a trot.

I really shouldn't have blown my cork that way, Dawkins thought, but then reconsidered: *That arrogant little asshole needed that. It just may keep him alive through the next couple of days.*

Ten minutes later, the pilots of MAG-21 were gathered in the tent that served as the briefing room. Three of the four sides had been rolled up, leaving only one narrow end wall behind the area that in a theater would have been the stage. Here, a bed removed from an otherwise destroyed Japanese Ford truck had been set up as a very rudimentary platform. It faced rows of simple plank benches. On the platform was a tripod made of two-by-fours. The tripod held several maps, now covered by a sheet of oilcloth.

Dawkins stepped into view from behind the canvas wall and made the slight jump onto the "stage."

"Ten-HUT!"

That was Galloway, Dawkins thought. For one thing, the command sounded like it came from a Marine, not from a recent graduate of the University of Michigan Naval ROTC program. And for another, a million years before the war, back when he was Technical Sergeant Galloway of VMF-211, Galloway had always taken pride in being the first to spot the commanding officer and issue the command that brought everybody to their feet and to attention.

Out of the corner of his eye, he spotted Galloway at the rear of the tent, standing beside Lieutenant Bill Dunn and Captain Dale Brannon, U.S. Army Air Corps.

Brannon commanded the somewhat grandiosely named 67th Pursuit Squadron, which had arrived at Henderson 21 August. Brannon's group, more or less informally, was put under MAG-21's command. It had only five airplanes, Bell P-400s. In Dawkins's opinion the P-400 was only marginally superior to the F2A-3 Buffalo, which was arguably the worst plane either side sent into combat in the Pacific.

Dawkins felt sorry for Brannon and his pilots; they would be going into combat almost literally with one hand tied behind them. Not only was the P-400 inferior to the Zero, but Dawkins had just learned that the oxygen system installed on the P-400s when they were supposed to go to the English could not be serviced by the equipment on Guadalcanal. That would limit them in altitude to maybe 12–13,000 feet. The book said that oxygen should be used over 10,000. The only hope Brannon and his pilots would have was in their superior armament (superior to the F4F, anyway): In addition to six .50 caliber Browning machine guns, the P-400s had a 20mm cannon, which fired through the propellor hub.

A hit with an explosive 20mm projectile was far more lethal than, say, ten hits with a .50 caliber solid nose or tracer bullet.

Dawkins was not surprised, somehow, when he noticed that Brannon and Galloway had taken up with each other.

All the pilots, Marine and Army, were dressed in gray tropical areas Naval aviator flying suits and boondockers. Dawkins would not have been surprised, either, to learn that the Army pilots' flight suits had come to them via Charley Galloway's VMF-229. Just before they left Ewa, a highly excited Navy supply officer at Pearl Harbor appeared, trying to locate a barrel-chested, bald-headed Marine Technical Sergeant who had been drawing supplies—including leather jackets and flight suits—with requisitions that turned out to be fraudulent. Dawkins told him he couldn't call to mind, offhand, if he had a barrel-chested, bald-headed Technical Sergeant or not. But if one turned up, he promised to let the Navy supply officer know right away.

Although there were some .38 Special caliber revolvers around, Galloway and Dunn and most of the others had Model 1911A1 Colt autoloaders in shoulder holsters.

Captain Brannon and his officers were all wearing battered leather-brimmed caps, from which the crown forms had been removed, ostensibly so that earphones could be worn over them. Dawkins recognized them for what they really were. They were pilots' hats, so that no one could mistake their wearers for some pedestrian soldier. Dawkins thought it was a classy idea—though he would not have shared this opinion with Brannon.

Galloway had a utility cap at least four sizes too small for him perched on top of his head. He had pinned to it his gold Naval aviator's wings and his railroad tracks. Dunn and most of the others wore khaki fore-and-aft caps, carrying the Marine insignia and the insignia of their rank.

I wonder what's going to happen to Dunn today? He's going out as Charley's exec, not as just one more airplane driver.

"Take your seats," Dawkins ordered. "Good afternoon, gentlemen."

There was a chorus of "Good afternoon, Sir," from the pilots, as they settled onto the plank benches.

"I am sorry to have to tell you that Captain Frankel is not available. Word has reached me that he was out carousing all night, and will not be sober until much later this afternoon. Consequently, I will handle this part of the briefing," Dawkins announced, straight-faced.

There was another chorus, this time of chuckles. There was, of course, no place to carouse; and even if there were, Captain Tony Frankel, MAG-21's S-2, was an absolute teetotal, and everybody knew it. And most of the pilots knew that Frankel had caught some kind of bug and had a spectacular case of the running shits. The scuttlebutt was that the Doc said he didn't know what it was, although he didn't think it was dysentery. Whatever it was, the Doc had grounded him.

Dawkins grabbed the oilcloth covering the maps and threw it over the back of the tripod.

A map showing the area from New Britain in the North to San Cristobal island, southwest of Guadalcanal, was now visible.

"For those of you who may have been wondering where the U.S. Navy is . . ." Dawkins began, and waited for the laughter to subside, "I have it on pretty reliable authority that as of midnight last night, Task Force 61 was in this area, about 150 miles east of here."

He used a pointer to show where he meant; it was made of a shortened pool cue, to which was fixed a .30'06 cartridge case and bullet.

"Task Force 61 consists of three smaller forces, each grouped around a carrier. *Saratoga* is out there, and *Enterprise. Wasp* and her support ships left the area yesterday so she could refuel; no estimate on when she will return.

"And we had, as of 2400 last night, *precisely* located the Japanese Navy as being *right* here," Dawkins said and waved the pointer over the map from New Britain to San Cristobal. His pilots correctly interpreted the move to mean that as of 2400 no one had any idea where the Japanese were.

More chuckles.

"At 0910 this morning," Dawkins went on, and his changed tone of voice indicated that the witty opening remarks were now concluded, and this was business, "a Catalina found the aircraft carrier *Ryujo* and its support vessels right about here. Just to the right—ten, fifteen miles—there's a transport force. Intelligence thinks it is safe to assume that the transports carry troops to be landed on Guadalcanal."

The tent was now dead quiet.

"At 1030 this morning, F4Fs operating off *Sara* shot down an Emily here. The *Saratoga* was then twenty miles away, which means the Emily got pretty close before they found it.

"About an hour ago, another Catalina found the *Ryujo* again, still on a course that would bring her to Guadalcanal. Nobody's said anything, but you don't have to be Admiral Nimitz to guess that *Enterprise* has mounted a rather extensive search operation, so as not to lose *Ryujo*. It's just as clear that *Sara* is preparing a strike. Or vice versa, with *Sara* looking and *Enterprise* preparing to launch an attack.

"We also have word that at about half past ten the Japs sent a hell of a lot of airplanes, about a hundred of them, down this way from Rabaul. The word comes from what CINCPAC chooses to call an Intell Source One. That means they think the poop is the straight stuff. *I* think it probably comes from the people the Australians left behind when the Japs occupied the islands between here and New Britain/New Ireland."

Dawkins paused until the murmur died down, and then went on: "About forty Zeroes escorting thirty Vals, ten Bettys, and fifteen Kates. Now, the odds are that their scouts are going to find *Sara* or *Enterprise*, or both, in which case I think we can presume that a good many of them will divert to make their attack. But some of them, maybe even most of them, will continue on to hit us. It's also just possible that they may *not* find either of our carriers. In that case, they will *all* come here, probably with all the aircraft *Ryujo* can launch coming with them.

"The best guess we can make of their ETA here is a few minutes after two. It's now," he paused to look at his watch, "1225. At 1300 we're going to start launching the SBDs as our scouts, in thirty-five minutes in other words. At 1330, we will start launching the fighters. First, VMF-211. And at 1345, VMF-229.

"If things go as scheduled—and they rarely do—at 1400 the SBDs should be at altitude here," he pointed again, "in a position to spot either the planes from *Ryujo* or the planes from Rabaul, or both. VMF-211's F4Fs should be about here, just about at the assigned altitude. And Captain Galloway and his people should be about here, *almost* at assigned altitude.

"We've been over this in some detail, so I'll just touch the highpoints: When the SBDs *positively* locate the stream of attacking aircraft, or when it is *positively* located by aircraft from *Lexington* and/or *Sara,* they will start to look for the *Ryujo,* fuel permitting. Fuel permitting is the key phrase. I don't want to lose any aircraft because they ran out of go-juice. When the SBDs *start* to run low on fuel, they *will* return here to refuel. I don't want any stupid heroics out there. I think I can guarantee there will be ample opportunity for the SBDs to take on an aircraft carrier, or carriers. It doesn't have to be this afternoon. Unless, of course, our estimates are way off, and you find them sooner than we think you will and can attack and still have enough fuel to get home safely.

"The mission of the fighters is right out of the book. They will locate, engage, and destroy the enemy. And they will do that in the knowledge that if they run out of fuel doing so, a scorned woman's fury can't hold a candle to that of your friendly commanding officer."

There was a murmur of chuckles.

"And something you haven't heard before: Stay off the radio unless you have something to say."

More chuckles.

"No damned idle chatter," Dawkins went on firmly. "When this thing starts, all I want to hear on the radio is business. I want a word with the squadron commanders and the execs. The rest of you may go."

"Ten-HUT!" somebody bellowed. Dawkins was surprised.

He was looking at Charley Galloway, and Galloway didn't even have his mouth open when the command came.

Colonel Dawkins jumped off the truck bed, walked behind the tent wall to wait for his squadron commanders and their executive officers.

(Five)
HEADQUARTERS MAG-21
HENDERSON FIELD
GUADALCANAL, SOLOMON ISLANDS
1715 HOURS 24 AUGUST 1942

Lieutenant Colonel Clyde W. Dawkins had decided early on that squadron commanders, and certainly air group commanders, really had no business being present when individual pilots were being debriefed by intelligence officers. With The Skipper standing there, pilots would be far less prone to tell the truth, the whole truth, and nothing but the truth, than if they were talking alone, and more or less in confidence, to the debriefing officer.

He decided that the debriefing of First Lieutenant William C. Dunn, USMCR, however, was going to be the exception to this rule. He sent word that when Dunn was to be debriefed, he wanted to be there.

The debriefings were conducted on the bed taken from the Japanese Ford truck. The debriefing officer had set up a folding wooden table in front of the map tripod Dawkins had used in the pre-flight briefing. He sat behind the table. As the pilots came in, one by one, to be debriefed, he waved them into another folding chair in front of his "desk."

Knowing the set up, Dawkins came into the tent carrying his own chair, a comfortable, cushioned, bentwood affair left behind by some departed Japanese officer.

He came around the tent wall as Dunn entered the tent from the other, open, end.

Dunn looked beat. He was hatless. His flight suit had large damp patches around the armpits and on the chest. When he came closer, Dawkins saw that his face was dirty; and, although Dunn had obviously made a half-assed attempt to wash, the outline of his goggles was clearly evident on his face.

Dawkins, smiling, made a gesture to Dunn to come onto the platform. And then he sat down, backwards, on his Japanese chair, resting his arms on the back.

Dunn eyed the debriefing officer suspiciously.

"Sir, where's Captain Frankel?" he asked.

When he was tired, Dawkins had noticed, Dunn's Southern accent became more pronounced. That had come out, "Suh, Whea-uh is Cap'n Frank-kel?"

"He's got the GIs, Bill," Dawkins said. "You know that."

"Don't I know you, Lieutenant?" Dunn asked, but it was more of a challenge than a question.

"Yes," the debriefing officer said. "I debriefed you after Midway."

"I thought I recognized you. I didn't like you then, and I don't like you now. Colonel, do I have to talk to this sonofabitch?"

Ah thought ah recog-nazed you. Ah didn't lak you then an ah don' lak you now. Cunnel, do ah have to talk to this som'bitch?

"With Frankel down with the GIs, I borrowed him to do the debriefing. It has to be done. You don't have to like him, Bill," Dawkins said calmly, "but you do have to answer his questions. Sit down!"

Dunn looked at him with contempt in his eyes, as if he had been betrayed.

"Sit down, Bill," Dawkins ordered again, calmly.

Dunn met Dawkins's eyes for a moment, and then shrugged and sat down.

"Before we begin, Lieutenant Dunn," the debriefing officer said, "I'd like to say this: If there ever were any questions raised at Midway about your personal behavior, your courage, to put a point on it, your behavior today has put them to rest for all time."

"Jesus!" Dawkins snorted.

"My report will indicate," the debriefing officer plunged ahead, a little confused by Dawkins's snort, "that you shot down four aircraft today, two Zeroes, and one each Betty and Val; that all kills were verified by at least two witnesses. That places you, Lieutenant, one aircraft over the five required to make you an ace. I would be very surprised if you were not given a decoration for greater valor in action, and it probably means a promotion."

"Fuck you," Bill Dunn said very clearly. "Stick your medal and your promotion up your ass."

"That's enough, Bill," Dawkins said. There was steel in his voice. Their eyes locked for a long moment.

"Yes, Sir," Dunn said, finally.

"Get on with it, Lieutenant," Dawkins ordered the debriefing officer.

"Well, as they say," the debriefing officer said, "let's take it from the top. In your own words, from take-off until landing. When I have a question, I'll interrupt? OK?"

"Every other pilot who made it back has been in here. How many times do you have to hear the same story?"

"Bill, goddamnit, do what he says," Dawkins ordered.

"You took off at approximately 1420, is that correct?" the debriefing officer began.

"Yeah."

"Was that the originally scheduled take-off time?"

"No," Dunn said, "we were supposed to take off earlier, at 1345, but the Colonel changed his mind, and held us on the ground. The SBDs hadn't found the Japs, and he wanted to conserve fuel. We took off when the goddamned radar finally found the Japs."

"Was the take-off according to plan? And if not, why not?"

"No. When the scramble order came, everybody tried to get into the air as quickly as possible. The Japs were just about over the field; there was no time to screw around waiting for the slow ones."

"And was the form-up in the air according to plan? And if not, why, in your opinion?"

"No. And I just told you. The Japs were over Henderson. It would have made absolutely no sense to try to form up as the schedule called for. And some airplanes are faster than others. Mine was faster than most."

"So, in your own words, tell me what happened to you after you took off."

"I guess I was eighth, ninth, tenth, something like that, to get off the ground . . ."

"Do you remember who was first?" the debriefing officer interrupted.

"Captain Galloway and his wing man, Lieutenant Ward. When the Black Flag went up, they were sitting in their aircraft with their engines already warmed up. They were moving within seconds."

"By the Black Flag, I presume you mean the Black Flag raised above the control tower signifying 'Condition I, Airbase under attack.' "

"Is there another black flag?"

"And once you were in the air, what did you do?"

"I started the climb," Dunn said. "Alone. I had been in the climb two, three minutes when I saw Lieutenant Schneider forming on my wing."

"That would be Lieutenant David F. Schneider?"

"Yes."

"Go on."

"Well, we finally got to 10,000 feet. By that time the bombers, the Bettys, had dropped their bombs, and were headed home."

"And how high would you estimate the Bettys were?"

"They were at nine thousand feet, I guess, and they were in a shallow dive, apparently to gain speed."

"There were no other enemy aircraft in sight?"

"There were Zeroes to the right," Dunn said. "They had seen us and were trying to keep us away from the Bettys. Captain Galloway and Ward headed for the Zeroes. I headed for the Bettys."

"Why?"

"Because it was pretty clear to me that was what Captain Galloway wanted me to do. He would take care of the fighters while I attacked the Bettys."

"Where was Lieutenant Schneider?"

"Shit. While *we* attacked the Bettys. He was on my wing. I told you that."

"And you did, in fact, attack the Bettys successfully. I have been told that you attacked from above . . ."

"Yeah."

"And that your stream of fire caused an explosion in the engine nacelle . . ."

"The one Schneider got, he took the vertical stabilizer off. Then it blew up."

"We were talking about yours."

"I got the engine. Schneider got the vertical stabilizer on his and then probably the main tank."

"Right. I have that. And then what happened?"

"Then the Zeroes showed up. Some of them apparently stayed to deal with Captain Galloway and Ward, but most of them tried to protect the bombers, and came to where we were."

"And then what happened?"

"I don't know. We got into it."

"Witnesses to the engagement have stated that during that engagement, you shot down two Zeroes. And you don't know what happened?"

"We were all over the sky. The only thing I know for sure is that Schneider got one, beautiful deflection shot, and he blew up."

"I thought you said Schneider was on your wing."

"I also said we were all over the sky. I don't know where Schneider was most of the time, except when I saw him take the Zero with the deflection shot."

"But you do remember shooting at at least two Zeroes?"

"I shot at a lot more than two. I'm sure I hit some of them, but I couldn't swear to anything but that I hit one good and he started to throw smoke and went into a spin."

"You did not see him crash?"

"No."

"Did you see Captain Galloway crash?"

"No. I saw Captain Galloway on fire and in a spin, but I did not see him crash."

"Was that before or after you shot the Zero you just mentioned, the one you said began to display smoke and entered a spin?"

"Before."

"Did you see Lieutenant Ward during this period?"

"I don't know. I saw a plane that could have been either him or Captain Galloway. I can't say for sure. They both came to help us when the Zeroes came after us."

"But you are sure that it was Captain Galloway you saw, in flames, and in a spin?"

"Yes."

"How can you be sure?"

"I'm sure, goddamn you. Take my word for it."

"Tell me about the Val," the debriefing officer said.

"He was a cripple," Dunn said. "I saw him down on the deck as I was coming home."

"Let's get into that. Why did you disengage?"

"My engine had been running on Emergency Military Power too long. I was losing oil pressure. My cylinder head temperature needle was on the peg. And I had lost fuel. A fuel line fitting had ruptured. I didn't know that. All I knew was the LOW FUEL light came on. Two of my guns had either jammed or were out of ammunition. So I started home."

"But you saw the Val and attacked it?"

"Why not?"

"Was attacking the Val wise, Bill?" Dawkins asked. It was the first time he had spoken.

"I was a little pissed at the time," Dunn said.

"Because of Captain Galloway?" Dawkins asked.

"He was one hell of a Marine, Colonel," Dunn said, and Dawkins saw tears forming in his eyes.

"Getting back to Captain Galloway," the debriefing officer said. "At the time Captain Galloway was reported hit, it has been reported that he had engaged a Zero and seriously damaged it. Did you see any of that?"

"Yeah," Dunn said. Dawkins saw that he was having trouble getting the lump out of his throat. Finally he cleared his throat. His voice was still unnatural.

"I am sure beyond any reasonable doubt that the Zero Captain Galloway was engaging the last time anybody saw him was in flames, missing his left horizontal stabilizer, out of control, and a sure kill."

"Very well, we'll put that down as 'confirmed.' "

"Thank you ever so much," Dunn said sarcastically.

"That makes it three and a half for Captain Galloway and two and a half for Lieutenant Ward, right?" Dawkins asked.

"Yes, Sir," the intelligence officer replied.

"What was the total, Sir?" Dunn asked. "Not, now that I think about it, that I give a flying fuck."

"Eleven this morning," Dawkins said. "And seven this afternoon. That makes eighteen. I think that's probably the most aircraft ever destroyed in a twenty-four hour period by any squadron—Marine, Navy, or Air Corps."

"We get a gold star to take home to Mommy?"

Dawkins ignored him.

"We lost five. Captain Galloway, of course."

"Of course."

"Close your mouth, Dunn," Dawkins snapped, and then went on. "Galloway, missing and presumed dead. Jiggs. We know he's dead. Hawthorne, ditto. Ward, pretty well banged up on landing. And Schneider, wounds of the legs and a broken ankle. Six aircraft lost or seriously damaged. That's not a bad score, Lieutenant."

"It didn't come cheap," Dunn said, "did it?"

"I don't want to wave the flag in your face, Dunn, but don't you think Charley went out the way he would have wanted to?"

"Charley didn't want to go out at all," Dunn said. He stood up. "I'm going to the hospital to see Jim Ward and Schneider," he said.

"I spoke to Ward," Dawkins said. "He asked me if it would be all right with you if he wrote his aunt and told her what happened to Charley. Charley apparently had her listed as 'friend, no next of kin.' I told him I thought you would be grateful."

"Yeah, sure," Dunn said.

"The other letters, you're going to have to write yourself, Bill. In my experience, it's best to do it right away. It doesn't get any easier by putting it off."

It took a moment for Dunn to take Dawkins's meaning. It is the function of the squadron commander to write letters of condolence to the next of kin of officers who have been killed. In accordance with regulations, Lieutenant William C. Dunn had acceded to the command of VMF-229 when the previous commander had been declared missing and presumed killed in action.

"As soon as I see the guys in the hospital, Sir," Dunn said. "I'll get on it."

"We're not through here, Lieutenant," the intelligence officer said.

"Yes, you are," Dawkins said. "Go ahead, Bill."

(Six)
160 DEGREES 05 MINUTES 01 SECONDS EAST
LONGITUDE
09 DEGREES 50 MINUTES 14 SECONDS SOUTH
LATITUDE
1820 HOURS 24 AUGUST 1942

Captain Charles M. Galloway, USMCR, had a pretty good
idea that he was going to die before the sun, now setting, rose
again. It could come violently, and soon . . . in minutes. Or
more slowly . . . he might last the night.

He could think of two possible violent deaths. The most
probable, and the most frightening, was from a shark attack.

At the moment he was floating somewhere in the Southwest Pacific. God knows where. It was a circumstance that
flung the thought of sharks right out there in the forefront
of his mind.

He remembered hearing somewhere a peculiar theory
about shark attacks. Peculiar or not, at the moment he took
some small comfort from it. This theory held that when a
shark bites something—or in this case, someone—it consid-
ers to be dinner, the force of the bite is so violent that the
person bitten doesn't feel any pain.

The shark bite was somewhat analogous to a gunshot
wound. When you're shot, the pain comes later, after the
shock has passed. When a shark bites, according to the theory, there'd be no pain at all: a shark would tear away so
much flesh—the powerful jaws of a shark could tear away
half a leg, or so he had been told—that you passed out from
loss of blood before the shock went away and the pain came.

The other sudden, violent death he could think of would
be self-induced. He still had his .45 automatic. It had been
underwater since he had gone into the drink, of course, but
he thought it would still fire. After all, he reasoned, ammunition was designed to resist the effects of water. The cartridge
case was tightly crimped against the bullet, and the primer
was coated with shellac.

Although they were badly puckered and a dead-fish white,
his fingers still functioned. He was reasonably sure he could
get the .45 out of its holster, work the action, put the barrel

against his temple or into his mouth, and then pull the trigger and see what came next.

It wasn't an idea that attracted him very much, even under the circumstances. In fact, the idea was repugnant. It literally made him shiver. When he was a young marine, for reasons that were never made clear, an old staff sergeant blew his brains all over the wash basins in a head at Quantico. The memory was bright in Charley's mind; he didn't want to go out that way, even if logic told him there wasn't much difference between a shattered head and having half your abdomen ripped off by a shark.

Given the imminent certainty of his death, he thought, it would have been better if he had been killed in the air. That almost happened. Now that he had time to go over it in his mind, he was more than a little surprised that it didn't:

He saw a Zero, a thousand or so feet below him, on Bill Dunn's tail. Bill was firing at a Val and didn't see him. Charley put his Wildcat in a dive and went after the Zero, to get him off Bill's tail.

He got him, almost certainly a sure kill. But as he started to climb out again, another sonofabitch came out of nowhere. Before he knew that anyone was anywhere near him, it was all over.

Parts of the engine nacelle suddenly flew off; a moment later, the engine stopped. Probably 20mms, hitting and shattering jugs, and freezing the engine.

Because he was in a climb when the power stopped, he decelerated rapidly. Moments later, the expected shudder announced a stall. And a moment after that, yellow flames came from the engine.

The nose went down, and the Wildcat began an erratic spin to the right. He reacted automatically. First, he shut off the fuel selector valve. There were probably shattered lines, but it probably wouldn't hurt. Then he pushed the stick full forward—the priority was to pick up airspeed and restore lift—and applied full left rudder.

He didn't remember how many turns he made—five, anyway, probably six—but getting out of the spin took a long time. By then he had a chance to look at the instrument panel. Most of the gauges were inoperative, and there were bulges and tears in the control panel itself, telling him that either explosive rounds had gone off behind it, or that the 20mms that killed the engine had sent shrapnel and/or engine parts into the back of the panel.

He had no doubt that it was time to get out of the Wildcat.

He held the stick between his knees, so that he could pull both of the canopy jettison rings simultaneously. If you didn't do that, the canopy might well jam on the remaining pin, trapping you in the cockpit; or else it might drag off into the airstream and hang there like an air brake, making control difficult or impossible.

The canopy blew off without trouble. All he had to do after that was unfasten his seat and shoulder harness, and climb out.

That turned out to be harder than he thought it would. He'd been a pilot for a long time, but he was still surprised at the force of the slip stream when he lifted his head and shoulders above the windscreen.

He went over the left side, bounced on the wing, then fell free. He watched the tail assembly flash over his head, alarmingly close, and then he pulled the D-Ring.

A moment after that, there was a dull flapping, thudding noise, and then a hell of a jolt as the canopy filled with air and suddenly slowed his descent.

For a while there was still some horizontal movement. When he bailed out, he was probably making right about a hundred knots. So when it opened, the parachute had to stop the forward motion before it started to lower him to the water.

He swung like a pendulum for maybe twenty seconds under the parachute, and then he looked down and saw the water. For a moment, it looked very far away, but the next it rushed up at him with alarming speed. Then he went in.

He remembered, at the last possible instant, to close his mouth. He even tried to get his hand up to hold his nose, but there wasn't time.

All of a sudden, he was in the water. It was like hitting hard sand. It wasn't at all cushiony, like water is supposed to be.

He remembered to get out of the parachute harness as quickly as he could. He worked the quick-disconnect mechanism and made sure he was free of the straps before swimming to the surface.

If you got tangled in the parachute harness, the shroud lines, or the parachute canopy itself, you could drown.

When he was on the surface, and sure that he was away from the parachute, which was floating on the surface of the water, he fired the CO_2 cartridge and inflated his life vest.

The sea moved in large, gentle swells. Nothing at all was in sight, not even aircraft in the distance. Using his hands, he turned himself around. He could see no land on the horizon. He was therefore at least seven or eight miles from any land—and probably a hell of a lot farther than that. In any event, he was too far away to try to swim anywhere, even if he knew where he should go; and he didn't.

He never felt so alone in his life.

He told himself they would probably look for him, either airplanes from his squadron, or Catalinas, or maybe even with Navy ships. But then he told himself that was wishful thinking.

If anyone watched him go down, they would have seen he was in bad trouble, and they'd probably figure he died in the crash.

He was in the water about an hour when the wind picked up and started making white caps. That seemed to put the cork in the bottle. He was a tiny little speck floating around in the great big ocean. It was difficult, but possible, for someone to spot the brilliant yellow life preserver against a calm blue sea; there was no chance anyone—from four, five thousand feet—could make out a couple of square feet of yellow among the white caps.

When darkness fell, Charley told himself that with a little bit of luck, he would be asleep when the shark—sharks—struck. That would be a better way to go than putting the .45 in his mouth, or of being sunburned to death when the sun came up again in the morning. He was already desperately thirsty, and that could only get worse, not better.

He went to sleep thinking of Caroline. They were in the marble walled shower of the Andrew Foster Hotel in San Francisco, with the water running down from the multiple shower heads over them.

(Seven)
USN PATROL TORPEDO BOAT 110
160 DEGREES 05 MINUTES 02 SECONDS EAST
LONGITUDE
09 DEGREES 50 MINUTES 14 SECONDS SOUTH
LATITUDE
0505 HOURS 25 AUGUST 1942

At 0400, Ensign Keith M. Strawbridge, USNR (Princeton, '40), relieved PT 110's skipper, Lieutenant (j.g.) Simmons F. Hawley III, USNR (Yale '40); but Hawley elected to remain on the bridge.

Ensign Strawbridge wasn't sure whether Lieutenant Hawley was staying because there was no sense trying to go below and get some sleep; or because he didn't really trust him to assume command of the boat; or whether—despite the heat, it was a pleasant night, reminding both of them of sailing off Bermuda—he just decided to stay for the pure pleasure of it.

After all, he was the captain. PT 110 was, in the law, a man of war of the United States Navy; and Sim Hawley was therefore invested with the same prerogatives of command as the captain of the Aircraft Carrier USS *Saratoga.*

If he wanted to stay on the fucking bridge of his man of war and play his fucking harmonica, there was no one to say him nay.

Having just asked his executive officer if he thought bathing the harmonica in fresh water would be a good idea, to combat the rust from the salt spray, Captain Hawley was startled and somewhat annoyed by a report from Motor Machinist's Mate 3rd Class James H. Granzichek (Des Plaines, Ill. Senior High '41).

"Hey, Mr. Hawley," he called. "Check out whatever the fuck that is on the left. The yellow thing."

Hawley did not like being addressed as "Hey, Mr. Hawley." He preferred to be referred to as "Captain," but thought it would be rather bad form to suggest it, much less order it. He also could not see where it was necessary for the men to use "fuck" every time the proper word did not immediately come to mind. And there was a proper Naval term for "on the left." Granzichek should have said, "to starboard." Or was it, "to port"?

But he looked for the yellow thing. First with his naked eyes, and then, when that didn't work, through his binoculars. The boat was shaking so much he couldn't hold the binoculars still.

"All engines stop," he ordered.

MMM3 Granzichek hauled back on the throttles that controlled the twin Packard engines of PT 110. She slowed, and then began to move side to side in the swells. This action tended to make Ensign Strawbridge feel a bit queasy, but it permitted Captain Hawley to see through his binoculars.

"Good God," he exclaimed. "It's a man in a life jacket."

"No shit?" MMM3 Granzichek asked, reaching for the binoculars. A moment later, he reported, "I think he's dead. He's not moving or waving or anything."

"May I have a look now, please?" Ensign Strawbridge asked, a trifle petulantly. Granzichek handed him the binoculars.

"How would you say, Granzichek," Captain Hawley asked, "would be the best way to take him on board?"

Granzichek, Captain Hawley reasoned, had been aboard PT 110 for three and a half months. He himself had assumed command only last Monday. Experience tells.

"Pull up alongside him, catch him with a boat hook, and then get a line on him," Granzichek said.

"Very well, then let's have a go at it," Captain Hawley ordered.

URGENT
CONFIDENTIAL
FROM PTSQUADRON-30
TO COMMANDING OFFICER
VMF-229
VIA CINCPAC
1. PT 110 OF THIS SQUADRON RECOVERED AT SEA AT 0530 THIS MORNING CAPTAIN CHARLES M. GALLOWAY, USMCR.
2. CAPTAIN GALLOWAY IS SUFFERING FROM EXPOSURE AND DEHYDRATION BUT IS OTHERWISE IN GOOD HEALTH. HE HAS BEEN TRANSFERRED TO HOSPITAL SHIP USS CONSOLA-

TION, WHO WILL ADVISE YOU OF ARRANGEMENTS TO RE-
TURN HIM TO DUTY.
BY DIRECTION:
J.B. SUMERS, LTCOM USNR